ALSO BY JERRY JAY CARROLL

Top Dog
Dog Eat Dog
Inhuman Beings
A Dog's Life
The Great Liars
The Horror Writer

END
TIMES

JERRY JAY CARROLL

SWAGGERING PRESS

End Times is a work of fiction:
The premise and plot are the product of the author's imagination

Book design by Dog-ear Book Design **www.dog-earbookdesign.com**

Published by Swaggering Press
34 Segovia Drive, HSV, Ark., 71909

Library of Congress Control Number 2018910683
ISBN: 978-0-9898269-6-9

This is dedicated to my wife, the poet,
and to my grandchildren, Jack and Tova Jaffe.

ESCHATOLOGY IS THE PART OF THEOLOGY CONCERNED WITH DEATH, JUDGMENT, AND THE final destiny of the soul and of humankind.

—*The Oxford English Dictionary*

CHAPTER 1

THE MAN STEPS WITH ATHLETIC GRACE FROM THE NEARLY FINISHED PAINTING IN A LOVELY ROOM washed in yellow-green light from the garden beyond the French doors. He is elegant in a white linen suit, pink shirt, blue silk tie, and hand-made Italian shoes. The room has an Isfahan rug, surely too precious to walk on, heavy but graceful furniture from a Bourbon palace, pale purple Lisianthus in a Han dynasty vase, a large mirror in a gilt frame, and a palette on a tripod with wet paint waiting for the artist's return.

He is impossibly good looking with dark hair and green eyes, a wide brow and firm jaw. He casually inspects the room, picking up objects—a Fabergé egg here, a Swiss cylinder music box there—to enjoy the feel of their weight in his hand. He wanders through the house looking at everything with pleasure. In the kitchen, he pours lemonade in a glass and drinks. The long-lashed eyes widen in surprise as the tartness floods his mouth.

He walks out the front door into the long-shadowed autumn afternoon across an emerald expanse of manicured lawn, down a winding dirt path nearly overwhelmed by undergrowth to a quiet two-lane blacktop road. He turns left without looking back, as if what lies behind has served its purpose. He is bewitched by all he sees, blue sky, pillowed clouds, light through the trees, walls clad in lichen, a string of geese honking overhead.

An older woman with a long, sharp face like one of the pinscher breeds stops digging in her garden and stands to glare as he passes her spiked iron fence and the stone lions guarding the driveway. This is not a neighborhood that likes strangers, especially on foot. He glances over at her and her nose begins to flood and spills over cupped hands as she runs for the house. It takes two jumbo boxes of Kleenex to handle the outflow.

Cars passing at long intervals make the burgundy and gold leaves dance and twirl merrily on the ground. Heads turn in the cars; such an elegant figure they think. Who is he and where is he going on this road that dead ends at a locked gate? As the shadows lengthen into twilight, he turns his collar up and walks with hands in pockets.

When darkness begins to fall, a police car draws near from behind and stops with blue roof lights spinning and an officer gets out. Sergeant Alex Randall is strongly built but doesn't hit the gym as often as he used to; the muscle is still solid but beginning to soften as middle age works its changes. As he approaches, limping a little from the IED in Iraq, he squares his hat with a tug at the bill. His Sam Browne belt laden with holster, cuffs and other gear squeaks with official authority.

"Where are you headed, sir?" he asks politely. That ice cream suit belongs in Southern California, he thinks; we're coming on to flannel and parka time here.

"I don't know." He seems mystified that he can't answer so a simple question. The man's voice is pleasingly pitched between tenor and baritone. A good looking guy, the cop notices. No, more than that, incredibly good looking.

"Where are you coming from?"

"Back there."

"Back where?"

"A house."

"What address?"

"I don't know."

"Could I see some ID?"

"ID?"

"Something that says who you are."

The man pats his pockets vaguely, wanting to be helpful but not sure how.

"What's your name?"

A slow, wondering shake of the head.

The policeman's suspicion normally would sharpen now, but something tells him this man is harmless and somehow different. He takes his old Canon digital camera from a pocket for a video recording of the interview. He means one day to string together bits and pieces as a kind of career diary for the twins to see what it was like to be a cop way back when. Not just accident scenes to warn against drinking and driving, but funny stuff like the firemen rescuing a cat from a tree. And weird stuff like this.

"Mind getting in the back of the car?"

"Not at all."

"You told me you don't know your name, correct?"

"I don't know my name."

"Have you been in an accident?"

"No."

"Do you hurt anywhere?"

"I feel wonderful."

Procedure is clear in these cases of mental confusion; call it in and drive to headquarters to let them sort things out, but at this hour that means a night in a holding cell. If it is busy, he'll share space with drunks, some of whom can be violent. Then tomorrow the legal and welfare machinery clank into action. He will be transported to the hospital and put in the lockdown ward for evaluation. People howl in fear or rage there or silently rock back and forth as they stare at nothing. The few times the policeman was there to dump off somebody he couldn't wait to leave. He has learned from experience to go by the book. It is protection from nit-picking superiors as well as mouthy arrestees and the lawyers they hire. But he thinks this should be an exception to the rules.

"If I were to drive you back, do you think you could recognize the house?"

The man shakes his head. "I don't think I could."

"It was your first time there?"

"I don't know." He looks apologetic that he can't be more helpful.

"Do you remember anything?"

He thinks about this. "Something I had to drink."

This was getting somewhere. "Booze?"

He doesn't understand.

"Liquor."

He still doesn't.

The cop mimes drinking from a glass and shuddering. "Whiskey, gin, vodka. Was it the hard stuff?"

"It tasted wonderful."

"Maybe it was drugged."

The officer takes off his hat and scratches his head, unconscious of the comic weight tradition has given this. He gets the official digital camera from the trunk and takes a picture for record purposes. He remembers a former rich man's estate up the road that is now a sanitarium for wealthy people. It is very posh and discreet; nobody outside your family need know you go off the rails from drugs or alcohol or didn't take your medication. He knows this from the visit to dispatch a rabid skunk on the grounds two years ago. He closes the door and walks around to the other side, removing his hat before getting in.

During the drive Sergeant Randall searches himself. Why am I doing this? A peek in the rearview mirror shows the man is as comfortable as someone in a rocking chair on his own front porch.

"I'm supposed to take you to the station house."

The man waits with an expectant look.

"Where I work. Somebody called in sick today; I'm doing his shift."

The explanation is sufficient and the man turns his attention back to the road.

"But I'm not taking you there."

The man turns back.

"It's a shit hole," says the sergeant.

"Where are we going?"

"To a place like a hospital. Maybe you got hit on the head and that's why you don't remember. You know what a hospital is?"

"Sorry."

"You speak good English, no accent or anything. How come you don't know what things are called?"

The man just looks at him with smiling eyes.

A few miles up the road a brick wall with ivy begins on the left side and a hundred yards beyond an iron gate stands open. A brass plate in the wall says Templeton Hall. A long tree-lined drive turns circular in front of an imposing Palladium-style stone mansion. Some electronic device has alerted the house and a man in a sports coat with leather patches and a white turtleneck comes down steps wide enough for a Verde opera.

"Is there a problem?" he asks as Randall gets out and puts his hat on. "I'm Dr. Marc Ashford." His long gray hair has modish swept back wings.

"Are you the director?"

"I'm the executive director." The distinction seems to be important to him.

"I found him walking on the road."

"Why bring him here?" He appears close to taking offense.

"I thought you could look him over."

"What's wrong with him?"

"I think he's got amnesia. He doesn't even know his name."

"There is a public hospital an hour away."

"He'd just be a number."

"I'm sorry… is it sergeant?"

"Can you just take a quick look?"

Ashford reluctantly stoops to look through the window and his manner changes. "Where did you find him?"

"A few miles south."

"So he's from one of the big houses."

"I would guess so."

This changes things. Ashford opens the passenger door with a broad smile. "Welcome, I'm Doctor Ashford." The man gets out and takes the offered hand. "You've had some trouble?"

"I went out for a walk."

"Why don't we all go inside where it's warm?" Ashford leads them to the grand entrance past where a knot of staff members has gathered. They pass through them and into his office where a blaze crackles in a fireplace. A big desk, overstuffed leather chairs and nice pictures on the walls. Randall removes his hat as he settles in his chair. His dark hair is peppered with gray.

"Now then," Ashford says, "can you tell me what happened?" You can't get a linen suit like his for under twenty-five hundred dollars, he is thinking. And the loafers are hand made.

"He doesn't remember anything," Randall says.

"I'd like him to answer," Ashford says sharply.

"I don't know what happened," the man says.

"You don't hurt anywhere?"

"I feel wonderful."

"You don't know your name?"

"No."

"You're not worried about that?"

"I'm getting the feeling I should be." He laughs easily.

"What is the last thing you recall?"

"Walking, and then I was picked up by the sergeant."

"Nothing before that?"

"A big house. Something good I drank."

"It could have been spiked with something," Randall puts in.

"There are several kinds of amnesia," Ashford says. He is not a hasty diagnostician, but the man might have the severe form known as global. Or perhaps it is dissociative amnesia where he can't remember personal information. These patients typically are aware they have forgotten but don't know what. They can boil an egg but they can't make an omelet. This amnesia lasts hours to days and usually comes after a severely stressing or traumatic event.

"The odds are very strong that your memory will return," he tells the man. "Your appearance suggests perhaps you are in the performing arts."

"My appearance?"

"You are very handsome, as you must know, extraordinarily so. Am I right, sergeant?"

"Like a movie star," the policeman agrees.

"And your clothes," the psychiatrist says. "They're very expensive."

The man looks down at them. "Expensive?"

"Very. What's the label on your jacket?"

The man looks. "Fioravanti."

"What does that mean?" the sergeant asks.

"The top of the bespoke trade," Ashford says.

Randall's radio crackles and he speaks into his lapel microphone. "Unit Four."

"Sarge, there's a report of a 10-14 on Wood Road."

"Mrs. Kletchner?"

"Affirmative."

The elderly woman lives alone in an enormous house because she can't keep servants. Mrs. Kletchner is good for three or four prowler reports a month. "So I can leave our friend in your capable hands?" he asks Ashford.

"Yes, of course," the psychiatrist says as if there was never any question about it.

A group of nurses are at the door when he comes out. They remind him of groupies at the Bon Jovi concert where he picked up a few extra bucks doing security. Who is that man, they ask.

"Beats me."

Before he drives away, he takes out the Canon for a panning shot of the outside of Templeton Hall. "This is where I left the nice man who didn't know his name," he says for the boys to hear one day.

CHAPTER 2

KLETCHNER WAS A COOKWARE MAGNATE AND THELMA MUST HAVE BEEN A YOUNG TROPHY WIFE AS
he has been dead these fifty years. "Where is Officer Cook?" is her first question.

"He's not feeling well tonight," Randall says. He is pretty sure Cook is driving home from a lake with a cooler full of trout.

"Men were looking in my windows."

She can't describe them or the car they came in, but she doesn't think they were peeping toms like before; they seemed to be looking for something rather than a glimpse of her in her nightgown. Starved for conversation, she chatters on. Her legs hurt and the headaches are worse. The man who delivers groceries was rude; the refrigerator is making a funny noise. Randall breaks free and checks outside with his flashlight. No footprints or signs of attempted entry, the same as all the other times.

He drives the cruiser home after radioing that he is 10-7. "Goodnight, Sarge," the dispatcher says. A cold wind has picked up, stripping off leaves that hurry in the headlights like commuters for the last train. The moon ducks in and out of the clouds and shadows move in the trees. Randall is not an imaginative man, but he has a creepy feeling as if dark things move just beyond the edge of his vision.

So he is happy to get home and close the door on the night, finding the suitcases just inside the threshold. His pretty wife, Abigail—a strawberry blond with cornflower-blue eyes—greets him with a kiss and the tow-headed five-year-old twins, Michael and Martin, swirl at his knees. "Daddy! Daddy!" Not to be outdone, the Lab mix Bub dances on hind legs and paws the air as he barks his welcome.

"Has everyone been behaving?" he yells through the clamor.

"I'm not a mom, I'm a referee," she says. "Why do boys fight all the time?"

"It's in the DNA," he says. "If it wasn't for guys you could lay off ninety per cent of the cops."

"Ready to go?" he asks her as he picks the boys up and kisses them.

They drive tomorrow to her mother's place in Oregon. Abigail is as efficient as she is pretty, so the question is unnecessary. He follows in two weeks and already dreads the nights with nothing but television to keep him company.

"All set," Abigail says. "A quiet night?"

"Mrs. Kletchner said someone was at her window."

"How many times does that make?"

"I lost count a long time ago."

"It must be awful to be so all alone."

"That's me when you guys leave."

"We had that discussion," she says firmly. "I'm all mom's got left."

She takes meat loaf from the oven and he uses the mixer on the boiled potatoes, adding enough milk to whip them smooth. Hoping to find creamed corn, he lifts the lid from the pot.

"Green beans are less fattening," she says, knowing what he is thinking.

"I actually prefer them."

"Try your reverse psychology on someone else," Abigail laughs. She tells the boys it's time to turn off the cartoons and come to the table.

"I picked up a guy walking on the road," he says over dinner. "He didn't know who or where he was. Nice guy; rich by the look of him."

"You took him to the lockup?" Abigail worked as police dispatcher before he took her away from all that. She says she would still be working graveyard if she'd left it up to him.

"No, I took him to Templeton Hall."

"But that's private."

"Yeah, I was afraid they wouldn't accept him. Looking rich helped."

"Why take him there?"

"I don't know… there's something different about the guy."

He downloads a picture on the computer and prints it. "My goodness," Abigail marvels, "what a handsome man."

"More handsome than me?" He gives her his profile.

"That's not possible, dear. Is that what you mean by something different?"

"It's hard to put into words."

"That's another thing about males I've noticed."

After he sees Abigail and the kids off in the predawn darkness, Randall goes back to bed. When he wakes in the stillness a couple of hours later, it's as if all the fizz has gone from the house like day-old champagne. Bub looks at him accusingly.

"Don't blame me," Randall says. "It wasn't my idea."

Next year he will put his foot down. No family vacation to see the leaves turn in southern Oregon, land of Jell-O salad with canned peaches and pears and a scoop of cottage cheese.

"We can watch the leaves turn here," he had said as he does every year.

"Mom's not well."

He wanted to say what's new? Her father dragged out illnesses for years requiring annual visits before he turned toes up, and it looked to him like the old lady was up to the same trick.

He lets the dog out to do his business, showers, puts his uniform on and pulls belt and straps tight. He pours a cereal like brown cardboard peelings into a bowl with nonfat milk. This mixture is supposed to be good for constipation, the curse of the desk-bound policeman. As he eats standing up, he is oppressed again by the house's quiet. Abigail has made a nice place out of it with curtains and throw rugs and other touches. The curmudgeonly owner—there appears to be something about living in the woods that brings that out in people—is an odd duck with tastes to match. The house has a steeply pitched roof and tight rooms like a fairy-tale dwelling where dwarves march off at dawn to dig for gold. He has to turn his torso sideways to climb the narrow stairs to their bedroom where the ceiling's slope matches the sharp angle of the roof and has left him with a more or less permanent bump on the head. He reckons in four years they can buy a modern house in a pleasant neighborhood and live like normal people. He has passed the lieutenant's exam and if Frudenthaler will just ease his fat ass into retirement life will be good.

"Don't do anything I wouldn't," he tells Bub. A flurry of indignant barking comes from inside as Randall walks to the cruiser.

"Things never did quiet down last night," Lieutenant Frudenthaler says at the station house as he looks up from the printouts. "Five calls and a dozen silent alarms. I think we're looking at a gang hitting at random."

"What did they take?" Sergeant Randall asks.

Leaning on the counter, Frudenthaler shifts a large haunch as he thumbs through the reports. He has a square head with a Junker's brush cut and protrubant eyes that give him a look of astonishment. His movements are so ponderous they call him Ellie behind his back, short for elephant. "It looks like nothing," he says. He raises eyebrows so arched and thin that the same wags joke about Maybelline.

"There goes your theory."

"Then it's teenagers messing around." He passes the reports to Randall.

After Frudenthaler lumbers to the coffee maker and returns with two cups, Randall says, "Teenagers in big black SUVs?"

"That would be different," the lieutenant concedes. "It's strange, whatever it is. I'll do the morning shape up so you can head this up in the field. Cook called in; he's feeling better so you don't have to fill in tonight."

"Did you ask how the fishing was?"

"He said a cold kept him in bed all weekend."

"Amazing how often that happens."

The lieutenant drifts away humming to himself. His way of dealing with personnel problems is to pretend they don't exist. A new world awaits Cook and one or two others when Frudenthaler shoves off, Randall thinks.

Randall spends the morning and afternoon driving to the homes the intruders visited. Only a few are still occupied this late in the season and he resets the burglar alarms. An elderly Filipina caretaker named Iris Corizon had exchanged the only words with them.

"I open upstairs window and say what you want this time of night? He tell me 'Shut the fuck up,' please pardon the expression."

"How many were there?"

"Four, five. Maybe eight."

"You didn't get a license number by any chance?"

"It too dark."

"You couldn't describe them."

"It too dark."

"Nothing taken?"

"No, they just look round with flashlights."

You didn't have to be Sherlock Holmes to connect this to the amnesia victim. Randall drives to Templeton Hall where a woman waits on the broad steps in welcoming mode. "Hi," she says. "Back again so soon?" She is Emma Rasmussen, head of the nursing staff. She is round and pleasant looking.

"Did we meet yesterday?" he asks, squaring his hat after getting out of the cruiser.

"I was one of the faces in the crowd."

"How's he doing?"

"Awesome except that he still can't remember anything."

"How's it awesome then?"

She hugs herself. "He's just so… I don't know… nice. We'd just about die for him. Nobody's ever met anyone like him."

Randall gives her the look he does to speeders who say the radar gun must be malfunctioning.

"No, I mean it," she insists. "There's some… quality."

Purity. The word pops into the sergeant's head. Was that the quality about him?

"Would you like to see Doctor Ashford?" She leads him inside as he removes his hat. Ashford is wearing a light blue turtleneck and gray slacks.

"Sergeant, so soon?" There is irritation in his voice.

"The case is still open. How's he doing?"

"He's adjusting well for someone who is basically a blank slate. Although obviously well educated, he doesn't know what day or month it is, who the president is, even what country he is in. On the other hand, he sat down at our piano and played like he makes his living at it."

"So he might be a musician?" If so, he would play at the Fairmont or one of the other classy places across the bridge; the locals who worked the joints on the Marin side were lucky if they cleared a couple hundred bucks for a night's work and their wardrobes showed it.

"He might be a hypnotist. He practically has my staff eating out of his hand. They call him Rex."

"Rex?"

"For king, I gather."

"I'd like to ask Rex a few questions."

Admiring staff people stand around him in what was a large game room and still has a covered billiard table; Rex is perfectly relaxed with one leg over an arm of his chair. "And then a car stopped," he is saying, "and..." He spots Randall. "And he picked me up." The staffers beam at the sergeant as if he had done them all a kindness.

He asks for a few moments alone with Rex and they file out. "Everything all right?"

"Everything is great."

"People like you."

"They told me what you do, protecting and serving—that's an honorable calling."

"You didn't know about cops?"

"I don't seem to know anything."

"You know how to talk. You'll pick things up fast."

"I think you're right," he says with a grin.

"I don't suppose you know why anyone would be after you?"

"Is someone after me?"

"I'm putting two and two together and coming up with four."

"Is that good or bad?"

"My guess is bad. They're trespassing on property and looking through windows. We'll have extra patrols out tonight to see if we can catch them."

"Do you know why they are after me?"

"I was hoping you could tell me."

He shakes his head. "No, I can't."

The sergeant asks a few more questions that don't get him anywhere. In the hall outside, a gangling, young, dreadlocked black guy in T-shirt, baggy shorts and yellow Converse high-tops introduces himself. He has a basketball under one arm.

"Hi, I'm Jameel. I'm the P.E. director." He smiles at Rex. "You ready to shoot some hoops?" To Randall, he says, "It's part of the therapy."

"Whatever hoops are," Rex says with good humor. Randall follows them outside to a full-size basketball court.

"People who lived here had lots of boys," Jameel explains. "Got stuff up the ass pipe—a tennis court, a puttin' green, a pitchin' machine and ball diamond and lots a other shit. Pretty sweet, huh?" He bounces the ball, shoots a three-pointer and misses. "That's why I didn't make it to the pros." He fires it back to Rex who effortlessly sinks a jumper from midcourt. A group of patients applaud.

"Woo! Not bad for somebody don't know what hoops is." Jameel retrieves the ball and misses another three-pointer. "Shit, man." He returns the ball and Rex scores again. "Lemme see you do that again." He sinks six more times. The patients are high-fiving.

Jameel comes over to the sergeant. "This rock star is a no-shit athlete. Somebody gotta know him." He turns back. "OK, man, one on one. Let's see how you shoot with someone in that pretty-boy face." He explains the rules and they start to play. Jameel wins the first one 21 to 12, but Randall can see Rex is learning fast. He wins the second game 21 to 14 and Jameel is blanked in the third.

"That's it, man," Jameel says. "You just playin' with me." He is angry leaving the court. "Man made a fool out of me in front of all these people," he says as he passes Randall. "Pretendin' he don't know the game! He good as LeBron."

"You made the poor guy mad," Randall tells Rex.

"What did I do?" He is genuinely surprised.

"You showed him up."

"He said the object is to win."

"When did you learn to shoot like that?"

"Just now." The patients mob him before Randall can ask more.

This is making less sense as time goes on, he thinks on the way back to the cruiser. The man sits down at a piano and plays like a pro. He claims not to know basketball, but shows up a former college player. Back in the office, he searches law enforcement data banks for a missing person who matches up. He becomes aware from the strong cologne—another source of droll comment around the station—that Frudenthaler is behind him looking over his shoulder.

"Who are you looking for, Sergeant?"

"A man with amnesia turned up at Templeton Hall last night."

"I didn't see it on the log."

"I dropped by to see if the gang had turned up there."

"That's miles away."

Randall doesn't reply.

"Did you call it in?"

"No, I didn't."

A disapproving silence falls. "It should've been logged."

"You're right. I'll get to it right away."

"Find anything on him?"

"Nothing."

"Do we really need four men working overtime tonight? Seems we could get by with three."

"Your call."

The lieutenant wanders off humming.

CHAPTER 3

IT IS LATE AT NIGHT AND REX IS STRETCHED OUT WITH ANKLES CROSSED AND FINGERS LACED behind his head. The door opens to reveal a bearded man in denim work clothes that have seen a lot of wear.

"Come on in," Rex says. People pop by his room all the time. The nurses bring him treats from the kitchen.

"Leave immediately."

Rex rises from the bed, accepting this as he accepts everything.

"Evil is near." The old man steps forward with uncertainty as if not sure how he will be received.

"What is evil?" Rex is hungry for knowledge.

"We have no time for that." The old man goes to the window and looks out.

"What should I do?" Rex follows him, as eager for direction as knowledge.

The man pulls a thick lump of cash from a pocket. "This is called money. This is a hundred dollar bill, the most valuable." He thumbs past them. "The twenty is five times less valuable. The ten is ten times less and so on. Put it in your jacket pocket and follow me."

They go downstairs to a side door where a car idles. "You may think you don't know how to drive, but you know more things than you realize. Go out the gate and turn left."

"Where do I go?"

"Wherever the car takes you. Quickly, there's not a minute to lose."

"Are you coming?"

"You're on your own for now."

When Rex looks back in his rearview mirror, the man has been swallowed by the shadows. He reaches the gate and turns left. Sixty seconds later, two hulking black SUVs turn into the grounds.

The phone rings at the bedside table and Randall answers. "Sarge," the dispatcher says in a constricted voice, "we got a 911 call from Templeton Hall."

"And?" From the long silence, it doesn't seem like the dispatcher is able to say more. She gathers herself. "A woman reported a break-in. I heard screaming and then the line was dead. All units are responding and I thought you'd want to know."

"You told the chief and lieutenant?"

"Yes, sir."

He gets there in twenty minutes. The flashing red and blue lights on the front of the stately hall create a carnivale air as if women with banana headdresses might samba from the shadows. Officer Regis Cantrell approaches, his features frozen in shock.

"Far as we can see, everyone's dead. Twenty-five or thirty people. Everybody was tortured." He is swallowing hard. "Excuse me." He takes two steps away and vomits.

The sergeant walks through the rooms as if in a bad dream. Bodies are everywhere, some stripped naked and others clothed. They lay flat on backs or faces or arranged in gruesome displays; one ensemble has mouths open like a barber shop quartet, another has heads piously bowed and hands linked as in a prayer circle. Ears and noses have been hacked off, eyeballs dangle from sockets and a third or more of the victims have genital mutilations. The intent clearly was to shock and sicken whoever discovered these demonic atrocities. Doctor Ashford's arms and legs with the shoes still on his feet were cut off on the billiard table and placed on the corner pockets. Randall feels like going home and pulling the covers over his head. Before that was just an expression, something people said when things really went south, but now it seems the smart choice.

"Get everybody outside and put the yellow tape up," he orders. State and federal investigators would be here by first light. Who knows what evidence has already been ruined. He hadn't bothered looking for Rex among the bodies;

there would be no need for torture if he had been here. Ashford probably stepped forward to say he was the executive director and was the first victim to show they meant business.

He tells dispatch to cancel the ambulances rushing to the scene from all over in keeping with the disaster plan drawn up after 9/11. He orders a cruiser to block the front gate and posts officers around the grounds to seal the crime scene. He surrenders command to the Chief Parker and Frudenthaler when they arrive with clothes over their pajamas. The lieutenant lumbers around, making a show of barking out orders, but Randall has done all that is needed. Chief Parker, a smaller version of the portly Frudenthaler except for a rosy face from sun or bourbon, sends an officer off to bring his best uniform.

"The media will buzz in here like flies to shit," he says. "And I wouldn't bet against our showboat governor showing up." He turns sad hound dog eyes from his shoes to the sergeant. "How many bodies?"

"I make it thirty three."

"Christ!"

The evening passes and then an interminable gray morning. News copters clatter over Templeton Hall and a fleet of trucks with roaring generators and satellite dishes take up station at the front gate. The reporters are nearly all beautiful women, future anchors with great hair and terrific figures. A catering outfit arrives with coffee and sandwiches for the multiplying number of investigators and forensic technicians. The governor helicopters in to tell the hot reporters that those responsible will be found and prosecuted to the fullest extent of the law. His chopper lifts off afterward, making sandwich wrappers and paper cups fly across the green lawn. Randall eats two polish dogs with fries, and indigestion kicks in almost immediately. Abigail has reduced fat and salt in the family diet for health reasons. It's because I'm out of training, he thinks when acid reflux rises like lava. He eats two more later in the day.

"The second string will come in tomorrow or the next day," a producer tells him. "The old, bald guys work the yarn from then."

"How long will that be?"

"A week anyhow."

Nothing like this has ever happened and everyone is hyper at headquarters. As soon as phones are hung up they ring again. The limping, pie-eyed janitor they call Molasses does his job in double time and looks for more to do. Abigail calls from Oregon.

"My God, what happened?"

"Pretty much what you see on TV."

"It must be hell."

"Worse."

"I won't keep you. We love you."

"Back at you."

At four o'clock, Randall is called to the chief's office where two state detectives look at him coldly; a guy in his fifties and a younger one with a wolfish look of ambition. It occurs to the sergeant that reputations stand to be made on this case.

"Sit down, Sergeant," says Parker. He peers at Randall over heavy tortoise-shell half-moon glasses.

"We'd like to ask a few questions," says the older detective. He is fat and balding with a broad, blunt nose with broken capillaries.

"What did you say your name is?" Randall asks, covering a belch. The indigestion is back with a vengeance.

"Ferguson. This is Napier."

"Okay, what do you want to know?"

"What can you tell us about the person you dropped off at the sanitarium?" asks Napier. He is thin with slicked-back hair that shows a lot of scalp.

"Not much." The sergeant describes seeing Rex on the road at twilight and determining he was an amnesia victim. "I took him to Templeton Hall."

"Why there and not headquarters?" Ferguson asks. "Or call in and get an okay to go straight to the hospital."

"It was closer."

"But it's private."

"They didn't have a problem."

"When was this?" Napier asks too casually.

"A couple days ago."

"But Frudenthaler said you didn't report it until yesterday," Chief Parker says.

"I got busy."

"You do everything by the book I'm told," Ferguson says. "Dot your i's and cross your t's."

Randall is silent.

"But not this time, it seems."

"Did you know this person before?" asks Napier. Randall guesses his is the theory driving this line of questioning.

"No." Randall notices a small tape recorder on the chief's desk. "Is that running?"

"Do you have a problem?" Napier asks.

"Aren't you supposed to tell me?"

Parker adjusts his half glasses. "This is an internal investigation."

"At this point anyway," Ferguson notes. "You suppose this amnesia victim had anything to do with what happened?"

"That's my guess."

"What's the connection?"

"That's the question."

"Got an answer?" Napier asks, studying his nails in a parody of nonchalance. "See, there's no evidence about who did it that we can see. No fingerprints, no tire tracks, no nothing. It's like somebody who knows what he's doing made sure no evidence was left. That doctor kept a log. That's how we found out you were a day late."

"It doesn't look good," Parker rumbles, turning his chair with a squeak to look out the window.

"He wrote my name in his log?" Randall asks. He wonders who else saw it.

"It was on the doctor's desk," Napier says. "Smeared with blood. What else can you tell about the guy with amnesia?"

"He's some kind of athlete. Makes three pointers all day long. You might check with the NBA. Or he might be a piano player."

"That's quite a spread," Ferguson says.

"He's quite a guy."

"You liked him?" Napier asks.

"Everybody did except the PE guy. Rex—that's the name they gave him—showed him up on the basketball court. He got mad about it."

"That would be the black guy," Ferguson said. "He'll never get mad again. It would be nice to have a picture of the guy you picked up. Isn't that SOP?"

"Half our guys forget," the chief admits.

Randall lets that be the answer. "He's six-one, a hundred and ninety," Randall says. "Dark hair, green eyes. Good looking."

Randall is excused after a few more questions and then called back in forty-five minutes later as the detectives depart without looking at him.

"I'm going to suspend you with pay until this is cleared up," Parker blusters.

"Is that what those guys said?"

"It's a question of appearances. Don't talk to anyone from the press—and that's an order."

"I wouldn't bank on this case getting solved if that's how they think."

"TV's already calling it the Marin County Massacre. That's all people will remember about my time as chief." Parker ponders this latest confirmation of life's unfairness. "Give your gun and badge to Frudenthaler pending resolution of this matter."

"This is mine. The Smith & Wesson is in my locker." He pulls the locker key from the ring and drops it on the desk.

"Your wife can pick you up?"

"She's in Oregon with the kids."

"Frudenthaler will drive you home. Stick around in case the state people have more questions. I gave them your phone numbers."

Randall walks into the silence that falls in the outer office where people pretend they are busy. "Sorry this had to happen," Frudenthaler says as he drives. "If only the proper procedures had been followed."

"Yeah, I know."

"You of all people."

"Drop me off at the trailhead sign up there."

"We're miles from your place."

"That's a shortcut over the ridge. I'd like some fresh air."

Eroded in places and overgrown in others, the trail dates back to the WPA era but is returning to nature because of budget cuts. Randall pushes his hat back on his head, loosens his tie and unbuttons his jacket as he climbs. He startles white-tailed deer and sees a raccoon, innumerable fat squirrels and chipmunks. The old crocks at the bait shop say the animals are storing up fat for the hard winter the Farmer's Almanac says is on the way. It is easy to imagine what the conversation will be tomorrow.

"Suspended," one will say. "Looks like Randall is in deep shit."

"Figure he had anything to do with it?"

"I always thought he was a nice guy, but nothin surprises me anymore."

The news people would be met with hostile silence when they turned up. Much as they like to chew the fat, the bait shop idlers don't take to strangers. The wind sighs dismally through the pines as if making a comment on the futility of existence. He detours around a washed-out section and hears something in the trees. He loosens the nine millimeter in its holster.

He reaches the ridge line and stops to listen, but whatever it was is gone. The sun is slipping below the horizon and the light goes away like someone turns a dimmer switch. His stomach groans like the timbers on an old sailing ship when it gets breezy. Polish dogs definitely were not a good idea. Abigail had brought home a trunk load of Lean Cuisine frozen dinners before she left, but you were hungry an hour later; sooner if it was Chinese. He microwaved two at a time, which she would say totally defeats the purpose. But she's not here so the question is moot, as the lawyers say. An owl hoots to signal the official start of night, and it is nearly dark when he reaches the cut off to his house.

Something is wrong.

Bub's ESP always knows when he is near; either that or he has the keenest ears in dogdom. He should be barking like crazy, but there is only silence. Even the wind has died.

Randall stops in the trees short of the clearing where the house sits silent and dark. Hitching trouser legs up, he squats to observe. Those killers got nothing out of the staff, but they might think the cop knows something. A small light shows in the kitchen window. The refrigerator door has been opened—someone else is hungry.

People had seen a couple of SUVs. How many does that mean—six men, eight? Even with darkness and surprise, the odds are stacked against him. His old pickup is parked next to the house, but the engine takes a while to warm up. Randall stands with effort—maybe Lean Cuisine is a better idea than he thought—and moves back the way he came. The wind picks up again and the racing moon plays hide and seek in the clouds. The Kleinschmidt house—he's a plumbing contractor and she's a school teacher—is a quarter mile away. Randall was asked to keep an eye on it through winter. He finds the key under a planter box too heavy for a burglar to bother with.

The Kleinschmidts are return-to-nature types who use a compost toilet and plan to bury their ashes to nourish a tree rather than scattering them at sea and add to pollution, so there is no electricity or other evidence of progress. He wouldn't chance the light from even one of their dim oil lanterns, so he feels his way up stairs to the bedroom and brings down the spread from the bed. He sits in an easy chair and wraps himself in it, gun in lap. He hopes he will hear any footstep on the deck.

Randall comes awake from a light doze an hour later, aware someone is in the room. The wind is back at work, but the moon gave up the ghost and it is utterly dark. He is hyper alert, heart beginning to hammer.

"I'm not here to harm you," a kind male voice says. "Put your gun down."

"Show yourself."

"Put it on the table, please."

"How did you get in?" Randall stalls, hoping to locate him and get off a shot.

"The key under a planter box." The reassuring voice seems to come from everywhere.

"How did you know it was there?"

"It didn't take much imagination."

"But it's heavy, you had to know."

"Please, the gun."

Randall considers this. "What happens if I don't?"

"I leave because of your mistrust."

Randall can't see him anyhow, so he finds the table with his hand and lays the gun down. "Okay."

"Thank you."

"How'd you know I was here?"

The question is ignored. "You helped a man."

"You're not with them, right? I'd be dead already."

"No, I'm not with them. They left an hour ago."

"So what's this about?"

"He's in danger."

"That's pretty obvious."

"Would you help him?"

"I'm suspended and might be looking for a new job because I helped him. You think I'd make the same mistake twice?"

"He needs help."

"What'd he do to piss off these people, steal a truckload of smack?"

"I can't give you any details," the voice says. "But it's impossible to understate his importance."

"Make sure the door shuts on your way out. That wind is cold."

"I understand: someone you don't know is asking for help and not telling you why."

"I couldn't put it any better myself."

A match flares and an oil lamp begins to glow showing a bearded man in work clothes; his face is as kind as his voice. There is gray at his temples and beard; a fiftyish man, Randall judges. He settles back in the chair Oscar Kleinschmidt made with hand tools. Randall tried it once and it's like a torture device from the Middle Ages, but this man doesn't seem to mind.

"Did you notice anything different about him?"

"A lot of things," Randall says. "He had amnesia to start with, couldn't remember a thing."

He nods. "Is that all?" His deep voice is like an old-time radio announcer. It has—how to put it?—a kind of weighty authority. Randall feels his racing heart slow and his breathing get back to normal.

"Wouldn't you say he was perfect, Sergeant?"

"Perfect?" Randall scoffs. "Nobody's…" Purity was the word that had popped into his head at the time, but wasn't perfect better?

"What if I told you the future of mankind is connected to that man?"

"You didn't go to all this trouble to make me laugh."

"I'm very serious." He crosses his arms on his chest.

Randall laughs. "Okay, are we done?"

"I'll pay you for your help," he says. "Shall we say a thousand dollars a day?"

"Who are you?"

"My name is Camael. This is ten days in advance." He pulls out a fat leather wallet. "Here and now."

"Whoa, hold on a minute. What do you want—a bodyguard? One isn't going to do it. That's a whole army of stone-cold butchers."

"You are one and they are many, but help can come in different ways. His whereabouts are hidden to me at present, but perhaps police methods can find him."

"Look," Randall says with impatience, "tell me all you know about this."

The bearded man looks tempted, but then slowly shakes his head. "There will be a time, but not now." He gives Randall a keen look. "Nothing you have ever done in your life is as important as this."

After he slips silently out the door, it takes a few minutes for Randall to notice the pain in his leg is gone.

CHAPTER 4

REX HAS BEEN DRIVING FOR A LONG TIME WHEN A RED LIGHT COMES ON TO SAY FUEL IS LOW. "Fuel" is a word he has seen at islands alongside the road that blaze with light. He pulls into the next one.

Five minutes later he is standing next to a pump with the owner's manual from the glove box. Two perky young women gassing up a Mini Cooper check him out.

"Trouble?" asks the smaller one, a shapely blond in a leather jacket with a fur collar. They giggle when he admits he doesn't know how to refuel the car.

"Wow, you must really come from privilege," says the other, a redhead with a cute dimple. His smile dazzles them. They explain he has to pay first with a credit card.

Rex pats his pockets. "I don't seem to have one."

"Well, cash then," the blond woman says.

He takes out his thick roll and offers it. "You want me to take the money in?" she says. "Okay!" She peels off thirty and hands back the roll. She returns and they show him how to use the pump.

"Now I know," he says, putting the hose back in the pump when the tank is full.

They are both falling in love. "My name is Sheryl," the blond says. "She's Maggie."

"Thank you both."

"Where are you going?" asks Maggie, the bolder one.

"I'm not sure," Rex says.

"Are you in show business?" Sheryl asks.

"I don't think so."

"You'd say that even if you were," Maggie points out.

Rex is surprised. "I would?"

"You're probably hounded by fans."

Rex thinks of the staff at Templeton Hall. Perhaps they were fans? "I like people."

"C'mon," Sheryl says prettily, "tell us where you're going."

"Evil is near," Rex explains. "I must keep ahead of it."

A moment later, Rex smilingly shakes his head as he watches their tail lights disappear. The rudeness of young people was often discussed at Templeton Hall. To turn and walk away so quickly.

He slides behind the wheel and resumes his journey. The towns are bigger and closer together and he sees signs inviting the traveler to rest. Slumberville one says in neon, Zzzzzz says another. He turns into the next motel driveway. The Tuckaway's sign buzzes and the 'c' and 'y' are dark. Two couples are leaving rooms on opposite sides of the low building. The place is weed-grown and the cinderblock walls are chipped where cars bumped over logs put there to prevent just such accidents. A junker is jacked up and in the mid-stage of cannibalizing for parts in the parking lot. The empty swimming pool, the relic of a brief prosperity some decades before, is covered with trash on the bottom. The women in tight dresses that emphasize heavy legs and big rumps teeter on spike heels toward the road. Their johns drive off in cars without another look.

"Yeah, whattayawant?" demands the manager who answers the night bell.

He looks preposterously like an old-fashioned movie villain with oiled hair, pencil-thin moustache and close-set eyes with bluish bags like poison sacs. His tatty Bills jersey has the number of a long-retired player.

"I'm tired," Rex says.

"Who you with?" The manager sticks his head out the door. "Where is she?"

"Who?"

"You're alone?" Testiness turns to surprise. "You want a room to sleep in?" Rex admits this is true. "In this dump?" He meets Rex's eyes and his manner softens.

A car with another man and woman pulls into the parking lot. "Wait while I take care of them." When he hurries back he seems to notice the office's squalor for the first time. Empty pizza boxes and microwave containers occupy most flat surfaces. There are dirty magazines, laundry, empty beer cans and over-flowing ashtrays.

"I gotta get this place straightened up one of these days," he says apologetically, wiping a hand on a pants leg evidently used often for this purpose. He extends it. "Vito Romano."

"Call me Rex."

The only chair is in front of a TV screen where a porn video is on pause. Romano switches it off and sweeps an armload of takeout containers from the sofa. "No, wait." He hurries off and returns with a clean towel for the cleared spot. When Rex is seated, Romano draws his chair closer. "So what brings you to my place?"

"It's time for rest."

"Christ, there are people around here who'd slit your throat for a nickel. Lucky thing you rang my doorbell." The meanness around his mouth is gone. "Where're you headed?"

"I'm not sure," Rex says, as comfortable here as Templeton Hall.

"Where'd you come from?"

"Nowhere."

Romano relaxes in his warmth, the knots of a bitter life loosening a little. "Not sure and nowhere—that's the story of my life." Say, he asks, you hungry? When Rex nods, he telephones for a pizza. "I give them so much business they throw in the extra toppings free."

Another car pulls into the parking lot and Romano excuses himself. "Must be a fuckin full moon." When the pizza deliveryman arrives, he says, "I got paper plates somewhere." Romano shows a broad bottom as he digs in a low cupboard.

"What do you call these?" Rex asks after a bite and sip.

"You jokin? Pizza and beer."

"They're good!"

"No kiddin."

"I mean it."

"You act like you never had it before."

"I haven't."

"You never had beer and pizza!?" The sheer impossibility stops Romano in mid-bite.

Smiling, Rex shakes his head.

"Jesus Christ, where you been all your life?"

"I don't remember."

The door flies open and a dumpy young woman with bleached hair woven in thin cornrows walks in. "The toilet's plugged up in Twelve… hey, what do we got here?"

"Out!" Romano screams, spreading his arms to block her view. She backs out, trying to angle her head to see. "If the dude wants it, I'll do him for nothing. I…"

"Get out!" He slams the door in her face.

Rex watches as Romano turns locks in the door. "Who is that?"

"Just some skank."

"What does she want?"

"What's an assbitch hoebag butt slut ever want?"

Rex's puzzled look gets him. As with beer and pizza, the man doesn't know. "What did you say?" he inquires politely.

"Listen, you need a place to stay?" he says. "I can fix you up." He pays off the cops but they insist on one whore-free room they can look into when ordered to check the place out.

Rex pulls out his thick roll of cash. "Take what you need."

Romano is horrified.

"It's called money."

"I know what it is, for crissake. Look, you don't show a wad like that, let alone hand it to somebody."

"Why not?"

"A lot of people wouldn't give it back. That's just for starters."

"Would that be called evil?"

"It would be called taking advantage of an idiot. Put it away."

They finish their beer and pizza as Romano gets stymied every time he tries to find something they can talk about. The Giants—Rex never heard of them. The 'Niners, same thing. He tries music, movies, even politics though he doesn't know much himself except everybody's a crook. He draws one blank after another except when he asks more about where Rex was before here.

"It is a large hall with beautiful grounds. The people are wonderful."

Romano has to stretch to imagine such a place. "So is it a loony bin?"

"Pardon?" Rex had observed at Templeton Hall that this was a polite way to seek clarification.

"A place for people with"—Romano taps his head with a finger—"mental problems?" Even if Rex doesn't yawn hugely at this point, Romano sees he doesn't understand. It must be because he is on a much higher plain than a schmuck like me, he thinks. "You need to crap out." He makes a pillow with his hands and lays his head on them.

"That would be nice," Rex says.

"There are decent places ten minutes from here. I'm gonna be honest, we got rats and cockroaches and the plumbing could use a big enema. You can do better, is what I'm saying."

"I think this will be fine."

Romano sees there's no point in arguing. Maybe he can get more sense from him after a good night's sleep. "Follow me." The room is the far end of the building from the office. A dusty smell comes from the heater when he turns it on.

"Is your suitcase in the car?"

"I don't have one."

If only I could float through life like this, Romano thinks. The red carpet treatment even at a fucking dump like mine. He maybe ought to resent it, but somehow that doesn't seem right. Rex is a totally good person; all you have to do is look at him.

After he tells Rex to lock the door, he returns to the office. What if somebody tricks him into opening the door? Says he's hungry or gives him some other bullshit line? Got any spare change? People have pulled that here, gone door to door. Rex would show that big roll of cash and that would be that. Or one of the hookers asks does he wants to party?

Romano ponders who he can trust. "For fuck's sake," he says finally. "The coldest fucking night of the year so far."

Putting on a watch cap, gloves and his heaviest coat, he sticks a revolver in a pocket and carries a chair and his portable TV to Rex's door where the light is out already. The sleep of the fucking innocent. He sees his breath and it only takes fifteen minutes for the cold to penetrate. I'm gonna need a sweater under the coat and maybe my hoodie, he thinks. At that moment, the woman in cornrows and another whore and their johns come out of one of the rooms, everyone high as a kite. The customers leave, but Kimberly leads the other one to Romano.

"What are you doing sittin out here in the freezin cold?" Kimberly asks.

"Mindin my own business," Romano says. "You might try it yourself."

"Where's your handsome friend?"

"I guess you didn't hear me."

"I know," Kimberly says to the other one. "I bet he's in there."

"I'd like to see him from what you said."

She's new to Romano and he looks her up and down. She is bird thin with tattoos and a don't-give-a-shit look. A serious druggie, he decides; she'll be dead within a year. Quitting that life was the smartest thing he ever did.

"So what are you, guardin him or something?" Kimberly asks.

"I got a vandalism problem, if you gotta know."

"So you're gonna to sit here all night?" She is incredulous.

"Gotta better idea?"

"So where's your friend?" the other hooker asks.

"Long gone."

The women exchange skeptical looks.

"You think I give a shit you don't believe me?" Romano bristles.

"Don't get all hot under the collar," Kimberly says.

"I don't like being called a liar."

"People call you worse than that."

"You wanna keep bringin johns here? Maybe you want to use the dump down the street where the nigger takes a bigger cut. You think I don't know that?"

Alarmed, Kimberly makes nice. "Take it easy, Vito. No need to be such a hot head."

They leave but as he expects word gets around that a famous rocker or Hollywood star—somebody big to drool over—is at The Tuckaway, probably to escape fans. All through the long night people drive up totally wired or like zombies from downers to where Romano sits. A few are merely drunk. Everybody wants to see who is in the room. He shows his gun to the persistent.

"Just say who it is, man." A fat white Georgia cracker with glue in his vowels, ball cap turned sideways rapper-style.

"You think I won't use this? You think that!"

Backing off, hands up. "Take it easy, dude. We're goin."

The night crawls. Once every hour he hurries to the office for a slug of bourbon. The warmth lasts about fifteen minutes. The batteries give out on the TV and there's nothing to do but think. He asks himself what the fuck he's doing.

Just another four hours, he thinks.

Just another three hours.

Only a couple more.

Gray to the east. Romano is so cold and stiff he can barely stand. Rex will want breakfast; the only meal Romano knows how to fix. He's got eggs, bacon, potatoes for frying after the microwave softens them up. Orange juice—yes, he's got that too. The office is too hot after the outdoors and he peels off the layers. An inch of whiskey still in the bottle; might as well finish it off. He sits on the sofa in the place cleared for Rex. God, what a night. Don't want to close my eyes because… He wakes with a start and looks at the clock. Nine o'clock! He rushes to the door but Rex's car is already gone. Romano's gaze is blurred by tears.

"Cryin—what the fuck is happening to me?"

He doesn't feel like making breakfast now. Warmed up pizza is what he usually has anyhow. He's got a couple of pieces in the microwave when he hears cars outside.

CHAPTER 5

MOLLY SIMON IS SIPPING A SKINNY LATTE WITH A TRIPLE SHOT OF ESPRESSO IN A CAFÉ THAT HAS chintz curtains and fake flowers on the tables. She is in her work clothes: dark skirt, plum-colored button-up sweater and silver necklace, an ensemble that says she is a nice person who can be trusted. The caffeine works its magic as she studies faces.

If she sees some quality she is looking for, she approaches the person and asks permission to take a photograph for the Trippit Agency. "Excuse me," her line is, "but you have the most interesting face. May I take a picture?" Roughly half are flattered enough to say yes and the others decline, sometimes impolitely. Once she was told to fuck off if she knew what was good for her. "Okay, no problem," Molly replies lightly. If you have a thin skin this is not the job for you.

When she gets an okay, the picture and the personal information go into a digital data base for a software program to scan, sort and evaluate. This face might be good for a campaign pitching an HMO or a cruise line to seniors. That one for a mock jury to help lawyers prepare for a big trial. There is a big market for ordinary faces that give authenticity to products and services.

Finding them is like being a casting director except harder. Molly reads faces for honesty and deceit, good character or bad, gullibility or slyness. She finds them in eyes, a noble or button nose, a weak chin or a jaw that is determined. Her work is so unusual she has been interviewed on television and followed around by an NPR reporter.

When she looks at her own face she sees a redhead with gray eyes and faint freckles as if a chemical removal process didn't quite get the job done. A pretty enough face, she will admit, but hardly in the famous-model league. She has discovered a few of those behind a cosmetic counter, under a Stetson in cow country, or in some other place nobody else bothers to look. Her own bones are too big, her manner too tomboyish to be considered chic, not that she cares. She eats right, works out and generally takes good care of herself. Yet she is aware the firmness of youth is giving way to the dreaded sinewy look of the fit older woman with ropy tendons and veins that stand out.

A woman sitting with a friend by the window interests her. She has a round-ish face, trendy hair she's let go gray and modish eyeglasses. Put the hair in a bun, trade the frames for old-fashioned spectacles and maybe she can be the face for a new line of lamps for the older reader. Or leave her as is for another direc-tion—the hip, age-defying older reader who still needs a stronger light. Others make that decision; she merely offers them possibilities. Molly is about to make her approach when the door opens and she is mesmerized. The best looking man she has ever seen has walked in. From the silence that falls, she is not alone.

Rex had veered off a freeway exit with tires squealing and air horns blast-ing around him and wended his way through streets to an attractive shopping neighborhood where the hanging pots that hold flowers on street lights await putting away for spring.

Their eyes meet. "Mind if I join you?"

Unable to speak, she nods yes.

"Breakfast is a fine thing," Rex says. "We ate it every morning at Templeton Hall."

It strikes her as a strange comment, but it is buried in a rush of tingly feeling.

"I liked the bacon and eggs," he continues, "but others said hot cereal and toast was better for you. And orange juice, of course." The others customers are talking again, but she thinks he is the only subject of conversation.

"Is that what you want?" asks the older waitress holding her order pad to her bosom like a smitten teenager with an autograph book. "Bacon and eggs?"

"Yes," he says with a smile that makes her sag. She gulps and hurries off.

"I'm Molly." She reaches to shake hands and his transmits a kind electrical shock. Her eyes automatically take in his glaze of innocence. "Are you from here?"

"No, I'm from a different place."

"And where would that be?" My God, she thinks, where did that coquett-ish voice come from?

He hesitates, seeming ill at ease. "They ask me that a lot." Molly thinks that is his answer, but then he continues. "I'm afraid I don't know."

"Where are you going now?" Her heart is melting.

"I don't know. I'm just… driving around."

"You need to see a doctor."

"Doctor Ashford said my memory might come back."

"And he just let you go?"

"The man who came to my room said I should leave right away."

"What are you supposed to do?"

"He didn't say."

"Wait a minute!" Molly exclaims. Then she lowers her voice. "Did you say Templeton Hall?"

"Yes, it's a wonderful…

"That's where that awful thing happened."

The waitress arrives with the orange juice and Molly motions not to say anything until she leaves.

"Nothing awful happened at Templeton Hall," Rex says. "My friends there are all…"

"People were killed there! Everybody was!"

"Killed?"

She stares into his bafflement. "As in not breathing anymore."

He tucks into the bacon and eggs, his face without expression.

"It's all over the news, how could you not know? That must be what the man was talking about, the one who came to your room. Evil, isn't that what he said?"

Rex slows in his eating and a frown appears. "Killed—so that is evil?"

"What else would you call it, for God's sake?"

"Who is God?"

"Oh, please, no jokes. He knew something bad was coming and wanted you to get out right away."

"God did?"

"No," she whispers fiercely. "That man."

"Why was everyone killed?" he asks.

"They were in the wrong place at the wrong time. Call it fate."

"Fate?"

"Or random chance. Whatever. You need to talk to the police."

"I talked to Sergeant Randall."

Okay, she thinks quickly, that base is covered. "What are you going to do now? You can't keep just driving around."

His expression says he is open to suggestions.

"Look, come with me," she says, surprising herself. "We'll figure something out. I've got a spare bedroom until you find a place."

As they walk out the door, Molly wonders just what they will figure out. And at a deeper level, she wonders why she—a confirmed believer in whatever—is getting herself mixed up in somebody else's trouble. She gives him a sideways glance. Well, she thinks, the answer is obvious.

"We better take my car." It might be illegal for someone in his condition to drive. He follows her down a side street. As he gets out, a woman in a parka and bandana tied under her chin is raking leaves in her yard.

"You're not going to park there for long?" she says, a warning in her voice.

"There aren't any signs," Molly says, answering for him.

"I like that spot left open."

"This is a public street, not your private property," Molly flares.

The woman stares indignantly.

"Where are we going?" Rex asks as Molly pulls onto the freeway.

"My place."

She has lived with a couple of men—one was in IT and the other a paralegal. Jimmy Fitzleigh and Al Murry are easy-going slackers as soft as brie. Give them beer and a big flat screen TV and they ask no more from life. They are both cases of arrested development; ideal roommates for one another except nobody would cook, clean or take out the trash. Every now and then one calls to ask can't they make a fresh start, but she hasn't got that lonely yet. It is a moment's work to get Rex to sign a contract making her his agent and manager and giving her a twenty percent cut of every deal.

"You seem pretty unconcerned," she says as Rex gazes at the passing scenery like a man without a worry in the world.

"I do?"

"You have amnesia and barely escaped being killed with those other people. That would shake most people up."

"Yes, I can see how it would."

Molly accelerates expertly into the fast lane. "I don't suppose you know what you do for a living. From your clothes, I'd say you make good money."

"I don't know what I did."

"Something interesting, I bet." With his looks it wouldn't be anything humdrum or nerdy like two guys she could name.

They drive to her apartment in Hays Valley, a neighborhood of storefronts and Victorians. The green armchair by the window was set out on the sidewalk for whoever wanted it; the Indian blanket hides where the stuffing comes out. Paintings by her artistic friends hang on walls and brass fireplace tools gleam before the fake fireplace.

"It's humble but I like it." She shows him the spare bedroom and he sits on the bed to test it. "This is a nice place," he says, and she doesn't think he's being phony.

"That suit is divine and I like the tie, but you're going to need more clothes."

She calls her boss Irv Trippit and tells him he won't believe the face she's found. "He's a Greek god, I swear. The thing is he needs some clothes."

"Bring him over and let me see what he looks like," Irv says. "We've got plenty of stuff around here that never got returned to the stores." On the ride the taxi driver keeps staring at Rex in the rearview mirror.

"Jeez," he asks Molly when she pays the fare. "Who is that guy? Gotta be somebody famous."

"Not yet," she says.

Waiting for an elevator in the lobby hewn of Carrara marble, the same stone that Michelangelo carved into masterpieces, is tawny-haired Cristobal, the imperious, five-foot eleven inches couture model who is so famous only her single name is ever used. Two gay men are with her.

"Who are you?" Cristobal asks Rex as the doors open and they all enter the elevator with mirrors and brushed steel walls.

"Rex," Molly answers for him. "Where are you going?" she asks the pages. The light scent of Cristobal Romance ($300 oz.) fills the elevator.

"Tenth floor," one of Cristobal's escorts answers. Both are awed by Rex, who politely smiles at Cristobal like an alpha god acknowledging a minor deity.

"We're going to the Cumberland Agency on Twenty-One," Molly lies. "Could you punch the button for me?"

Cristobal has put long crimson-tipped fingers on Rex's arm. "Can we talk?"

"We're already late," the button-pushing companion reminds her in a heavy French heavy accent. "Eet's the Ford account and Hal says zee are death on late."

"As soon as I get out of that meeting?" she whispers to Rex.

"Come up to the Cumberland Agency," Molly says. "We'll be there for an hour or two."

"The Twenty-First floor?" the other page says. Molly nods and waits as the doors open on the tenth floor.

The rubber edges of doors keep bumping against the foot of one of the men as Cristobal tries to free herself from Rex's spell. "Really, Cristobal," he protests as the elevator begins a frustrated buzzing. When the doors finally close, Molly pushes the button for Thirty-One.

Irv has seen enough great faces to be jaded, but his mouth falls open. "My God," he manages to get out. "Where did you find this guy?"

"A coffee shop in Danville."

"Danville? You are shitting me."

Rex is looking at them with affable curiosity.

"Bring me a blank contract," Irv says. "We've got to sign this guy right away." He is a tall, dark man with cadaverous looks. The vivid cravat and old fashioned pince-nez glasses on a ribbon point to a streak of vanity.

"I'm his agent," Molly says.

Hiding his disappointment, Irv shifts into schmoozing gear. "The name's Irving Trippit, Irv to you. Have a chair, my friend." He hits the intercom. "Hold all my calls."

These are lean times for advertising, but Irv sees a world of potential in this hunk. Not just fantastic looking but tall and well built and not gay from the vibes he gets—a major bonus in this business. He is perfect for men's fashions, obviously, but more possibilities occur to Irv. He's got definite brand potential. From cologne to the face of a financial investment firm, the guy would fit anywhere. Molly is aware his mind is speeding up. She'll have to handle Irv carefully.

"So you want to be a model," Irv says.

"A model?" Rex turns to Molly for explanation.

"He just wants to borrow some clothes for now," she says.

"Take what you want." He shows Rex an adjoining room with clothes on hangars and shirts and socks in drawers. "Load up."

When Irv returns, Molly says, "There's something you should know. He's got amnesia. Can't remember anything, including who he is."

"Shut up!"

"I'm not kidding. He walked into that café with no past except for Templeton Hall."

"Jesus Christ! Where all those people were massacred?"

"He left before it happened."

Irv is momentarily speechless. "Do the police know?"

"He already talked to them." Molly thinks that's all Irv needs to know.

"Is that what caused the amnesia?"

"He wasn't there when it happened, Irv."

"Yeah, but the shock when he found out?"

"I don't know."

"So you don't know what he does or anything? He might already be under contract."

"Wouldn't we recognize him? A face like that."

"Yeah, you're right." Irv chews his lip.

"So do you see the potential I do?"

"Are you crazy? It's huge, mega! He's Cary Grant and Brad Pitt with a little of George Clooney thrown in. I can tell you right now who will be the next *People*s magazine's sexiest man of the year."

CHAPTER 6

RANDALL TELEPHONES THE NON-EMERGENCY NUMBER FOUR TIMES AND HANGS UP EACH TIME. HE gets Penny on the fifth. "Things still hopping?"

"It hasn't let up," she says. They'd had one of those teasing office things that could have gone somewhere if they hadn't both been happily married. Now, like him, she had put on weight, and picturing her in bed wasn't quite what it was before. "I think what they did to you was rotten. Whatever happened to the presumption of innocence?"

"They're scared so they're being stupid. Happens all the time in life."

"Nobody I talk to thinks it's fair."

"It'll all get sorted out." But Randall thinks of the people he arrested who went to prison even though they were probably innocent of the charge though guilty of a lot of others.

"It better get sorted out," Penny says.

"Want to do me a favor?" he asks.

"Sure."

He gives her the license number of the car the bearded man said he had rented using the name A. A. Sephirot. "See if that turns up anywhere. If it does, let me know."

"Does this have to do with Templeton Hall?"

"I'm not sure. Don't do anything that gets you in trouble."

"I don't care about that. Greg and I are getting tired of the rat race. We're thinking about Arizona."

"Property is cheaper," Randall says.

"That's a big part of it."

While he waits in line at the bank to buy a CD with the cash, he wonders how to break the news to Abigail about Bub. They put a bullet in his head just inside the door. Brave, steadfast Bub; he had made it clear they would get in only over his dead body. Sobbing, Randall buried him up on the ridge, the first and last place you could see the sun rise and set. He had always hoped heaven had dogs. How could it not if it was perfect? He has to wipe his eyes.

Bub is just one of the things he has to explain to Abigail. The list already includes his suspension, the bearded man, and being hired for ten thousand dollars. He wouldn't tell her about the SUVs full of killers. She would be on the road back home with the twins as soon as she hung up.

"Wow! Did you win the lottery?" Ernestine Dowd says when he takes the rubber band off the roll of currency and begins counting out the bills.

"A hot streak at the Indian casino."

"I won two hundred bucks there once, but lost my shirt every other time." She watches with envy. "I think I just might take another crack at it."

He thought of hiding the cash, but what if something happened to him? Rocky Marciano buried his money in places no one had found yet, and you heard other stories like that. You had to tell where it was hidden and that put whoever you told in jeopardy. The bank would notify the IRS, of course, but Randall didn't mind. A man ought to pay his taxes.

He had fallen asleep after the visit and woke up in full daylight. The killers were long gone, as the bearded man had said. Apart from Bub nothing was wrong. No vandalism, the drawers hadn't been rifled, and they hadn't eaten anything. No surprise there. The light from the fridge door that had alerted him showed bagged carrot sticks and celery stalks, low-fat milk and yogurt. Abigail had been so hopeful.

He drives into town in jeans and flannel shirt to George's Café for its Lumberjack Special, ham steak with eggs and stacked pancakes smothered in maple syrup. He also orders a double side of cottage fries on a separate plate. When he is chewing on a toothpick, his cell phone rings.

"Hi, honey," Abigail says. "Are things still crazy?"

More than you can possibly imagine, he thinks. "About the same."

"It's on the news just about all the time. They're saying there are no clues."

"I can't comment on that."

"Oh, don't be so official, it makes you sound pompous. It's horrible to think that could happen in our own backyard. I can't even think when the last murder was."

"Eleven years ago."

Broderick Dunbar had killed his wife for fooling around with the handyman and then shot himself; people talked about it for years. The massacre would be good for at least a century of conversation. The ghost hunting shows would be turning cartwheels.

"How are the kids?"

"They're eating their Cheerios now. Did you have your special cereal?"

"Breakfast was delicious." It wasn't a total lie.

"How much are you doing on the case?" she asked.

"They brought in experts from the state police to run things." Not the truth, but also not a lie.

"That must be hard."

"It's easy, actually."

"You guys don't mind them butting in?"

"The old saying, many hands make the work light. How's your mother?"

"She's perked up seeing the twins. We miss you."

"Same here. Listen, there's another call coming in."

"I'll call you later."

"Frudenthaler here. How're you doing?"

"Fine," Randall said. "Nice of you to ask."

"Sarcasm never helps a situation. You at home?"

"George's Café."

"Their Lumberjack Special can't be beat."

Randall removed the toothpick. "What's up?"

"Look, I want you to know I don't think you had anything to do with this other than not logging in. Neither does the chief, just between us."

"He has my permission to tell other people."

"Those state guys put him in a corner from the get-go and he felt he had to go along with them."

"Isn't that called not having a spine?"

"I predict you'll be back at work in a week or two, anyhow as soon as the district attorney's office signs off."

"Signs off on what?" Randall asks.

"That you didn't have anything to do with it. One of them is here now talking to the chief. A little bird tells me those two state cops are going to get a dressing down. I'd go fishing if I were you; have some fun on the taxpayer's money."

"Good idea. Thanks for the call."

Randall drives back home, keeping an eye on the rearview mirror. When he pulls up to the house, the world gets blurry. Up to yesterday he heard dancing claws on the floor when he got to the door. He has to sit down until he stops crying. The killers hadn't shit on the coffee table, a way of salting the wound in many burglaries. They had even used cereal bowls instead of the floor for their ashtrays.

"You won't believe this," Penny says when he answers his cell phone.

"What?"

"Do you have a cold? You sound stuffed up."

"Allergies."

"The car you're interested in was spotted where a man was murdered."

"Anybody else there know yet?"

"Not yet."

"Keep it under your hat for now, okay?"

"You got it."

Randall drives to the hamlet of Pinedale and parks in front of the small police department. He shows his badge to the gum-chewing young woman holding down the fort.

"You want to talk to the chief," she says before he can speak, "he's out at the scene."

She gives directions and he drives to the motel where all three of the police department's cars are parked and crime scene tape keeps a bunch of kids on bikes from coming any closer.

A stout man in a business suit with a thick walrus moustache is just coming out of the office as Randall bends under the tape.

"I'm Bill Noble," he says, sticking out a hand. "You from the state?"

"What's up?" Randall says. He didn't exactly say he was from the state if it came up later.

"A guy tortured to death. Better have a strong stomach."

Romano has been carved up with the same finesse as the Templeton Hall victims. "Looks like he held out a long time," Noble says. "Wonder if they wanted something from him or were just having fun. The shit that goes on these days."

"Did anybody see anything?" Randall asks.

"One of the hookers took down a license number."

"Did she say why?"

"The driver was some handsome dude she wanted to see more of."

"Did she explain how she was going to arrange that by writing down the number?"

"She might have someone in the department who'd look up an address. We don't pay the salaries you state guys make."

"Any other leads?"

"We've asked for one of your forensic teams to come over from Templeton Hall. Maybe they'll find something."

Randall thinks the manager could have given up what he knew and saved himself all that pain. They would have still killed him, but it would have been a clean bullet to the brain to save time.

"Anything taken?" he asks routinely. The thought occurs that the victim wasn't talking because he was trying to protect Rex.

"How could you tell?" Noble said, looking around. "There could be a pony in here and you wouldn't know. Looks like he lived on beer and pizza."

"It beats carrot sticks and celery," Randall said.

"Is your wife doing that to you, too?"

The coroner's van pulls up and Randall leaves them to gather up the various parts of the late Mister Romano. He calls Penny. "Looks like the same people were involved in this one. Better tell the chief and Frudenthaler."

"That car you're looking for turned up again. It was towed in for a parking violation." Randall gets the address and drives east. The woman in jeans and flannel sitting on a stool to dig up bulbs for winter storage has a busybody look.

"If you're selling something, I'll tell you right now I'm not buying."

Randall flashes his badge. "I wanted to ask about the car that was towed."

"People who work in the shops think the law doesn't apply to them. The sign says four hours but they leave their cars all day."

"What can you tell me about the driver?"

"The woman he was with had a smart mouth, I can tell you that."

Randall puts on his most attentive look.

"They had separate cars. His was the one parked in front of my house."

"So did you get a look at him?"

"Just his back."

"What about her?"

"I took down her license number. I've had people throw eggs at the house when I turn them in. They come back at night."

He got the number and telephoned Penny. "Still busy?"

"There are so many investigators hanging around we have to make coffee every half hour. I don't know why half of them don't go home and get some sleep. They're no good the way they are, yawning and rubbing their eyes."

He waited while she ran the license number. "A party named Molly Simon. She lives in the city." He got the address and drove to Hays Valley. License plate numbers from two eyewitnesses—this was too easy.

CHAPTER 7

THE ONE-TIME PLUMBING PARTS WAREHOUSE IS ROCKING. A PNEUMATIC DEVICE BENEATH THE FLOOR makes it dip and shudder so straight off you get a reeling-drunk feeling, just one sign that Party Time at the Clown House has the out-of-control vibe that is so cutting edge right now. Ship rigging and rope ladders are overhead and a mirrored disco ball flashes. Ten bartenders in nautical uniforms work a hundred-foot bar like the hull of an America Cup yacht. The trance music is so loud it seems almost visible and people writhe on the small dance floor as if falling to the floor and speaking in tongues is next.

Because she is connected with the scene, Molly Simon doesn't have to stand outside hoping the slab-muscled bouncers in tight black suits and shaved heads let them in. The velvet rope lifts and they get a good table; she doesn't kid herself that the awestruck looks are for her. Rex in jeans, black T-shirt, and leather jacket borrowed from the agency looks like he is sponsored by GQ.

A wizened gnome of a man in a velvet frock coat and an awesome head of dark hair advances with a springy step. "Hi, I'm Mick." To Molly he is like a figure from Madame Tussaud's waxworks that has had a really cool animatronics update. "Mind if I sit down?" He shakes their hands, gripping only the tips of fingers.

"You've gotta be in show business, mate," he tells Rex.

"Why?" Rex says, smiling.

"Not just hoping to be, but in show business. So how come I don't know you? Where's your entourage? Your manager, the bodyguards, your agent, the rest of the lot?"

"I'm it," Molly says.

He doesn't take his eyes off of Rex. "So are you in rock and roll, the cinema—what is it you guys do?"

"We aren't…" she starts.

"I played the piano at Temple…" Rex begins

"At temple," Molly cuts in.

"I've got a lot of Jewish friends; so shalom. The club asked me to do a set a little later on. You interested?"

"Interested?"

"In sitting in." At Rex's look, Mick continues. "You know, playing with us. Everybody knows Satisfaction. The chords are so simple, man. We've got sheet music if you need it."

"That sounds like fun," Rex says.

"Wait a minute," Molly says.

"I'll give you the high sign from the stage," Mick says, springing up nimbly for man of his advanced years. The visit to his table by a historic figure in rock and roll intensifies the interest in Rex. Molly is so busy fending off table hoppers, including women who sit down to openly stare, that she asks a bouncer to help.

"You," he says jerking a thumb at them, "move it."

Meanwhile, there is a stir in the crowd as new musicians filter onto the stage; they are recognized by the cognoscenti as Mick's sidemen. The music stops and there is a hush until a voice says, "Ladies and gentlemen, we have a special visitor tonight…" The rest is drowned by the crowd's roar.

Mick does a few of the numbers that made him a billionaire and then squints into the bright lights. "I've got a friend out there who's gonna help us on the keyboard for the next number." He raises both arms. "Give it up for my friend Rex."

Rex wends his way through the tables as hands grab at him. He gains the stage and turns to wave to the crowd. As Mick gives shout-outs, the keyboardist whispers to Rex and shows him chords. Molly is blown away by the sangfroid, by how totally relaxed he is. Mick launches into the number he's done a thousand times, but never like this. It is electric, explosive! He pauses in his skipping and capering to point at Rex, caught in a second spotlight grooving to the music and giving the chords masterful riffs not heard in the original.

"Fabulous!" Mick cries as the music ends. "Ladies and gentlemen—Rex!"

A storm of applause.

After raising their hands overhead and bending in a bow so perfect it looks rehearsed, the two disappear into the wings. Molly squeezes her way through the mob.

"I need to get back there," she tells one of the bodyguards fencing off the stage. "I'm with Rex."

"Everybody's saying they're with Rex," he says, thick arms folded implacably against his chest.

"I'm his agent for crissake."

But he won't be moved and she has no luck with others she tries. After an hour of waiting, a band technician that she asks says Rex left the building with Mick.

She feels a sense of loss, but it is comforting she has the signed contract that goes straight into the safe deposit box tomorrow. She understands the mesmerizing power of glamour and the cleverness of lawyers and won't be surprised down the road if they tried to pick it apart. She kicks off her shoes back home and switches on a news program where the Templeton Hall massacre still has top billing. A psychiatrist and a retired FBI profiler are interviewed. Then old men at some bait shop in hicksville are on the screen; she knows these old-fart types from her work. She sees the tug-of-war between their suspicion of outsiders and their hankering to be on television. They'd work well as scoffers in a TV commercial; by the end of the spot they are totally won over, singing the praises of the new product—constipation relief or false teeth cleanser now with Foam Power—as the best thing since sliced bread. The reporter is asking them about a policeman who was taken off the investigation. The old duffers trade guarded looks. "I know him," one offers, "but I don't know nothin about that." The others don't either.

Long after she has gone to bed there is a soft knock at the door. Going to the peephole in her pajamas, she sees Rex standing outside. "Sorry to be so late," he says. "There was a party with a lot of interesting people. Why didn't you come?"

"They didn't let me." God, she thinks, I must look like hell in ratty pajamas and my hair sticking up.

"But you're my friend."

"They wouldn't listen when I told them. Tell me about the party."

"There were lots of really neat people called celebrities and guys who play sports for money. Mick sure knows a lot of people. A guy asked me to come by the ball park tomorrow and meet the team. Man, I'm tired…"

"Am I invited?"

"You're going to drive me there." Rex hesitates, uncertain. "I hope."

"I might not let you out of my sight again," she jokes. "What kind of team?"

"He said they play baseball; the Giants. Do you know them?"

"They need pitching."

Rex stretches and yawns hugely. "Mick has a new song he wants me to sing for his next album."

"What!"

"It's not bad, but I think I can make it better."

"I didn't know you sang."

"Oh," he said casually, "there are a lot of things I do."

"You were amazing tonight."

"Well, thanks."

Was anyone ever less impressed with himself? "Weren't you nervous or anything?"

"Not a bit."

"Why doesn't he sing his own song?"

"He says it's about birds. I thought at first he meant, you know, with wings, but it's women. Young, beautiful women with long legs. He said it wasn't age appropriate for him because he's a great grandfather and all, though he still has those thoughts."

"You didn't sign anything? Like a contract?"

"No," he says with a smile, "you're my manager, remember?"

Molly wonders if she should invite him into her bed, but thinks better of it. It is hard enough as it is to keep her head clear. In the morning while he is in the shower she gets coffee and Danish from the neighborhood Starbucks. Afterward, they drive to AT&T Park.

"He said to check in with the guard at the player's entrance," Rex says.

After walking through a tunnel they emerge on the emerald playing field where men are lazily throwing the ball or taking swings at the batting cage. It's weird seeing the field from this angle. She usually has nosebleed seats.

"Rex," cries one who trots toward them. Molly recognizes Felix Fernandez, the hawk-nosed home run champ. "Glad you could make it, dude." He chest bumps Rex and shakes her hand. "Glad to meet you."

"I'm such a fan," she gushes.

She got hooked on the Giants going to games with her two former boyfriends. She has seen Fernandez exchange post-game banalities with announcers countless times on television. "I just try to stay focused" is usually worked into the conversation.

"How about this guy, though," Fernandez says. "You shoulda heard him last night. He plays the axe better than Eric Clapton, swear to God."

"The guitar?" she says, turning to Rex. "You play the guitar, too?"

"A little," he says. "I seem to have a knack."

"A knack," Fernandez says, laughing. "Listen to the man. Mick wants to build a new band around him. Did he tell you?"

"I thought it was just one song."

"I think he got a little carried away," Rex says.

"Hey, you want to throw some batting practice? Fernandez asks. "I'm up next. Nothing fancy; just lob them over the plate or come as close as you can."

"Sure," Rex says with a smiling shrug.

"I'll meet you at the cage. I gotta get my gloves." He trots off and Rex asks, "What's throwing batting practice?"

Molly points. "Like that man there." A coach behind a protective screen is tossing balls to a batter who cracks them into the outfield.

Rex watches, noting the ways the leg is lifted, the half turn and throw. "That looks easy enough."

Fernandez has his batting gloves on and is standing in the batter's box by the time Rex reaches the pitcher's mound. "Hey, Charlie," Fernandez yells. "Let the new guy throw."

Charlie, a middle-aged man with a face the color of glove leather from the sun, hands Rex a ball and stands behind the screen. Fernandez shows where he wants the ball. Rex puts it in the strike zone with an easy motion and the balls fly into the stands.

"Put a little mustard on it," Charlie says.

"Mustard?" Rex asks.

"You know, throw harder."

"How much harder?"

"How about as hard as you can?"

The ball blazes past Fernandez's bat and catches the catcher in the face mask.

"Jayzus," he yells. "Why didn't you say you were throwing a heater?"

"Hell," the coach says, "that had to be in the high 90s."

Fernandez is slow getting his bat around on the next three pitches. "I was out late last night," he calls to a knot of assistant coaches.

"Bennie," Charlie yells, "get the radar gun on this guy." A coach runs into a tunnel and comes back with it. The next pitch zips over the plate clocked at 107 miles an hour.

"My God," the coach exclaims to Molly, "where'd he get that arm?"

Players stop to watch. Rex's next pitches come in at the same speed.

"C'mon, man," Fernandez yells, "you're making me look bad."

"Can he throw a curve?" the coach asks Molly.

"I didn't know he could throw a fast ball."

"You the girlfriend?"

"I'm the manager."

The coach takes a phone out of his pocket and walks to the third base line to make a call. When Fernandez steps out of the box with only a couple of foul balls for his efforts, others take turns but nobody can hit the fastball. Molly hears them talking in awed tones.

"Man, Bob Gibson didn't throw that hard."

"Neither did The Rocket."

When Rex takes a break they gather to pepper him with questions. They been hiding you in the minors? You been playing down in the Dominican to be so loose? Did you play in college? How come nobody's heard of you, man?

Charlie is at Molly's elbow. "The GM wants to talk to you."

"What about?" she says.

"He's coming right down."

A few minutes later, a silver-haired man with a pugnacious jaw look walks quickly toward them. "Ethan Margolis," he says. "Charlie says you're his agent."

"Manager."

"Let's go to the dugout. It'll give us a little privacy." They sit on a bench close enough for her to smell the mint with an undertone of bourbon on his breath. She remembers reading he was a big party guy in his playing days.

"Charlie tells me your client has a cannon for an arm." His extra chin wobbles from excitement he is trying to restrain by force of will. "How many offers?"

"Offers?"

"From other teams."

"You think he's a ball player?" Molly says in surprise.

"Well, isn't he?"

"He seems to be a lot of things."

Margolis ignores this. "I'll get our player personnel people together and put something on the table this afternoon. It isn't the world's biggest secret we need pitching. Charlie says he's got an amazing fastball that jumps around and he's the best judge of pitchers in the majors."

"Well," she admits, thinking of Mick. "He does have one offer."

"We'll match or beat anything you got. Does he have a curveball?"

"I doubt it, but he sure is a fast learner."

"How old is he?"

"I never asked. Mid-twenties, early thirties?"

"Charlie thinks that's about right. These days a guy his age can expect another ten, fifteen years if he stays in shape."

Molly explains about Rex's amnesia but leaves Templeton Hall for later.

"So we don't really know anything about his background?" He makes a clucking sound. "Look at the way the guys crowd around him," Margolis marvels. "The guy's a natural leader. Amnesia's not a problem for us; we'll get him the top doctors. Stanford is just down the road."

The cell phone rings in her bag and she excuses herself and steps away to take the call.

"What's new with you?" asks Doreen, her friend in the New York office. Like practically everyone she knows, Doreen used to be a model; but beneath those abundant dark curls is a sharp mind.

"Everything."

"Do tell." She pictures Doreen kicking off her shoes and leaning back in the chair.

"I picked up this guy in a coffee shop."

"I guess it beats a bar. What's he look like?"

"He's the handsomest man in the world."

"I'll give that the usual discount."

"I'm serious."

"I wish I could tell you how many men I thought were handsome looked like diseased weasels the morning after. Once, I couldn't stop myself from screaming."

"Irv Trippit thinks so, too."

"Wait a minute, Irv?" Molly pictures her sitting up straight. "He called first thing this morning and got the higher-ups in a tizzy over some new god on the West Coast."

"That's him. He's got amnesia."

"Wait a minute! This man you picked up in a coffee shop is the guy Irv is talking about?"

"One and the same. I introduced them."

"And how do you know he has amnesia?"

"Because he can't remember anything. That's what amnesia means. He was at Templeton Hall."

"Oh, my God!"

"He got away before it happened. He was just driving around aimlessly when I found him. He has no memory of it."

Silence does not come natural to Doreen, but this one lasts. "So the shock made him lose his memory?"

"Maybe the doctors the Giants hire can help him find out."

"You're going to have to explain that."

"The Giants want to sign him as a pitcher."

"He's an athlete?"

"And a fantastic musician. Mick wants him to go on tour."

Another long pause. "Molly, you are so full of shit."

"It sounds crazy, I know."

"Handsomest man in the world I can maybe buy when I see the picture, but a rock star and a major league pitcher? I'm sorry."

"He's neither yet," Molly pointed out. "They're just what you'd call possibilities."

"How could you have time for both?"

"Athletes start bands."

"Not worth listening to. You said Mick wants him?"

"They're going to write a song together."

"When did you meet this guy? You haven't said a word before now."

"It was just the day before yesterday and it's been wild ever since; there hasn't been time to call you. And, look, I don't have time now. We're at the ball park and the general manager is talking to me."

"Why is he talking to you?" Doreen asks.

"I'm Rex's manager."

He is in the batter's box now, everyone silent and watching. Gene Kelso, the pitching ace, is winding up. Rex blasts his first offering over the center field fence.

"Who's Rex?" Doreen asks.

"The guy. Bye."

Ten pitches, ten cracks, ten balls rocket into the stands. Margolis doesn't try to hide his excitement.

"So are we on for this afternoon?" he asks Molly. "One of the owners is flying in personally. I just talked to him."

"I can't commit to that. I'm not even sure he wants to play baseball."

Margolis rears back in disbelief. "With talent like that?"

"He's got a lot of talents, Mr. Margolis."

"The man fires a 107-mile-an-hour fastball, lady, and that last ball he hit is probably still in the air. There's no way he can be better in something else."

"I can see how you'd think that, but this is one special guy."

His smile is knowing. "Okay, you're softening me up, but I'm telling you it's not necessary." He gives her his cell phone number. His arm goes around her shoulder and his voice drops. "If he signs with us, we'll take care of you on the side."

"On the side?"

He winks. "Whatever it takes."

Sitting in his car outside the player's entrance, Randall has just finished making quacking sounds on the telephone for the twins, having fed Abigail more lies. He can justify them because she's not crazy out of her mind with worry... but the time is coming. He pictures her set jaw and flashing eyes. She will want to know why the hell didn't he tell her the truth?

Randall had pulled up just as Molly and Rex drove away from her place in her red Honda that racked up thirty thousand miles a year in her search for new faces; he follows close enough not to get stranded by a light changing to red. If they're friends, he thinks, that means Rex has some memory back. But the man is so likeable she could just be a chance encounter. Keeping an eye on the player's gate from a coffee house across the street, he sips coffee and eats Danish with thick frosting. Abigail would be horrified, especially when he orders a second. He is licking his fingers when he sees Rex and the woman coming from the gate.

He leaves the coffee shop to intercept them. "Hi, Rex."

"Sergeant!" Rex gives him a bear hug so powerful the policeman grunts.

"Next time let's just shake hands," Randall says. "Who's your friend?"

"I'm Molly," she says with a firm handshake. "I'm his manager."

"You've got a manager already?" he asks Rex.

"Is it about Templeton Hall?" Molly says, not quite aggressively but enough to hint that she could be trouble.

"Can we talk inside?" Randall says. "There's a nice coffee shop right over there." He wouldn't mind another Danish if the truth was told.

"I think I should see some identification," Molly says as they order coffee.

"The sergeant is a nice guy," Rex says.

"No, she's right," Randall says, letting her take a long look at his badge and then his police ID. "Is your memory any better?"

"It's still like the world began the afternoon I met you."

"Have they made any progress?" Molly says.

"Men were seen in SUVs. That's about all we know."

"So you don't know why they killed all those people," Molly says.

Randall nods at Rex. "The only thing I'm sure of is it has something to do with our friend here."

Molly lays her hand protectively on Rex's forearm and he slowly withdraws it, all attention on the policeman.

"Have you ever heard of a motel called the Tuckaway?" Randall asks.

"I stayed there."

"Did anything happen?"

"The manager's a nice guy. We talked for a while and then I went to bed."

"What happened then?"

"Nothing."

"Is there something else?" Molly interjects.

"I left before anyone was up. I drove around until I met Molly."

She repeats more firmly, "Is there something else?"

"The manager was killed. It was the same guys in the SUVs."

"Oh my God," Molly cries. People at the other tables look over.

"They came for me too," Randall says. "Before they got the manager."

"You?" Rex says. "Why did they do that?"

"They probably thought I knew where you'd gone."

Rex looks pensive but not afraid. Randall thinks the lack of fear is strange.

A waitress is being roundly abused by a regular, a heavy-set bully with purple wattles that judder from his anger. "I ordered a whipless dry double double with room," he said. "Can't you get anything straight?" He slams a hand on the table making a dish with his double-chocolate chunk brownie jump.

"I'm sorry," she says, cringing. She is tiny and gamin-like and wears gold-hoop gypsy earrings too big for her small head.

He is about to continue when Rex glances at him and his expression changes from fury to alarm. "Oh, my God," he cries. He lunges to his feet and hurries to the men's room with quick short steps and buttocks clinched.

One of the gray-haired ladies sitting at a table gets up, grimaces and waves her hand at the odor that hangs in his wake. "Young man," she says to Rex, "would you mind sitting with us for a moment?"

"It would be a pleasure," he says.

"What a nice guy," Randall says, watching him being introduced to the women.

"Everybody loves him," Molly agrees.

"Not everybody."

Randall watches him charming the ladies. "What were you doing at the ball park?"

"Watching him pitch."

"Let me guess, he's good."

"None of the Giants could hit his fast ball, that's how good. The owners want him to sign a contract."

"From what I've seen, the guy can do anything."

"I'm glad to hear you say that, I'm at a total loss what to think." She tells him about Mick. "So right at this point he can be a rock star or a baseball star, his pick."

"Assuming he survives," Randall says.

"But why would anyone want him dead?"

His mind had been resisting going there but now it gives way like an earth berm in a spring flood. He leans back in his chair.

"I think we ought to take a step back," he says. "This is not natural what we're dealing with here."

"If it's not natural," Molly says, her eyes big, "are you saying it's… supernatural?" She watches as he chooses his words.

Randall tells her about Camael's visit and what he said. "He told me keeping him safe was the most important thing I'd ever do."

She is silent and looks out the window for a long time. It's just too big to get her arms around. "Rex mentioned an old man, too, but, sorry," she says, "like the song, I'm a material girl in a material world. I just can't believe something like that."

"Make up your own mind," Randall says, "but to me it's looking like a good versus evil thing."

"But that's like… so old-fashioned." She rakes a hand through her thick red hair. "The way we think now is that good-evil stuff is just… I don't know, relative." She recalls bits of a lecture in college. "What's bad in one culture might be acceptable in another and who's to say which is right?"

He thinks about Templeton Hall, the tortured bodies in their sticky pools of blood and the many other crime scenes when he was a cop in San Francisco. Wives and children murdered by drunk or crazy husbands. Or they were cold sober when they picked up the cleaver. They had worked out what had to be done and took the necessary action. Alongside the ordinary horrors in the headlines, beheadings and cannibalism were on the rise everywhere you looked. Killers videotaped themselves eating the hearts of their victims or their livers. Then they put it on Facebook and YouTube so you didn't have to imagine the details. So, yup, he was totally on board with the existence of evil.

"I'm not saying killing isn't totally wrong," Molly says. "That's stupid."

"What are you saying then?" The sergeant doesn't claim to understand the younger generations except that every ten years or so you looked back and things seemed to have changed for the worse.

"Motive! They killed all those people for a reason, not because they were evil. You have to find out what it is to catch them."

"They want Rex, that's your motive."

"But why?"

"The guy seems perfect. He's great at whatever he does."

"And?"

"I haven't figured 'and' out yet."

Rex is disengaging himself from the old ladies.

"Don't say anything," Molly says fiercely. "It would so totally mess up his head."

"I wonder what's going on in that head."

Rex remains a blank slate. He accepts things as they come, not forming an opinion unless he gets a cue about what to think. An important critical faculty appears missing along with his memory.

"I don't think you should take him back to your place," Randall says. "Park him in a hotel. That might be a good idea for you, too. Let me know where you're staying. Pay in cash instead of a credit card. Give them a phony name."

"Where will you be?"

"I'll be in touch." He gives her one of the pre-paid phones he picked up at Best Buy. "Don't use your smartphone or any of your other gadgets. Pretend like you're on Lost."

"That was so long ago I hardy remember."

"How about Survivor?"

"You don't have to paint a picture, you know. I'm not stupid."

He drives through South of Market to the Mission District trying to sort things out. When he nearly gets in a rear-ender because he wasn't paying attention, he pulls in front of a graceful, Mission-style Episcopal Church artfully framed by tall palm trees. The cool, lofty interior has a high arched ceiling and rich wooden pews; long, narrow banners are hung to celebrate the church season; candles gutter in the nave. He takes an aisle seat to think. The light through stained glass windows depicts Christ at various stages of His life, death and Resurrection. A priest comes from the sacristy behind the chancel and moves objects around on the altar.

This is too deep for a simple cop like me, Randall thinks. I'll give the money back and work around the house until they call me back to the job. A dead tree needs taking down and the rain gutters are clogged, and Abigail has plenty of other stuff on the honey-do list. He feels moving air and looks up. The priest is smiling in welcome. His thick hair shot with gray is expensively cut and his teeth whitened. He wears a natty dark gray suit and his dog collar is like a hip accessory.

"New here?" he asks. "I'm Bill."

"Just passing by," Randall says.

"Please stay as long as you like. If there's anything I can do."

It's a getaway line, but Randall pounces. "There is something." He slides down the pew to make room.

The Reverend William Masters takes a seat and assumes an attentive manner, smile lines deepening. He reminds Randall of a youth leader who made a smooth transition into middle age, the enthusiasm still there but on a tighter leash. He leans his chin on his fist to signify he is giving his full attention.

Why pussyfoot around, Randall thinks. "I think I had a visit from an angel."

Masters' smile fades. This is San Francisco and St. Timothy's is all too familiar with mad people from the street. If they begin to shout, police are called.

"An angel," Masters repeats brightly, removing his chin from the fist.

Randall shows him his policeman's badge. "I'm not one of the neighborhood crazies."

The clergyman inspects it. "That's a relief."

But he is wary. The more advanced elements in the church have put angels behind them; some in a private moment will even admit to skepticism about God. The old rituals and rites are necessary because congregations must be humored, but social justice and the environment are the thing.

"When did this, um, angel visit you?"

"The night after Templeton Hall."

"That horrible massacre! We held a vigil for the victims."

"One got away."

Masters rubs his jaw thoughtfully. "Angels." That came up in his seminary days. The professor's heart wasn't in it and they skimmed through the material.

"Let's see, what do I remember? The term 'angel' means messenger. They are mentioned in Hebrews, Luke and a few other places. Revelations, of course; there are a lot of strange things there. Angels are immortal but not eternal, having been created by God in the first six days. Knowledgeable but not omniscient, powerful but not omnipotent. Is this the sort of thing you want?"

"Whatever you can tell me," Randall says. "He was an older party. He looked like somebody who might work in a hardware store."

"How did this apparition appear? By some accounts, they are invisible."

"He was very visible."

"And yet the Bible describes some as glorious, radiant or brilliant in appearance. The Scriptures have many contradictions."

Randall shakes his head. "Like I said, ordinary looking."

"Angels are neither male nor female, according to Luke, so there's another problem." Masters taps his head to jog memory. "They are immaterial, but can move physical things."

"He had to move a heavy planter box to get a key."

"You say someone got away? I don't remember that from the news."

"The old man, Camael, said watching over him was the most important thing I'd ever do."

"Did he give a reason?"

"We didn't get around to that."

"You follow every lead no matter how far-fetched, that's why you're asking about angels?"

"Something's not far-fetched when you saw it yourself." A thought pops into his head. "There were bad angels in with the good ones weren't there?"

"Yes, a third of them followed Lucifer and got thrown out of heaven with him. Fallen angels, they're called. According to Scripture, they are evil and depraved spirits with no second chance for salvation. Our Baptist brethren are more into this sort of thing; you might want to touch base with them."

Randall ignores the brush off. "Who is this guy and why do they want him so bad they'd kill all those people, that's what I want to know."

"Did he insult Islam by any chance?"

"He has amnesia so he wouldn't remember if he did."

"He doesn't remember anything?"

"There's another thing, he's as innocent as a baby. Oh, and he can do anything. Whatever you can name; not just do it, but do it better than anyone. He's perfect."

"Perfect? How old is this man?"

"Early thirties, I'd say."

Masters has a thin smile. "Okay, I get it now, it's the Second Coming but with a case of amnesia. Good joke."

Of course, Randall thinks, let angels in the picture and can Jesus Christ and Moses and the rest be far behind? "You think that's who it is?"

"I don't think anything of the sort," Masters says. He stands up, the smile gone and his manner cold. "Is there anything else I can help you with?"

Randall thanks him for his time and heads for the door. There are dry wells that waste time but others yield a clue or evidence that connects dots. He now knows more about angels than he did before, having never thought about it. He is stopped in traffic when Molly calls.

"We're checked into the Andrews Hotel on Post Street," she says. "And before you ask, yes, I paid cash for the rooms." It had a kind of faded elegance with high ceilings and moldings. "They wanted to see a driver's license, but I said I didn't have it with me."

"Where did you park the car?"

"The underground garage at Union Square."

"I know the Andrews. It didn't have a restaurant when I was a cop in the city."

"There are plenty in the neighborhood."

"It might be a good idea to stay put. Order a pizza or something."

"Are you talking about the YouTube video? It was a cell phone and you can't see that well. The sound is good though."

"Say what?"

"You don't know about that? It's him and Mick; a million views already. It might set a record for so fast."

Randall pulls to the curb. "This is not good."

"The club has a rule against photography, but there's no way they could enforce it without an army. Hold on, I've got a call coming in. No, never mind, I don't need to take it." She has been telling clients she's on an emergency leave of absence, sorry for any inconvenience. Some are not taking it well; a text message from a big one said to consider the bridge burned.

"How's Rex doing?"

"Totally relaxed as usual. He's watching television in his room. He acts like he's never seen one before. I had to show him how to use the remote. Oh, the Giants want to send a private detective."

"You didn't tell him where you're staying?"

"I didn't know yet. They want to ask some questions and fingerprint him to see if he has a criminal record. It's what they do before they sign a player."

"Very wise." The alarm bell must have rung in the legal department with the kind of money they're thinking about. "Tell them Rex is too busy, but you'll get back to them."

"Won't that sound funny? Normal people jump at the chance to make millions." In all honesty, she has to admit a selfish interest. Her cut of a Giants contract would banish the fears of ending up as a bag lady that haunt every single woman her age. The middle management people she works for seem younger and crueler each year. Sometimes she has to fake an understanding of the pop culture references they toss off with rat-a-tat-tat speed. If there were still sins, dating yourself by not knowing the latest ironical reference would be one of them. Old and slow is as filled with as much peril as in the fashion world as around the watering hole.

"Tell them about Mick," Randall says.

"It wouldn't be a lie. His management company wants to fly us to Lake Como."

"Why Lake Como?" Where is that, he wonders, Switzerland?

"He has an estate there. He's there all next week."

"The Giants will understand. It might even make them sweeten the pot."

"I'll just say he's busy," Molly says.

They hang up and he pulls back into traffic headed back for the Golden Gate Bridge. West Marin is still pastoral thanks to the national seashore Congress created. But the wealthy Silicon Valley tech people who made San Francisco hell are nibbling away, buying up all the private property that comes on the market for their weekend retreats. A wind brings cold fog in over the hills from the Pacific that muffles sound.

CHAPTER 8

THE SOUND IS BY SOMETHING THAT LEFT THIS TARRY NETWORK OF HAWSERS FOR HER TO CLAW through. As Molly struggles, her hands sticky with the residue produced by some vile process in a body cavity, she realizes it is a web spun by the monstrous spider on the other side of the door.

Oh, crap!

Saying it wakes her and she is flooded with relief. Just a dream. But the noise resumes; someone is softly but insistently knocking. The clock says three-thirty; she throws back the covers and hurries to the door. "Who is it?"

"It's the night deskman. We met when you checked in."

"What do you want?"

"The police called. They're checking all the downtown hotels. I think they're looking for you guys."

Molly opens the door but leaves the chain in the slot. Yes, she remembers him. Thin, dark gay guy in a blazer with the hotel logo on his breast pocket. "Why do you think that?"

"The descriptions match, a woman with a really handsome dude." He hands her a card. "My home number is on the back; if he needs help, tell him to call." A slightly awkward pause. "You, too." He tells her how to use the back way out.

It takes Randall four rings before he picks up. It isn't likely to be good news and he has had enough of the other kind. "What?" he says.

"The police are coming after us; we're on our way to the Union Square garage to get my car."

"No, don't," Randall warns. "Don't go near your car, they'll be watching."

"How would they know it's there?"

"A surveillance camera saw you drive in and it's got a sneaky little tracking device even your mechanic doesn't know is there. They put them on when cars are assembled."

"What should we do?"

"Grab a cab and go somewhere," Randall says, "an all-night restaurant or something." He needs more sleep or he'll be good for nothing. When he was a SEAL they took pills to stay awake; they worked, but you didn't want to get in the habit.

"The streets are not exactly crawling with taxicabs," Molly says. "And this phone has zero aps. "Should I use my mine?"

"That would not be a good idea. Look, I'm so tired I can't think straight, I'll call you in a bit."

She calls Rex on the house phone. "We've got to get out of here fast,." She has barely got her clothes on before she hears him at the door. He is composed and perfectly groomed.

"Is there a problem?" he says with his easy smile.

"The cops are coming!" she cries, pulling with a brush at her tangled hair as she balances to put on a shoe. "Did you sleep in your clothes; no, you don't have a single wrinkle." He follows her down stairs to the service entrance. The wet fog and a security light give the alley a sheen like raw meat. "Let's leave the suitcases here," she says, setting hers down, "they're a dead giveaway."

Molly sees two young men in hoodies under a street light that has a swirling cowl of fog. Their heads swivel as they look to see if anyone else is around.

"Those men walking toward us."

"Is something wrong?" he says.

"I think they're dangerous."

"Well," Rex says genially, "that's not good."

He has no sooner said it than one man turns and hits the other in the face. "Muthafucka!" Then they are fighting with fists and kicks until the man getting the worst of it breaks off and runs off, chased by the other.

"I think we just dodged a bullet," Molly says shakily. At his look, she adds, "It's a saying. Look, there's a taxi." Headed their way, it passes the running men. She steps into the street and waves; the driver rolls down the window.

"I can pick you up if you don't mind going on a rush job with me." He has dark glossy hair and a thick moustache and sounds Middle Eastern. A gold incisor reflecting the street lights seems to wink a code as he speaks. "Otherwise, I call the dispatcher and on my honor he's a friend and you get a ride five minutes tops."

"We don't mind," she says, jumping in the back and sliding over for Rex.

The driver looks in the rearview mirror. "Those men running, a drug deal gone bad, I promise you. This a dangerous time of night, mostly bad guys on the streets. You are tourists?"

"From Idaho," Molly says without hesitation. "What's the rush job?"

"They're making a movie at Fisherman's Wharf. I got pastries in the trunk, all the bakery had. It's a big crew, cold night. They have coffee, but no pastries. They order and I deliver. Movie people—big tips." They follow the cable car tracks over Nob Hill and drop down to the bay side and the wharf where floodlights blaze in the parking lot for the fish restaurants.

"Where you go after I drop this off?" the driver asks.

"Just say we're with the bakery," Molly pleads. Whispering to Rex, she says, "I want to be with lots of lights and people." She takes money from her purse and hands it to the driver through the slit in the bullet-proof glass.

"Hundred bucks! Okay!"

A uniformed security guard is at a saw horse blocking access to the set. "These are the pastries," the driver calls to him. Molly lowers her window. "Fresh from the oven," she calls cheerily. "You want yours now?"

"I better not before my break," the guard answers. He comes closer and lowers his voice "The supervisor's a real asshole and he's around somewhere."

"We'll tell them to save you some," she says.

He moves the saw horse and waves them through. The driver finds a place amid a fleet of vans and SUVs; they get out while he opens the trunk piled with warm boxes of pastries.

Clumps of people stand around in hats, heavy coats and mufflers by a restaurant doorway where motion picture cameras on dollies are deployed with spindly boom microphones hovering around them like eavesdroppers. An extra leans against a truck waiting to wrestle a wooden box of live crabs from the bed.

"Molly Simon, is that you?" cries a voice.

A small woman detaches herself from one of the huddled groups and hurries to them. "Ellie!" Molly screams. They embrace and kiss on the cheek.

"It's been so long," Ellie cries.

"Forever!"

"I can't believe it. I look over on a freezing night and there you are. What are you doing here?"

"I brought the pastries."

"Pastries?" Ellie Pico is an elfin woman with a face like a wised-up fairy. They know each other from dozens of TV commercials that were the stepping stones to Hollywood for Ellie.

"The ones somebody here ordered."

"The commissary shut down because of the union and everybody was starving because you wouldn't believe the body heat you lose out here. But what have you got to do with pastries?"

"It's my bakery," Molly says. She is appalled at how easy lying is in just the last couple of days. Did she always have this mother lode of duplicity waiting to be tapped?

"No way!" Ellie cries. "What happened to finding new faces?"

"Oh, I still do that; we're connected to the culinary academy to exploit student labor. My job basically is to loom up unexpectedly to keep people's noses to the grindstone. I'm back in bed by six and up by nine for my day job."

"Molly, you always were like a force of nature."

"This is my friend Rex."

Ellie turns to him and it's like her knees buckle. "Oh, my God!" She pretends to swoon and extends an arm to Molly for support. "Are they bringing him in to save this movie?"

"Does it need saving? Rex, meet Ellie."

"How do you do?" he says politely.

"Where have you been?" she asks dramatically.

"Have we met?"

"I mean all my life!"

Rex looks to Molly for explanation. His expression asks: another problem with my memory? "Ellie is very dramatic," she explains.

"You are one gorgeous hunk of manhood," Ellie blurts.

"Go ahead, get it out of your system," Molly says, laughing. "Everybody has the same reaction. Tell me about the movie, what's wrong with it?"

Ellie turns her eyes from Rex with reluctance. "What's wrong? Everything is wrong! It's a revolving door here. A hundred-million budget and the studio thinks the dailies are shit. We're on our third producer and six writers so far. Let's go sit in a trailer; I think I'm getting hypothermia again."

They follow her and she yanks open the door. "Anybody here?" When there is no answer, they follow her in and make themselves comfortable on built-in sofas. A large bowl of fruit sits on a hinged table that folds into the wall when the trailer is on the road. "This is nice," Molly says without meaning it.

"You mean it's warm; this is a sardine can compared to what the stars have. They've got hot tubs and saunas and every other creature comfort their agents could think to put in the contract." Molly watches Rex look around, perfectly at ease.

"What is the movie about?" she asks.

"You tell me," Elie says. "It started with aliens called Trucs and a private eye who discovers them thanks to a fortune teller with psychic powers. Now it's a gay cult leader who learns the creatures are among us, and his helper is professor of botany who lives in a big house full of kids and a wife barely coping because of personal issues you wouldn't believe. It looks like one of the kids is turning into a demon and… well, I could go on but you get the picture."

"Is it a comedy?" Molly asks.

"That's just it! It's not; it's deadly serious but also deadly boring. They ought to throw the whole mess in a fire and start all over, except some of the financing is Russian and they're afraid of the gangsters. That's supposed to be a secret, by the way. But you didn't answer my question: is this our Superman or Batman dropping in from the sky to save us from a dire fate?"

"He's not an actor," Molly says.

"The man looks like a god! He could read from a cereal box and people would think it's Shakespeare. I know you can talk, Rex, because you did a minute ago. What's with the Sphinx act, darling?"

"I'm not sure I understand the question," Rex says.

"He chooses his words carefully," Molly says.

"He's even more handsome when he smiles!" Elie shrieks. "Do you have an agent?"

"Me," Molly says. "Actually, I'm his manager."

Elie stares at her dumbstruck. "What, do you never eat or sleep?" She leans in. "You do look tired. We've got to seriously catch up. Seriously!"

Molly changes the subject. "What's your job on this doomed project?"

"Assistant director, one of three," Elie says dejectedly. "Hollywood is hell for women; I'm beginning to think I'll never climb higher. The men are bad, no surprise there, but the women are worse. It's supreme bitchery wall-to-wall if they see you as a threat, which of course any other woman is. If you're an assistant director long enough they assume you don't have what it takes and you go back to reading crap scripts and doing notes—if you're lucky."

"What about romance?"

"Don't get me started. Work in Hollywood and you become a misanthrope. You can't help it! Brainless actors and career-crazed wannabees with as much talent as my little finger. Anyhow, everyone is gay or think they have to pretend to be. What about you, Rex, what line of work are you in?"

"Well…" Rex begins.

"He's a Jack-of-all-trades," Molly says.

"Except speaking for himself?" Elie says, an eyebrow cocked.

"I like your hair. Is that color called burnt umber?"

"Thanks, if you're paying a compliment, but I'm going back to shocking pink. It's more bang for the buck to stand out in the crowd. I couldn't help notice you changed the subject." She tilts her head with perkiness that Molly remembers from when they were close friends. Perkiness in women isn't all that attractive after a certain age, Molly thinks, and sadly Elie is close. She has to find a nice way to tell her pink might not be a good idea.

"What are they waiting for out there?"

"Fog."

"It seems there's plenty."

"That's the problem, too much. They planned on foggers for the look the cinematographer wants, but then the real stuff moved in. He wants mood but not moody-mood."

"On a commercial shoot we'd just work around it," Molly says.

"On a commercial shoot you don't have raging egos and raving insanity. Oh, guess who's a second banana in this so-called movie? Hickory Carson. You wouldn't recognize him from the Polydent days."

Hickory had been one of Molly's greatest finds; a long-distance hauler discovered eating fried chicken at a huge truck stop outside Menden, Nebraska. He had what Madison Avenue thought was the perfect flyover-land face—tanned and craggy with crinkly smile lines radiating from the corners of blue eyes—a face as honest as the day is long, as far from sophistication as you get, but nobody's fool. Hickory reminded you of the Marlboro Man before he got lung cancer. His grin said I'm listening but don't try to bullshit me, Pilgrim. It was easy to imagine him squatting on booted heels alongside a campfire at the end of a day in the saddle, shifting position to free a fart. He was the face of a host of over-the-counter products—corn and bunion removers, soap for hands that worked on machinery, a stool softener, gold coins—and then came the Polydent jackpot. He had a way of speaking lines that made it sound like he had just turned from another old friend to wink and bring you into the conversation. No matter the product, sales spiked after Hickory started pitching it. Noting his Everyman appeal, Hollywood casting directors came calling, giving him walk-ons in small movies at first. As time passed, the roles got bigger, if still secondary, and so did the movies. He played wise counselors to junior corporate executives in Wall Street movies and in TV series as a well-meaning teacher in the ghetto, a police commander with a head in the clouds unable to see the corruption around him, a feed lot operator who chewed a toothpick and viewed life grimly (Oscar buzz for this role tapered off because the movie was released too early in the year), and a buffoonish TV weatherman who drank.

"Second banana," Molly says, "that's a step up from the buddy roles."

They need a place to stay until daylight and someone—a dialogue coach or lowly technician—could walk in here any minute and kick them out. "I'd love to see him."

"He's got a bit with the crab delivery scene, so I know he's awake. I'll give him a call." Ellie uses her cell phone. "He wants you to come over." She leads them to his trailer and says goodbye. "I've got to get back to work before someone yells at me." She pulls a walkie-talkie from a coat pocket to show them. "But later?"

"Wild horses couldn't stop me."

The door opens and Hickory's honest face appears. "Wal, hello there, sister," he says, drawing her in for a bear hug. "It's been too long, darlin'. C'mon in and put up your feet; she was just leaving." A pretty young woman with dark hair gives them a tight smile as she eases through the door. Hickory is barefoot and in a silk dressing gown. He does look different, an expensive haircut instead of a ten-dollar one and the teeth are capped, but the impression of rugged openness remains.

"Hello, stranger, they call me Hickory," he says, gripping Rex's hand. "You joining up with us?"

"We're just visiting the set," Molly says.

"I'd say it's more madhouse than set," Hickory says with a chuckle. "I got some coffee and a runner just brought over some delicious pastries. Hell, they're still warm from the oven. I need some help eating them because my contract says I can't pack on more than two-twenty while we're shooting, which is gonna be a long time the way things are going. They weigh me once a week, the bastards."

"We'd love some," Molly says. They sit around a table with the pastries and the coffee Hickory pours from a Starbuck thermos. He leans over the table for a closer look at Rex. "You wearing makeup?"

Rex smiles and shakes his head.

"Don't let 'em put it on. You're fine the way you are."

"He's not an actor," Molly says.

"He ought to be, good lookin' like that." He got a sheepish look. "How you been keepin,' Molly? We kind of fell out of touch."

"That sometimes happens when a person doesn't return e-mails, phone calls or text messages," she says lightly. "It's rare, but it happens."

"They're keeping me crazy busy, but you're right, that's no excuse in this day and age. I'd still be driving a big rig and eating fried chicken at Gert's Grits and Gravy in Menden if it wasn't for you." A wistful look crossed his face. "Those were good times, looking back. You did real work instead of waiting around to say something like, 'You lookin' for somebody?' in front of twenty people you're pretending aren't there, and saying it six more times because the director is wearing the rag." The mood passes and his eyes twinkle. "But this sure as hell pays a lot better."

"Life is full of trade offs," Molly says.

"Ain't it the truth? What are you folks doing up so early?"

"I read in the Hollywood Reporter you were in a movie they were making on Fisherman's Wharf and we talked our way onto the set," Molly says, struck again by how easily she lies. I take to it like a duck to water, she thinks.

Hickory is pleased and flattered. "Try one of those cream buns when you finish that one, they're amazing." He is as loquacious as she remembers, telling story after story about the movie business. It's crazy, he says, just crazy. "If someone tells you they've got your back, the odds are fifty-fifty it means they got a knife waiting for a chance to stick it in."

His cell phone rings. "Yes, Csaba, ready for me? Oh. Sure, come on over. Give me a couple of minutes to change." He hangs up. "I gotta get dressed; the director wants to talk. But don't move. He doesn't waste much breath on me because he thinks I'm as dumb as a box of rocks; one of the sound guys told me that. In this industry they never pass on good comments, only bad ones." He grins with palms up, a look that says what-are-you-gonna-do? He leaves the room to get dressed.

"He seems like a good guy, like at Templeton Hall," Rex says, startling her. She's not used to him beginning a conversation. Rex takes a bit of pastry. "That was smart of you."

"What was?"

"Saying we were delivering these."

"More lucky than smart." She sees he's thinking about what she said. "Oh, don't go all moral on me, sometimes you have to tell a lie."

He nods. "Understood."

Their eyes lock and she is afraid she can't swim fast enough to keep from being pulled under.

There is an aggressive pounding at the door and then a massive man barges in with long hair and a dense reddish beard that starts just below his eyes; the ursine look is amplified by an ankle-length fur coat. "Vere iz Hickory?" Csaba Balušík speaks in a furious thick accent. The famed European film director with his thick mane of hair that is oiled and combed straight back is so tall he must stoop in the tight trailer.

"Here I am, boss," Hickory says, tucking in his shirt as he comes. "These are some old friends of mine. They…"

"Send zem away! We must…" He stops when he sees Rex. "Who is this man?"

"Why," Hickory says agreeably, "his name is Rex and she's Molly. Folks, this here…"

"The studio sent you," Balušík bellows. "The swine! A new leading man and you," he says to Molly, "must be the new producer." He seems on the verge of violence.

"Hold on, pardner," Hickory says soothingly, "these are just ordinary folks, nothin' to do with Hollywood."

"Look at him!" Balušík thunders. "You tell me he is not actor, dis, dis… pretty boy?" He begins choking on his own rage and the part of his face visible above the beard turns purple.

"Do something!" Molly cries. "Give him the Heimlich maneuver!"

Hickory gets behind and tries to encircle Balušík with his arms, but the auteur's girth and fur coat stop his hands from linking. The two reel around the trailer, knocking over a lamp and a bowl of fruit. Balušík's eyes bulge in terror and there is froth on his lips.

"Help him, Rex," Molly screeches.

"He'll be fine," Rex says calmly.

Balušík bursts from Hickory's embrace and sinks into a seat, gasping until the dangerous color leaves his face.

"Christ Almighty," Hickory says, winded himself. "That was like waltzing with a bear that didn't want to."

"Děkuji," Balušík says. "Thank you, my friend. There is much passion in my soul. It runs over its banks, but never so much."

"Yeah, I'd say you got kinda bent out of shape." Hickory swipes away imaginary sweat from his forehead with a finger. "Whew." He pours coffee for Balušík, who takes a silver flask from a pocket and pours a splash of brown liquor into the cup.

"You wanted to talk about the scene we're gonna shoot?" Hickory says.

"Is not important," Balušík says. "You fine, maybe show less fear. Skeptical, not scared."

He looks down into his coffee and Hickory winks at Molly. "You got it, boss," he says.

"Studio sends airplane for me at dawn," Balušík says. "It is like execution they send me to but no blindfold and last cigarette." He drinks down the coffee in one long swallow.

"You come with me on plane," he says to Rex. "To L.A."

"He's with me," Molly protests.

"Then you come, too."

"Why do you want us to go?"

Balušík nods at Rex. "He will be great movie star. This my guts tells me."

"He's not even an actor!" Molly cries.

"This is piffle, anyone can be. It's how you look in camera. I teach him to act in one week, two. How to move, what to do in close-up. I teach hundreds of actors. You come with me?" His dark, emotional eyes are pleading.

CHAPTER 9

RANDALL HAS OFTEN PASSED THE TABERNACLE SITTING BACK FROM THE ROAD AS PLAIN AND white as bone bleached by the sun. It doesn't even have windows, which he believes has to do with the stern beliefs preached at Bethany Primitive Baptist Church. A notice on the door gives a number in case of emergency.

Pastor Barton Philpott doesn't mind discussing angels. He is a brawny man with a ruddy face and a jolly manner who pulls up in a tow trick twenty minutes after Randall telephones. He takes out a thick ring with dozens of keys and finds the one that opens the door. The church is as spare inside as out; no stained glass and rows of folding chairs in rows instead of polished pews. The narrow pulpit has a bare wooden cross on the white wall behind it. There are no rivals for attention for the gospel preached from the book.

"You've got a nice piece of property here," Randall says. The parcel goes all the way out to the road; goats and a single cow graze in the broad, green pasture.

"Yeah, rich guys pop in every couple of weeks or so wanting to buy us out. It's like money doesn't mean anything anymore, the offers they make."

"Like they say, they're not making land anymore."

"Is that what they say?" the pastor answers dryly.

"The real estate people, that's what they say."

"God made everything you see—and what you don't see for that matter."

"For sure," Randall agrees, hoping not to get into that. He tells him about his meeting with Masters.

Philpott shakes his head. "They've strayed so far they might as well go all the way to Roman Catholicism, which is what we call the Whore of Babylon. He recommended you get the low down on angels from a true believer, that right?"

"Yes, from a Baptist."

"Well, you have to mention what kind of Baptist, 'cuz some have been back-sliding pretty fast and far themselves. It ain't easy to stick to the straight and narrow these days, your Reverend Masters being an example." They go to a small kitchen in the rear of the church and Philpott gets mugs from a cupboard and pours coffee from a thermos. "That wind is colder than an Eskimo's outhouse."

"You got that right."

"I've seen most of the guys doing patrol duty out here, but you're a new face."

"They got me behind a desk nowadays, but I used to be out here quite a bit. Charlie Morgan had the tow truck business."

"He sold it to me after his back got stove up."

"Keeping you busy?"

"It's 'bout usual. One or two bad ones a month. Young people drunk and old people who shouldn't be driving at night."

"Some things never change," Randall says.

"Human nature ain't changed since the Garden of Eden. We're all sinners like Adam and Eve."

Pastor Philpott leans back in his chair. "You're thinkin' there's a satanic angle with those murders at Templeton Hall like with Charlie Manson. Those killings are all people talk about these days. You even got liberals for strict gun control buying firearms, but they deny it if you ask. Not that guns are gonna be any help with Satan."

"That's an approach we're following," Randall says. "But I'd appreciate it if you kept it quiet."

There is a good chance the FBI will get around to Philpott at some point, so he has to be careful. A surveillance satellite overhead would have already logged his visit. It would go to a computer file on a huge server farm.

"All that killing for the sake of it.'" He takes a well-thumbed Bible from a jacket pocket. "That was pure evil in operation, what happened at Templeton Hall." He puts on reading glasses and leafs through pages. "You know Lucifer is a fallen angel, right? Let's see, in Ephesians 6:11, 12 bad angels are called rulers, authorities, powers, and spiritual forces of evil." He turns pages and his thumb tracks down the text. "In Luke 7:21, 8:2 they are evil, perverse, depraved spirits. Revelation 12:7-9 tells us being fallen angels, they are less than the holy angels, not possessing their intellect and wisdom, and they are weaker. Having followed Lucifer in the rebellion against the Almighty, they are wretched and miserable because they will never see God." He closes the Bible. "So evil, perverse and depraved, that's pretty much what happened at Templeton Hall. It has Lucifer's handwriting all over it."

"We think there were several bad guys," Randall says. "Is it possible they were…" He clears his throat. "… also fallen angels?" It is not a question he would feel comfortable asking Masters.

Pastor Philpott thinks for a minute and shakes his head. "I'd say more likely they are humans possessed by demons. Guns will deal with them just fine."

"How about the other kind, the good angels?"

"What about them?"

"What would they look like, for one thing."

"Matthew and Luke say the holy angels are brilliant in appearance. So does Acts."

"So one wouldn't look like ordinary."

"No, sir, not if you go by the Bible." He gives it a thump. "Which I do. That is why I believe the End Times are upon us. Never before in the fifteen hundred years since the signs began have they been so clear. Daniel 12:4 says 'even to the time of the end many shall run to and fro, and knowledge shall be increased.'" Philpott is on his feet pacing like he addresses the faithful. "Look at the explosion of knowledge over the past hundred and fifty years. Look at the internet. We are definitely running to and fro—everyone complains about how busy they are—and we have knowledge like never before. The Bible says in the End Times no man might buy or sell, save that he had the mark, or the name of the beast, or the number of his name. Is that the credit card system or what? Genesis 6:13 tells us in Noah's day the earth was filled with violence. And in Jude 1:7 it says that in Lot's day, Sodom and Gomorrah had given itself over to fornication and strange flesh, that being a reference to homosexuality."

Philpott stops pacing and reopens the Bible. "'Now the spirit speaketh expressly, that in the latter times some shall depart from the faith, giving heed to seducing spirits, and doctrines of devils. Look at TV and the movies and what do you see? Harry Potter and Lord of the Rings. Hosea 4:3 says, 'Therefore shall the land mourn, and every one that dwelleth therein shall languish, with the beasts of the field, and with the fowls of heaven; yea, the fishes of the sea also shall be taken away.' The oceans are dying, jellyfish are proliferating, and the bee colonies are collapsing."

Randall takes a covert look at his watch; Philpott catches him and grins. "I get carried away, don't I, and you're a busy man."

"Yeah, I've got a few things I need to do."

"Let me leave you with one last thought. Matthew 24:4-5, 11 said 'many shall come in my name, saying, I am Christ… and many false prophets shall arise and deceive many.'"

Night is falling and the fog is thicker. Randall stops for a take-out sandwich at what used to be a mom-and-pop store but now is yet another lair for the foodie tribe. In the old days he would buy a baloney and cheese with limp lettuce for a buck and a quarter. He pays fifteen dollars for an artisan sandwich in a fancy carton: ribeye with caramelized onions, sun-dried tomato, and sweet basil mayonnaise on toasted Turkish bread. A bottle of beer, also artisan, is another five. He wonders if the Romans were this occupied with their bellies when the lean barbarians emerged from the dark northern forests. He drives to a hostel favored by vacationers who hike the trail over the ridge to the ocean; he knows from past years business will be light and there will be room. He pays cash and the sunny young blond woman in jeans and a thick sweater gives him a key attached to a piece of driftwood. Have a good evening, she says cheerily. The window has a view of the entrance to the hostel so he would see the headlights of the killers when they turned in if they were dumb enough to leave them on, which he doubts. Checking the back window, he is relieved that it lifts smoothly. His guess is they are staking out his home again on the reasonable assumption he must be as stupid as a box of rocks to be mixed up in this business. He is watching Monday Night Football when Abigail telephones.

"Did you forget you had a wife and family?" she says with exasperation. "Is that a football game I hear?"

He hits the mute button. "I just this minute got home. I was waiting until I had enough strength to put a Lean Cuisine in the microwave."

"Poor baby. I called on the land line. No answer."

"I turned down the ringer because of the telephone solicitors." You had to be quick on your feet with Abigail.

"The story is on the national news the second night in a row," she says. "Mom doesn't know what the world is coming to."

"I thought she never watched the news."

"It's because you're involved."

"I wish I was eating Jell-O and cottage cheese with you and the kids."

Her voice gets husky. "I know it must be awful for you."

Randall stifles an urge to tell her how much worse it is than merely awful. "How are the kids?"

"They're coming down with something," Abigail says. "They're whiny and both have a fever. Mom is hunting around for a thermometer; she is so disorganized since dad died."

"They picked up something on the road, I betcha," Randall says. "Kids are magnets for virus. Maybe it's one of those 24-hour bugs."

"There's no such thing with them. They're 48-hour or 72-hour bugs, or they last a week. Your voice sounds strained."

"Good thing I don't have any singing emcee jobs this week."

She laughs. "Well, take care of yourself. I have to run to the drugstore for baby aspirins before they close. It's raining, of course."

"It's always raining. Every time we've been there."

"I know it's a pet peeve of yours."

"Is it a big drug store?"

"One of the chains. I want to say Walgreen's."

"Buy a prepaid phone to call me on." He gave her his number.

"What's wrong with our cell phones?"

"The FBI is super-paranoid about the media listening in."

"Really?" Abigail says skeptically.

"You know how good they are these days? They can hack into your electric toothbrush and you get emails saying its time to see your dentist."

"You're full of it, but I'll get the phone."

CHAPTER 10

SERGEANT RANDALL IS AWARE THERE IS ANOTHER PRESENCE IN THE ROOM. HE SWITCHES ON THE nightstand lamp and sees Camael sitting in the room's straight back chair, leaning forward elbows on knees and staring at him with frowning intensity.

"You must call your wife right now. She has to take the children to the hospital."

"It's just a little fever, they get them all the…"

"Now," he says firmly. "They are dangerously ill, you can't waste a minute." He takes a small vial of something from a pocket. "Mark them on the forehead with this when you get there. Put it in your inside pocket with the zipper so you don't lose it."

His heart in his throat, Randall digs the throwaway phone from a coat pocket and calls Abigail. She answers right away, fear in her voice from a call at this hour.

"The kids are really sick," he barks. "Call an ambulance and get them to the hospital right away."

"Why are you saying that?" He hears her footsteps over the phone. "Oh, my God, they're burning up with fever." Then she turns calm the way she does in a crisis. "It's faster to drive. Call the emergency room and tell them we'll be there in ten minutes. Mom, put on your coat and carry Michael out to the car, I'll bring Martin. No, just do it!" She looks up the hospital number, gives it to him, and hangs up.

"My wife and my two kids are coming in," he tells the nurse who answers in the emergency room. He tries to keep the panic out of his voice. "They are four-year-olds with really high fevers, cause unknown. She'll be pulling up to the entrance in about nine minutes."

"We'll be waiting for them," she says.

He switches off the phone and turns to the chair, but it is empty. With the light out, he goes to the window and parts the curtain, not really expecting to see anyone in the fog and darkness. Then he sits down and clutches his head, trying to slow his whirling thoughts. Okay, getting to Abigail and the kids as soon as possible is top priority. He throws his things together and climbs out the back window to circle the building; the few lights are just yellow blurs in the fog. It takes only seconds to reach his car, and a minute later it crunches over gravel to the road. He heads east to hook up with Highway 101 and turn north for the Oregon border; it will take seven maybe eight hours of hard driving to get to the hospital. He feels like a punching bag and the day has barely begun.

He stops at the first open gas station to fill the tank and calls Molly on her throwaway phone. "It's me," he says.

"Guess where we are?" she says in a spent voice.

"I hope you're going to say Dunkin' Doughnuts."

"San Carlos Airport. We're on our way to Hollywood by way of Burbank International."

"It sounds like a long story I don't have time for."

"Is there something wrong? I mean something new?"

"My kids are in the hospital; I'm driving to Oregon."

"What's wrong?" Both children? Don't let it be an accident, she thinks.

"They both got high fevers. I got to hang up; it's foggy and I'm driving fast." Five minutes later, it rings.

"I can't talk," he says. This is a part of the road where deer make kamikaze dashes.

"Wait!" Molly says. "Pull over. We've got an idea."

Randall finds a shoulder on the road and brakes to a stop. "Make it fast."

"We can meet you at the airport in Santa Rosa and fly you to Oregon. It's a Gulfstream jet and the pilot says it goes five hundred miles an hour. Where are you now?"

"Fairfax is just ahead."

"We can be in Santa Rosa before you." He hears her talking to someone. "Go to the private plane part of the field, not the terminal," she says.

"I'll see you there."

Wheeling back onto the two-lane road, the fog is a gun-metal color as dawn breaks. His mind jerks in all directions and he strains to focus on driving. If the old man hadn't wakened him for that warning, the kids… no, he doesn't want to go there. He reaches Highway 101 and turns north, squinting at the dazzle of headlights from the vanguard of commuters head for the city. The GPS tells him the Santa Rosa Airport is about an hour away. He knows the highway patrol boys will want a jump on the ticket quota nobody admits to, so he stays just under the speed limit.

It is too early for the first scheduled flight and the terminal shows few lights. He follows signs to the general aviation area and sees an ivory Gulfstream on the apron, its landing lights ablaze and a blue strobe flashing from the tail. The hatch is open and the ladder down. The sergeant parks and locks the car and hurries to the small building nearest the jet, the disposable phone to his ear. The connection is bad and all he can hear Abigail say is "went into seizures."

"There you are," Molly says. "The crew is ready to go."

The pilot and co-pilot are showing Rex the instruments in the cockpit when they climb aboard. He joins them in the back and they buckle up in their seats as the Gulfstream begins to move. It has a spotless, white-leather interior that looks sterile enough for brain surgery.

"Molly says your children aren't well, Sergeant," Rex says, laying a sympathetic hand on his shoulder.

"The pilot says we'll be on the ground before eight," Molly says. "An Uber car will be waiting." She points to a phone on the bulkhead. "You can call your wife when we reach cruising altitude."

"I won't even try to thank you," Randall says.

Blowing out her cheeks, Molly sags in her seat. "I feel like I could sleep for a week, have breakfast and sleep for another week. I must look like a bag lady."

"You look fine," Rex says. Randall notes her blush. This was only a matter of time, he thinks.

"You want to know what happened?" she says. "When we were chased out of the hotel because the police were coming, we were nearly attacked in the street by two thuggish-looking guys. We caught a cab taking pastries to a movie set, where I met an old friend who introduced us to the director. He was going to Hollywood for a budget meeting at the studio and invited us to go along because of our friend here." She jerks her thumb at Rex. "He thinks he can make him the biggest movie star ever because he… well, you can guess. Then I get an idea. Let's give him a ride to Oregon on this beautiful jet. The director, Csaba Balušík—I never heard of him either, but my friend Hickory said he has a huge reputation in Europe—tells me, 'Are you out of your mind?'—bellows it actually, he's a big, very loud man—and then Rex steps in. Tell him what you said, darling."

Rex shrugs matter-of-factly. "Just that if you didn't get a ride to Oregon, we don't go to Hollywood."

"Now you have to understand," Molly says, "this guy is a tyrant, totally used to getting his way. I thought he would blow his top, but he just shrugged and said okay, if that's the way it is." They will pick him up and continue on to Hollywood after dropping Randall off.

There is a glimpse from a porthole of the Pacific Ocean and its fog bank, and then the plane levels off on a northeasterly heading. Rex excuses himself. "The guys up front said they'd show me what they do."

"He's changed," Randall says when the cockpit door closes.

"I know what you mean. He seems more together, more confident, like he's becoming his old self."

"Nobody knows what his old self was like."

He has her go through what happened since he saw them last. "These punks were heading toward you when they suddenly started fighting with each other?"

"One said something about the other's mother."

"Did you hear any other words?"

"Just that."

"Then the cab shows up?"

"It passed the guy chasing the other. I forgot to tell you the director had some kind of choking attack in the trailer. Hickory was trying to give him the Heimlich thing, but he was thrashing and twisting too much."

"Hickory?"

"That's my friend. His real name is Owen, but I convinced him to change it. Owen doesn't leap off a resume like Hickory; sometimes it's the little things with casting people."

"What happened next?"

"I asked Rex for help and he said Csaba would be all right and, sure enough, he calmed down right away, no more choking. You've got a look on your face, what are you thinking?"

"You're about to be mugged and you're not, and a man stops choking when Rex says he'll be all right, that's what I'm thinking."

Molly's eyes widen. "You think Rex did that—like the power of positive thinking?"

"Positive thinking doesn't explain two guys coming after you and then deciding fighting each other is what they really want to do."

She thinks. "Maybe I was wrong about them coming after us, I could have been imagining it."

"Look at it this way," Randall says, "a lot of good things happened in row. You get tipped the cops are coming, the punks fighting, the cab takes you to where you meet a friend who just happens to know a man with a jet."

"It's not his, actually. It belongs to the studio."

"That's just detail."

"I think I know what's coming next," Molly says.

"I don't like it any better than you. Do you know how I learned my kids were sick?"

"That man you say is an angel?"

"I'll use another word if it makes you feel better."

"Sorry, I'm just too rational. It's the way I'm built."

"I saw him again. He was in a chair as close as that porthole. If he hadn't warned me, I wouldn't have called Abigail and she wouldn't have rushed them to the hospital."

"I definitely believe in telepathy," Molly says. "Maybe your wife was sending you a message."

"For me to wake her up with a telephone call so I could warn her the kids were sick? That seems a little round about, doesn't it?. And Camael warned Rex at Templeton Hall, remember?"

"Oh, that... well." She frowns.

He unbuckles his seatbelt and uses the telephone on the bulkhead to call Abigail's cell. An automated voice says the number he called is not available at this time and please try later. The different nurse he gets in the emergency room says she is not authorized to give him information.

"I'm their dad for God's sake."

"I don't make the rules, Mr. Randall." He knows the type from her bureaucratic tone. "I'll speak to your wife when I see her, but we're very busy right now. There was an accident with multiple victims."

"I think hospitals make you to turn off your cell phone," Molly says when he returns to his seat.

"You know what?" he says. "When Rex comes back from that cockpit he is going to know how to fly this plane. I guarantee it."

She laughs like he made a joke.

"I'm serious, Molly."

"It takes months to learn that, maybe years. People go to pilot school."

"Since I met him on a country road, the man has learned how to play basketball at least at the college level, been offered a major league baseball contact, and sat in with Mick Jagger."

"Mick wants Rex to write a song with him," Molly admits.

"And now you're headed to Hollywood. Is there any doubt they'll see him as the next George Clooney?"

"Rex is way more handsome and Csaba says he can teach him to act. He'll be another Daniel Day-Lewis."

"Sometimes I find myself almost forgetting all this started at Templeton Hall."

"Yes! That already seems like last year. But remember it didn't start there, it started when you saw him walking down the road."

"I wish I'd never stopped," Randall says. "Just pulled around him and hit the gas pedal."

Did the big roulette wheel drop the ball on his number by chance or was the game fixed? Maybe when he stopped the car, circumstances, for want of a better word, were set in motion that plays out to the end. But wouldn't that mean a chain of events stretched back to when he was born and as a kid decided he would be a cop when he grew up? In which case he never really had a choice: he had to turn on the roof lights and stop the car. In a way, that simple act doomed all the people at Templeton Hall. If he had only followed policy and taken Rex to the slammer, those people would still be working on their problems at that fancy spa. The jet passes over rich valley farmland below and Molly drops off to sleep, lightly snoring. She's probably used up a year's worth of adrenalin, he thinks. A sudden thought turns him cold. If he had driven past Rex, maybe his kids wouldn't be in the hospital this very minute. Something malevolent had sought them out and the old man warned of the danger just as he had advised Rex to leave Templeton Hall. It was one thing to take a thousand dollars a day to watch out for Rex because supposedly it was the most important thing he would ever do, but what could be a higher priority than his kids?

A patch of rough air wakes Molly up and brings Rex back from the cockpit. "I've got a stiff neck," she says. "Have I been asleep long?"

"Just a few minutes," Randall says as he watches Rex buckle into his seat. "I bet Molly you would know how to fly this airplane by the time you came back."

"I probably could," Rex says easily. "Those guys explain things really well."

"Oh, Rex," she says, "he was only joking around."

"It mostly flies itself except for takeoffs and landings, but I think I could handle that, too."

"See?" the sergeant says.

"Why is everything so easy for you?" Molly says almost despairingly.

"I don't know," Rex confesses, lifting his shoulders. "They just are."

"You know that old man who told you to get out of Templeton Hall?" Randall says.

"Sure, a wonderful guy."

"He calls himself Camael. I think he's an angel."

"I don't!" Molly exclaims.

Rex is thoughtful. "There was a woman at Templeton Hall who talked about angels. She said they are guardians and guides. When somebody asked, she admitted there is no proof."

"I'm having the same trouble with Molly," Randall says.

"There would be a lot of oddball ideas flying around at a place like that," she says.

"Like telepathy?" Randall responds.

"There have been experiments that prove telepathy."

"Why would an angel be interested in me?" Rex asks.

"That's the big question, dude," Randall says. "But isn't it obvious you're different?"

"Special?" Molly prompts.

"You can do anything better than anyone else," Randall says. "You could strap yourself into the pilot seat and do a barrel roll with this jet."

"Yes, I suppose I could," Rex says.

"Not only can you do all this stuff, you do it better than anyone," Randall says. "Don't you think that's strange?"

Another shrug. "Everything comes easy for some reason."

"That's just the point. Haven't you wondered why?"

"It just seems natural."

"It's not natural, it is literally incredible. And even that isn't strong enough. Impossible is more like it."

"If we only knew more about you," Molly says. "What if you're from outer space?"

"I doubt that," Rex says with his smile.

"But how would we know?"

He thinks. "I guess you wouldn't."

"Nothing has come back to you from before?" Randall asks.

"No," Rex says decisively. "Look, this is getting us nowhere."

The jet begins to descend. "Everybody buckled up back there?" the pilot asks.

"That didn't take hardly any time at all," Molly says.

"I'll have them send the jet back for you when you're ready," Rex says.

It is a smooth landing and the Uber car is waiting. Bright sunshine, no threat of rain. Molly hugs him and Rex grips his arm before he goes down the steps. It is a Ford Mustang, a classic muscle car from the '70's, driven by a hip young guy in a goatee, porkpie hat, and shades. "I'll have you at the hospital in ten minutes."

As they drive, Randall thinks about that sudden change in Rex. He cuts off the conversation about his amnesia and promises to send the jet back.

CHAPTER 11

A STUDIO CAR IS WAITING FOR THEM AT BURBANK INTERNATIONAL. CSABA WAS MUMBLING OVER his laptop on the hour's flight from San Carlos, and Molly has a feeling he is whipping himself into a fury, eager to close with the enemy. Her guess is he clashes often with Hollywood bosses—a titanic personality like his would— and experience has shown him this strategy works with bean counters; they would see it as the normal behavior of a temperamental genius. But he must not feel as certain about the outcome this time or he wouldn't be bringing Rex along as insurance.

She catches a quick glimpse of herself in a window. Unshowered and without makeup, her thick hair wild and the clothes she had thrown on wrinkled and mismatched—she must look like a bag lady. As usual, Rex is cool and immaculate and draws long looks as they follow the striding director muttering to himself in a foreign language.

The airport gets a lot of celebrities passing through and onlookers try to place Rex. If they weren't moving so fast Molly thinks they would be pulling out autograph books or scraps of paper to sign. He would stop to sign every one, nice guy that he is. Awe-struck, they would look at the signature and puzzle over why they never heard of such a great looking dude as light on his feet as a wide receiver.

Or maybe he wouldn't be so nice. There was nothing she could put a finger on, but something told her a tipping point had been reached. Rex is coming out of the stage of a sponge soaking up information and was beginning to act on what he knew; it showed in his ultimatum about the airplane and she suspects the world will see a sharper edge from now on. Csaba's psychic antenna, sharpened by dealing with unstable actors who need to be soothed and coddled, had also picked up on it.

A young production assistant with spiked hair in jeans and a T-shirt with a surfer scene holds a sign that says Magnificent Productions; not that there was any mistaking who the bearded Csaba was as he bursts through the crowd, his unbuttoned fur pelt flowing and his eyes ablaze. The assistant lowers the sign and trots behind as humbly as a serf dogging the footsteps of the Czar. A door stands open when Molly and Rex reach the Esplanade in the no-parking zone, a chauffeur behind the wheel.

"Are they coming too?" the assistant is asking when they get there.

"Get out!" Csaba bellows.

The assistant cringes before his Magyar fury and slips out the other side and closes the door noiselessly. Molly watches him walk back to the terminal, shoulders slumped and hands in pocket. The lowly people in Hollywood eat all kinds of shit, she thinks—a yard every day.

They pull away from the terminal and soon are on the inevitable freeway swollen with slow-moving traffic from dull suburbs that stretch in all directions. Signs for fast food franchises call out varieties of previously cooked protein heated up by microwave or plunged into hot fat. She and Rex decline champagne from a bottle on ice in a bucket. "No need for glass then," Csaba says, taking a long swig and wiping his mouth with the back of his hand. Molly is reminded of an autocrat from the Middle Ages glowering at the world from a swaying carriage.

"I do talking only," he says. "I know dees people. Dey is vermin."

"You really want us at the meeting?" Molly asks. They bought time getting out of the Bay Area, but she hasn't a clue what to do next. I suppose we just keep going with the flow, she thinks.

"It will be interesting," Rex says pleasantly.

He has put another opinion out there, she thinks, the blank slate slowly filling. It might be an unworthy thought, but she is glad his signature is on the management contract. Worse comes to worse, she gets bought out with an extravagant number.

The Esplanade leaves the freeway and travels on surface streets until they reach the Moorish arched entrance to Magnificent Pictures Studio. The uniformed man at the security kiosk waves them through and the chauffeur salutes him with a light beep-beep. They pass sound stages and arrive at a clump of cottages in manicured landscaping. Csaba explodes from the car and heads at a trot for one with a brass sign that says Magnificent Productions. Nearly at the door, he grabs a hamstring and cries out in pain. "Jézus!"

"Are you okay?" Molly asks when they catch up.

"My leg! Sum-ting ees wrong. Ago-nee! I am in ago-nee!" Sweat has sprung out on his brow. "But show must goes on."

Still clutching at the hamstring and crying out in pain, he leads them past a receptionist too stunned by his overpowering presence to protest. They press on through mahogany corridors to an office and an arrogant-looking woman in a tailored cream suit; her glossy dark hair is pinned back in a severe manner.

"Is something wrong, Mr. Balušík?" she asks evenly. She has a mid-Atlantic accent—a posh education in England with the cut-glass accent flattened some by years in the states.

He has flopped down and is shaking his big head back and forth and beating a chair arm with a fist. He gives her an outraged look, unable to speak.

"He hurt his leg just now," Molly explains.

The secretary gives her a look and Molly knows she has sized her up from the unbrushed hair and thrown-together look, not even wearing lipstick. You are nothing, she has decided. Then her eyes move to Rex and the coldness vanishes. "My God," she exclaims.

"We get that a lot," Molly says. The woman recognizes a claim is staked and her manner changes instantly.

"Lazarus," Csaba gasps. "Tell him I'm here."

"Mr. Lazarus is in a meeting," she says apologetically. "He expected you two hours ago." Regina Welborne-Smyth is the name plate on her tidy desk.

"We were held up," Rex says with easy confidence. "Tell him we're here."

She picks up the telephone and pushes a button. "Mr. Lazarus, Csaba Balušík and his party are here to see you."

"Send them in," says a voice on speaker phone. Irving Lazarus, one of Hollywood's rulers, is a small man in a dark suit and vest; he is in his sixties crafty eyes in a vulpine face and a mop of gray hair.

"You," he says to Rex, ignoring the director. "Have you done a screen test?"

"No," Molly says.

"And you are?" he demands.

"She's my manager," Rex says.

"Are you signed with anybody?"

"Just me," Molly says.

"That's the first order of business." He punches a button on a large telephone console. "Regina, set up a screen test with Brad. Tell him I want it in fifteen minutes; walk them over there yourself."

"Yes, Mr. Lazarus."

"You look great to me," Lazarus says, his smile crafty, "but I've been fooled by you gorgeous guys before. The camera either likes you or it doesn't; some guy you wouldn't give a second look are great on film and the opposite's true. It's the same with broads."

"He weel be vonderful," Czaba says through gritted teeth. "I tell you."

"What the hell's wrong with you?"

"My leg!"

"He hurt it coming in here," Molly says.

"Don't try that shit on me, Czaba. My company's got liability insurance and their guys are pit bulls when people fake injuries."

Regina is at the door with a smile. "If you'd like to follow me," she says. As they leave, Czaba is rocking back and forth and Lazarus looking at him like he's crazy.

"So, where are you guys from?" Regina asks Rex as they walk toward one of the sound stages.

"We're from up north," Molly says.

"I love the Pacific Northwest," Regina says. "Is that where you mean?" The question is addressed to Rex.

"What's going to happen with Czaba?" Molly asks, running interference.

"I don't know, but I can tell you that Mr. Lazarus is worried about the project." She arches her brows conspiratorially. "How are you guys involved?"

"We're not, actually," Molly says.

Regina waits to see if she is going to elaborate. When she doesn't, she asks Rex, "Are you guys friends with Czaba or something?"

"We just met him today," Rex says.

"He sure knows how to make an entrance." She can't take her eyes from him. "He has a reputation, but I've always dealt with assistants."

"We don't know him," Molly says firmly.

"Oh. Well, I thought…"

"He flew us to Oregon and then down here," Rex says.

His smile makes Regina look like she goes a little weak in the knees. "I guess that explains why you were late," she stammers.

"We weren't late," Molly says. "Czaba was."

"I'm not sure he's authorized to change flight itineraries," Regina says, making a face. "Mr. Lazarus might not like it."

"Not our problem," Molly says brightly.

They reach a sound stage and Regina leads them down a passageway to a room where a crew is setting up lights and a camera. A gaunt man with dark hair tumbling over his forehead rushes into the room with a bag under his arm.

"I've got everybody on standby to do this… Whoa, I can see why the boss wants it right away. The name's Brad Shafer." He shakes Rex's hand and has him sit in a chair; he pulls a script from the bag. "You're going to read from Gary Cooper's role in *High Noon*. Ever seen it?" Rex shakes his head smilingly. "It's a Hollywood classic." He turns to a page. "When I say Action, just start reading the lines like you're the character."

"Wait," Molly says. "He doesn't know anything about the sheriff or what went on before."

Brad takes a frantic look at his wristwatch. "Okay, a gang of bad guys are in town gunning for you," he says rapidly. "The townsfolk talk a good game about law and order, but they won't back you when it counts. Nobody could blame you for running away, in fact you've got a deputy who wants to be a hero to his girlfriend who used to be your girlfriend, but he can't be if you're around for the showdown. He's, like, begging you to get on a horse and vamoose. And to tell the truth you've been thinking about it, but you're a man of honor."

"Don't forget the wife," Molly prompts.

"Right. So the sheriff just got married an hour ago —to a Quaker! Meaning she's opposed to violence and will leave him if he gets mixed up in the trouble."

"The sheriff is conflicted," Rex says after briefly thinking about it. "He's being asked to stand up for law and order for people who aren't worthy of his sacrifice if he's killed."

"Yeah, yeah, you got it. They're a bunch of hypocrites. Ready, guys? Give us the clapboard. Okay, Action!"

Rex seems to be pulling the strings of the story together in his head. He takes another look at the script, and then he speaks to the camera. 'Look, Harv, I thought about it because I was tired. You think about a lot of things when you're tired—when people cross the street when they don't want to look at your face… And with everybody there telling me I ought to get out. For a minute there I began to wonder if they weren't right… But I can't do it.'"

"Cut," Brad says. "Damn, what a reading, every line nailed—the man's got a helluva memory. It reminded me of Coop himself—the stoic goodness, not calling attention to itself but solid to the core, wanting to be anywhere but there." He pulls another script from the bag. "This is *On the Waterfront*, the scene where Brando wises up to his brother selling him out." He explains what went before as Rex listens carefully. The clapboard is used again and then the camera is rolling.

"It was you, Charley," Rex says with anguish. "You and Johnny. Like the night the two of youse come in the dressing room and says, 'Kid, this ain't your night—we're going for the price on Wilson.' It ain't my night. I'd of taken Wilson apart that night! I was ready—remember the early rounds throwing them combinations. So what happens—this bum Wilson he gets the title shot—outdoors in the ballpark!—and what do I get—a couple of bucks and a one-way ticket to Palookaville. It was you, Charley. You was my brother. You should of looked out for me. Instead of making me take them dives for the short-end money."

Reading from the script, Shafer says, "I always had a bet down for you. You saw some money."

"See! You don't understand! You don't understand! I could've been a contender. I could've had class and been somebody. Real class. Instead of a bum, let's face it, which is what I am. It was you, Charley."

"Cut," Brad says and the crew breaks into applause. "Wow! Brando didn't do it that good." He's not rushed now and wants to talk. "Where did you learn acting? I bet it was with the Brits. The Royal Academy?"

"He's not an actor," Molly says.

"Oh, come on!" He is offended someone thinks he could go for that line.

Regina is on her cell phone. "We're done Mr. Lazarus." She holds her ear back from the blast on the other end. "I'm not kidding," she protests. She hands the phone to Shafer. "You tell him."

"We're all done, chief," he says. "One take each for two scenes, that's all we needed. They're gonna blow you away! I'll email the video as soon as the guys download them. Yes, sir, right away." He hugs Rex, looks at his watch, and rushes off.

Molly watches Regina as they walk back from the sound stage. She is clearly awed. "Is that true," she asks timidly, "you never saw those movies? I mean, how could you not? They're part of the canon."

"No, I never saw them," Rex says matter-of-factly, looking up at an intricate web of white jet contrails in the blue sky. "Not that I remember, anyhow. I bet they're good."

"They won a ton of Oscars."

Molly interrupts before Rex can ask what Oscars are. "We're going to need a place to stay."

"We have an arrangement with the Beverly Hills Hotel," Regina says. She is bending over backward to be helpful now. Couldn't be nicer.

"And a car and driver."

"That is no problem at all."

The great Hungarian or Czech director, Molly is not sure which it is, is stretched on the floor, a studio nurse crouched at his side. "Call an ambulance or something," Lazarus is telling her impatiently. "I got work to do."

"Yes, Mr. Lazarus," she says.

"My leg!" Czaba howls.

"You guys follow me," he tells Rex and Molly. "Regina, I don't need you." He leads them into another office with a computer and a large screen on one wall. He dims the light and taps some keys on the computer; the screen shows the chair in the screen test room. The camera and sound men are heard commenting and then Rex settles himself in the chair, the clapboards are brought together with a crack, and they hear Shafer say, "Action."

Lazarus watches the scenes twice. "I'll be goddamned," he says to them. "I never saw anything like it. I wouldn't think it was possible, but he looks even better on camera. And that's not all. The average good actor would have to go through some Actor's Studio ritual and need ten takes to come even close to what you did off the top of your head in one." He looks at Molly. "Look, I'm a plain-spoken guy. What do you want? Give me a figure."

"We're looking at some other offers," she says with smiling vagueness. Lazarus would think they were both crazy if she tells him what they are.

"I'll have my legal department draw up a contract and you fill in the numbers," Lazarus says. He stands and spreads his arms. "I'm gonna tell you straight, I've never done that before."

Marveling at her own nerve, Molly says, "We can give you a week. If yours is the best offer we get, we'll sign on the dotted line."

"You're giving me an exclusive option only for a week?" Lazarus says with disbelief. "That's not the way we work. I answer to a board of directors."

"The option will cost you fifty thousand dollars. In cash, this afternoon." It's the first figure that popped into her mind, and she doesn't know if it's low ball or preposterously high.

"Fifty grand for a week! C'mon, get real."

"Take it or leave it," Rex says in a quiet voice.

Lazarus darts a measuring look like they are poker players and all the chips are heaped up in the middle. "Are we talking business days?"

"No, all seven from right now," Molly says, looking at her watch. "You're on the clock."

"Jesus," Lazarus says, "where did you learn to negotiate? There's supposed to be give and take."

"Be happy I'm not asking for seventy-five."

"You got some balls, sister. I like that."

Sure you do, Molly thinks. Get your face ready before you tell a lie like that.

"Let's say for the sake of argument…" he begins.

"Take it or leave it," Rex says again. The impact on Lazarus is like rolling thunder from the mountaintop. He actually flinches.

"Okay, okay," Lazarus says, one palm up like a traffic cop. "But you must think we're run like a drug cartel. We're honest businessmen; we don't have fifty thousand bucks in a drawer. I'll have to call the bank, and they'll want Brinks to deliver it. It'll take a couple of hours."

Molly thinks that smile he has now must have taken in a lot of innocent suckers. He must have practiced before a mirror.

"You need anything right now?" Lazarus says grandly. "Ask and ye shall receive."

"We might need your airplane to pick up a friend in Oregon," Molly says.

"Sure," Lazarus says. "Whenever you say."

"We're not sure about timing."

"Just let my girl know."

The cabana at the Beverly Hills Hotel is sumptuous, fit for royalty. Regina has called ahead and they are met by the manager himself at a side entrance used for publicity-shy celebrities.

"The first thing I'm going to do is shower and fix my hair," Molly says when he leaves them. "Then I need to shop for clothes and cosmetics. I look like a rag picker. Did you see that look Regina gave me at first?"

"Want some company?" Rex asks when she comes back from the bathroom with her wrinkled clothes back on and toweling her hair.

"No, thanks. There would be a mob wanting your autograph within fifteen minutes, even though they don't know you; not to mention the paparazzi that hang out around the shops hoping to catch a celebrity shopliftng. You're supposed to stay out of sight, remember? Stay here and chill."

Rex shakes his head in a bemused way.

"I'm so used to you being the best at everything, I expect it now," Molly says. "If only we knew who you were before you lost your memory." She pauses. "You know there are cases where people get knocked on the head and have a brain injury and when they wake up they speak a language they never knew before."

"I suppose that's possible." But his manner says he doesn't think so. It is a beautiful cabana with antiques and cut flowers in vases and large windows with views of palm trees and gardens. "This reminds me a little of when I woke up, though not as nice. The other room led outside to a garden. I guess you would call that room perfect."

"Like you," Molly bursts out. "You are a flawless man."

"I started walking and it's been like what they say a dream is."

"Who says?" Molly asks.

"It was a TV program we watched one night at Templeton Hall. A man didn't know if he was awake or dreaming." Rex gazes into the distance. "Having had a try at it myself now, I realize the acting wasn't very good."

"This is not a dream, sweetheart. You are definitely alive. And you're catching on more about things as time passes. I have that feeling, don't you?"

He contemplates her and she feels like she is shrinking to nothing before his gaze. "Yes, but I'm still waiting to figure out who I am."

"I can't tell you how many times I've heard people say that," Molly says.

Rex sees through that clumsy attempt at consolation. "This is different."

"Maybe if we could find that room something would click in your mind. Or there would be someone you knew and it would all come back. Sergeant Randall knows the road. We could use Google Maps or go door to door."

Rex's nod is non-committal, his mind evidently elsewhere. She is almost afraid to think what is going through it.

The concierge desk calls to say they have a visitor from Brinks and a gray-haired man looking like an accountant in a business suit knocks at the door a moment later carrying a briefcase full of cash in various denominations.

"I thought there would be more of you," Molly tells him as she signs a receipt. "Men in uniform with guns."

"Sometimes it's better not to be noticed," he says pleasantly. "But we do have additional personnel on the premises." He says it was nice doing business with her and have a nice day.

The chauffeur drives her to Rodeo Drive, where he carries an ever mounting armload of packages from store to store, and they are back in two hours. "You'd be surprised how little fifteen thousand dollars buys these days," she tells Rex. "But this is like play money, so I didn't even care." She had caught one store clerk rolling her eyes as she counted out the currency. She probably thought I was laundering money for one of the cartels.

CHAPTER 12

ABIGAIL SITS OUTSIDE INTENSIVE CARE, TRAGIC AND ALONE. WHEN SHE SEES HIM, SHE FLIES INTO his arms and he hugs her tightly. "Oh, Alex, I'm so scared."

"How are they?"

"They just lie there breathing so fast, but the doctors brought the fevers down a little. I told you they went into seizures?" Her natural bubbliness is gone, replaced by this flatness.

"Yes."

"The connection was so bad I couldn't tell. I'm so glad you're here." A thought occurs to her. "How did you get here so fast?"

"I flew." This was no time to try to explain it all even if he could. "Where's your mom?"

"Gone to get coffee."

Her mother, Esther, normally slow afoot, turns a corner with two paper cups of coffee at a good speed. She has a long, plain face with a bony nose that makes her seem bird-like. Abigail's good looks came from her father, who ran a tree service. Esther wears a sweater buttoned over a housedress, the only combination Randall ever saw her in except at the funeral.

"We're going to get through this just fine," she says to Randall, forcing a bright smile. "We'll have those kids home before you know it."

"No doubt in my mind," he says, calling up a hearty manner himself. The glance they trade says be brave for Abigail.

He is allowed in the intensive care unit to see the children; they are unmoving and their faces under the oxygen masks have a hectic flush. He is horrified by the medical paraphernalia crowded around their beds, the IV bags, the tubes, the beeping electronic monitors making spikey tracks on screens. A pretty, young, dark-haired nurse in green scrubs is changing cold compresses. "I think they're better." Instinct tells Randall she is only saying that. "The medication makes them sleep."

"Do you know what's wrong?" Abigail had just shaken her head wordlessly when he asked her.

"Nothing is jumping out at us," the nurse says, "but you better wait for the doctor."

As always, he is struck by the kindness of the people who work in this intense setting; duty has required him to interview victims or eyewitnesses injured enough to be hospitalized. It must be when they rise in the hierarchy that they become cold and official like the one on the telephone.

He and Abigail and her mother walk down corridors in the glare of fluorescent lighting for breakfast. "I don't think I can eat anything," Abigail says, sinking into a molded plastic chair in the cafeteria.

"You have to try, honey," Esther says. "You'll get weak if you don't and then we'll have to look after you too. My, the light is bright in here, isn't it? It shows every line and wrinkle a person's got."

"I'll see what's to eat," Randall says.

He grabs a tray and joins the line of people pushing theirs along the lip of a steam table. The scrambled eggs are rubbery looking and the bacon as thin and dry as a layer of dust. He loads the tray with coffee, what passes for bagels with silver rectangles of cream cheese, and dishes of canned fruit. Two doughnuts for him.

"Well," Esther says, "it's better than nothing." She fusses over Abigail, nagging at her to eat. "At least try the peaches, the sugar will give you energy."

Abigail is looking off into space. "They've always been so healthy except for the little stuff all kids get."

"Lord, there are so many children living here now who have never had a vaccination in their life," Esther says. "Their parents are fanatics or from another country where they never heard of them."

"They didn't say, but I think they were almost gone when we got them here," Abigail says in a dull voice.

"I didn't hear that," Esther says, amazed.

"Didn't you see their faces?"

Randall swallows the lump in his throat, unable to speak.

Abigail continues in a dreamy voice, "The doctor kept asking if they'd gotten into something poisonous, pills or a plant of some kind. Like they even would; I can never get them to eat their vegetables."

The sergeant remembers the vial the old man gave him. He pats his jacket and locates them in the zippered pocket. "Excuse me," he says. "I've got to make another call."

He returns to intensive care. Through a window he sees nurses bent over what he assumes is someone injured in the big accident. He steps behind the curtain surrounding the kids, who are unchanged. He unscrews the top and smells it; it is some kind of odorless oil. He makes a horizontal line with it on each forehead. Then, as an afterthought, he goes back and adds the intersecting vertical line.

The curtains are yanked open. "I'm sorry, but you can't be here." The voice from the telephone belongs to a woman in scrubs with short hair going gray and snapping blue eyes. "What did you put on their faces?"

"Something to help them."

"I'm wiping that off right now." A dry wash cloth appears like magic in one hand and she starts to go around Randall. He moves to block her.

"Patient care—if that's what you're doing—is hospital staff only," she snaps, trying again to get around him. He stops her again.

"I can keep this up all day," he says warningly.

She takes a step back, her face flushed with anger. "Do you want me to call security?"

"No."

"Then step out of the way."

"No."

If one of the Old Masters were to paint this scene, Randall thinks, he would call it Authority Thwarted. Her expression says, "I'll show you" as clearly as if she had spoken the words. She spins on her heel and he pulls the curtains closed; their skin is quickly absorbing the oil. An automated voice like one in the big box stores says on the intercom, "Code Three in ICU." It is repeated twice.

A skinny young man parts the curtain a moment later in a cheap blue uniform too big for him; the Eisenhower jacket has Security in white across one pocket. "Excuse me, sir." His high voice is weak and whiny. "I'm gonna have to ask you to leave."

"Beat it, kid."

The guard decides this is a matter for higher command and disappears. Randall watches Michael and Martin until their foreheads are dry. He kisses them and leaves the unit. Another accident victim has arrived and ER nurses with backs to him are dividing their time between the two. A siren grows louder outside and he hears someone say Jaws of Life. In the corridor he passes the security guard, his head turned in earnest conversation with a tubby middle-aged man at his shoulder.

"We call the police if he doesn't," the older man is saying.

Randall turns into the cafeteria. "My, that was a long call," Esther says disapprovingly.

"I told her it was probably about Templeton Hall," Abigail says in her flat voice.

Everything is, Randall thinks.

"What I was always telling your father is there's a time and place for everything."

"Fine, mother. Is there any change?" Abigail asks him.

"I couldn't tell."

She looks at his doughnuts. "I see you went off your diet," she says.

"We can talk about that later."

"I don't even care anymore."

"Look," he says, "we're going to get back where we were and everything will be great again." You don't know how much you have until you lose it, he is thinking—people have been saying it for thousands of years but nobody really pays attention until it happens to them. They sit in silence, wrapped in gloom. Words are useless and even if they weren't, it doesn't seem like there is anything to say. At last, Esther can't stand it any longer.

"How is that case of yours coming?" she says.

"A lot of blind alleys."

"You're working too hard," Abigail says. "I see it in your eyes; and when was the last time you shaved?" That jogs her memory. "I still don't see how you could have got here so fast. What was it, three hours?"

"Private jet," he says. "It's a long story."

"Those things cost a lot of money," Esther says. "I think they say a hundred dollars an hour or something outlandish like that."

"A lot more," Randall says.

"You'd have to sell the house for that," Abigail says, coming out of her shell a little.

"It was a gift from somebody in the case."

"From what I heard," Esther says, "there were a lot of rich people at that place." She natters about how bad times are compared to when she was young. "Why, you never heard of half the stuff that goes on today." Normally, this chin wagging made Randall restless because he had heard it all before, every last story and comparison with the golden past, but he welcomes it now. It is better than silence.

Esther interrupts herself. "Oh, there's that nurse."

Randall sees the pretty, young woman sweeping the room with her eyes. When she spots them, she almost runs to the table.

"They woke up!" she cries.

They rise as one. "Good God above, our prayers answered," Esther calls out. Faces around them smile.

Abigail grabs his hand tightly and they quickly follow the nurse to intensive care. "I can't keep up," Esther says from behind, "but I'll get there when I get there."

The twins are sitting in bed, color back in their cheeks and hair sticking up every which way. The Randalls give them kiss after kiss.

"I'm hungry," Michael says.

"How did we get here?" asks Martin, always the more curious. "I'm hungry, too," he adds.

A doctor in a white coat rushes into the room. "I'm Clint," he tells Randall. "Hi, kids. What's going on here?" He is a lean, young guy who runs to stay in shape, from the look of him.

"We're hungry," they say as one.

"They just… woke up," Abigail says joyously, beginning to cry.

"His temperature is back to normal," says the young nurse, holding a probe to Michael's ear. She transfers it to Martin. "And so is his."

Dr. Clint Martin does not hide his bafflement. "An hour ago they were in a coma." "I thought they were just sleeping," Abigail protests.

"Sometimes we say that so peoples don't freak out," Clint replies uncomfortably.

The overbearing supervising nurse enters the room, but her belligerence changes when she sees she is outranked. "Hello, doctor," she says. "I understand we have some good news here." She smiles at Abigail but pointedly ignores Randall.

"I'd say so," Clint says. "Just look at 'em."

Esther arrives, breathing heavy. "I'm so glad to see you kids looking so good!"

"Hi, Grandma," Martin says.

"Hi, Grandma," Michael says.

"I said it first," Martin points out.

"No, you didn't."

"Mom?"

"It doesn't matter," she says.

"Why are you cwying?" Martin asks.

"Because I'm so happy," she says.

"I cwy when I'm sad," Michael says solemnly.

Other doctors and nurses crowd into the room, the masks of detachment momentarily set aside to celebrate a come-from-behind win over death.

In the midst of the jubilation, Randall thinks, what's to stop this from happening again, maybe next time to Abigail? Joy is replaced by the seep of dread.

"Do you think they could have cereal with banana?" he hears Abigail ask as he slips from the room. "It's what I give them at home."

They could take the kids and hit on the road, drive from state to state to put behind the malignant spirits that almost got away with this. A blur of motels and family restaurants, always on the move—but how long could they keep that up? The kids would be restless and whiny strapped in their car seats all the time, and adult tempers would wear short. And there was no guarantee an out-of-control eighteen-wheeler with air horn blasting wouldn't knife across the divider one day, coming at them head-on faster than he could react.

He calls Penny on his smartphone for better reception; his location is already known. "It's me," he says. "What am I missing?"

"Sound and fury signifying nothing," she says. She was an English major in college and likes reminding the criminal justice types from time to time.

"Okay, I guess I should know who said that."

"Two men were killed in San Francisco and the talk is the same perps as Templeton Hall. Torture, blood all over. One guy's nose was hacked off and glued to the bathroom mirror. They think he was made to watch while they did it. It makes you sick."

Randall pushes the image from his mind. "Any idea why they were picked?"

"Not a one so far. Where are you?"

"I'm in Oregon with the family."

"Well, that was fast; lucky you." Penny senses something when he doesn't answer. "Everything all right?"

"Peachy keen."

"You might get called back. The chief got some spine stiffener from somewhere and is telling the FBI he's thinking about un-suspending you; I think he's tired of being pushed around. He also doesn't like that he has to pay Frudenthaler overtime to fill your shoes." She switches to her joking voice. "Not that they could be. Ever!"

"They say we'll all be replaced by robots one day."

"Then one day the robots will realize they don't need us and put us down like dogs," Penny says.

But he's in no mood for their usual banter. "What's the connection between these two guys in San Francisco?"

"They're digging into it, but nothing so far. The first read is they were just ordinary city hipsters as cool as the other side of the pillow. Want their names?"

"Let me get out my pen and notebook." He pats his coat and notices the vial is gone. Didn't he put it back in a pocket? "Okay, shoot."

The first guy lives in Cow Hollow, or I guess you'd say lived, meaning a little bit of money there."

"Everybody in San Francisco has money except the people who wait on them in restaurants," Randall says.

"His name is James Fitzleigh, thirty-eight years old. Single white male, works as a software designer at the foot of Market Street. His family is in Indiana. They've been notified."

"I pity the poor bastard who had to tell them, especially if they started to ask questions about the details." Randall has had that job a few times. He went home shattered.

"The other one," Penny says, "is Al Murray, thirty-five years old, SWM. He also does something in IT. He had a sleeve of tattoos on his left arm, which they found in the living room. The rest of him was in a bedroom."

"Is he the guy with the nose on the mirror?"

"No, that was the other one. I don't see how they could rent those places again, but they will. They'll even jack up the price; people won't care because everybody wants to live in San Francisco, but I couldn't stand the fog in the summer. And that wind." Penny drops her voice. "Here comes the chief." Randall hears her say good morning and then Parker talking in the background. "Will do, chief," she says brightly.

After a small pause for him to get out of earshot, Penny says, "He wants you to come back to work. I can say I can't reach you because nobody answers on the land line and your cell is turned off."

"You're the greatest."

"I know."

He wanders outdoors past the pariahs taking quick, greedy drags from cigarettes and follows a sidewalk to a Garden of Reflection with benches on paths among the shrubbery. A green metal sign in the ground says it is maintained by the Evening Primrose Club of Klamath Falls. He has to get Abigail alone to tell her the whole story; she would be furious at not being told earlier, and she would cry about Bub. When she got control of herself maybe she could come up with a better idea than taking to the road.

CHAPTER 13

"ARE YOU SERGEANT RANDALL?" ASKS THE HEAVY YOUNG WOMAN WITH A NOSE RING OF SILVER claws that climb a nostril of her pug nose. A green snake tattoo winds around her neck, the scales so meticulously inked they look real. Throw in the thick plugs in her earlobes and the egg-yoke yellow hair and it came to a total rejection of the world and what it thinks.

He had watched her approach the Garden of Reflection where he sits on a bench. She has a scuffling walk in laced boots that emphasize thick calves; her jeans are so tight a mighty struggle must be necessary to pull them on. Cheeks as plump as dumplings give her dark eyes a slitted wariness.

"How did you know?" he asks. Nothing surprises him anymore.

"He said you'd be here," she says truculently.

"Who did?"

"He said you'd be here," she repeats, raising her voice as if she had been contradicted. "He said to give you this." She pulls an envelope from a rear pocket, hands it to him and walks away. The view from behind is no more attractive than head on.

"Dear Sergeant," it reads, "you and your family are welcome at the monastery." It was signed Brother Mario Roberti on stationary from The Order of Cistercians of the Strict Observance at St. Benedict's Abby in Snowmass near Aspen.

Randall catches up to her as she plods toward the parking lot. "Hang on," he says when he intercepts her. "What did he look like?"

"I couldn't see 'cause it was dark."

"So it was last night?"

"More like this mornin', early. I thought I was dreaming it, but it was on my night stand when I woke up. I thought somebody was playin' a trick, and I still ain't sure."

He sees now she has the hurt eyes of someone who has been the butt of cruel jokes. The self-sabotage—the in-your-face look, the surly manner—are her defense against mean people. The sergeant sees it all the time in teenagers who can't stay out of trouble.

"Was he young, old? Tall short?"

"I would say sorta in between? Sorry, but I gotta get going. I'm late already."

"This is for your trouble." He takes a hundred dollar bill from his wallet.

"Oh, wow," she says. She reaches for it, but then pulls back. "No," she says, shaking her head. "I can't accept it. He asked me as a favor and I can't take money."

"Can you tell me a little more about him?"

"Well… he was kind. I felt good when he was there and I still do somewhat. So, no thank you, sir."

"How did he get in?"

"That's the funny thing. My mom and me have four dogs and three cats and none of 'em woke up."

Randall watches her continue trudging to her car, an old one with dents, patches of bare metal where the paint has worn away, and a missing hub-cap. The busted muffler makes a snarling roar as she leaves the parking lot bound for what he guesses is a dead-end job. When she turns onto the road, he sees it has a doughnut tire on the passenger side. She could have used a hundred bucks.

He returns to the bench to think some more. It was obvious who paid the visit to the young woman at the same time he was visited in Marin, and equally clear he wants them to go to that monastery in Colorado. That was a long drive, and the vision returns of the 18-wheeler jackknifing across the freeway divider at them.

"Mom and a couple of the nurses want to have a party for the kids with cake and ice cream," Abigail says, collapsing on the bench alongside him. "Did you board Bub?"

"Bub's dead."

"Oh, my God," she says hand to mouth.

"He was shot by the people who killed everyone at Templeton Hall."

Stunned, she begins to cry again. "But that's miles away! Bub would never roam that far."

"He was at home. They were looking for me." His words are hammer blows that make her flinch. He takes her into his arms and holds her as she sobs. At last she raises her tear-stained face from his chest.

"Why were they looking for you?"

"It's all guesswork at this point."

"Did you find evidence they didn't want getting out?"

"They're looking for that guy I picked up walking. He was acting confused, so I took him to Templeton Hall. I got suspended for not following procedure. The FBI seemed to think that was a big deal."

"Suspended! Oh, Alex."

"With pay and they want me back, so no problem."

"Why didn't you tell me all this was going on?" she cries.

"It sounds lame, but I didn't want to worry you."

"You always talk to me about the job."

"Not the really bad stuff."

"Who was the man?"

"He had amnesia and still does, the really bad kind. He doesn't know who he is or what he was doing before I picked him up, that being the biggest mistake in my life."

"That's your job."

"You'd be surprised how much is choice—get involved or pretend you don't see something and keep on going."

"Not you, you're a good cop."

"Every cop is until something like this happens—most of us, anyway. There are bad apples in every barrel."

She is silent for a moment, and then says, "Have you told me everything?"

"No, we're going to Colorado."

She swipes her eyes with the back of a hand and gives him a hard stare. "Why are we going to Colorado?"

"We'll be safer."

"From what?" Then fear darkens her eyes. "Are those killers still after you?"

He keeps his voice matter-of-fact. "They're still looking for the guy I picked up, so it's smart to be careful."

"Wait, wait. Why wasn't he killed with the rest of them?"

"He was tipped off and left before they got there." Randall doesn't think this is quite the right time to bring an angel into the story. "You'll have to talk your mother into Colorado." As much as he hates the thought of dragging Esther along, he can't take a chance on her being abducted and used as a bargaining chip.

"How do you know he got a tip?" Abigail asks. "You must have talked to him afterward."

"I traced him to San Francisco."

"And he's not in protective custody?"

"I think he's in Hollywood right now."

Abigail looks like she is ready to tear out her hair. "What is he doing there?"

"All I know is that's where he is at the moment. I'll call later and find out what's going on."

Abigail gives out a burst of wild laughter. "Do you know how crazy this sounds after the night I've had?"

"Yes, Crazy and I are close friends now." He has a manic urge to press on like the TV pitchmen and say, "But, wait, there's more."

Abigail takes a sudden veer to her practical side. "That's a lot of money," she protests. "I haven't budgeted for it and we'd have to dip into savings. And anyhow, our car is too small for three adults and two little kids. Mom gets car sick unless she rides in the front."

He has a brainstorm. "We'll fly there." If Rex and Molly can swing it. "We're going to stay at a place near Aspen."

"Flying," she explains in a fake patient way, "is more expensive than driving. And what is this place?"

"It's a monastery."

"Oh, brother," Abigail says. "I've heard everything now."

Not by a long shot, he thinks. "I'm sure the rates are reasonable."

"Do they know we're Presbyterians?"

"I don't think that matters so much these days."

Abigail eyes him narrowly. "How did you arrange all this?"

"It hasn't been easy, believe me."

"That doesn't answer my question."

"Look, I'm asking you to go with the flow for now." When she fixes him with her fierce eagle stare, he says, "Have a little faith in me right now, Abigail."

Her generous nature overcomes the anger and she grabs him and holds tight. "Of course the boys and I have faith in you. You're the best husband and father ever there was!"

They drive to a bakery for a cake and stop at a grocery for a gallon of ice cream, and he tells her as much as he thinks she ought to know at this point, skipping over the torture bit. The murdering is bad enough.

"So this man is both a musician and a baseball star," Abigail says. "That's so unusual, isn't it?"

"He's not a baseball star yet."

"And performing on the same stage as Mick Jagger. To have so much talent, that's something! I wish you had taken more pictures so I could see if he's as handsome as you say. And don't say only you come close." She gives him a punch on the arm.

He smiles, glad her spirits are recovering. They will need all her smartness and toughness to get through this.

He has cake and ice cream as the boys perform for doctors and nurses coming in and out of the room they were moved to from intensive care. Michael and Martin are born show offs and compete at being the funniest. They make faces and take exaggerated falls to the floor. Randall sees the genes Abigail's brother has; he is a goof who does silly walks to get a laugh. If you don't smile, he keeps up the hijinks until you fake one, otherwise you'd be there all night. Randall calms the boys down when they threaten to go over the top like Uncle Bart. He hands them off to Abigail and slips outside to call Molly on the throwaway phone.

"It's me," he says. "What's happening?"

"How are your kids? We've been really worried." Rex hasn't actually mentioned them, but she's sure he feels the same.

"They're fine now. I'll fill you in later." He doesn't feel like another discussion of rationality and how she just can't do a darn thing about it.

"You won't believe what's happened now," she says.

"I bet I will."

"We're having dinner tonight with the famous Irving Lazarus."

"The movie man or the dentist?"

"I didn't know you had a sense of humor."

"You have to hang around the gallows more."

"They want to give Rex a movie contract," Molly says.

"The whole world wants a piece of the guy."

"They're putting us up at the Beverly Hills Hotel until we hear the details. It is unbelievably swanky."

"I bet they don't have a free breakfast like Motel Six. What's our friend up to?"

"He's still changing," she says in a lowered voice.

"Is he where he can hear you?"

"No, he's watching TV, no, more like studying it. He has such a concentrated look; I think he's looking for cues on how people behave."

"If he can't hear you, speak up. They saved money on the reception part when they built these phones. What are the changes?"

"It's like he's starting to take total command of his life."

"What about his memory?"

"It's bothering him more how he can't remember anything. I had an idea. You know that road where you picked him up? Why not go door to door and see if you can find the house he came from? There can only be one with a room like he's told us."

"I assume the FBI already did that." Never assume anything, he reminds himself. "But it wouldn't be a bad idea to double check. Maybe they missed something."

"I gave them one week to come up with their proposal. Guess what they're paying for that? Fifty thousand dollars! We've got it in cash right here in a briefcase."

"In your room?" Randall says with disbelief. "As soon as I hang up, put it in the hotel safe." He gave her credit for more common sense.

Molly gets huffy. "You don't want me using credit cards, remember?"

"Yes, but fifty thousand?"

"I spent fifteen thousand alone on clothes today. I had to get us both stuff to wear because we left everything behind in San Francisco. Rodeo Drive isn't cheap, believe me."

"Isn't there a Wal-Mart in town?" Molly doesn't bother replying.

Let it go, Randall tells himself, they might need that cash. "Are you still bud-dies with the director? Can you have them send that airplane to fly me and the family to Colorado?"

"I have a feeling he's out of the picture in more ways than one," Molly says. "Something happened to his leg. He grabbed it and he was, like, howling. The last time I saw him he was rocking back and forth on the carpet, but I bet we could swing it for you. Lazarus is eating out of Rex's hand."

"We're in Klamath Falls and we need to go to Aspen," Randall says. "Then I want to shoot back to the Bay Area after I get my wife and kids settled. Think you can set that up?"

"Let me run it past Rex." He hears her calling to him and explaining the situation. "Rex says sure, no problem." She lowers her voice. "See what I mean about taking command?"

"The sooner you guys can get the plane here the better." Life is moving like one of those speeded-up film where a seed grows into a flower.

Then Esther gets in the picture and it slows down to molasses-as-usual.

"Mom's not sure she wants to go," Abigail informs him, "and if she does it'll take her a couple of days to take care of things." What things, he asks. "She has to get someone to feed the cat. Maybe that someone can water her plants, but if not she will have to get somebody else. She's choosy who she lets in. One of her windows is sticking and a repairman is scheduled, and she doesn't have a thing to wear."

"She can grab a few things from her closet," Randall says. "Monks won't care."

"You don't know women and when did you become an expert on monks?" Abigail says.

"They have renounced earthly things, which include noticing what old ladies are wearing."

"Don't let her hear you say that."

"And the rest of that stuff sounds like a couple of phone calls."

"She has her programs she watches, and I doubt a monastery has a TV."

"Talk her around, Abby," he says patiently. "Tell her it's for the children. It never fails when politicians say that. Missing a few episodes of Days of Our Lives is not a huge sacrifice."

"I'll try," she says tiredly, "but don't be surprised if she says no."

"You would be amazed how unsurprised I am these days."

"I know it's been hard for you," she says sympathetically. "I'll get the boys ready while you get us out of here."

It's a whopping bill, but their insurance takes care of most and the business office will send a bill for the deductible. They hurry to the car as fast as it is possible to move with a lagging old woman and two children with short legs.

"I've been to Colorado and didn't much care for it," Esther says in the front passenger seat she claims in the name of her car sickness. "Why would you want to go there anyway?"

"A free vacation?" Randall says.

That puts the matter in a different light. Esther's passion is discounts and bargain bins and nothing beats free. Well, being paid to go on vacation is even better, but those opportunities were rare outside of game shows where in her opinion any fool could answer the questions.

"I don't see why we have to be in such a hurry," Esther complains. "There are things I have to take care of."

"Mom," Abigail says from the back seat, "you already agreed."

"I know I did, I'm just saying."

"It's a tight window," Randall says.

Esther doesn't like his terseness; her style is to wander from one subject to another with maximum garrulity. "Did you win the trip in a contest? I had a friend who…"

"It has to do with a case and, sorry, I can't say more."

"Oh," she says, submitting to this flourish of legal authority.

Her Craftsman cottage a half an hour from the airport is filled with heavy furniture, chintz curtains and cushions, and pictures of the twins. He watches the boys play in her backyard while she and Abigail choose which clothes to pack, a drawn-out process that takes place before the mirror. He telephones Molly and tells her they're ready to go.

"The crew is on standby, so I'll pass the word. Do you want them to wait in Aspen until you're ready to go back to the Bay Area?"

Randall says that would be perfect. They must really want to land our guy, he thinks.

Esther's friend can both feed the cats and water the plants if they are gathered in one spot so she doesn't have to worry about finding them in different rooms and maybe forgetting one so it withers and dies and she would be responsible. This is a conversation of thirty-five minutes by Randall's watch.

"Yes, it is very sudden," Esther tells her friend. "I don't know why a person couldn't be given a little warning, but that's just me." Randall senses the woman on the other end can't hide her envy.

"We're not going through Portland," Esther says importantly. "A private jet is picking us up." That floors the friend. "I'm sorry, but I'm afraid it's... I guess you'd say a secret mission, but I can't go into the details." After a few more words, she hangs up, clearly satisfied with the effect. "She once told someone I lead a humdrum life," she says to Abigail.

"That sounds divine to me at this point," her daughter replies, looking up from washing Michael's face and ears with a cloth. "You're next, buster," she tells Martin. He takes to his heels and Randall has to run him down.

The cat gets out and has to be lured back, they assemble the luggage, strap the boys into their car seats, look for a scarf Esther can't find, and finally leave for the airport. "Why does it take as much time as it does to get an army on the move?" Randall asks.

"I don't know," Abigail answers, calm as usual in the face of his exasperation on this subject, "it just does."

"We're just going to leave the car in the parking lot, I guess," she says as they are unloading the luggage and children and the paraphernalia that goes with them.

"One car at the Santa Rosa airport and the other at the Klamath Falls airport," he says. "How does it feel to be a jet setter?" She has to laugh.

Everyone is impressed by the sleekness of the Gulfstream when it lands and taxies to the apron. "It must be a job keeping this clean," Esther says, looking around the interior. "Whoever owns it doesn't have little kids."

"If they do," Abigail says, "they have nannies to watch them every minute." She takes things as they come and this showy aircraft interests but doesn't impress her.

Before long foothills and then the craggy peaks of the Rockies are rising below them, and then the jet is on its final approach. They follow their luggage on a cart to the general aviation terminal where a taxi is summoned for them for the eighteen-mile drive to Snowmass.

The women marvel at the beauty of the scenery and wildlife, but Esther thinks it must be bitter cold in winter. "I'd leave before the first snowflake."

"Let the kids stretch their legs," Randall says when they pull up forty-five minutes later at the monastery set in trees. "I'll get the lay of the land."

St. Benedict's Abby is a collection of buildings with steeply pitched roofs. He is aware of an abiding stillness when he walks through the front door under a sign that says PAX. He is expecting people in robes, but he is met by a man in jeans and a long-sleeved print shirt. He raises his eyebrows questioningly but does not speak.

"I'm looking for Brother Mario," Randall asks.

"I'll take you to the abbot." The man beckons him to follow to the administrative wing and they set off down a stark corridor with a polished floor and the smell of beeswax. Brother Mario, a tall, balding man, large nosed, wearing a robe with a rope belt, is in a small office furnished merely with desk, chair and lamp. They shake hands and Brother Mario waits for him to speak.

"I got your offer." Randall shows him the envelope and letter.

"This is the original," Brother Mario cries. He gives Randall a long look. "I wrote it at midnight and it was to go out in this morning's mail. It's impossible for you to have it."

"Another miracle," Randall says.

"I was asked in a dream to write that invitation. I awoke and did so without further thought and returned to bed. Help me understand this."

"I'm a cop," Randall says, showing his wallet with the badge. "This all began when I stopped a guy walking down a road in the Bay Area." He goes through the whole story without interruption from the abbot.

When he is finished, Brother Mario shakes his head. "I truly don't know what to make of your story."

"I had a head start and I don't either."

"I was asked to provide refuge to your family because of grave danger." He gazes at the wall, remembering. "He was a humble man with a beard, some kind of outdoor worker."

"Did it seem like more than a dream, that he was actually there?" Randall asks.

"Yes, now that you mention it. I wouldn't have written that note just because of a dream. It was a presence... he had a warmth and yet an unmistakable urgency."

"The same for me."

"It's more disturbing the more I think about it. Ordinary miracles are one thing, but this... Yet there are many records of divine visitations through the ages."

"I heard about the Christmas one when I was kid," Randall says. "That's about it."

"That was much later in biblical history. In the Old Testament angels told Abraham that Sarah would bear him a child; later the angel stopped him from sacrificing Isaac as proof of his faith in God. I thought into my early adulthood that the evidence was angels were best avoided. They appeared to Mary at the Annunciation, a huge and joyful event, but then there was her agony as a mother over his horrifying death. Those nails pounded into his flesh, the slow suffocation. Shouldn't the angel Gabriel have warned bad would come with the good?"

He shakes his head sadly as if it happened a week ago. "I thought then that angels dealt only with big events and great people, the mighty kings of early times and so forth. Then I became aware how common their visitations are to ordinary people in all cultures. As a simple academic, I had regarded them only as archetypes shaped over time. But I came to see them as intermediaries between God and humans at critical points in lives. Their frequency is the stuff of tales in literature and now TV and films."

"I don't watch TV much or see that many movies," Randall says. "There's so much crap."

"So I am informed by our visitors." A silence falls between them. "Do angels exist in their own right in celestial realms," Brother Mario muses, "or are they a vibration of light and energy from the eternal source that take on a form consistent with our cosmology when they interact with human consciousness?"

"You lost me there," Randall says.

"The modern mind scoffs and seeks worldly explanations—illness, obsession, delusion rooted in madness. And nowadays there is a great flowering of neurological theories in the name of reductive materialism."

"Think of me as just a dumb flatfoot and we'll save time." Not even a hint of this stuff was on his mental radar before. "Listen, my family's outside. Do you suppose…"

"Yes, yes, of course," Brother Mario says hastily. "We have guest quarters for our visitors. I'll have Brother William get them settled." He leaves and returns. "That's taken care of and the cab driver paid," he says. "What nice children."

"I don't think they're going to be very good with the silence thing."

"The hermitages are a mile away, far enough that the brothers in the cloister aren't disturbed. And we're not totally silent here, you know, necessary conversation is allowed. Would you like a look around while we talk?"

Brother Mario shows him through the library, the refectory, the hall where the brothers take their meals. "We have sixteen monks with cells on the second floor." They climb the stairs and he opens the door of one. A bed, a desk and chair, a lamp for reading, a crucifix on the pale wall.

"Pretty simple," Randall says.

"That's the idea."

They walk outside to a quadrangle in bright sunshine with a high-mountain bite; Randall jams hands in his pockets to warm them. "The universe is far more complex than we imagined," Brother Mario reflects. "Dreams and angelic visitations such as you and I had point to a form of non-rational and mystical knowing beyond the five senses. They understand this better in the East."

"Like I keep saying, go much beyond police work and the water is over my head in a hurry."

"That's true of most of us. There are many brothers here who find the Holy Scriptures have answers to all questions that interest them. The world of mystics, shamans, and spiritual guides in a universe that blends body, mind, and spirit is as foreign to them as it is to Richard Dawkins."

"I guess I should know the name," Randall says.

"He is," the abbot dryly says, "what you might call a celebrity atheist. I'm told the media is quite fond of him. There is something called the sensed presence that has been studied, but that's not what you and I experienced. Mountain climbers and solo sailors and others in life-or-death situations speak of feeling someone helping them survive. Twenty-four years after his flight, Charles Lindbergh finally wrote about the presence in his cockpit that kept him awake with advice and suggestions. He was a brave man, but not brave enough to endure scorn for sounding foolish. Scientism would have us believe it's the effect of chemicals released in the brain under great stress, but then it would, wouldn't it? Quite a lot of first-person stories about sensed presences come out, but not as many as happen. People sometimes will say, 'Something told me' and leave it at that."

"Do I smell cookies?"

"We have a small bakery and sell our cookies all over the country from our website; FedEx comes every day. It's one of the ways we support the Abby."

"The kids will like that."

"They will be safe here. I have a feeling the angel wouldn't have directed you to bring your family here if that wasn't true."

"I can't tell you what a load off that is." Strangely, Randall actually feels looser and lighter as if the weight was physical.

"Did the angel say his name?"

"Camael."

"In early times he was seen as one of the seven archangels, the first created by God to protect the world from demons. The name means 'He Who Sees God. But he isn't listed in traditional Old or New Testament scripture; that is why the Vatican banned Camael from its teachings. One or two of the New Age religions have taken him up in modern times."

"So the Vatican thinks he's a phony?"

"I guess it would depend on who you ask. Why is this Rex so important?"

"That's the big question, one of them anyhow. Finding who killed all those people at Templeton Hall isn't exactly a small deal."

"The killers might be incorporeal beings you will never bring to justice, but God has judged them already."

"The law says we have to try."

"The Scriptures say they are immortal, but not eternal; powerful, but not omnipotent. Theirs is a realm of darkness; they are wretched and miserable and share Lucifer's burning hatred for us. What joy they took in the torture and slaughter at Templeton Hall." They walk in silence, the abbot deep in thought.

"We at the Abby don't follow the news," he continues, "but people who come to our retreats are sad by what they see on TV." He stops and turns to Randall. "You have to go back to the Middle Ages to match the modern glorification of savagery. Oliver Cromwell's body was dug up after three years, torn apart, and his head stuck on a pike to rot for three years. I used to find such hatred and barbarity unimaginable, but no longer."

"No need to imagine nowadays, it's all on YouTube."

"The Devil did not bother to hide his hand back then. The modern mind smiles at him as a metaphor or a superstition we have long outgrown; even the church rarely mentions the Devil today. It is as if he is an embarrassment that got swept under the rug and was forgotten."

"You're saying—what?—that he didn't just go out of fashion, he just went into hiding?" Randall feels a cold that is not from the mountain air.

"Some say this skepticism about the Devil suits his purposes. Do you know the author C.S. Lewis?"

"Afraid not." Abigail recommends books now and then, but he is not much of a reader. He would rather be down in his shop doing stuff.

"The Screwtape Letters dealt with that very question; I read it as a young man. It's light-hearted, but serious. That's hard to bring off, but you have to entertain people to get them in the tent for the message."

Randall makes a half-hearted promise to himself to look it up if he has a chance, but he is pretty sure that won't happen, not with everything going on.

"You describe Rex as perfect," Brother Mario says musingly.

"I couldn't think of a better word. An Episcopalian priest thought I was making a bad joke about the Second Coming."

"All the Abrahamic religions have a second-coming element. We think Jesus Christ was the Messiah, but the Jews and Muslims believe differently—to put it mildly. Yet all agree such a figure will appear in the End Times to do battle with a false messiah, a being of concentrated evil. These final days will come with unrest, strife, famine, and natural disasters. The Buddhist and Hindu traditions also agree the final days will be turbulent."

"Things aren't exactly peaceful today," Randall says.

"They must get far worse according to prophecy, but the trends are certainly not encouraging." Randall is glad to go back inside where it's warm.

"You don't mean that this man Rex is actually perfect," Brother Mario says behind his desk. The point clearly troubles him. "You're exaggerating, corect?"

"Except for the amnesia, he sure seems perfect. People love the guy. And why not? He's handsome, charming, kind, great personality. There would be something wrong with you if you didn't like him."

"There must be something you don't know yet."

"It's hard to find out what that might be when his mind is a blank about the past." Randall works to keep his voice from dropping. "Doesn't this quiet ever get to you?"

"At first," Brother Mario admits matter-of-factly. "But you get used to it, or you find another vocation. And after time passes it's hard to imagine life any other way. Don't his fingerprints tell you anything?"

"They haven't had a chance to lift any. It's been go-go-go since Templeton Hall." Penny would have mentioned it if the FBI found prints they couldn't identify, but on the other hand there must be hundreds to sift through.

"You said you have a plane waiting for you in Aspen. If you like, I'll run you down to the hermitage to say goodbye to your wife and children."

They drive in a pickup truck with a load of fence posts. "Living next to the wildlife preserve, we have to keep the animals out or they eat everything," Brother Mario explains.

The kids are off walking on the grounds with Esther. "We want to wear them out so they take a long nap," Abigail says, running a hand distractedly through her hair. "Mom and I are running out of gas, and I would kill for a hot bath." She gives him a searching look. "Are you going now?"

"Time to saddle up," he says with a feeble show of jauntiness.

"I'm so worried."

"You'll be safe here."

"I know that; it's a special place, you can just tell. It's you I'm worried about." There is pleading in her eyes. "Can't someone else do this?"

"I wish there was, but I can't think who."

"Will you call every day?"

"Count on it." A last embrace and then, wiping his eyes with a sleeve, he goes out to where the abbot waits in the pickup. They drive in silence toward Aspen.

"I've been thinking about what our angel said to you," Brother Mario says at last, "that Rex is somehow connected to the fate of the world. Did he say this connection was good or bad?"

"He said the 'future of mankind'; he didn't say one way or the other."

"You've been assuming your job is to guard him. Maybe it's to watch him."

"For what reason?"

"To be on the safe side," Brother Mario says taking his eyes off the road to glance Randall's way. "Nobody is perfect."

CHAPTER 14

MOLLY'S EXPERIENCE PICKING FACES FOR TV COMMERCIALS IS GOOD BACKGROUND FOR JUDGING the men and women who drop by the booth at the Polo Lounge. They are young and fit upward-strivers or middle-aged men who watch their weight and spend money on good plastic surgery. This second group is in mid-career and their hyper-alert manner says they are all too aware of the razor edge they walk between the kingpins above and the young dudes climbing the ladder below. The men vary from sham geniality to thin smiles that do not mask cut-throat ambition.

The women have a bright, brittle charm, but Molly sees through them. Strip away the phony tinsel of Hollywood, someone said, and you find the real tinsel. The woman have priced to the penny her new Seafarer flared velvet pants and mauve silk Gucci blouse. They push a gushy welcome-to-the-Hollywood-sisterhood line, but she doesn't buy it for a minute. They are here to feast their eyes on the most gorgeous hunk of man they have ever seen. In the jeans, red turtleneck and leather jacket she bought for him at Zazzle's, he calmly receives the homage.

They come in relays, sliding across the pale leather banquette during her aperitif and appetizer of lightly smoked Hawaiian amberjack, the almond-crusted Dover Sole entre with buttered New Potatoes and winter truffles, and the finale, spiced chocolate Gateau. At some signal from Lazarus after self-ies with Rex, one delegation finishes drinks or leaves them untouched and is replaced by another. All are senior executives of one sort or another, the production head, a chief of marketing and another of finance, lawyers, people savvy about talent and deals, charmers and tough-nosed negotiators. It is clear Lazarus is exposing the studio's entire leadership team to Rex to justify the

rich offer he means to make. And it is just as clear that his box-office potential blows them away.

They see in him a decade and maybe two of summer tent pole action-thrill-
ers that will gross billions in the domestic and global markets. Then there will
be the smaller prestige films that rake in Oscars and advance the studio to
the artistic front rank. Goodbye to comic book movies and dreary sequels
with diminishing returns that earn the contempt of the creative types whose
approval they covet but never get. These Big Data wizards and talent spotters
can tell all this just by looking at Rex. Surround him with top talent—writers
and directors and production designers—and their bonuses and stock shares on
top of salary increases will make them wealthier than they have ever dreamed.
Molly is struck by a middle-aged woman beautifully turned out in diamonds
and a deep purple Prada outfit who is introduced only as Leah. Her dramatic
eyes devour Rex with a connoisseur's appreciation, brightening when his passing gaze around the table lingers on her briefly before moving on. She follows
Molly to the ladies room.

"I'm Leah Loraine," she says when Molly comes out of the stall. "You're his
manager? I'd like to see him alone."

"That won't happen," Molly replies, looking into the mirror and reapply-
ing lipstick.

"You know who I am?"

"Sure, you're the famous casting director. If they gave Oscars for the job
you'd have ten."

"Well?" Leah says with impatience.

"He's not ready for one-on-one."

"He's an actor, isn't he?" Her tone is imperious.

"He's a lot of things," Molly says, putting on her lipstick, "maybe actor is
one of them."

Leah is affronted by her flipness —this is the beating heat of the popular culture… *Hollywood*. "He'll have to do a screen test," she sputters.

"That won't be a problem," Molly says, turning from the mirror to look at
her. "Not for him."

"I can help him with a monologue for the test; I'm thinking of something
by Shakespeare or Chekhov. Looks are one thing, acting ability is another."

"You've seen him out there," Molly says over her shoulder on her way out, "he could read a menu and still knock 'em dead."

Rex has no awe for the powerful people at the table. At a meeting like this some tension over stakes this high is expected, some minimal anxiety about pleasing them. Instead, he is so laid back he politely stifles a yawn at one point. They are ravished by the dazzling smiles he dispenses like coins thrown to beggars, and lean forward to catch his humdrum remarks about the news or the Sports Channel and rear back in amazement as if they have heard pearls from Oscar Wilde. This is far from ordinary Hollywood sycophancy, Molly realizes, it is as genuine as it gets for these people.

She is aware others in the lounge are taking a sharp interest in their group. They bob up from tables for better looks and to take phone videos; the boldest make excuses to drop by and say hello. Evidently, Lazarus gave orders for a quick brush off and they back away with lingering looks at Rex. An older, deeply-tanned man with dyed black hair combed forward approaches with a regal pomp that needs only horn music and an ermine-trimmed robe for the picture to be complete. Molly guesses from the looks of awe that he is one of the uncrowned heads of Hollywood. He wears slacks with a razor crease, a monogramed blazer, an open-collared shirt that shows white chest hair, and a thick gold chain. A gold Rolex encrusted with precious stones winks at one wrist.

"Lenny," he says patronizingly to Lazarus. The lesser executives at the table dim in his aura like figures wavering in the afternoon heat of the Sinai. "Where ya been? I haven't seen you in a dog's years."

"I been around, Marty," Lazarus says tightly, and Molly senses deep animosity. "Where *you* been?"

"Don't you read the trades, for crissakes?"

"We're busy here, Marty, what can I do for you?"

Marty Cohen flinches as if slapped. He has been at the top so long he can't remember when anyone spoke to him like that, but he recovers and leans on the shoulder of the marketing chief like that is what he is for and sticks out a hand to Rex. "Who's the new boy?"

Lazarus bats his hand away. "Beat it, Marty. We're talking business." This is public payback for some past humiliation, Molly realizes. The group at the table is frozen and silent.

"They call me Rex."

Cohen, pale beneath his tan, turns his molten glare from Lazarus. "You got an agent, Rex?"

"She is," Rex says with a nod to Molly.

"See me before you do a deal with that shmendrik," Cohen tells her. He gives Lazarus another long stare and turns away. A glance around the room tells her that everybody saw the seismic event. There is a general movement of cell phones from pockets and purses.

"Maybe you don't know it," Lazarus tells Rex and Molly, "but this town is full of fucking assholes."

"There are a lot of bad people it seems," Rex says mildly.

The response around the table is as if Rex had uttered a koan of deep wisdom. They nod in agreement or shake heads like they can't believe how smart this guy is.

"He's the worst, believe me," Lazarus says.

Cohen suddenly stumbles in his stately progress and falls over a table, stripping it of its linen and bringing down an avalanche of plates, glasses, cutlery, and a candle in a holder of modern design. The people at the table leap to their feet except for a white-haired man in a three-piece suit who has gone down under Cohen; women put hands to mouth or shriek. The famous transgender celebrity Molly hadn't noticed before does both. A few seconds of silence follow except for the canned background music that suddenly seems loud. Then everybody begins talking and the wait staff converges from all parts of the room to assist Cohen and the man to their feet and begin a rapid clean up. The white-haired man in the suit has an actively bleeding nose he is not aware of at first.

"That's Lesley Hopkins from Credit Suisse," the studio finance chief tells Lazarus. "He's in town for some deal with Fox."

"The poor schmuck," Lazarus says. "Looks like he's got a broken nose. Ha ha! Look at Cohen; he can't believe this is happening to him." Some friend or associate is helping the unsteady movie magnate from the room; the layer of food crushed into his chest is like a gaudy painting of the Expressionist school.

Lazarus leans closer to his chief of corporate communications and Molly hears him say "Slip it to the trades he got drunk and fell down; say it happens all the time now. By the time his people get out a denial, it'll be in the *New York*

END TIMES ⊕ 133

Post." He sweeps the room with a peevish glance. "Christ, where's the paparazzi when you need them?"

The excitement takes a while to die down. By that time, the golden spell Rex cast has been broken for one of the lawyers at the table, a dark stiletto of a man called Goddard.

"What do we know about you, Rex?" he asks.

"What do you want to know?" Molly answers.

"Everything," he says with a shrug. "Let's start with his last name. We're sitting here calling him Rex, which is short for king if I'm not mistaken, or maybe emperor, and we know bupkis about him–or you, for that matter. Shit, do we even have a phone number?"

"Shut up, Goddard!" Lazarus thunders and the room goes quiet again.

"Boss," Goddard protests with a stricken look, "I'm just starting some due diligence here. We don't…"

"Later for that," Lazarus commands, making it sound like Goddard has some contemptible bit of nit-picking in mind. He lays a hand on Rex's arm. "We're just getting acquainted here, right, Rex?"

"Right, right," Goddard says abjectly. "Sorry, Rex. Sorry, Molly."

Molly looks at her watch. "Good grief, is it that late?"

"It's only nine o'clock," Lazarus says, looking at his.

"We've got to be in Malibu in half an hour."

"You're not gonna make it," someone says. "Not with the traffic."

"I'll call from the car. C'mon on Rex, let's make tracks."

Rear ends slide across the leather banquette to release them from the booth, and they shake hands all around. Looking back as they leave, Molly sees they are like mourners at a funeral. It is as if a rich prize dangled before them had been snatched away. Lazarus is berating Goddard, who has a hangdog look.

"They were starting to ask questions, even the first of which we can't answer yet," she explains as they wait outside in the soft Southern California night for the car to be brought around.

He smiles. "I guess we'll have to think up a second name."

"Better we should find out the real one."

She is about to say more when an earnest middle-aged man loitering outside the Polo Lounge approaches in a suit more Main Street than Hollywood

Boulevard. With the eyeglasses in heavy dark frames and the carefully-parted hair, he could have stepped directly from *Dragnet*, the 'Fifties TV serial.

"Excuse me, folks," he says. "I'm with the San Francisco Giants organization." He shows them a laminated card from his wallet that confirms this. Ralph Buford is his name. "Can I have a minute?"

"We're waiting for our car," Molly says, "and here it comes now." The studio's Escalade swishes to a stop and the chauffeur pops out to open the door for them.

"They just want to know how to get in touch with you," the man says.

"Tell them we'll get back to them as soon as we can," Molly says as they get in; the chauffeur, who is well practiced in dealing with fans and other pests, shuts the door on him. "Where to?" he asks behind the wheel.

"Pacific Coast Highway," Molly says. "Malibu." She knows the driver will report where they go. They head west and join the eternal traffic jam on the inevitable freeway—just another corpuscle in a vein of Southern California's restless bloodstream. "If there was no other reason to hate this place, this would be it," Molly says, looking out the window.

"It seems there's a lot of energy here," Rex says.

"If you're from the Bay Area, it's, like, a law that you have to hate Southern California."

"Where in Malibu?" the driver asks after a few moments.

She doesn't know Malibu and hasn't a clue. "We'd like a quiet place for a drink. What's that place with a bar off the dining room?" That's safe enough; what restaurant doesn't have a bar off the dining room?

"There are quite a few," he says over his shoulder. Molly figures he is an aspiring actor paying the rent with this chauffeur's gig.

"Sort of… sort of French or Italian?"

"Up in the hills, looks like a chateau?"

"That's the one."

"Bonjour," he says. "The locals like it and the tourists don't know about it."

It is intimate, a place of dark wood and glowing brass and small rooms with bead curtains. A hostess dressed in a rustling brocade dress and combs in her hair like a lady-in-waiting leads them to a quiet corner. She gives Rex a long look as she seats them and seems about to speak to him when Molly says sharply, "Thank you."

"When you're ready," she responds.

"I'll give you the high sign."

"Do you ever get tired of the way people look at you?" she asks him.

"I don't notice," Rex says. "Do you think I should?"

"I'd get tired of it, I really would."

"A good thing it's not you in that case."

Molly feels stung as if she has been reprimanded, and she feels a blush burn her cheeks. She searches his face as he examines the drink menu; is another side being revealed?

He lifts his eyes to hers. "Not that you aren't beautiful."

She softens like candlewax in the refulgence of that smile, but she has had time for more thinking. It would be fatal to fall for him. His charisma would attract great men and women, good and bad, who would use him and be used in turn. She was just a little person, a small-time talent scout, who would soon fade into the background, replaced by power people in a position to advance his prospects. It was best to keep their relationship strictly business as long as it lasted. They order two glasses of a Napa chardonnay.

"What did you think of all that?" she asks.

"I guess they want us to sign with them."

"Are you kidding, there's no guessing about it. So what's your preference, baseball star, rock star or movie star?" Irv could forget about the modeling.

"Why not all of the above?"

Another first, she thinks—a sense of humor. Then the thought that is never far from front and center in her mind breaks in again. It's as if with the rush of everything that's happened we keep forgetting how it started with unspeakable horror.

He says with nonchalance, "It would be a matter of scheduling."

No, she realizes, it's not a sense of humor, he's serious. "The baseball season is half the year, and, sorry, but it's full-time."

"The guys told me a pitcher only works every four or five days."

"And the rest of the time you're making a movie or doing a concert?" Molly hopes her amazed disbelief gives him an idea of how crazy the idea is. But it's like he's off in a dream world, not even paying attention.

"Scheduling and logistics would be the main problem," he says, thinking aloud. "Fast planes for point-to-point travel, helicopters and cars to meet us. The musicians are ready for rehearsal sessions when I get there; I arrive an hour before the concerts and leave right afterward. The same with film crews, everything set up, the actors prepared with their lines, no more than two takes per scene, and the green screen technicians ready to go. A catcher travels with us for workouts." His focus returns to her with a laser intensity. "This can be written into the contracts."

"Everything would have to be perfect for this to work," Molly protests. "The timing, the people—everything."

"You can write in robust penalty clauses if they fail," Rex says imperturbably.

"Do you really think people would go for this?"

"If they don't, somebody else will."

The strange part, Molly thinks, is he's right. If not the Giants, the Yankees. If not Mick, Lady Gaga or some other pop idol. If not Lazarus, Sony Pictures. Somebody would be greedy or desperate enough to agree to whatever he demanded, there would even be bidding wars. He's figured all this out.

"We'll need to hire people to help," he says. "A first-rate management company; ask around for the best one." He takes a sip of his wine. "This is a nice chardonnay." Then, after thinking about, "But I bet it can be improved." He holds the glass up in the light and she wonders if he is thinking how. A little less acidity, another year in the barrel, soil higher on the slope? He glances at her. "They had wine at Templeton Hall," he says idly, "but it was for the staff."

All of them are dead now—she feels like saying it. Instead, she excuses herself to go to the ladies room. The hostess is before the mirror putting on lipstick. Her eyes slide to Molly.

"I wasn't going to hit on your boyfriend, if that's what you were thinking," she says. "I don't like guys too good looking, they're nothing but grief." She turns to face Molly. "And, boy, someone that gorgeous is gonna be a lot of trouble."

"Save it for *Downton Abby*, Lady Mary," Molly says, closing the stall door.

"Just sayin'," the hostess says in a breezy manner as she goes out.

She must be married to the owner to be that familiar with a customer, Molly thinks. Not that she was wrong. Handsome men do face temptations, and most surrender in a blink of an eye, lying about it later with a wide-eyed look of injured innocence. She learned that as a young woman specializing in rotters. Straying wasn't a worry with Jimmy or Al, her ex-boyfriends; only women into nerd collecting would give them the time of day. You could count on them being there and being there on time; that and a few laughs were about all there was to the upside. The downside included a large helping of boring.

She sees the kitchen staff peeping at Rex from their door as she returns to the table. "When we finish our drinks, it would be nice to look at the ocean in the moonlight." To give it a practical purpose, she adds, "Maybe it'll trigger a memory."

"Sure," Rex says with neither enthusiasm nor a lack of it.

They both look up to see the man in the suit from in front of the Polo Lounge. "I know I'm being a pest," he says, "but if I could just have a few words."

"You didn't follow us from there," Rex says with interest. "You didn't have time to get to your car; how did you find us?"

"I'll be honest with you," he says. "I put a tracking device on the bottom of the car while you were in the restaurant."

"How did you know we were at the Polo Lounge?" Molly says challengingly.

"The agency has a source at the Beverly Hills Hotel. He tipped the agency, the agency tipped me."

"What agency?" Molly asks.

A slight hesitation. "The FBI, but that's just between us, okay?"

"Is it possible anymore for people to be somewhere where they don't have to worry somebody is watching or listening?" Molly says with eyes flashing.

"Well," Buford says a little sheepishly, "if that's a serious question, I'm afraid the answer has to be no. I put my tracking device next to one someone else put on the car, so the movie people know where you are, too. I wouldn't be surprised if they got somebody outside watching."

"But why?" Molly asks helplessly.

"It's all about data points," Buford says. "Information is power."

Rex sees the connection. "And power is money."

Buford's shrug is eloquent. "Is there any other way to look at it? Maybe the other way around, money is power."

"To follow that reasoning, when intelligent machines have all the information, they'll have all the power," Rex says.

"I won't be around for that, thank God," Buford says. "But listen, folks, the

Giants want to talk to you very urgently." He pulls a cell phone from an inside pocket. "The owner and his top people are sitting by a speaker phone right now. You can be talking to them in the time it takes me to dial. They know you've been talking to Lazarus and they're willing to top any offer."

"They don't know what the offer is," Molly bursts out. "We don't know what it's going to be!" This is utter insanity.

"My job," Buford says humbly, "was to find you guys, tell you what I just told you, and get you on the phone with the Giants. I've got two-thirds of it done. If you let me make the call, I can go home to my wife and kids."

The throwaway phone rings in Molly's new five-hundred dollar clutch purse by Henri Bendel. It barely fits with all the cash stuffed in there. "I better take this," she says, sliding from under the table and stepping away.

"It's me," Randall says. "Tell me what's happening."

"More craziness is what's happening. We're in Malibu at a restaurant. At dinner, Mister Lazarus offered Rex the sun and moon and a few of the planets. And someone from the Giants followed us; he wants us to call the ownership, and I suppose they'll offer us the rest of the universe."

"Don't accept Uranus; I've heard bad things."

"Very funny. Are you still in Oregon?"

"I left the family there and I'm back in the Bay Area. The Giants have somebody tailing you?"

"He put a tracking device on the studio car; he said there was another one there, too. I think he has some connection with the FBI." There is a thoughtful silence on the other end.

"It looks like pretty much everyone interested in Rex knows where he is or has a pretty good idea," Randall says at last. "You guys have to get out of there."

Molly has to stop her voice from rising. "How are we going to do that, pray tell?"

"Have the guy from the Giants drive you."

"To where?" Molly says with exasperation. "To fucking San Francisco? I seriously doubt he'd be willing to do that; he's antsy to get home to his wife and kids as it is. And how do we know his car doesn't have one of those tracking things? I don't know what they look like and I doubt Rex does. Anyway, it's too dark to go crawling under a car."

"Good point," Randall says calmingly. He senses she might be close to losing it. Totally understandable.

"Thank you."

He forces himself to be chipper. "Sarcasm never helps, Miss Simon."

"Sorry," she says, "but I am under a little strain right now."

"Let me check something." Molly crosses her arms, elbow in hand, and taps her foot. She can see from his rapt look that Buford is already spellbound. "Drive to Santa Barbara and catch the Coast Starlight," Randall says when he comes back. "It's running late because there's been an accident. If you leave right now you can make it. Get the keys from the Giants man."

"He'll give them to us just like that?" Molly scoffs.

"If Rex asks him."

He's right, of course, Molly thinks. Rex could talk the man out of that wife and family he wants to get home to. "Why the train?"

"There are stretches at night on that highway where you don't see headlights ahead or behind. I'll let your imagination do the rest."

"I haven't been on a train forever."

"Call me if you make the connection."

After only the smallest hesitation with their promise to call the Giants, Burford leaves to drive the car to the back of the restaurant where they won't be seen coming out the kitchen. "You're going to call, right?" he says to Rex as Molly gets behind the wheel. "I can tell them that, right?"

"You can tell them that," Rex says.

"We'll let you know where we leave the car," Molly calls to him.

"What a simpleton," Rex remarks as they head for the coast highway.

Molly steals a look. Another side of him has heaved to the surface from hidden depths. Was it always there or is he learning the evil ways of the world? No better school than Hollywood, she thinks. Rex is silent, his classic profile lit by the blue light from the dash.

"Tell me why the sergeant wants us back in San Francisco?" he asks as if he has been turning over the question in his mind.

"He thinks too many people knew where you were."

"And why take a train? Why not the jet?"

"He didn't say, but maybe the idea is not to do what's obvious or what we did before. You can ask him yourself." There was a small silence. "He's on your side, you know."

"I know."

The way he said it makes Molly think that was good enough in the beginning, but maybe not anymore. The highway leaves the coast and turns inland toward Ventura. He keeps switching the satellite radio stations and listening with odd intensity, as if he is deconstructing music chord by chord. He switches from dry and cerebral jazz to boisterous, heart-filled gospel, listening a bit to each form and moving on to the next. Hillbilly and rap, big band and Latin; there is no telling if he likes one better than another. Symphonic and soul, the Mormon Tabernacle Chorus and elevator music.

"A penny for your thoughts," she says when there has been no talk for a long time.

He gives her a cool, sidelong glance but doesn't answer.

"Is anything wrong?" she asks after a moment.

"I'd say everything was right except for this detour."

It makes her uneasy... not so much for what he said as the snarky way he said it. The Coast Starlight arrives at the depot ten minutes after they do. She has bought tickets for a compartment with a Lilliputian bathroom and beds that pull down.

"I wish we'd had time to go back to the hotel and get our things," Molly says mournfully. All those expensive new clothes.

"If wishes were horses, beggars would ride," Rex says.

"Where did you get that from?" Molly says. Horses and beggars? People hadn't talked like that for, like, a hundred years. "Maybe you're starting to remember. From a class you had?"

"I think it means people want what they can't have." He thinks about this. "Maybe," he adds coldly, "because they shouldn't."

"Why shouldn't they?" she objects. "It's a free world and..."

The look he gives makes her feel like a silly schoolgirl. As the train lurches into motion, he wants to take a look around. When the door closes behind him, she fishes out the throwaway for a call before the cell phone towers are left behind. "We're on the train," she tells Randall.

"I wouldn't say you're safe, but you're safer."

"What could happen to us on a train?" she says incredulously.

"Probably nothing."

"No one even knows we're on it."

"That's why I said probably."

"Rex is changing."

"I know, you said that before."

"But the changes are… not for the better. It's hard to put into words, but he seems darker. I think he's sorry we're leaving Southern California." She hears voices in the background and phones are ringing. "Can you talk?"

"I'm at the cop shop. They had to bring in some desks and chairs for the FBI and their laptops. Stadium seating will be next. The agents are trying to keep it down to a dull roar, but they need more practice."

Molly quickly fills him in on what has been happening and gets a succession of uh-huhs in return. "Is there anything new on your end?" she asks.

"They found two more guys carved up in San Francisco, but what the connection is nobody knows."

A terrible fear strikes her with a sudden force that is almost physical. "What are their names?" she asks in a small, tremulous voice.

"Hang on, let me look it up." The pause seems to go on forever as she listens to the background noise of voices talking. It can't be, she tells herself… but that flash of intuition had pierced her soul.

"Albert Murry and James Fitzleigh," Randall says. He holds the phone away from his ear because she is screaming.

CHAPTER 15

RANDALL CALLS RIGHT BACK BUT THERE IS NO ANSWER. HE GOES OUTSIDE TO GET AWAY FROM the talking and ringing phones. He could ask that the train be stopped, but on whose authority? A sergeant in a small-town PD wouldn't cut much ice with Amtrak bureaucrats, who without any doubt are as slow as everything else in the company. They would want authorization from higher up the ladder. Chief Parker, a veteran buck-passer who welcomed him back with a few insincere words and a playful go-get'em punch on the shoulder, would tell the feds as soon as Randall walked out the door. CYA was the creed he lived by.

"I gotta tell you I'm tired of this shit."

Randall turns to see Lieutenant Frudenthaler's bulging eyes. They gave him a look of never-ending astonishment. "I told the chief he ought to make the FBI move their damned command post," he said. "There's not enough room for all these snotty bastards. For criminy's sake, they haven't accomplished nothing worth a fiddler's fart that I've seen." Frudenthaler's out-of-date slang was another source of merriment for the department.

"Who found the guys that were killed in San Francisco?" Randall asks.

"The San Francisco cops. The FBI seems to want to make a big thing of it, but I say they're just copy-cat killings." The protuberant eyes sweep the area as if looking for someone to argue with about it. "I wish I had a couple days off like you. I'm too old to work these hours; neither body nor spirit is willin'."

"Why not ask the chief; you got the time coming."

"I don't know how he'd take it, the biggest crime of the century and so forth, all hands on deck." Frudenthaler rubs his buzz cut and stares morosely at the half-dozen TV trucks parked nearby. "Those guys are still hanging around waiting for some crumb from the Fucking Bullshitters Investigation, which is what

I call them. They weren't gonna show us the stuff on the two dead guys. I had to ask a friend on the SFPD."

"Do they think it was a copy-cat?" Randall asks.

"They're not saying," Frudenthaler admits. "That's my theory from working homicide in Bakersfield. One cartel was always trying to blame the other so they rigged the crime scenes. If La Linea left a knife in somebody's rectum as their trademark, Barrio Azteca started doing it. Did the chief mention you need a shave?"

"No, but he noticed." Randall takes out the throwaway phone and steps away. "I've got to return a call."

"Where'd you get that thing, a five-and-dime?"

"Those went away a half-century ago. I guess you haven't noticed."

"Walmart then or one of those Dollar stores."

"My phone is recharging. I'll catch you later."

There is still no answer on Molly's end. He returns to the computer terminal and notices the hand-written sign he missed before that says POLICE USE ONLY. NO FBI. He looks up the addresses Frudenthaler got from his contact and drives across the Golden Gate Bridge to the upscale Cow Hollow home of James Fitzleigh off Union Street. Yellow crime scene tape makes an X across the apartment door. He knocks on three others before someone answers. The young, dark-haired woman in pajamas and a thick robe looks scared and keeps the chain on. He hears someone say Templeton Hall on the television.

"Are you another policeman?" Her voice is trembly.

He shows his badge. "I know we talked to you before, but I just have a follow-up question."

"Okay," she says, "what is it?"

"Did James have a girlfriend with red hair?"

"He went by Jimmy. Yes, her name's Molly. Is something… did something happen to her, too?" She is dissolving into tears.

"No, she's fine," Randall says. "We're just following up on loose ends."

"They haven't been a couple for, like, a year."

"So we understand, just confirming it. Thank you and keep that door locked."

He could go to the other address, but he is sure the story will be the same if he can even find a neighbor who will talk. People shy away from further involvement with whatever horror came out of the blue and upended their lives. They just want to get on with it, the healthy ones anyway. Unstable people tip over the edge and become obsessive or paranoid, or both. They lose weight or eat their way to obesity. They can't sleep at night and develop mental or physical tics. They have to learn every little detail about the crime, or dread locks them into total denial. La la, it never happened. Look, there's a squirrel!

The killers hoped for a lead to Molly once fingers and toes and the nose were chopped off, but how did they find the connection to the old boyfriends in the first place? And why the need for shoe leather with the Devil himself on the case? Wouldn't he steer them to… then he remembers the Baptist preacher saying Lucifer was not all-knowing. Maybe an FBI mole was funneling information or someone in the National Security Agency—or some other Big Brother outfit nobody even knows about.

As he drives back across the bridge, he wonders if it is safe to go home. His eyes are red in the rearview mirror and he has been in these clothes so long he feels like a vagrant. He has to put on a clean uniform before he goes back to work or Parker will draw him aside for his canned talk about the importance of professional appearance. It lasted five minutes, according to those subjected to it, but it seemed more like an hour of Parker's clove-scented breath in your face. It didn't take much to catch his eye, a missing button was enough. So it was take a chance nobody was watching the house and get cleaned up or call in sick. That would only work a day or two before Parker would be on the phone.

The search might be more focused and the department didn't know it because the FBI held the cards so close to its vest for fear of leaks. The last he heard was a man and a red-haired woman were being sought for questioning. They would get Molly's name from the car when it was towed from the public garage; they would put two and two together and the search would pick up speed. Or maybe they already did and that was how the killers connected her with the ex-boyfriends, meaning the mole theory was looking like a good bet. He stops for a double-cheese burger, french fries and a shake at the In-and-Out and is sleepy at the first belch. He shouldn't have asked for onions.

He parks near the old WPA trail where Frudenthaler dropped him off what seems like a century ago, takes the flashlight from the glove box and hikes up the trail toward the ridgeline. Walking settles the meal and he is mentally sharper. The moon dims the blanket of stars that tucks in the world at night when there isn't fog. As before, he studies the house from the shadows of the trees; it is dark and silent. Gun in hand, he makes his way to the back door and listens again. With still no sign of life, he enters and moves through rooms so familiar he doesn't need the flashlight. Relaxing, he reaches the bedroom and takes off his shoes and rubs his swollen feet. Lord I'm tired, he thinks. He sets the alarm to meet the Coast Starlight when it reaches Oakland. He has just enough energy left to get his clothes off and burrow under the covers.

Lulled by the train's motion and the wheels clicking on rails, Molly cries herself to sleep, not hearing Rex when he comes in. The train stops in San Luis Obispo to pick up passengers and continues into the night. An hour later, the blast of an air horn rips through the night; the brakes howl and screech as the train bucks and lurches.

"What's happening?" Molly cries.

"We're stopping," Rex says from the berth above.

She sits up and is forced to a lean by the rapid deceleration. Before the train fully stops Randall's phone rings him out of sleep as deep as any he's had.

"What's wrong?" he says groggily.

"The train stopped for no reason!" Molly exclaims. "Just all of a sudden." All thought about the old boyfriends is pushed to the back of her mind.

It takes a few seconds for Randall to pull his wits together. He turns on the light and rubs his face. "Where are you?"

Molly looks out the window. "It's so dark I can't tell."

"You guys need to get out of there. There's got to be a town nearby with a cell phone tower or we wouldn't be having this conversation."

"You mean get off the train?"

"Run for it. Hang up now!"

"We have to go," she tells Rex, peeling the blankets back and stepping into the high heels worn to the Polo Lounge. She crams the phone into the stuffed clutch purse.

"Randall?" Rex asks.

"Yes."

Rex slides down from the upper berth and puts on his shoes. He runs a hand through his hair and it springs into place as if he just got up from a stylist's chair. "The compartment has an emergency window." He pulls a red handle that removes the rubber molding and then another that frees the glass from the frame; chilly night air fills the compartment. He slips through the frame feet first and she follows; it's a long drop and she dangles by one hand before letting go. He breaks her fall as easily as a matador catching a bouquet. It is foggy and the sound of raised voices is muffled by the time they reach a planted field alongside the tracks. From this angle they see a dazzling light on the tracks ahead of the train.

"Is it another train?" she asks.

The light is mounted on some kind of frame straddling the tracks. Back-lit figures move quickly along the train; prying open the doors of the coaches and disappearing inside. Molly carries her high heels through the lettuce rows; it seems like miles and miles of them. Her velvet pants and silk blouse are like wearing nothing and Rex gives her his leather jacket. They are far from the train before she looks back. Flashlights stab the darkness alongside the tracks, and then the bright beam that stopped the train begins a search of the fields on the far side. They drop to the ground when it sweeps their way. When it passes over them and returns to the other side of the train, they hurry across the vast field to a dirt road separating the lettuce from another planting just as big. This is the Salad Bowl of America—she read it in a magazine. Rex breaks into a shed that looms in the darkness and comes out with a canvas tarp.

"This will keep you a little warmer," he says. He drapes it around her and threads a rope through grommets to pull it tight. It is stiff and sweeps the ground like a ball gown "This road must lead to a bigger one," he says.

"But which way?" Molly asks.

"Toward the ocean, that way."

There are small, sharp stones underfoot and soon she is hobbling; they stop so she can put back on her high heels. Reaching a paved country road, they turn north. The moon has set, the fog is gone, and the cold stars are tiny diamonds in the dark sky. She calls Randall.

"We're off the train and walking on some random country road."

"When they're finished with the train…" he begins.

"I think they already are. The light is gone."

"What light?"

"There was one on the tracks, really bright, like another train. That's why we stopped. People from outside were going in."

"When they're finished with the train, they'll start looking for people on foot," Randall says. "Is there someplace to hide?"

"It's just flat lettuce fields. There was a little fog at first, but it's gone."

He listens to her breathing hard into the phone and tries to think.

"I hear a dog barking far away," she says. "Do you hear that, Rex?" Randall doesn't hear his answer.

"If there's a dog there will be a house," Randall says. "Head that way."

"It's over more fields," she protests.

"You don't want to be on the road," he says. "Those guys are going to regroup fast."

"Okay," Mollie says and hangs up. Rex is more sensed than seen next to her. "He wants us to go where the dog is barking."

"It stopped."

"It was that general direction," she says.

They leave the road and traverse the field. The dragging canvas keeps catching on heads of lettuce. "I don't know how much more of this I can take." The nervous strain is getting to her; if only she were ten years younger. Her head is swimming and she thinks she might faint.

"You all right?" His tone is detached.

"I'm fine," she says. "Never better." The false bravado bucks her up: it's the power of positive thinking, she thinks. Maybe the people in the house with the dog will take them in. No, she realizes a few steps on; positive thinking gets you only so far. At this time of night, they would more likely call the cops and even likelier to open fire if they are scared enough by her Bride-of-Frankenstein look. She feels a burst of crazy laughter close to the surface. Near the house they come upon a dirt road and a battered pickup; worthless enough that the keys might be in the ignition. The bent door sounds like a hammer blow on sheet metal when Rex wrenches it open. No sign of keys on or under the dusty dashboard.

"I'll check the sun visor," she says. There they are, the third place a new farm hand would look when sent for the truck.

"We better push it down the road from the house before starting it," Molly says. "You push and I steer."

She squirms out of the tarp, throws it in the truck bed and slips behind the wheel. The upholstery is ripped and decades of heavy bottoms made a hollow in the seat. Rex puts his shoulder to it and gets the pickup rolling to brisk walking speed toward a dark stand of trees. When they get there, she taps the brake as a signal and Rex gets in on the other side, not even breathing hard.

"Here goes nothing," she says, turning the key. The engine turns over slowly, reluctant to obey the feeble current from the battery. Then it catches hold with a roar and off they go, bumping over the dirt road lit by the pick-up's wavering yellow lights until they reach pavement a quarter mile away.

"I heard of a bucket of bolts before," she cries over the busted muffler, "but I never knew what it meant." The truck was probably used for minor jobs and never left the fields. An illusion of speed comes from the loose springs and fenders and tools jangling in the back. The shaking hood seems to want to rise in a salute and the muffler's contact with asphalt scatters a comet's tail of sparks in the rearview mirror. The transmission whine rises like the voice of a diva, reinforcing the mistaken feeling of speed. The bouncing speedometer barely visible through smeared plastic doesn't make it past thirty-five miles an hour. She steals a quick look at Rex; he seems as composed as ever.

"A red light came on in the instrument panel," he calmly informs her.

"I'm surprised it took so long." We'll ride this until it dies, she thinks. A vehicle traveling at great speed with high beams on appears far ahead; it closes the distance with astonishing quickness and passes so fast she can't see who was in it through the windshield opaque with dirt. The pickup buckets side to side in the backwash of wind from the speeding car.

"I bet that's them," Molly says, heart in her throat.

"They're doing a hundred and forty," Rex says. "Will this go faster?"

"I've got the pedal to the metal," she says. "Literally." The floor mat must have worn out in the disco era.

They hammer on through the night with their tail of sparks until the muffler is ground away. A sign picked out by the shaky headlights says a freeway onramp is ahead but she doesn't dare take it; a highway patrolman would pull them over for sure. They are on what looks like an old farm-to-market road that draws only local traffic now. Another sign, dimpled by bullets fired by young males from car windows, says Monterey is ten miles ahead. They travel eight before there is some kind of detonation in the engine compartment and the loose hood leaps like a stag. The feeble lights go out and the pickup carries on a bit longer before subsiding to a halt. The silence of the rural night rushes through the windows and with it her memory of Jimmie and Al.

"Oh, God," she weeps, "do you know what happened?"

"The truck stopped."

"They're dead, both of them!"

Rex gets out on his side and comes around to jerk the beat-up door open. "Who is dead?"

"Two of my old boyfriends. They were murdered."

Rex makes the connection. "Because of me?"

"Yes, but why? What did you do to cause all this?"

"That's the question, isn't it?" Like before, he seems removed. They leave the sprung door standing open and she puts on the scratchy canvas cloak again. "It seems I can do anything, doesn't it, and do it without effort."

"Y… yes," she says.

"Maybe that's why they want me." But it doesn't seem to worry him. It's like it would be the most natural thing in the world.

Before he was so warm and open but now he is Olympian, almost disdainful in his remoteness. Instead of knowing him better as time passes, it seems he recedes further into mystery.

Or maybe it's just that she thinks he should show more sympathy. They continue in silence except for the click of her high heels on the pavement. She had never been more than fond of Al and Jimmie, both of them nice, regular guys; they wouldn't set the world on fire, but they were there for you. Maybe it should have been enough for her, but she got restless. It was like the Peggy Lee song, *Is That All There Is?*—not that bored and jaded, of course, but maybe the beginning. Everybody moved on after the breakups, but they still texted when something funny happened or they sent a viral video to share. Now they had died, she thought almost certainly horribly, for the sole reason they knew her. She sobs into her hands. "Oh, God." His hand catches her elbow when she stumbles.

"It's not a good idea to get close to others," he says. It is as if he had pondered the matter.

"How can you say that?" she says through her sobbing. "That's an awful thing to say."

"It's what I see."

"We have to have friends or what would life be? You'd be so lonely you'd want to die."

"I liked the people at Templeton Hall; I didn't know them well, but I suppose we could have become friends. Then they were killed. The friends you referenced were killed, and look at you now, you are extremely sad."

"Of course I'm sad, they're dead. Who wouldn't be sad? It's called grief."

"That's a small word to describe this discharge of emotion." He makes it sound like a weeping sore.

"Would a bigger word be better?" Molly cries, "for this *discharge*?"

"You need to control yourself."

His manner says the subject is closed, but it isn't for her. "What about families? Aren't people supposed to be close to their families?"

"I wouldn't know about that."

Of course Rex wouldn't know what it is to feel emotion. How could there be any given that blank state Sergeant Randall found him in, his mind wiped clean by who knows what. It must be like the deep isolation of severe autism; she had seen a documentary and felt so sorry for the victims. They might know the words but not the music; no wonder he seemed as cold as marble. He could mimic responses to cues discerned from observation, but only up to a point. He smiles easily, but she could not remember him giving himself up to laughter. He accepts there is such a thing as grief, but cannot feel it. Compassion for him struggles with the grief that threatens to engulf her.

"I'm sorry, Rex," she says. "I didn't mean to hurt... " She was going to say his feelings.

"Not a problem."

The sky in the east shows a faint light. He is right, she must get control of herself. She brushes away her tears and they trudge on. Fifteen minutes later, the telephone rings in her purse.

"Tell the sergeant what happened and then let me talk," Rex says.

"I didn't want to call before in case you were hiding and someone was nearby," Randall tells her.

"We stole an old truck that quit running and now we're walking to Monterey."

"Any sign of the bad guys?"

"A car passed us going really fast, but we haven't seen them since."

"I'm sorry about your friends."

"I can't talk about it now."

Randall takes a sip of the strong coffee he brewed to wake himself up. "Monterey is a fair-sized city so it'll be harder for them to find you; but don't underestimate these... people."

"Rex wants to talk to you." She passes the phone.

"Sounds like you had some close calls," Randall says.

"Do you have a recommendation, sergeant?"

"They'll be watching everything—public transportation, airport, the car rental places. It'll take me hours to get there and you don't have that much time."

"So what is your recommendation?" Rex says evenly.

"Get to the marina and charter a boat. Pay whatever they say to bring you up the coast to San Francisco. The other side won't think of that." At least I hope they won't, Randall says to himself. He is about to continue when Rex says, "Fine" and hangs up.

"Do you know where a marina is?" he asks Molly.

"I have a rough idea."

"The sergeant wants us to charter a boat."

"A great idea if we can get to the marina."

They move to the side of a dark country store when headlights appear ahead; it is a van dropping off newspapers. On an impulse, Molly sheds the canvas and approaches the driver when he slides open the door to pull out a bundle.

"Our car broke down," she says. "Can you give us a ride to the marina?" she asks. "We'll pay you."

He is a friendly-looking middle-aged man in a parka and blue watch cap. "Sure," he says. "I'm on my way back to the office anyways."

CHAPTER 16

IT'S CLEAR HERE, THE DRIVER SAYS, BUT SOCKED IN CLOSER TO THE OCEAN. HE MAKES A SHOW of refusing a hundred-dollar bill when they reach the fogged-in marina, but she insists.

"You folks have a good day," he says with a big smile.

"Money makes people happy," Rex says, "The more the better."

"It makes the world go round, so they say."

He turns to her, heart-catchingly handsome, maybe even more so with his dark stubble. There was a time when all the ad agencies insisted that models needed a shave. "Is that what you think?".

"There are other things," she says. "Love, for example."

"I wouldn't know about that," he says.

"I hope you do one day," she says in a small voice.

Early as it is in the dawn smelling of the ocean out there in the fog, fishing boats are readying for sea with people that pay a big price for the chance of pulling in choice denizen of the deep, ideally salmon. Crewmen are hauling aboard beer and masses of sandwiches in shrink-wrap; day fishermen loom from the mist in heavy coats, hats and gloves carrying poles and gear. Molly asks at wharf offices, but no boats are available for charter. A stout man in a heavy sweater and a weathered face with a tan line where his hat goes does an amazed double take when she asks him.

"This time of year everybody's booked," he says, "that's twenty thousand dollars in tickets right off the bat, not counting the extras like brews, lunch, cleaning the fish and so on."

"I'll pay you thirty thousand in cash," she says.

"What would I do with my customers, kick them off the boat? Some are regulars who've been going out for years; I'd never see 'em again." He shakes his head. "No can do, and the other boats will say the same. It's a strange thing to ask anyhow. Hell, you could buy a new car and drive there in three hours."

"My husband and I are on our honeymoon and we thought it would be a special thing to do," Molly says, raking a hand through her unruly hair. What a sight I must be, she thinks.

"You guys one of those new Silicon Valley multi-millionaires?" he asks. Envy, sharp and unpleasant, glints in his eyes.

"Sort of," she says.

"Your best bet is walk along to the yacht harbor yonder. There's hippies with trust funds that might be willing."

Gayle Hunnicut in her yellow slicker and orange watch cap crouches to adjust a fender to keep her sailboat from rubbing on the berth. She is a meaty-looking woman with a thick neck.

"Are you available?" Molly asks. Mid-thirties, she guesses.

Ruddy-faced, Gayle looks up sideways from a fender. "For you I am," she says with a coarse laugh.

"We want to go to San Francisco."

"I didn't see that man behind you." The way she says "man" carries a negative charge. "Sorry, not in my plans."

"We'll pay well."

"I wouldn't do it for five thousand dollars," she says abruptly, turning back to the fender.

"How about ten?"

Gayle fiddles with her knot. "Okay," she says at last. "When do you want to leave?

"Right now," Rex says, stepping forward.

"Chrissake," she says involuntarily, rising to her feet, "what are you, a movie star?"

"Let's not go there," Molly says.

Gayle pulls off her cap and scratches her buzz cut as if it aids thinking. "I've got a full load of diesel, but I'm light on groceries."

"We don't care about that," Molly says.

"The fog is supposed to lift mid-morning, I can stock up."

"We want to leave now," Rex says, stepping aboard. He extends a hand to Molly and she follows. "You have navigation equipment?"

"Yes, Furano radar and a GPS-enabled laptop PC that runs on Nobeltec software. I guess I better see your money before anything else. Step into my office."

The saloon is compact with a head and small galley; it is what Molly guesses is called shipshape with everything in its place. "It seems small," she says. "Is it safe out there on the ocean?"

"Galloper is a twenty-seven-foot Erickson coastal cruiser with a sloop rig and lead keel heavy enough to keep you out of trouble. She has a Yanmar twenty-horsepower engine if I have to drop sails, not one of those cheesy outboards like some. I wouldn't want to test my luck with her in the Southern Ocean, but only fools do that anyway."

She watches Molly count out the money from the purse and does it herself twice. Then she chooses a hundred dollar bill at random and takes it to a small desk with a strong light and examines it carefully on both sides. "I used to be a bartender in the Castro District and I learned to spot the phonies."

"Those are not counterfeit," Molly says. Rex has kicked off his new Salvatore Ferragamo loafers and stretched out on one of the narrow settees with hands behind his head.

"No, I can see they're legit." Gayle settles heavily onto a settee. "Not that I care, but I suppose you're drug dealers."

"No," Molly says, "we just have a lot of money right now."

"It's none of my business and that's how I want to keep it." Gayle's eyes cut to Rex. "Your friend doesn't talk much, does he?"

"He's got a lot on his mind."

"There's a mind goes with all that? Impressive."

A half hour later they are motoring through the fog with a jib and reefed mainsail. "There's trawlers and party boats all around us," she says at the tiller, "but we each got radar and everybody will stay out of everybody's hair. That wind's got teeth; keep the hatch closed and help yourself to the sweaters and stuff under the bunk that lifts up on your left."

They are neatly stacked and Molly picks out heavy turtlenecks for her and Rex. "She is really organized," she says. Even the pencils in a coffee cup are the same length. Rex pulls his blanket over his head and turns his face to the bulkhead for sleep; his breathing is deep and regular after only a moment. She lies in her berth exhausted but her mind is racing too fast for sleep. The ride gets bumpier with the boat heeling and seeming to twist through the water.

"You'll need a slicker if you're coming out here," Gayle says when she opens the hatch. "You'll find them in up there in the bow." Molly puts on a yellow one with a hood and comes out again.

"It seems a lot rougher," she shouts, taking the seat Gayle points to on the windward side of the cockpit. The bow flings up a curling wave that throws a fine drizzle over them.

"The Monterey Canyon is below," Gayle says. "It funnels blue water into the bay and you get a lot of commotion, especially if there are these six-foot swells from the northwest. It'll bring in big sneaker waves that carry people off; there's a place the locals call Mortuary Beach because of all the drownings. You'll be standing in the sand with your shoes not even wet and the next thing you know you're carried out to sea. Some grown-up kids saw their mother pulled in not long back. They lived in Texas and she paid for a vacation here so they wouldn't feel so bad on the anniversary of her husband's death, which came the same day the ocean got her. They said she liked to swim, but she was used to gulf waters, not these big currents. I felt sorry for the people she left behind. There are signs on that beach, but they didn't see them or paid no attention."

"That's so sad."

"It would cost the county a quarter-million dollars a year, salary and benefits, to keep a lifeguard presence there, so they don't."

She says they will sail west seven miles before turning north. "The water is deeper and that makes the ride smoother." Gayle is like a different person now, invigorated and even elated. At the Marina she seemed sullen and with a chip on her shoulder, but now she is completely in her element. The fog parts for a moment giving them a view of a party boat with people hanging over the side.

"There go all those hearty breakfasts," Gayle says with laughter. "Dudes should have stuck with coffee."

The fog thins to patches until they leave it behind and Gayle turns off the engine, roller-furls the reef out of the mainsail, and sets a course north. "This is beautiful," Molly exclaims. Blue sky, deeper blue water festooned with long seams of white. The wash of waves and hiss of the hull are the only sounds except for the seagulls that wheel overhead shrilling crossly.

"This is the only time I feel alive," Gayle calls over the spanking breeze. "Just the three of us—me, the boat and the sea." Then, her tone darker, she adds, "Sometimes I wish I could just keep going and never go back."

That sounds like a world of trouble and Molly doesn't feel up the details. She can cope with only so much and her personal limit has topped out. Despite the sweater over Rex's leather jacket and the slicker over both, she hugs herself for warmth. "How long have you been doing this?" she asks after enough time has passed so Gayle knows there will be no sisterly letting their hair down.

"Living on Galloper? Not that long, three years. My partner died and left me some money; she owned the bar where I worked. Cancer. I knew I'd never find anyone like her again, so I decided to go on my own."

Because she is curious, Molly takes a chance this won't unleash a flood of weeping recollection. "Isn't it lonely?"

"I got a little TV I watch, nature programs mainly. I have a few friends around the marina who are live and let live. There's a bar in Monterey where us girls go, but I'm tired of that scene. How about you guys, are you a couple?"

"Not really," Molly says. "We're, like, just in business together."

"He didn't seem like it, but you look really tired. I think you ought to get some sack time like Mister Handsome."

"I think you're right."

Molly slips back into the saloon and closes the hatch behind her. Just being out of the wind is lots warmer and makes her sleepy. She peels off the wet slicker, arranges herself on the narrow settee opposite Rex, and pulls a blanket up around her ears. The boat's movement soon rocks her into deepest slumber. It is afternoon when she wakes and looks over to see Rex's bunk is empty. She dons her slicker again and sticks her head out the cabin.

"The man is a born sailor," Gayle shouts. She is exuberant and even ruddier than before.

Rex has not only mastered a new skill, Molly thinks, but seems to have charmed Gayle out of her dislike of males—this one anyhow. He is at the tiller looking as much a sea dog as Fletcher Christian in the Mel Gibson version of Bounty. He smiles and gives a little half wave that lifts her heart. It takes so little, she thinks ruefully; just a crumb from his table. I hate it that I'm such a pushover.

"It's decision time," Gayle says in her new jolly manner. "I say we put in at Pillar Point Harbor for the night. We can get a good dinner and a better breakfast at Ketch Joanne Restaurant, but it's up to you guys."

"Well…" Molly begins. They haven't eaten a bite since the Polo Lounge and the sea air has made her ravenously hungry. A big steak with a salad and garlic mashed potatoes and a glass of Merlo would be heaven.

"We'll continue on to San Francisco," Rex says.

"Cheese sandwiches then," Gayle says with disappointment. "I'm sorry to say the bread's a little stale."

"I'd eat cheese on hardtack," Molly says, "or just hardtack." Rex asks what hardtack is; she has noticed he is sometimes curious about the oddest things.

"That's what they ate back in the days of sail, Gayle says, "it was wooden ships and men of iron and a girl in every port. The wives were back home with the kids or having more babies, half the time hoping the men would come back and half afraid they would."

The hours pass and the sun passes overhead and sinks into the ocean. "You almost expect steam to rise," Molly says as it dips below the horizon. A few hours later staring into her radar screen, Gayle says, "That's funny."

"What is?" Rex says alertly.

"See that big old girl?" Molly says, pointing to a point on the radar screen. "She's a container ship that just changed directions fifteen degrees. They usually never vary their route because it costs fuel."

Rex surrenders the tiller to her to look for himself. "They're on a course to intercept us."

Gayle laughs mockingly. "Oh, I doubt that."

"How fast do those ships go?" Molly asks.

"It used to be twenty, twenty-five knots, but now they slowed to what the clipper ships did, fourteen to seventeen knots. It saves money and cuts pollution."

"How fast are we going?" Rex asks quietly.

"Probably eight knots."

"We can go faster?"

"We can pick up a couple of knots, but it means more tacking back and forth."

"Do that."

"What's going on?" Molly asks, putting hand to chest to quiet her already pounding heart.

"A ship that turns our way is something we want to think about," Rex says calmly.

Gayle snorts. "You don't think it made that course change for us?"

"Let's watch it a while."

"You're the boss." Despite her scorn, Molly sees Rex has made her think. Giving him the tiller, Gayle clicks on her laptop to a website that tracks maritime traffic. "She's Chinese and bound from Los Angeles to Oakland." She taps on her laptop again. "Longer than a football field, but that's nothing these days."

Molly can feel the wind fresher on her face as Galloper picks up speed. She looks back but there is only blackness. Rex asks what the radar range is.

"I can see out six miles or so," Gayle replies. She is watching the website waiting for the ship's position to be refreshed. "God," she says, "they've increased speed to twenty-two knots."

"They're coming after us," Molly says.

"That ship left L.A. the day before I met you in Monterey," Gayle says in a let's-be-reasonable voice. "How could they know you're on my boat? And why would a Chinese skipper be interested in you guys in the first place?"

"There are things we can't say," Molly blurts.

"Now, now," Gayle says, reaching out an arm soothingly as if it occurs to her there is a danger of hysteria, a scary thing on a small boat. "There's no need to get all worked up."

"They'll catch up in an hour or so," Rex says matter-of-factly. "What's that light way up there?"

Gayle crouches to keep her footing on the heeling boat. "You must have good eyes, I can't see anything; but it might be the Point Montara Light Station."

"What's around it?"

"Some public beaches this side, otherwise you got rocks."

"Aim for it." Rex says.

"You plan to swim ashore?"

"Do you swim, Molly?" he asks.

"Lap swimming at the health club."

"In a heated pool," Gayle says. "This water is cold, in the mid-fifties. I wouldn't dream of going into it; the surfers wear wetsuits and that's daytime."

"Do you have a water-roof bag?" Rex asks.

"Why do you need that?"

"For our clothes."

"You are bananas!" Gayle cries. "Molly, you're not crazy enough to go along with this?"

"Put a check next to the undecided box."

"I take that to mean you've got at least a little common sense." Galloper buckets along on the new heading, phosphorescence streaming like cold flame from the bow wave; it underscores the dark menace and power of the ocean.

Rex keeps his eye on the radar screen. "We should be able to see it now," he says. Molly looks back, her eyes straining. Yes, there it is, a tiny pin-point of light in the blackness.

"What are you afraid of?" Gayle demands. "The Chinaman on the bridge wouldn't dream of bringing a ship that size so close to shore."

"Ships run aground all the time," Molly says, feeling she should stick up for Rex. "I've seen it on the news. That Italian cruise ship."

"Not on this kind of milk route. They don't really need people anymore; computers will do everything before much longer."

"The captain of that ship might not be in charge," Rex says. He holds a hand up in a listening attitude. "That's the surf breaking on the shore. You can get in closer, right?"

Gayle looks at her depth sounder gauge. "Yes, I've got fifty feet of water under me."

"And your draft?" Rex asks. Gayle says it is just under thirteen feet. She checks the maritime website. "That big sucker behind is about 39 feet depending on her load." With Rex at the tiller, Gayle goes into the saloon to rummage around.

"It's not totally water proof," she says, returning. "But it's got a tight seal." Ablaze with light like a stadium, the container ship comes on fast. Rex shucks off his shoes and then his trousers.

"Are you coming?" he asks Molly, no tension at all in his voice. On an impulse, she peels her clothes off quickly and both stand in a state of nature. Gayle's state is one of disbelief at what they are about to do. Rex takes another look at the container ship. A smaller light rises from it.

"That's a helicopter," he says. "How far to the shore?" he asks Gayle.

"Seventy-five yards, a hundred," she says in a constricted voice. The smaller light wings their way.

"You first," he tells Molly as he drops her purse in the bag and cinches it tight. "I'll make sure you get there." With a shudder of anticipation, she puts palms together and knifes into the water. It is astoundingly cold as if poured from a cocktail shaker. She looks around for Rex after a dozen strokes.

"I'm on your other side," he says close by. "Keep going."

She takes a quick look and sees his head, and then concentrates on the Australian crawl learned in childhood. The boom of the waves on the shore is louder. She is lifted by a roller and stretches out arms and legs hoping to plane to shore like a body surfer, but she is tumbled over and scraped over the sandy bottom. A strong hand yanks her upright as she chokes and coughs up water. With his help she is able to stagger a few steps through chest-deep surf before another wave puts them back in the tumble cycle. This is repeated until they make headway against the backwash sucking them back into the breakers. Her long hair hanging down over her face and eyes burning from the salt, Molly stumbles until she collapses in wet sand above the tide line.

"We've got to get off the beach," Rex says. He squats on his heels at her side. He is breathing fast but isn't wiped out like she is. The bag is beside him.

"I…I can't move," she says feebly. She is shivering uncontrollably. He'd put a water bottle from the cockpit in the bag; he has her open her eyes and washes the salt from them. She can see a little now but still can't stand up. Rex scoops her up and, the bag over his shoulder, trudges through the sand as if she weighs nothing. She is dimly aware of a sound behind like popping champagne corks. They reach a small parking lot with an empty booth and gate at the far end. He sets her down to break a small window with the heel of his hand and reaches inside to unlock the door. He takes the plastic sign listing parking rates to push the broken glass into a corner. "You'll be out of the wind here."

"Where are you going?" He is pulling on his trousers and stepping into his shoes. "I've got to wipe out our footprints."

Strength slowly returns and she dresses herself, but it's hard because she is shaking and her fingers barely work. She worries about hypothermia. How do you know if you've got it? She hears running feet and Rex is back. "Duck down," he orders.

The whap-whap of helicopter blades is barely heard over the thunder of the surf and then rises in pitch as it comes closer until it is so loud Molly puts fingers to ears. A bright light overhead sweeps the parking lot and moves on.

"They're looking in case we didn't go down with the boat," Rex says, breathing hard from his sprint.

"Gayle's boat sank?"

"You must not have heard the gunfire. Those popping sounds?"

"Oh, my God! What about Gayle?"

"She's dead." He acts like it should be obvious.

It feels like she's been punched in the gut. "We're responsible," she says as the helicopter noise fades away.

"No," he says crisply, "they're responsible."

"If we hadn't hired her…"

"I've noticed people put a lot into *if*."

She feels a welter of emotions, from gratitude and admiration for his heroism—he saved her life!—to shock over what happened so soon after the train terror. And Gayle was dead. She had been cranky and blustery, a butch lesbian and all that; she would never have even known Gayle in her normal life, much less spend hours in a confined space beginning to see her behind her defenses. How could life end so suddenly? She has lost all concept of time, but it couldn't have been more than twenty minutes ago. No wonder soldiers came home with PTSD after seeing buddies killed, guys they knew for months or years. She tries to not weep because it seems there is no room for that in Rex's mental universe, but she can't stop herself.

Then they heard a colossal grinding sound from the ocean followed by a human-like shriek like a torturer had turned a wheel on the rack. "That ship went aground," Rex says.

CHAPTER 17

SERGEANT RANDALL WATCHES LIEUTENANT FRUDENTHALER MOVE IN HIS STATELY WAY TOWARD the chief's office, heavy rear end swaying like loose cargo.

"The chief is getting on him about his weight," Penny Osmond says, "he says it's unprofessional." She makes a comic rueful face. "Frudenthaler is talking again about turning in his retirement papers. He says he doesn't need all this Templeton Hall stress in his life."

"He doesn't look stressed to me," Randall responds.

"You haven't been around. The chief has him handling liaison with the feds. They were making him so mad he dumped it on Frudenthaler. I guess they can be pretty snotty. It makes him so nervous I bet he's eating a dozen doughnuts a day."

"How is that any different?"

Penny punched him on the arm. "Have a little sympathy for the poor guy."

"Like he's had for me?"

"Oh, well. Look, don't take this the wrong way, but you don't look so good. Haggard is the word."

"Thank you."

"I'm serious. Are you eating right, getting enough sleep?" There was a maternal side to Penny that all the officers liked.

Frudenthaler comes out of the chief's office a moment later and plods toward them with his heavy tread. "The chief said okay but make sure they know you're our contribution to the mutual aid pact." He turns and retreats to his cubbyhole of an office where there is always a game of solitaire on the computer screen.

"Are you going down to that ship that went aground?" Penny asks. "The news is full of it this morning. It was on *Good Morning America*."

"They'll probably put me to work directing traffic."

He needed to keep tabs on the manhunt so he couldn't blow off his job, but also needed a cover story to reach Rex and Molly in somebody's weekend retreat they had broken into. The mutual aid pact idea came to him on his way to work. At first, he was just going to put in an appearance and say he didn't feel so well and was going home, but now he had both bases covered. He congratulated himself for getting smarter as he got older—or more cunning, which was even better.

"Any new developments?" he asks Penny.

"If there are, the feds still aren't saying. They've cleared out of here, as you may have noticed, and moved their operation to San Francisco, I think because the restaurants are better. Or is that being cynical?"

"I'd do the same if it was the taxpayer's dime."

The news said salvage operations would try to unload the Chinese ship in the hope it could float free. That meant cranes hoisting hundreds of containers from holds and transferring them to lighters. It could take weeks, they said. The crew had been found in a safe room built on the ship in case of boarding by Muslim pirates. Nobody had been able to question them because they spoke a dialect the first translator couldn't understand. Chinatown in San Francisco was being combed for someone who could talk to them.

Randall checks a black-and-white out of the motor pool and drives to a Dunkin' Donuts to call Abigail. "Things all right?" he asks.

"So far, so good." She sounds cheerier than he thought she'd be. "Mom's already complaining about how quiet and peaceful it is, though. She can't believe there isn't a TV anywhere."

"Tell her to get in touch with her inner self. Or read a book—there's an idea. They say it's good for you."

"You think it's funny, but she's got her programs she watches. She hangs on every word Laura Ingram and Tucker say."

"How are the boys doing?"

"They're behaving themselves, but I don't know how long that will last." They chat a few minutes and ring off. Randall decides to take the scenic route down Highway One rather than fight the Silicon Valley traffic. Daly City is as usual misty silhouettes of buildings; he has never been there when it wasn't foggy. As he nears where the ship went aground, orange traffic cones appear and the highway patrol is busy with rubberneckers. A grinning young patrol-man, delighted at this break from dull routine, sticks his head in the window.

"So they're pulling guys in from the boondocks," he says. "The command post is the first turn on the right and take it all the way down."

Randall makes the turn and reaches the end of the road that is so full of first responder vehicles it has its own traffic cop and an area marked off with lit-tle yellow flags fluttering in the breeze. "Park up there next to the Belmont PD car," he says. The scale of the grounded ship is so immense it is disorienting; it is as if a city of steel came to a toy neighborhood. He reports to the long white trailer that says Emergency Command Post in big black letters.

It is an organized hive of activity with men in uniform squeezing past one another, telephones ringing and radios crackling with cryptic messages. An expert on emergency management after Templeton Hall, Randall thinks this is a picnic in comparison; people tortured and murdered made all the differ-ence in the world; some darkness lingers even after the bodies are gone. He is pointed to a square-built man with sandy hair and glasses sitting at a desk with a little sign that says Incident Commander.

"All the way from west Marin," he says. Randall thinks from his put-upon sigh that his presence is more annoyance than welcome.

"The chief wanted me to make sure we're listed as participating in mutual aid."

"Duly noted," is his dry reply. "We've got plenty of people, actually." Randall takes this as an invitation to get lost.

He hooks a couple of doughnuts laid out on a table by the Red Cross and walks to the water's edge to gaze at the big ship. Two news choppers are circling and a number of small boats are standing off. "She's a big one," says a fireman in full rig including a helmet. He doesn't appear to have anything to do either.

"Anybody know what happened?" Randall asks.

"Somebody said a bunch of people with guns and masks landed on a heli-copter and the crew went to a hidey hole. Next thing they knew, the helicopter was gone and then the ship went aground. There's wreckage of a sailboat far-ther up; somebody said it's got bullet holes."

"Any body found?" Randall asks.

"Not so far."

Returning to the car, he wonders if Rex skippered the boat up the coast; it wouldn't surprise him, there was nothing the man couldn't do. He drives to the first residential street as Molly had said, the third house on the left. It is small and he would say quaint, a getaway for rich people with simple tastes. He drives to a garage hidden to neighbors by foliage. Molly's ashen face and tangled hair are in the back door window. She looks like the goddess of a small, weird cult.

"You can't believe what we've been through," are her first words. Speaking in a hushed voice in the kitchen garlanded with an array of expensive copper-bottom cookware hanging from racks with anal-retentive attention paid to size relationships, she fills him in. Despite her appearance, it seems to Randall she has bounced back fairly well. What doesn't break you makes you stronger, he thinks; some of those old maxims still hold water.

Rex is in the living room, relaxed and feet up, watching the TV coverage of the ship. He stands with a smile and gives him a firm handshake. "The family all right?" They're just fine, Randall says. He sees that Molly was right, Rex is in charge

"I've been thinking, sergeant," he says. "You probably were right that other ways of escape were under observation, but wouldn't it have been better to charter a seaplane? Our exposure would be hours instead of days. I looked it up in the telephone book over there; there are a couple of companies that give tourists sightseeing flights around Monterey Bay. In foggy weather there's no business for them."

"On the other hand," Randall replies, "they might have found out when the pilot filed his flight plan and hired a faster plane. They could have blasted you out of the sky with automatic weapon fire. Hell, a couple rounds of buckshot would do the trick."

Rex considers this and is satisfied. "Yes, that is a possibility." The sergeant thinks he passed a test—if only barely. The idea of a seaplane had never occurred to him.

"My director of security has to think about all the contingencies," Rex remarks.

"Is that what I am?"

"If you want the job."

"To do it right would take a lot of money, a whole lot of money. Is this what you have in mind?"

"Think big; the people that are after me do. However much you think it would take, double the budget and then double it again. If you need more money after that, let me know."

"That sounds like a million dollars," Molly says.

"Way more," Randall tells her.

"What I'm saying," Rex tells him, putting a little more steel in his tone, "is not to worry about the money."

"Message received," the sergeant says.

"But where is the money coming from?" Molly asks with bewilderment.

"The management company you are going to hire will make some telephone calls," Rex says. "The rock star, the baseball team, and the movie people. Ten million dollars from each for a start."

"I don't think—no, I know I'm not qualified for that. You need someone who knows business. I'm just a talent scout for agencies."

Rex gives her one of those looks that always make her knees go weak. "And the sergeant is just a policeman, but none of that matters. You both took me in when I was a stranger, and I know I can trust you."

They are silenced by this avowal of trust… and strangely touched; Molly turns to hide welling eyes. How could they say no? For all of his phenomenal gifts, Rex was alone in the world and stalked by brutal, incomprehensible evil. The answer had to be yes.

It is settled without any more said, and Randall drives them to a hotel in Santa Cruz, dropping them off on a side street to reduce exposure to people in shorts and flip-flops. Rex wears sunglasses and a cloth cap pulled low that Molly bought for him on the way. It seems a dead giveaway to Randall—here comes a celebrity who doesn't want attention, but it's the best they can come up with. Molly also bought herself slacks, a sweater and sensible shoes because the out-fit she wore to the Polo Lounge was ruined. He calls from thet lobby and Molly tells him the room number.

"Got it. How is the place?"

"It was probably nice in the 'Eighties."

He had gone back and forth about mentioning Camael. No, he decided, best keep that quiet for now. But it wasn't playing straight with Rex, and that makes him feel guilty after what he had said about trust. Camael must have a reason for hiding his cards that was in Rex's best interests. Randall wishes now he hadn't mentioned the angel to Molly even though he had told her not to say anything. "Don't worry, I don't want him thinking I'm crazier than I am," Molly answered in an ironic voice. But it was bound to come up sooner or later.

CHAPTER 18

SILICON VALLEY ISN'T BAD THIS TIME OF DAY; THE YOUNG BILLIONAIRES AND MILLIONAIRES AND their legions of worker bees are in their office parks and campuses instead of on the road, so he takes 280 back to San Francisco and across the Golden Gate Bridge to Marin. He turns west on Sir Francis Drake Boulevard and travels through San Anselmo into the countryside, arriving at the spot where he first saw Rex. The road leads over the ridge to the ocean; bosky estates along here lay hidden up the wooded slopes. He sees shiny American Vigilance System reflecting signs at the foot of many driveways; Templeton Hall clearly had been a jackpot for home security firms. He winds up drives to houses that range from rustic knock-offs of Frank Lloyd Wright to minimalist structures like pads for extraterrestrial landings. The doors are opened to him by housekeepers or young nannies with foreign accents and children at their knees, the owners being away making even more money they had no time to spend. Nobody remembers seeing a man walking on the road; they seldom go down there unless they are driving somewhere.

This looks like a dry well until he reaches a house built close to the road with an iron fence and stone lions on either side of the drive. He stops before a gabled cottage with a hipped roof and an enormous English garden spread before it with mixed borders and formal hedges that would be gorgeous in springtime. Abigail is tired of living in forest shade and made it clear that when they buy a house it will have room and light for a garden, but obviously nothing on this scale. An older woman in gardening clothes who has a sharp, nosy look comes in response to his thumping with a knocker on her studded half-door.

"Yes, what is it this time?" she says, opening the top half as if already exasperated beyond words. Sergeant Randall tells her he is investigating a missing person case. "Who is missing?" she demands.

"We don't know his name, ma'am," Randall says.

"Then how do you expect me to know anything?" She is the sort who bullies when treated courteously, thinking it is a sham or a weakness for her to exploit.

"He was seen walking on the road out there a few days ago. Tall, good looking."

"Oh, him. Yes, him I saw."

"Can you describe the man?"

"Well dressed, is what I noticed. I had a terrible attack of allergy and had to go inside, so that's all I can tell you. I thought my nose never would stop running. I was gagging at one point."

"Any idea where he might have been coming from?"

"The only other house down that way is the old Adam place, but nobody goes there."

"Why is that, ma'am?"

"It's been tied up in litigation for decades. The family all hate one another; they are stubborn people and never let anything go. They might even be dead, but the heirs would fight on. The place is probably a ruin by now; rats and bats and who knows what else."

"How do I find it?"

"There is a road a half-mile away; it has a gate but it's so overgrown with acacia and boxelder I couldn't see it last time I looked." He thanks her and the door slams as he turns back to the car. Every bit of generosity has been squeezed out of her, he thinks. The garden must take it all.

He drives past the gate twice before finding it nearly swallowed by undergrowth. The lock is so rusted by years of weather it would take a hack saw to separate it from the chain. He fights through branches to climb over the gate and heads up a drive nearly obliterated by brush and saplings; he guesses it will be altogether gone in another year. As he follows it past a faded sign that says Entry Forbidden, he becomes aware of a deep silence with a creepy feel. There is no birdsong or insect hum and the leaves are motionless. He feels the hair on the back of his neck rise—the awakening of some early-man instinct that danger is close. Leave this to the FBI, he thinks, they're in charge. But he presses on, hand on the butt of his holstered gun. After an eighth of a mile, he comes to the crown of the hill with a view below of a glen that inevitably would be called Hidden Valley if a developer got his hands on it. Instead of the ruin he expected, there is a beautiful three-story mansion in colonial style with pillars and wrap-around porches surrounded by an immaculately groomed grounds. It wouldn't a stretch to see slaves, fields of cotton and a whistling steamboat coming round the bend as pickinnies caper.

"Baliel loves luxury," whispers a voice at his side. "And so, of course, do his creatures like Abaddon."

Randall is so startled he yanks the gun half out of the holster. "Man, don't scare me like that."

"And ostentatious display," Camael says, "the more awe it inspires the better. His marbled palaces with their columns and fountains were marvels of past ages."

"Who is Belial?"

"It is one of Satan's many names; he has forty at least. That thing down there is the hostile and evil archon Abaddon, the closest to him."

"I think that's where Rex came from," Randall says.

"You shouldn't be here. Violent men with vicious dogs guard Abaddon. Where is Rex?" His worried eyes in the weathered face search him.

"I've got him stashed in Santa Cruz with a woman who's a friend."

"Is it safe... is he safe?"

"I don't think he's safe anywhere; it's one close call after another with the guy. They stopped a train and ran a ship aground to get him, and that's just in the last couple of days. He wants me to hire a security team to even the odds, but you need to step up to the plate. This job is too big for me; I'm used to a chain of command with support services."

"I cannot," Camael says with a shake of his head. "Abaddon is a coward and won't show himself while I stand watch, but he is cunning and it takes all my power to keep him confined. If I were to leave, he would know."

"You mean it's a standoff?"

"It is more like a siege."

"So," Randall says, dismayed, "you're stuck here?"

"Think what would happen if instead of only being limited to dark influence

Satan could freely work his evil through Abaddon. There would be brazen acts in full daylight instead of whispers in the dark. The war and pestilence we now see would be nothing compared to the havoc he would bring. Abaddon is the Angel of Death."

Randall feels like he has been flung back to the time of sandaled people in flapping robes beating donkeys with sticks, to sand and desert and mad or holy men muttering beneath a scorching sun. This—he can't stop the thought—is effing primitive. "Why is this going on now?" the sergeant asks.

"For all his cunning, Satan cannot see into the future. Perhaps he himself believes in portents that say the End Times are coming." His gaze returns to the plantation house. "Or maybe he just wants us to think so. He is a liar able even to fool God if He is not paying close attention."

"What's Rex got to do with this?" Randall asks.

"He might be the Anti-Christ of prophecy…" There is a troubled pause. "Or was meant to be. Let's walk back down to the gate before the dogs catch your scent."

Randall is as dazed as if he took a solid punch to the jaw. They walk back down the slope through the snarl of undergrowth. The Anti-Christ. I'm a simple cop with a wife and two small kids. How many billions of people are in the world— six billion, or seven by now? Why me? I was just doing my job when I stopped to question a man on a country road. Why not pick a guy playing fantasy football in San Diego or eating pie in Bangor? Why not a woman for that matter, a drum majorette or somebody in a sewing circle. Plenty of CEOs would love taking on a challenge like this, the results-oriented sorts who got their teeth into problems and didn't let go. Then there are the hero types, stars of the movies that run in their heads. What greater glory than saving the world from evil? It would make someone bigger than the pope and the president put together and throw all the pop celebrities under the sun into the equation. If it were known, of course— but it wouldn't be. The lid would be screwed on tight so people didn't run out into the street to confess their sins. Hysteria would be uncontrollable and societies would buckle. It makes him tired just thinking about it: there wouldn't be enough cops or military personnel to handle the chaos. He tries to make as little noise as possible but sounds like a marching band compared to Camael. It is as if physical things bend before him and then spring back into place.

"You said 'meant to be,'" Randall says when they reach the gate. "What did you mean?"

"Satan was interrupted before could he completed his incantatory painting, probably leaving a small animating detail for a fine brush at the end; a subtle point of light on a button or a wisp of hair over an ear. He is a perfectionist and who you call Rex was to be the very summit of his dark art, a man outwardly perfect in every respect to be put to use for his evil purposes."

"So you interrupted the process?"

"An infinitely greater power interceded. Satan must have known the truth the instant he saw his creation was gone, but he would just as quickly deny it to himself; he is as self-deluded as at the beginning of his rebellion. He might have thought some minor flaw could be remedied when the figure was returned to the frame. Or, in fury at a revolt against his own authority, he might want to destroy the wicked wonder he labored so long to create. The model he chose for emulation was clearly Jesus, who he tempted in the wilderness with the all the splendors of the world."

"So… wait a minute, is Rex like Satan or Jesus?"

Camael turns uneasy eyes to the policeman. "This is the question. He might be one or the other. It might be possible he is both in one."

"But why wouldn't you know?" Randall asks, bewildered. "You're an angel. You've got a pipeline to the top."

Camael shakes his head. "Angels are only the humble foot soldiers of the Almighty. He orders and we obey; we ask no questions."

It is so overwhelming that Randall has to concentrate on just his piece of the puzzle or his head will explode. "What do I do now?" he says as he climbs over the gate.

"What you've been doing—watching Rex and keeping him safe until we know his nature and intent."

Randall nods numbly and returns to the car; when he looks back Camael is gone. He drives back to the cop shop and stops by the chief's office. Parker is going over some papers and lifts his head with an unfriendly look.

"Hell, you look like you've seen a ghost."

"I need a leave of absence," Randall says.

"What for?"

"I need to work out some family problems."

The chief's face softens. He has been divorced three times and well knows the policeman's life is not a happy lot, as Gilbert and Sullivan had it in the operetta. He also knows the policeman's wife's lot is often worse.

"You've never taken a leave, I believe."

"That's correct."

"How long?"

Randall picks a figure out of the air. "Three months."

"When do you want to start?"

"When I walk out the door."

"Sign the forms and tell Frudenthaler to get me the paperwork by tomorrow morning. Good luck to you."

The lieutenant is not happy about it. He half rises from his chair, but thinks better of setting all that mass in motion. "That puts me in the soup. How am I going to plug the hole in the schedule?"

"That's why they're paying you the big bucks."

"I've been thinking about retiring." Frudenthaler seems to think dangling the possibility might change Randall's mind. When there is no response, he says irritably, "Why do you want a leave anyhow?"

"Parker will tell you if he thinks it's any of your business."

"You don't have to be shitty about it." This time he does get up and lumbers to a filing cabinet for some forms. "Fill these out and return them to me."

"The chief said all I have to do is sign them."

"All right," Frudenthaler sighs. He is looking at the personnel schedule on the wall when Randall leaves. Penny intercepts him on his way out of the building. She has a worried look.

"You're not overdoing it, are you?" she asks.

"Overdoing what?"

"Overdoing the booze with Abigail and the kids gone. You look like you've been through a wringer."

"I'd say I was underdoing the booze, if anything. But you're right; I'm taking a leave to rest up."

"Templeton Hall has taken it out of all of us," she says, her eyes warm with sympathy. "You can't get a smile out of anybody these days. It's like everybody carries the weight of the world on their shoulders."

"I'd like to keep up with developments in the case," Randall says. "Can I call you now and then?"

"You better call me," Penny says, grabbing him by his arm. "I want to know how you're doing."

He drives home and his heart goes hollow when there is no joyous barking. Gun drawn, he goes from room to room the way the SEALS taught him. There is no sign anyone had been there since he left. After dining on Lean Cuisine, he goes to the basement where the camping gear is kept. He pitches the two-man tent up the hill where it is concealed but has a clear view of the house. It takes a long time to get to sleep on the air mattress with the slow leak he can never find; a fitful wind in the trees wakes him a couple of times. He is up at the first hint of dawn, the mattress flat as usual. He showers, shaves, and heads to a diner off the freeway that opens early for commuters. He telephones Abigail to tell her he misses them.

"Right back at you," she says, "urgently, passionately. How're things going?"

"The kids all right?"

"They love it here, I just wish mom did. Her television is going all the time at home. The quiet gets on her nerves."

"What doesn't?"

"I'm serious. She tries talking to the monks and they give her a few words to be polite and then excuse themselves."

"They don't want to listen to her complaining? Very strange."

Abigail laughs. "You're so funny. Did I say I missed you?"

"You can say it again if you want."

"How much longer do we have to stay here?" Then her voice has more of an edge. "You haven't asked how I like it."

"It's something we have to put up with for a while, honey."

"I don't want to pin you down, but could I get a rough idea?"

"When I get a rough idea, you'll be the second to know."

"Who's the first?" she asks, not pleasantly.

"Me."

That makes her laugh again. "You are such a comedian. Did you sleep at home last night?"

"They're not letting me do that yet." It was not a total lie, but not the total truth. How easily a man could slip into half truths, especially with his record of unswerving marital fidelity; he could have a woman on the side and Abigail would never know. He cuts off the thought and wonders where that come from. "An abundance of caution, they call it," he tells Abigail.

"It's weird being so cut off from everything. Anything new on the case?"

"We're still waiting for the breakthrough."

"What if it never comes, what if it will be one of those unsolved mysteries that go on for years?"

"Life will get back to normal, I guess. We'll go on as we did before." Suddenly, that life seemed humdrum, dull beyond sufferance, and he thinks again of a mistress. It would be so easy and put the mustard back in his sex life. It might even make him a better husband, more thoughtful and considerate to dispel suspicion... He beats the thought back again.

Reginald Pricewater II runs Southeby's Marin County real estate affiliate but the supercilious toff in cravat and blue blazer the name suggests could not be more different. He is portly, casually dressed in corduroys slacks and an open collar; he is outgoing in a vaguely familiar manner that Randall can't put his finger on at first. Then it comes to him. Pricewater looks like chuckling Thorny Thornberry, Ozzie and Harriet's next-door neighbor in the TV show made at the beginning of time or close to it; his mother-in-law never misses it on the Retro channel that caters to the aged. People were more real then, she says.

"Yes," Pricewater says when Randall points it out the resemblance, "I used to get that in my twenties. That generation is dead or doesn't remember a thing anymore. What can I do for you?" He looks at his watch.

"I'm looking for a totally private place to lease."

Pricewater doesn't quite give him an up-and-down look, but Randall thinks he is tempted. "We deal with ultra-high net worth individuals," he says.

"So do I," Randall says. "It has to have room for a large security detail."

Pricewater is transformed. "Royalty? We have sold property to several families in the Middle East."

"This has to be absolutely secret."

"We operate with complete discretion."

"Discretion is one thing, secrecy is another. You have to handle all the details personally."

"No one will know," Pricewater says, warming to the task. "May I ask what price range we are thinking?"

"The sky's the limit."

"And for how long?"

"Let's say a year to begin with. Off the beaten track a little, but not isolated."

"If money is no object, I think the Bluff Point Estate might be right for your principal. It changed hands for only the second time in a century and the new owner built a wonderful home across the channel from Angel Island. Forty-eight million dollars for the house alone. The property is priceless, of course. Unfortunately, he died in a sailing accident and never had the chance to live in the palace he built. I'm not exaggerating, the palace. I can take you there now; a caretaker is on the property."

Randall wasn't aware of this hidden spot off Paradise Drive where it takes a hard turn west toward downtown Tiburon. "The property alone sold for thirty-nine million dollars, but like I said it's priceless."

They descend a drive in his Mercedes and pull up at before the cream-colored building that reminds Randall of an elaborate pastry dessert, ridiculous but beautiful. It looks out grandly across water to pretty sailboats ghosting on a downwind reach in the breeze through the Golden Gate. "And then Mr. Hamlin built this. There is not a property like it left in the Bay Area. They finished it about the time his boat went down five months into the around-the-world Volvo Ocean Race. His widow was so heartbroken she moved back to Argentina. There was a lot in the papers. All the networks did documentaries."

A caretaker as meek as a serf waits to show them around the main residence with fifteen bedrooms, two guest cottages and an au pair unit, all with their own small kitchenettes. It has a curved pool, spa, sauna and steam room, tennis court, large level lawns and manicured gardens, recreation room with a billiard table and wall-size television, and an adjacent wine cellar. The elevator stops at all levels of the main residence. A garage holds four cars and a carport three more. The entry door leads to a foyer with a grand staircase and chandelier, large formal living and dining rooms, paneled library and kitchen area. The furnishings are as grand as the setting. "The interiors were designed by a protégé of Juan Montoya," Pricewater says in a superior way. Randall wonders if someone is born a snob or it's learn-as-you-go.

"The en-suite bedrooms are large with generous closet space," he says upstairs, opening a door and stepping back dramatically to give Randall the full effect, "and the master suite offers a huge lounge and fireplace. Take a look at the view from the window." It takes in Mount Tamalpais, Sausalito, the Golden Gate Bridge, San Francisco, and the East Bay.

"It'll do," Randall says.

"We are asking seven hundred and fifty thousand a month," Pricewater says, "and that is firm." His eyes narrow as if he suddenly thinks he should hit the brakes. "The first six months in advance by cashier's check or wire transfer."

"That won't be a problem," Randall says. If it is, it won't be his. "No background or credit checks."

Pricewater is as grave as a judge. "Sotheby's has certain requirements. I'm afraid they have no bend, unfortunately."

"We'll make it worth your while," Randall says with a wink. "Something on top of the monthly rent." He waits a beat. "Cash."

Pricewater crosses his arms and looks at the floor for a moment. When he looks up again, greed glints in his eyes. "Yes, I could arrange it."

"I've got a couple of calls to make," Randall says. "Do you have an office I can borrow?"

The affable Thorny Thornberry returns. "You can have my office for as long as you need." Pricewater gives him a matey slap on the back. It's easy to be a con man, Randall thinks, if the mark wants to believe badly enough. If I weren't a straight arrow I could be rich. Not super-rich like Mr. Hamlin—the man clearly was a special case—but rich enough so the kids would grow up with advantages and go to Ivy League schools. And Abigail would be well fixed if things went sour between them.

Pricewater's secretary is a young brunette with an hour-glass figure. Randall wonders if she is something Pricewater has going on the side; he chats her up while her boss takes a phone call. It wouldn't take much to peel her away from Thorny Thornberry, especially if she thought he was rich. Her boss's fawning manner certainly gave her that impression.

"Come right in and make yourself comfortable," Pricewater says. "I'll shut the door so you have privacy."

Randall reclines in the big leather chair behind the massive mahogany desk and uses the computer to look up the website of Inflexible Security, the company that tried to recruit him when he separated from the service. In effect, it is a private army whose world-wide clients include NGOs, telecommunication companies, oil and gas corporations, mining and financial firms. He calls the number listed and says he is interested in a contract for guard service, and is passed up through a couple of layers of management filters until Christopher Finnese comes on the line.

"How can I help?" he says.

"I need a security detail for dignitary protection."

"Sorry, and you are?" He is both polite and firm, the voice of a man to trust when things go seriously wrong. Randall pictures a retired special forces guy.

"Alex Randall. You wanted to hire me when I left the SEALs. You probably still have my file."

"We never delete them. Yes, I see you're a cop."

"You knew that?"

"We keep up. What's the job?"

"Anybody listening in?"

"I can call you back on an encrypted line if you like."

Randall goes to the door to say he is expecting a call. By the time he is back at the desk the phone is ringing. "Guaranteed NSA-proof," Finnese says.

"I have a subject that requires a high level of protection. That means at least a dozen highly-qualified personnel. The job include escort with decoys and premise defense on a property that needs security enhancement. Travel will be frequent by private aircraft with advance parties coming and going."

There is a small silence on the other end. "That's a lot of money, Alex."

"I know."

"When do we begin?"

"Immediately."

"As in now?"

"Affirmative."

"You're calling from a Northern California number. I can have… hang on." A minute later Finnese is back. "I can have three people with you within four hours."

Randall gives him the name and room number of the Santa Cruz Hotel. "Have them ask for Mr. North."

"We'll need some money up front, two hundred and fifty thousand. We bill twice monthly."

"Sounds good."

"I'll fly out tomorrow with the contract and we'll go over the details. The security enhancement of your facility is additional."

"Understood."

"Who is it we're protecting?" Finnese asks.

"I'll explain when I see you."

"Is the Santa Cruz location where I go?" Randall gives him the Paradise Drive address.

"I'm Googling it." Randall hears a whistle on the other end. "Jesus, what a spread." Another pause. "It says here the owner is dead."

"This is someone else."

After he hangs up, he calls Molly. "Hello," she answers in a guarded voice. There is a television on in the background—Rex doing his homework.

"I've rented us a place and hired security."

"So fast? That's awesome."

"Things are easy when you throw around a lot of money."

"How… how much money?" she asks.

"Tell Rex he is already on the hook for better than five million bucks, and that's just the start."

"You tell him."

She hands the phone to Rex and he listens. "That's fine," he says and gives it back. He is sprawled in an easy chair watching quarreling women on The View.

"I'll be there in three hours, traffic willing," Randall tells her. "If some strange guys get there before I do, they're our security detail. If they ask for Mr. North, let them in. If they ask for someone else, go out the fire escape."

Molly hangs up and looks at Rex. "He wants five million dollars." It might as well be the moon, the way she sees it.

"Call Lazarus," Rex says, eyes still on the argument between the women. "If he says no, tell him we'll get the money from Cohen."

"Don't you think…" she begins.

"You want me to make the call?" he says in an even voice.

"No, not at all," she says, aware her frequent doubts might make him question whether he really needs her. "The sergeant says some men will be coming. They're security people."

"Good."

She steps into the bathroom and telephones the studio. Lazarus is not available, but Goddard the lawyer comes on the line.

"Molly, how can I help you?" he says with phony cordiality.

She keeps her voice level and firm. "We want five million dollars by the end of the business day."

There is laughter on his end.

She looks out the window at a small savings and loan building in her line of sight. "Send it to an account I'm opening in my name at Santa Cruz Consolidated Savings."

"You cannot be serious," says Goddard.

"You talked to your casting director."

"Leah?" He is surprised.

"Well?"

"She said Rex has potential," he says guardedly.

"She told you he's got a lot more than that."

"Did you talk to her?"

"For about five seconds in the ladies room."

"She has no authority to speak for Magnificent Pictures. You should be clear on that."

"If you won't give us this advance, we'll go to Cohen."

There is stunned silence and Molly thinks his career must flash before his eyes like a drowning man. A misstep that made the studio lose Rex and he would be on the street. "Even if I wanted to," Goddard says weakly, all corporate arrogance crushed, "I couldn't make a commitment like that without the approval of Mr. Lazarus and the board of directors."

"The end of the day. I'll tell you where to send it."

"We still don't even have a phone number for you," Goddard says helplessly. She gives him the number of the disposable phone and hangs up, trembling. High finance was like walking a high wire without a net.

"I told him," she says to Rex. Eyes not leaving the TV screen, he nods as if acknowledging a routine fact. "Now, I have to go down the block and open a bank account." This is what delirium is like she thinks in the elevator, this total loss of any sense of reality. She walks to the savings and loan with the purse stuffed with cash and asks for the manager, leafing as she waits through a magazine whose words and pictures don't register.

"Good morning!" The manager is a cheerful, large-bosomed woman in her middle years with dark hair that has high lights. She is cinched into a grey suit too tight with a corsage pinned to a lapel. She bustles Molly into her tidy office where a colorful poster on a wall says Santa Cruz Has Flower Power. Two other employees standing behind counters await customers; it doesn't seem a bit busy. Molly fills out the forms to open an account.

"I want to deposit fifteen thousand in cash in savings," she says when they are completed. She pulls a folded wad of currency from her purse.

"Oh, dear," Evelyn Beatty, the manager, says as it is counted out. "We'll have to tell the government, Miss Simon. I'm afraid it's the law."

"That's fine. I'm expecting a wire transfer of five million dollars later in the day; there might be ten million more in a day or so."

"Oh, my goodness," Mrs. Beatty says, reeling back in her chair and fanning herself with one hand. "This is very unusual for a little office like ours. I mean, it's never happened!" Recovering her poise with some effort, she says, "May I ask who will be sending the wire transfer?"

She is afraid it's drug cartel money or worse, Molly thinks. "Magnificent Pictures."

"Oh," Mrs. Beatty says with relief, "you're a Hollywood person."

"We're considering a real estate investment here."

"You won't be sorry!" Mrs. Beatty exclaims. "We're a progressive, dynamic community here. As a director of the chamber…"

"I'm sorry," Molly cuts in, "but I'm in a hurry. You can tell me later."

"Yes, yes, later." Molly wonders if Mrs. Beatty, her face hectic and flushed, will need to lie down and bathe her wrists with cold water. She accompanies Molly to the glass door that leads outside as if reluctant to let her go before she has answers to the questions that fill her mind.

"That's done," she tells Rex back in the hotel.

"Call Mick and the Giants."

That sounds like the title of a kid's movie, she thinks. She would say so but Rex has not given any sign he has a sense of humor. Seriously, she tells herself, who in his shoes would find anything funny? The London office says Mick is in St. Kitts and they'll have him call.

CHAPTER 19

ETHAN MARGOLIS OF THE GIANTS CANNOT CONCEAL HIS RELIEF. "DAMN IT I'VE BEEN ON PINS AND needles. When can we meet?"

There is no sugar-coating this pill, Molly thinks. "Rex needs five million dollars up front."

"Up front of what?" Margolis says with puzzlement.

"The negotiations."

"We have to pay him to negotiate with us?" His rising voice says he can't believe what he just heard. "That's crazy! In the first place, the league would be against it because the other teams would go through the roof. And that's without what the front office here would say; which, excuse me, is really what's in first place. What have you been smokin', crack?"

"This is just between us," Molly says quietly. "Nobody needs to know."

"It's wacko; I never heard anything like it."

"Teams are signing players to contracts worth a quarter of a billion dollars. This amounts to chump change dug out of the sofa." How can I be this brazen, she wonders.

"It's not up to me. I don't sign the checks around here; the front office does with the okay of the ownership."

"You can tell them."

"Tell them what?"

"Rex needs five million dollars up front."

"There you go again!" Molly remembers from an ESPN profile that he was famous for blowing his stack as a player and coach. He stuck his face in an umpire's and yelled until sometimes he was thrown out of the game. The story was he chewed raw garlic on game day.

"You do want Rex on the team," she says sweetly.

"You know we do, goddammit. He might be one of those guys that comes along once a generation, the way he was throwing the other day. And pounding the ball a mile. Maybe he's once in a lifetime."

"We'd like an answer by tomorrow."

There is a moment of stubborn silence when she is supposed to cave in, but she outwaits him. "All right," he says grudgingly, "We want the guy bad enough to do just about anything next to murdering our moms, but this is just between you and me. Right?"

"Right."

Rex had muted the TV to listen to her end of the conversation. "They'll say yes," he says with matter-of-fact confidence. He turns off the arguing women. "Television doesn't give you a true picture. People aren't that good or bad."

"Ya think?" Molly flutters her eyelashes.

"Funny." It is apparent he doesn't think so and she should stop trying to be comedienne. He goes to the window and stares out with a brooding look.

Two hours later the cranky old lady who checked them in calls from the lobby. "There are visitors for Mr. North." She sounds subdued and Molly sees why when she opens the door. Dressed in jeans and windbreakers, they are burly and radiate extreme competence with a salting of lethal menace. One goes directly to the window and draws the curtains and another stands with an ear to the door. Introductions are made, Ron, Mel and Todd. The one named Todd asks, "Do you have luggage?" Molly says no and they go down the back stairs and leave Santa Cruz in a dark blue Range Rover with tinted windows. The conversation is minimal, which she knows suits Rex. The two in front constantly scan the traffic and check the rearview mirrors. Twice, Mel the driver suddenly veers onto off-ramps and later rejoins the freeway. He changes speed, fast to moderate and back again, without pattern. Ron glances regularly at a radar detector.

When they reach South San Francisco, Molly's phone rings. "Lazarus," the voice says. "The money has been wired to your bank. Now, when do we see you again?" This is so easy, Molly thinks. She gives him the news with her eyes and Rex nods.

"I'll let you know… tomorrow," she tells Lazarus.

"You're not talking to Cohen?" There is something close to desperation in his voice. "I told Goddard he should have said yes, contract or no contract. I said you're honest people and should be treated like that."

"This was soon enough," she says graciously. "Thank you."

"Cohen?"

"We are not talking to him."

"Can I have a word with Rex?"

"He's not here right now." She is aware of sharpened interest from the security men.

"There is a special project we need to discuss. It has a vital time element."

"I'll call tomorrow and you can explain." A shot across the bow to let him know there would be no going over her head. At least for now.

"Morning is best for me," Lazarus says pleadingly. "The sooner the better. Six is not too early."

"I'll be in touch," Molly says nicely. She hangs up and telephones Mrs. Beatty at Santa Cruz Consolidated Savings, who confirms the money was received from Magnificent Pictures via its New York bank. "Just minutes ago." She is still fluttery from excitement.

Despite their sangfroid, even the security guys are awed when the Range Rover comes down the driveway, giving a panoramic view of the palatial mansion and grounds of Bluff Point Estate. Todd gives a low whistle. "Nice," Mel says with humorous understatement. Randall is standing out front to welcome them.

"It was the best I could do on such short notice," he says. "A year's lease with an option to renew."

"Good work, sergeant," Rex says, rewarding him with a fleeting smile. Molly has noticed that they are rarer with the new serious Rex, the commanding Rex.

"The security set up needs tightening," Randall says. "A guy is flying in tomorrow."

Randall shows them around the place, but it is the strolling Rex who is clearly the lord of the manor; it shows in every inch of him. He is a god and this a worthy temple; the sergeant remembers what Camael said about Satan's love of splendor. But he reminds himself he picked this place without in-put from any other source. That he knows of. That gets him thinking about the sexual fantasies teeming in his mind like a randy teenager's. It began with the idea of inviting Pricewater and his secretary over and at some point giving him the sign to scram—there would be an understanding beforehand with a sweetening of the pot—and then making moves on that luscious babe. He got the feeling from guarded looks that she wouldn't mind a bit of fun, but maybe his imagination had run wild. More lately, it is Tenderloin whores partying with him in the big hot tub, their pink-tipped bubbies floating in the water. Clean whores, young ones, he would see to that; he could look up pimps and madams he collared back when he worked vice in San Francisco. There'll be lots of weed, cocaine, and fine wine brought up from the late owner's cellar.

He stops, aghast. He would never, never… no, to be completely honest, under the right conditions like now, Abigail and the kids gone and heavy travel looming for Rex and his bodyguards… Not noticing that he has stopped dead, Rex moves on up the grand staircase. The security detail pauses for the sergeant to finish what it was he was saying. Which was what? Randall sheepishly becomes aware of their stares. He wipes off the lewd expression he is sure is on his face.

"Sorry, guys," he says. "I had one of those mind freezes."

"Looked like a good one," says one and the others laugh. They continue up the stairs.

After the tour, the security people—all ex-Delta Force he has learned—scatter to inspect the lay of the land, especially the perimeters. Rex sinks into in a deep chair in the mahogany-paneled study lined with books and portraits under spotlights of boats plunging under full sail through storm-tossed seas. Molly can't bring herself to look at them after the recent experience. Inspecting a few of the books, Molly judges from the unknown authors that they were bought by the yard from second-hand stores. She read that interior decorators like the look of shelved books even if all they and their clients look at is their smartphones.

"These guys look like they eat like horses," Randall says.

"I'll order take-out for tonight and line up a private chef," Molly says, glad for something to do. Daily meals for a dozen people or more: whoever is hired will need helpers.

"Now is a good time to start the search for a management company," Rex says from the chair.

She retreats to a room where the owner kept his computers, orders a meal for delivery from different restaurants—Chinese, Mexican, pizza, gourmet hamburgers with thick-cut fries—and surfs the internet for a chef and management company. She picks Margie's Chef Services because she likes the down-home sound of her name. Margie Weston herself answers; a warm voice but she also sounds efficient. "Three meals a day for a dozen people?" she asks, a little flustered.

"It might be more," Molly says. "We're a start-up company."

"How soon?"

"Can you start tomorrow?"

"Oh, dear, breakfast? I don't think…"

"I know this is sudden, make it lunch." Men who had lived on MREs in some godforsaken dump of a country should be able to handle leftovers one day. Margie wants to go over menus and talk about staff "and the other details," but Molly says she will leave that up to her to start with. Early doubts evaporating, Margie starts to get pumped up. "I'll do my shopping first. Watch for the white van with my name on it."

That was easy, Molly thinks, but what do I know about management companies? The only thing to do is plunge in and pick another name that appeals to her, which is what Rock-Steady Mgt. Ltd. on Montgomery Street does. She speaks to a young male; a junior executive from his voice, or maybe even an intern. "I need a company to help manage a personality." Standing at a window as she talks, she sees six new additions to the security detail arrive in two cars. They are greeted by the other three with high-fives and some playful wrestling. Finnese wants them all bunking in one of the guest cottages to establish esprit de corps.

"We haven't done any work with… personalities," Philip Dickson says cautiously. "I'd have to check, but I don't think that doesn't mean we wouldn't be open to expanding into that area."

"What do you do?" Molly asks.

"Business-change programs, post-merger integrations, and pre-merger analysis. We work together with the client to determine the strategic direction of the firm, and develop the plans and materials necessary to pursue goals. This typically involves developing financial and market-analysis documents, pursuing partnerships, and creating intellectual capital."

It sounds pretty dry. "What do you mean by intellectual capital?"

"Oh, case studies, white papers, and articles for publication." There is more

MBA jargon that is as unintelligible to her as a foreign language. Then he asks, "What is the name of the personality?"

"Maybe we should call him a pre-personality."

Dickson doesn't say anything for a moment. "In what area is he a… pre-personality? I don't think I've actually heard that term before."

"When you meet him, you'll understand," Molly says.

"What is the field of interest—his, I mean?"

"Sports and entertainment."

"It would be helpful to know his name."

"If wouldn't mean anything to you, he's pre-famous."

"A pre-famous pre-personality, then." Molly believes he must be wondering how to escape this conversation.

"I'll send a car and driver to pick you up. You can have dinner with us."

"Ah…"

"This is opportunity knocking, Phillip."

In the silence that falls, she senses him steeling himself. "All right," he says suddenly, as if releasing a long breath he has been holding. "I don't see what harm there would be, it being on my own time. Or do you want me to ask some of our senior people? I'm not sure they would come—probably not, this being so unusual and they're tightly scheduled, but I could ask."

"No, let's keep things simple at first."

"I see, okay," Dickson says half-heartedly. "Well, see you tonight then."

Molly sees the awe when he arrives, primly seated in the back of the Range Rover. The mansion is ablaze with light and the moon over Angel Island spreads a pale glamor over water to the iconic bridge and the less alluring sister-span to the East Bay. "My God, what a place," he says to Molly on the wide steps that lead to the entrance. His former reluctance has vanished. "There's a man at the gate with a gun," he says with puppyish enthusiasm. "An automatic weapon."

"Security," Molly says. "We have lots of it."

"That driver is pretty quiet isn't he?"

"They don't waste words."

He is tall and narrow with a mop of hair, dressed in an off-the-rack suit and stiff shoes that say he either doesn't have the slightest idea of style or is careful with money. She is disappointed by the soft face and turned-up nose; it hasn't seen enough of life for character to be imprinted on its roundness. Her first impression is he is the nerdy, chess-club kind elected to Boys State in high school and a possible mama's boy.

She leads him inside to Rex, where Dickson is quite frankly stupefied as if seeing one of the wonders of the world, which Molly has to admit is the case. Still, the stumbling over his feet and blushing to the roots of his hair is not a good first impression. He is like a gaping yokel from an olde-timey place where plodding horses wear straw hats.

"This is Phillip Dickson from Rock-Steady Management for an interview," Molly says nervously. Rex will know she just threw a dart to come up with him.

"I...I..." Dickson says rapturously, accepting Rex's extended hand like he means to bow and kiss it.

"Have a seat, take a load off," Rex says. Molly recognizes the line from a Bonanza episode they watched in Santa Cruz waiting for the security detail. "What can you bring to our picnic?" Another line from it.

Dickson looks around for a chair to drop into like his legs are about to fail him and leans forward on it with elbows on knees and hands gripping one another, the picture of wretched inadequacy. "I attended Philip Andover, Yale and Harvard Business School before accepting my current position as an associate... in training." That last seems forced from him in the interest of full disclosure. "My work with clients includes engagement leadership, relationship management, and the creation of deliverables for our clients."

"What does that mean?" Molly asks.

"In addition to what I told you earlier, Molly, this typically involves managing other consultants and client resources, interacting with clients to keep them up to speed on the progress of the project, and creating, or managing the creation of, documents like presentations and spreadsheets that succinctly convey the lessons and conclusions of a project."

His face is rosy and shiny. Flop sweat already. Please don't take out a handkerchief and mop your forehead, she thinks.

"Last week," young Dickson continues, pausing for a throat-clearing, "we hosted a day-long workshop for the top team where we presented information collected from the rest of the organization. Some of this was very challenging, and the day was very powerful, with a lot of soul-searching about work-life integration challenges. It ended with some very clear resolutions that will mean large changes for the way the organization works. My task right now is to draft a memo from the CEO to the staff letting them know what was decided at the workshop and what the next steps are. It will go to our visual graphics production office in India. They will produce slides and send them back for presentation. I have also been tasked to do some right-brain thinking to overcome some of the change-management challenges that we are facing."

He is kind of a flunky, Molly realizes with a sinking feeling. He reaches with a trembling hand for an inside pocket and out comes the handkerchief for his sweating forehead. The chance of a lifetime and he's blown it. She doesn't dare look at Rex.

"Your company has lawyers, accountants and so forth?" Rex asks. "There is a lot of legal stuff we need to do. Creating an off-shore corporation for tax avoidance is one thing."

Where did he come up with that, Molly wonders.

"Oh yes, sir," Dickson gulps. "We are fully staffed with offices in sixteen foreign countries, including…"

"You'll do," Rex interrupts. He rises and leaves the room. Dickson is dumbfounded.

"Is that it?" he asks Molly with disbelief.

"It looks like it."

"But he only asked one question."

"He believes in instinct." Could there any other explanation? He had picked her and she chooses this juvenile trainee. Where was any evidence of thinking through a problem? Yet he sometimes took advice, or had in the past anyhow, and everything seemed to work out—so far.

Dickson stares at his knees as if he can't believe they're his. Then begins to pull himself together. "I have to know what he does," he says. "Silicon Valley, Wall Street, one of the Fortune 500? That's the first thing my company will ask me."

"Magnificent Pictures wants him. So do the San Francisco Giants and, I think, Mick Jagger."

"W…w…why?" His bewilderment is so comic she has to laugh. Welcome to my world, she thinks.

"He'll be a movie star, a sports hero, and a rock star. You see why I said pre-famous and the need for a management company. We'll have a travel schedule that needs split-second timing to work."

Dickson shows a smorgasbord of reaction—shock, wonder, misgiving, hope, and then excitement. "But how can he be all three?"

"I don't know… he just is. Or will be."

"But…"

"The studio gave us five million dollars just to think about signing with them; he's already had a tryout with the Giants that blew them away and they are in the same process; and he's been on stage with Mick Jagger, who wants him to write music."

"Oh, my God."

"All this can be verified, but it must be totally secret for now."

Dickson jumps up. "I need to go back to the city. Our CEO is having a private dinner at Huxley and I'm going to gatecrash it and ask to talk to him." He swallows hard as soon as he says it. "I've never actually met him." Then a surge of confidence washes over him. "Like you said, this is opportunity knocking."

Molly picks a figure at random. "Tell them we'll put down a hundred thousand dollars in advance." She doesn't know if that would be impressive or chintzy. "Or whatever."

"Wow." He asks permission to take a picture of the outside of the mansion and then leaves with the same car and driver.

She finds Rex reading about chess in the library. "This looks like an interesting game."

"Do you think he's a dud?"

"He'll be just fine," he says abstractly, his attention on the book.

"He's so young, though."

"It's a big company, yes?"

"One of the biggest. I'm sure we'll get a more senior person."

"No," Rex says, looking up from the book. "Keep him as the point man. He's eager, he'll learn the ropes fast, and in a short time his loyalty will be to us first."

That's a shrewd way to look at it, Molly realizes. Except for empathy, his psychological skills are increasing by leaps and bounds. Maybe that sense will come in time.

"See if you can find a chess set," he says.

"Aren't you coming down to dinner?"

"No, send something up on a tray."

She hunts around until he finds chessmen and a board, both beautifully carved from rare wood. "I suppose you'll be beating grandmasters in a month."

"Think it will take that long?"

CHAPTER 20

CHRISTOPHER FINNESE OF INFLEXIBLE SECURITY HAS FLOWN OUT ON A RED-EYE, ARRIVING BEFORE dawn with a briefcase and a watchful air. "Call me Chris," he tells Randall when he comes down in the elevator to what he thinks of as the lobby but probably has a fancier name. He is yawning and rubbing his eyes; sleep had been fitful, full of violent erotic fantasies. Finnese is pretty much as he pictured; a high and tight haircut and as squared-away as a sergeant-major. He gives an impression of clarity and resolve; Randall thinks he would have been a major or even a young colonel before leaving the service. You can always tell leaders of men, but as the old joke had it you can't tell them much. Randall got along okay with the type back in the day if they didn't have a hunger for glory. Those were dangerous to a warrior's well-being.

"I brought two more guys with me," Finnese says. "They're having coffee in the kitchen. The others will be here by the afternoon." He looks around. "This is quite a place."

"I haven't seen all the rooms yet," Randall said. He had slept in a four-poster bed in a princely chamber, but it was modest compared to Rex's suite fit for an emperor on the opposite side of the mansion; it had room enough for a court jester who tumbled. Both had high ceilings with crown molding and a chandelier, also doors that led to balconies with magnificent views. Silk sheets matched the silk wallpaper.

"What's the deal?" Finnese says simply.

Randall guesses he would see through any bullshit. "This is totally secret, okay?"

"You want me to sign something?"

"No, I trust you. Rex was at Templeton Hall."

"Rex being?"

"The guy you're protecting."

Finnese takes this in, eyes narrowing a little. "I thought no survivors."

"He was gone before it all came down."

"You a cop on the case?"

"I've taken a leave. The FBI is hogging the show anyhow."

"Their way or the highway."

"The people who did the Templeton Hall killings are still after him."

"The reason being?"

"We don't know." Randall explains how he found Rex walking on the road. "He still doesn't know his name. Total amnesia. Rex is a joke name the Templeton Hall staff came up with."

"They say the Witness Protection Program works pretty well, why do you need us?"

"The FBI doesn't know about Rex."

Finnese shifts in the gilt Regency chair. "Not sure I like the sound of that."

"Don't remember I said it."

"Maybe he double-crossed a cartel or the Russian mafia."

"We could sit here all day spit-balling theories and not know if we were close." Lucifer and the archangel might even come up if they kept at it long enough. Even hint at that, Randall knows, and Finnese and his men would burn tire rubber getting away as fast as they could. They were serious people in a serious business.

"Why not lawyer him up and let the FBI in on the secret?" Finnese asks. "They can protect him at the same time they get to the bottom of it. You're talking about spending a ton of private money to keep him safe. I'm not seeing your upside in this."

Molly in robe and slippers approaches with coffee on a tray. "This might help everyone think." Finnese gives her an appreciative look that goes on a beat too long. She had put on lipstick and ran a brush through her hair and thinks she doesn't look too bad to be seen in public. She settles into an easy chair opposite the men.

"This is Molly Simon, Rex's executive assistant," Randall says.

"Executive vice president," she says. As they are creating titles out of thin air, she thinks hers ought to be grander than a nice way to say secretary.

"I'm senior executive vice president," Randall says, deadpan. She makes a face at him that Finnese doesn't catch.

"He was just asking why we don't bring the FBI in on this," Randall says.

"That would screw things up royally."

"How is that?" Finnese asks.

"He is about to make a fantastic amount of money that he won't if the government gets into the act."

"Rex is a freak of nature," Randall explains. "He can do anything better than anyone."

"He's a great athlete and musician and who knows what else," Molly says. "And he just might be the handsomest man who ever lived, which is why Hollywood wants him." She tells him about the offers on the table. "But don't take our word for it. Seeing is believing."

Finnese's mask of imperturbability is gone. If he had a hat he would tip it back on his head and whistle. "He can do all that stuff?"

"And who knows how much more?" Molly says. "He was teaching himself chess last night. I said he'd be at grandmaster master level in a month. He doubts it would take that long."

"Is he real… I mean, is he a kind of intelligent machine from some lab?"

"Flesh and blood just like us," Randall says.

"You'll see," Molly adds.

Finnese adjusts in mid-stride like a good officer who has been ambushed in battle. "We've had a couple of clients with what you might call unusual problems. We had them take out insurance riders for legal problems, criminal or civil. They were on the hook for fines, penalties, and compensation for time our people might spend in prison. It never came to any of that, fortunately. But I warn you these riders aren't cheap; they require you to hire the best lawyers for litigation and appeals and all the court costs."

"Put it in the contract," Randall says.

"The lawyers at Rock-Steady Management will look it over for us," Molly says.

"They're on your team?" Finnese says, clearly impressed. "Those guys are major players."

Young Dickson had texted her from the restaurant to say the CEO had given his approval. "It was the 100k. C U noon w/contract."

"You can help us with another problem," Randall says. "We need an identity for Rex. With the kind of money that's on the line, people are going to want a name and background they can check out."

"We have that capability."

"It's got to be air tight. And fast."

"Understood."

Randall asks Molly if Rex is up so he can meet Finnese. "I think he only sleeps, like, four hours a night," she says. "I heard him on the treadmill when I came down."

"Other than Templeton Hall," Finnese asks, "have there been other attempts on his life?"

"Two more," Randall says. "You know about that container ship that went aground, but did you hear about the train stopped in California?"

"There was a little story in the *Washington Post*," Finnese says.

"Both were attempts to get abduct Rex or kill him. Molly was with him both times. Tell him what happened." She fills Finnese in and then with a tragic air says to Randall, "Look at this, gray hair! I saw it in the mirror this morning."

"I can't tell from here," the sergeant says.

"I can," Molly replies.

Finnese, who had listened without expression as she described the train and ship incidents, says in a flat voice, "We need another dozen men."

"Whatever you say," Randall says.

"Money still not a problem?"

"Not for me."

"How about the big guy?"

"He told me spend whatever it takes."

They take him upstairs to meet Rex and like everyone else Finnese is awe-struck. The fitness room has free weights and a dozen machines. "Your men can use this room when they want," Rex says after they have chatted for a few minutes.

"Thank you, sir," Finnese says.

"We want them in top shape."

"Yes, sir."

Randall notices it is top down with Rex now, no pretense at equality. It wasn't long ago that he was everyone's friend.

The security people bought up what must be every disposable phone in Marin County. Molly picks one from an overflowing box and takes it to her bedroom, chosen for its view of the Golden Gate Bridge. She calls Doreen, her friend in New York.

"Where have you been?" Doreen cries. "I've been worried sick. Do you know how many times I called?"

"Sorry, I haven't been able to use my phone."

"I almost didn't pick up because I thought it was one of those damn solicitors."

"This is one of those throwaways that can't be traced. They call them burn phones."

"The last time we talked you were at the Giants ballpark."

"That seems an eternity ago, so much has happened."

"My next hour is yours, more if you need it. God, speaking of that, it's nine o'clock here. When did you start getting up so early?"

"I am so sleep deprived you wouldn't believe it."

"Did your Mr. Wonderful sign with the team?"

"Doreen, this is strictly between us."

"Of course, what do you think I am?" She sounds wounded even though she told two girlfriends who don't know Molly and also a guy she met at a bar.

"He hasn't signed," Molly says, "not yet."

"I thought it was too good to be true. Is the thing with Mick off, too? That wouldn't surprise me. This guy you picked up has the golden gift of gab, but I wouldn't..."

"No, he still might go with the Giants and Mick, though we haven't talked to him lately. We're also looking at a Hollywood offer. We flew down there with a director who says he has a lot of potential, and the head of Magnificent Pictures agrees so much he gave us five million dollars."

There is a moment of silence before Doreen speaks in a strange voice. "This is a little hard to believe, Molly. Wait, you said your phone couldn't be traced. What's up with that?"

"That five million is just a carrot to sit down and negotiate. I chose a management company to help me with Rex's career; I can't do it all. By the way, we're staying in the most beautiful mansion you ever saw."

"We?" Doreen asks.

"Rex, me and the police sergeant. His name is Alex Randall."

"The police are involved?" Doreen says slowly. "You didn't answer my question about the phone."

"He's for security, a nice guy—married, two kids. There are people who want to kill Rex, so Sergeant Randall hired a private army to protect us."

"Who wants to kill him?" Doreen says even more carefully.

"We don't know. That ship that went aground, did you hear about it?"

"There was something on the news."

"That ship came after us. We had to jump off a sailboat they sank and swim to shore. Rex thinks the skipper, a lesbian, must have drowned. They sent a helicopter to look, but we broke into a house and hid. Before that they stopped a train and we had to run across lettuce fields to get away."

"My God, Molly," Doreen bursts out. "You need to get to a hospital. Tell me where you are and Irv will pick you up."

"Oh," Molly says, almost laughing, "you think I'm crazy?" Reflecting on what she had said, she sees how Doreen would think that. Of course. If positions were reversed…

"Crazy's not the right word." Doreen dials it back to soothing. "But you need to see a doctor and get something to, you know, bring you back?"

"Bring me back?"

"You know, when your back gets out of alignment and you have to go to a chiropractor for adjustment, it's like that. Honestly, just about everyone I know is on something for anxiety or depression. Nobody thinks anything about that anymore; it's the times, Molly, it's nothing to do with you personally. The times have made everyone… you know, sorta, kinda disturbed."

"I'm not disturbed, Doreen. I'm telling you what happened."

"No, no, no. I'm not saying what you said didn't really happen."

"What are you saying then?"

"In your mind they happened! That's all that counts, is what I'm saying. Minds are tricky things. We still don't understand what goes on with minds, you know? But there are medicines."

"Well, forget about Irv picking me up. We're pretty much in lockdown status here. There's something else," Molly says with a catch in her voice.

"There's more?" Doreen cries. "How could there be more?"

"You remember Jimmy and Al, my old boyfriends? They're dead...murdered." The grief returns with a rush and she sobs. "I have to go."

"Don't hang up..."

Molly throws herself on the bed for a long cry. She feels a little better afterward and even better after a hot shower. Laying everything out like she did for Doreen let her see how utterly mad all those things sound; they are a blur that ends up in this beautiful place... for now! Who could be blamed for thinking they were the demented jabberings of a nut? No wonder Doreen wanted her to check into a hospital, and in a way it clarified how the level-headed Randall could come up with that supernatural stuff. He hadn't brought it up again—no doubt embarrassed, which is the reason he asked her not to mention it, not to anyone—but maybe he still believes it at some level. We're both crazy people! Maybe an angel that appears is a mental anchor that keeps him from being swept away for good. She remembered that sad saying, Whatever gets you through the night. Oh, God. She begins crying again.

CHAPTER 21

SHE MEETS MARGIE HARTLEY ON THE STEPS WHEN SHE ARRIVES IN HER CATERING VAN WITH TWO Mexican women. "Oh, what a grand home," she marvels. She is a beaming woman in a crisp chef's jacket and hair up in a bun. I'd choose her for a pancake package, Molly thinks automatically; show her with a spatula on a box with the product name in an old-fashioned type face. Maybe a dialog bubble over her smiling face saying, "Try my flapjacks." She escorts them through the twenty-foot front doors with a tall ship under full sail in bas-relief. They must weigh a ton but are as light as a feather because of some pneumatic mechanism that causes a generator to leap into ear-blasting action in the deep basement that doubles as a bomb shelter. On an inspection tour, Finnese said you would have a shot at surviving a nuclear weapon even near ground zero.

Margie oohs and aahs and the Mexican speak in hushed Spanish as they pass through magnificent rooms on the way to the kitchen. "Why, this is big enough for a hotel," she says, taking it in with an admiring eye. The walls are banked with gleaming stainless steel ranges, grills, sinks, and refrigerators.

"They look like they've never been used," she exclaims. The Mexican women begin carrying in boxes of food. "I thought I'd fix Spanish omelets with Romesco sauce for lunch," Margie says. "It's quick and easy and a real crowd pleaser." Molly says the staff is expanding in the days to come. Margie is eager to engage her in talk about menus, but Molly says she is leaving all of that to her.

"That's quite a vote of confidence," the flustered chef says.

"Just do your best. Bill us weekly or monthly, whatever."

"Well," Margie says with a deep breath, "I'd better get going."

A different Dickson, jaunty over the bold stroke that won over the boss, arrives in time for lunch with a contract for someone to sign. "Is it you or Rex?" he asks.

"I'll sign to get the ball rolling," Molly says, thinking that is what a decisive executive would say. He follows her to the bedroom where the checkbook from Santa Cruz Consolidated Savings is still in her purse. She writes out a check in deliberate cursive for a hundred thousand dollars. "I never heard of this bank," Dickson says. Molly tells him he will like Mrs. Beatty.

At lunch with Molly, Finnese and a couple of the security guys, he listens with shining eyes to their war stories from Iraq and Afghanistan. The omelets with Romesco sauce are a hit and Margie comes to the table for a bow. Finnese gives Dickson the Inflexible Security contract with the insurance rider faxed from the Virginia headquarters. "We'll get back to you today after our lawyers go over it," Dickson says in rather a grand way.

"So far so good," she tells Rex on the balcony where he sits with feet up, remote in Olympian thought.

"Keep it up," he says. He spends the morning being fitted by tailors from Wilkes Bashford.

She telephones Lazarus and is put through right away. "When can we talk?" he asks with close to a tremble in his voice. "I'll send our jet to pick you up."

"We'd rather you came up here," she says, agog at her own audacity. If it weren't for Rex, she would be a gnat too insignificant for someone like Lazarus to notice.

"Okay, okay, whatever."

"We'll have someone pick you up in Santa Rosa. Dinner?"

"Yeah, yeah, sure. I'll bring a few of my people. I'm a vegan, by the way."

"I'll tell our chef."

When he arrives with his party, all are in dark suits. They don't include Goddard, who apparently was condemned to movie Siberia. Lazarus is not as bowled over by the estate as she expected. "New, isn't it" he asks, "you can always tell new. Take away the view, which I grant is terrific, and it's not all that special. If you want special check out Trump's place in Florida, Mar-A-Lago. I've stayed there a few times. That place is fuckin' beautiful."

"Oh, it's lovely," agrees Leah Loraine, the casting director. "But this is nice, too, these ravishing views." She is going out of her way to be nice. "Is that necklace by Anne Paloma Ruiz-Picasso y Gilot?"

"I didn't know she had all those other names," Molly says coolly.

"Lovely woman."

"We gonna have drinks before dinner?" Lazarus asks. "And bring a bowl of mixed nuts, would ya." Doubling as a waiter, one of the bodyguards serves the drinks.

"Seems like you got a lot of muscle around the place," Lazarus observes. "You got enemies?"

"They're to keep Cohen away," Molly says.

Lazarus looks at her with astonishment, and then gives out a bark of laughter. "Funny! You got a sense of humor, I like that." He circles the room restlessly, martini in hand, stopping at the bowl and popping nuts in his mouth on each circuit. "Where's Rex?" he says impatiently.

He enters the room as if he had been waiting for that cue and all eyes are drawn to him. In the blue wool sports coat, blue five-pocket wool trousers, and blue linen polo shirt, he is the zenith of male fashion. "Gentlemen," he says with a nod to the guys, walking to Loraine to bow and kiss her hand. A blush rises from her neck to her cheeks as if she is burning inwardly; this will give her a lifetime of dreams, Molly thinks, forcing herself not to feel jealousy. Rex is just playing up to Loraine for business reasons. She makes the best of what she has, but could not be called a beauty. With all that sexual power at his command, wasting some on Loraine does not diminish it any more than a teaspoon's worth drawn from the ocean.

"Errrup." Lazarus breaks the spell with a long, noisy clearing of his throat. He crosses the room to pump Rex's hand with both of his.

"Let's take a load off," Rex says with a sweeping motion; they all take seats and lean in his direction. One leg carelessly over the arm of his chair, Rex inclines his head as if a signal for Lazarus to begin.

"If you read the trades—you don't read the trades, I'm gonna guess—but if you did you'd know we're in big trouble with a project. And when I say big trouble, I mean Heaven's Gate trouble. You know that turkey? Hollywood's biggest catastrophe! But we're gonna leave it in the dust the way things are going with *When the Day Comes*, a crap title but we were gonna change it before release. I was outta action with my stroke—scariest thing that can happen to you—and the idiots in charge let this egomaniac director shoot ten miles of film, fifty-seven takes for one scene in San Francisco to give you an idea. They're scared at the time to tell me for fear it will finish me off and I go through rehab not knowin' a thing. When I'm finally half way back to normal, they let me know and it nearly does kill me. But, you know, I've been around the block a few times. With all that footage—real film, mind, not video because the director wanted high class—a smart editor can put lipstick on a pig that won't fool the critics but the masses will pay ten bucks to watch and maybe with luck we break even. Then you know what happens?"

Rex gives a slow, barely perceptible shake of his head that says he looks down from a height far above such paltry strivings.

"The leading man dies of an overdose!" Lazarus throws himself back in his chair. "Can you beat that? Rupert Kingsley, a Shakespearian actor from the Royal Academy no less, a cinch for a knighthood they said, young as he was. And the idiots hadn't even begun to shoot the third act, let alone the ending. The studio is gonna go bankrupt and I personally will lose everything except the clothes I'm standing in, so you see how totally fucked we are."

"We're ready to help any way we can," Rex says. His tone is graciousness itself, the emperor throwing a purse to the crowd.

"This is my idea; we use technology to put your head on the guy's body in every frame of the movie. We can do that now, it's amazing. Every big star that ever was is going to have a second career. These pipsqueaks we have today like Ben Affleck and Rosamund Pike; you could walk them down any street in the country and no one would notice. D'ya think that would be the case with Gable or Monroe and the other old-time greats? No, there'd be riots! Those ridiculous star salaries we been paying—twenty million for Jim Carey when he was a joke nobody laughed at—is a thing of the past. This deal I'm talking about, everything stays the same, the other actors and the extras, the sets, costumes, scenery—exactly the same. The only difference is we digitally put your face on his shoulders and you put on a green suit and lip sync his words on a green stage, a lot of which we can drop because, frankly, the dialog ain't so good. The director kept hiring and firing writers while they were filming. We might have to bring back a few actors and shoot some new scenes with you for continuity."

Rex looks at Molly. "That seems workable," he says. All heads swivel to her.

"The scheduling will have to be super tight," she says, "because of other irons in the fire. You can work out the details with Rock-Steady. I'll be the in-between person for you two... and the others."

Lazarus and the others are unpleasantly surprised. "When did they get in the picture? And you say the others, who are they?" he asks.

"Is there a problem?" Molly says brightly.

"I thought we had a handshake deal. You got five million bucks from us."

"That's for *When the Day Comes*," Rex says lazily, leg still hooked over the chair arm. "We're the Seventh Cavalry saving you from what you yourself say is bankruptcy."

"We're also talking to a baseball team and a famous rock star," Molly puts in.

They exchange pop-eyed glances. "What are you talking about?" Lazarus manages to say. One of the bodyguards comes to the door and motions to Molly. She feels every eye following her.

"Two things," he says in the hall. "One is our guy on the roof with a scope spotted someone in the woods watching from Angel Island; it was pure luck he saw him. I'm telling you because Randall checked out hours ago. The other thing is some clown's on the phone saying he's Mick Jagger's personal assistant."

Molly clutches her necklace. "What should we do?"

"Our guys are on high alert. You want me to tell the creep on the phone to get lost?"

"No, I'll take it."

"Hello," Jagger says on the line, all jaunty charm. "I'm calling for Rex."

"Just a minute, Mr. Jagger, I'll get him."

"Aw, c'mon, I might be Sir Michael to the world now," he says with a light laugh, "but it's Mick to me friends." She pictures the large voluptuary's lips form-ing the words in that bogus working class accent—estuary English they called on Wikipedia. "You'd be Molly, right?" He is calling from some island in the Caribbean where all the neighbors are other billionaires.

Molly returns to the room. "It's Mick Jagger for you," she tells Rex. The Magnificent Pictures delegation is thunderstruck.

"Is... is this a gag?" Lazarus says after Rex strolls out the door.

"I'll ask Rex to put him on the phone if you have a question," Molly says. Putting him on his back foot, she adds, "If you think I'm lying."

Lazarus puts one hand to his heart. "I didn't say that. Don't say I said that. No, no, no."

Rex returns and looks around with his easy smile. "Cat got everyone's tongue?"

"What's up with Mick?" asks Mark Aronson, a smiling man in his late twenties, precocious even for Hollywood; he was introduced as the head of production for Magnificent. He has small hands and neat feet. He strikes Molly as a man who is good with details.

"He's fine," Rex says carelessly

"No, I mean what have you got going with him?"

Rex glances at Molly. "It's early days," she says, answering for him. "But there might be collaboration on song writing and touring. Mick sees Rex as the new him."

There is an intake of breath around the table. "And the baseball team," Aronson says, "what's up with that?" He's asking the questions in everyone's mind.

Molly looks at Rex, who nods. "Rex has a fantastic fastball. The Giants are interested. Very interested."

Dazed and on the ropes, Lazarus is a moment recovering his power of speech. "He's… he's a pitcher, for gawdsakes?" When Molly nods with a polite smile, he asks incredulously, "How can he make movies and do all this other stuff?"

"Tight scheduling," Molly says. "Your people work it out with our people."

Lazarus flaps his arms like a bird trying to lift off a perch. "Do you know how much time it takes to make a fucking movie? Do you have any idea? Twelve, sometimes sixteen hour days!"

"I've been on sets," she says. "I saw how much time is wasted fiddling with lighting and equipment while the stars are in their trailers are smoking dope and flipping through magazines." She looks at Lorraine. "You saw his screen test."

"Yes," the casting director says.

"Did they tell you how much rehearsal time he needed?"

"They said none, basically." She casts a scared look at Lazarus as if guilty of disloyalty.

"Everything is ready when Rex flies in, says his lines and shuttles out. No displays of artistic temperament, no time wasted. When you are ready again, he does the same. Everybody understands this going in, including the other actors. You can cast B-listers opposite him and nobody will care. They'll be crowding the theaters for Rex."

After a long cathedral-like hush during which Rex stares at the ceiling as if thinking thoughts too lofty to share, Aronson says, "It's possible. And if he's got so much heat on his fastball the Giants want him and if he's the next big thing in rock, it would make for some very interesting synergies."

CHAPTER 22

TRAFFIC IS DEFINITELY GETTING WORSE, RANDALL THINKS, AND ROAD RAGE IS DEFINITELY A BIG PART.
A disabled eighteen-wheeler blocks the next-to-last freeway exit and a little later some maniac keeps him from taking the last one by roaring past on his right just as he is about to turn, forcing him to continue onto the bridge into San Francisco. He gets a glimpse of the driver's face contorted with berserk fury—late somewhere and people in his way. There ought to be a new test for mental stability before you get a license to drive, Randall thinks; that would thin the traffic a lot. He had been on his way to the cop shop to catch up on what's new with Penny before her shift ended, but now that he is in the city he has a sudden yen to revisit the Tenderloin he patrolled with partners when he worked vice. He doesn't kid himself that this nostalgia is not related to the fantasies he has been having, but it wouldn't hurt to walk around and relive those old days before returning to reality, if life with Rex can be described as such.

The modern way to think of them is sex worker, but the old Irish sergeants he worked under still called them whores and prostitutes. They thought the way things were going they would be turning tricks on church steps at noon and nobody would turn a hair. But those old cops didn't care, by then they'd be long gone on good pensions; they had seen the best of it. The city was a modern Sodom and Gamorrah and it would take the big earthquake to straighten things out, that's how far gone it was. The young officers listened to them with straight faces but laughed behind their backs.

Randall parks in the Fifth and Mission garage across from the *Chronicle*, which was well into its long decline when he was a rookie cop; it now shared its Industrial-Gothic-style building with dot.com companies whose workers would never dream of reading a newspaper. He walked up Fifth to Market Street and then west on Eddy. You saw all sorts in the Tenderloin, mostly the bad after sundown. They were down-and-outers, crazies, muggers, drug addicts, lurk-ers; now and then you saw scared-looking tourists who had wandered there by mistake. It had always been a toilet that resisted gentrification. When he was on uniformed patrol, he and his partner would roll down the window and call out to the innocents with maps in hand that they were in Indian country. Then a memo came down against the use of that or other insensitive variations. "Crime-ridden" was tried but businesses complained, so "undesirable" was agreed on. It was so far from doing justice to the hazard that most officers didn't bother saying anything.

He stops for a beer at McGirt's, a marshaling yard for tarts long before Pearl Harbor. If it weren't for the myriad of neon beer signs it would be as dark as a tomb. Raddled women with makeup as thick as clowns turn from drinks when he walks in. The beer is drawn by a depraved-looking bartender who slams the mug down with a leering smile.

"Five bucks," he says. "Anything else you want tonight?"

"Not just now," Randall replies. This is the lowest strata of hookers; they take customers to the fleabag hotels nearby and are back on their stools a half hour later. A man could do better working his way up toward Union Square, where the sisterhood was younger and not so beaten down by life. In time, they ended up at McGirt's or some joint like it and then disappeared. The theory in vice was they died or went to the Central Valley where the competition wasn't as stiff. Randall drains the mug in a couple of swallows and motions to the bartender. "A little less foam this time."

"You getting your engine warm? Want a shot of Early Times with that? Six-fifty." His evilness is so extravagant it is theatrical. In the old days, Randall would have parked him in the backseat of the patrol car and run a check with records for the fun of it; you generally found something that let you put them in the pokey.

"Just the beer. Where's the gent's room?" It was down the hall to the right. Randall is standing at the urinal when the door to the single stall opened and Camael quietly steps forth. "I've been waiting for you."

Randall is so dumbfounded he nearly forgets to zip up.

"Satan is tempting you," Camael says. "This is an unclean place and you should leave." Their eyes lock in the mirror.

A glassy-eyed woman with bleached hair and a crooked smile stands outside the door. "Hi, darlin'," she says to Randall.

He pushes past her and runs out of McGinty's followed by mocking laughter. He feels scalded by shame on the walk back to the parking garage. He had nearly been sucked in. A couple more drinks and he would done a swan's dive into the sewer without a thought for Abigail and the kids, pushing his dick into the hot flesh of a diseased streetwalker for starters. Sin and debauchery and words like it were rim-shot lines now, as old-timey as moustache-twirling villains. The old sergeants had traced the decline back to the 'Sixties when they were fresh-faced rookies themselves. Men and women copulated in Golden Gate Park with a crowd watching, a first even for San Francisco. Just doing their thing. The homely hooker Margo St. James became a media celebrity after forming C.O.Y.O.T.E, short for Call Off Your Old Tired Ethics. The center gave way and gay men strode stark naked down the street and gave each blow jobs in broad daylight as was now their right. The dissolving of morality in the acid bath of the new culture was one of the reasons Randall took a job in Marin; boring was better than deviance flaunted in your face. Molly peers at him when he returns. "Are you all right?"

"Why do you ask?" Near miss, dodged a bullet, by the skin of the teeth; every one fit.

"You look different. Did something happen?"

Randall ignores her question. "The guy out front told me they're on high alert."

"Our man on the roof saw someone watching with binoculars on Angel Island. How could they find us so fast?"

"They have help," Randall says.

"The government?"

"What's been happening while I've been gone?"

Molly tells him about the meeting. "Lazarus blew up at first but one of his people talked him round. He didn't like the vegetarian casserole Margie made special for him and I think her feelings got hurt. Being so new to the job, she's sensitive."

"That's hard cheese."

"I thought you were the one who doesn't like sarcasm. And as it happens, it had a layer of soft Trugole cheese from Asiago. Margie said she should have used Cheez Whiz."

He goes upstairs to the bedroom and calls Abby. When she says hello he feels such a surge of emotion he can't speak at first. The eighteen-wheelers and the berserk driver were not coincidences; they were to funnel him to the Tenderloin.

"Hello," she repeats. "Alex?"

"Just checking in," he croaks.

"What's wrong with your voice? Are you taking your allergy pills?"

"I forgot," he says more strongly.

"You know how you get. You want to hear something crazy?"

"Yes, I don't get enough of that at work."

"I swear, your sense of humor. I think mom is getting adjusted to this place. She's even trying meditation. One of the monks taught her the breathing and all that."

Randall tries to imagine Esther in the lotus position. "How are the kids?"

"They keep asking where you are and when you'll come back. Michael fell down and skinned his knee and I put Martin in time out for laughing. When will you be coming?" she asks yearningly and his throat gets tight again.

"Just as soon as I can, honey."

"Any new developments in the case?"

"A few, but I can't talk about it now."

They speak for a few more minutes and end with Abigail telling him to remember his allergy pills. "I promise," he says. After he takes a long, hot shower to wash off the Tenderloin, he wanders downstairs to the game room and is watching the news about the attempt to free the grounded ship—bunker oil is leaking now—when Finnese calls.

"A contractor and his crew will get there first thing in the morning to put up lights and a ten-foot security fence with razor wire," he says. "You're paying a hefty premium for getting moved to the top of his work schedule. Our own people will put the movement sensors in the ground. The rest of the security team will be there by the end of the day. We have Rex's new identity; Rex is for Rexford, Todd Daley Rexford. He went by T.D. for a while. He is thirty-five, born in Lancaster, California. An orphan, poor guy. Rags to riches from wildcatting in shale."

"He doesn't look that old," Randall says.

"He's lived a clean life."

"I guess I don't need to know who the real one was."

"The fewer the better."

"I'm good with that."

"I'm sending the bio. He should memorize it up, down and sideways."

The talking head on the news said the FBI was looking into the possibility the ship was hijacked by Muslim terrorists who fled after putting it on its course to shore. "But this has not been confirmed, our sources say." There was no more mention of the sunken sailboat.

CHAPTER 23

THE CONSTRUCTION CREW ARRIVED BEFORE DAWN TO BEGIN WORK AND THE FENCE WENT UP FAST.
In the mid-morning, Pricewater was stopped at the gate until Randall said it was okay to enter. He is so upset his pink jowls are quivering.

"That fence is in violation of the zoning laws and it'll have to come down," were the first words out of his mouth. "I got a call from one of the neighbors."

"Take it up with them," Randall said, giving him Dickson's card.

That afternoon Dickson called. "Our lawyers say the law is on their side, but we can file a suit on Constitutional grounds. We'll lose but can tie them up in court for months."

"Sue the bastards then. Molly wants you sitting in tomorrow at a meeting at Magnificent Pictures."

"She already told me."

She and Rex had been closeted all day reading the script of the movie the studio had in production, the project he was to save. "The problem according to him," Molly says, "is it's crap."

"Isn't everything they do crap?"

"Rex the film critic now says they have to make up their mind if they want a thriller or a comedy. It has something of both, but not enough of either. "

"Sorry to say that's above my pay grade," Randall said. "Back in the good old days I was a simple flatfoot, remember?" The good old days a lifetime ago.

He and Finnese had worked out on a secure line how to get Todd Daley Rexford to the meeting in Hollywood. The scenario they came up with seemed off the wall but sort of okay. The new fence had a gate on the bay side with hidden hinges. While SUVs formed a convoy in front with plenty of lights and noise, they would sneak down to the estate's tiny beach where an inflatable boat would take them to a sailboat ghosting on the slack tide. Once clear of Angel Island, sails would be dropped and they'd motor to the Redwood City Marina where a car would to take them to the San Carlos Airport and the private jet.

"Is moonlight a problem?" Rex asks when Randall presents the idea.

"The moon will be low."

"Let's do it," he says casually and turns his attention back to the chessboard. Randall looks over his shoulder. "It's the 1956 game between Byrne vs. Fischer," Rex says.

"Yeah?"

"They say the greatest game of the century, but it was poorly thought out."

"You played before?" A sprig of hope springs up. Maybe his memory is returning.

"No, I found a book about chess yesterday."

They are up at three in the morning for the rendezvous with the sailboat. The security detail in night-vision goggles leads them down to the beach through the screen of oak trees, madrone and bracken fern. As lights go on at the mansion, voices shout, and car doors slam, the inflatable boat glides noiselessly ashore. They board, hands shove it back into the water, and a motor that murmurs on the transom pushes them to where the sailboat gently rocks under a bare mast. They climb up a short ladder, sails are hoisted, and they glide east in silence. When they are well past the influence of Angel Island, the diesel engine comes to life and they power toward the marina in Redwood City.

"Aren't the bridges beautiful at night?" Molly says. "The Golden Gate looks like the stage for a grand opera by Verdi."

"Joe Green," Randall says. The boat is far bigger than Galloper and Rex has gone below to sack out.

"Pardon?"

"I read somewhere that Giuseppe Verdi would be Joe Green in English."

"Leave some romance in life, please."

One of the security guys sitting nearby touches his earpiece and stiffens. "Jesus Christ, they took out the middle car in the convoy," he tells Randall. "They pulled Roland from the wreck, but they don't know if he'll make it. Sounds like it was an RPG."

"An RPG?" Randall repeats dumbly.

Molly remembers Roland, a fun guy nearly as wide as he is tall with lots of tattoos he keeps covered on duty because of company policy. "I've spent like twenty thousand dollars on them," he proudly told her in a down-time moment. He seemed more open than the others with his ready laugh, and she confided to him that she wants gun control. She didn't know anyone in San Francisco who doesn't.

"So do I," he had said, a smile spreading. "But spend enough time on the shooting range and you'll learn how to control your gun just fine."

"The bastards must have guessed Argonaut would be in the middle car." She puts a name to the face she now recognizes under the watch cap: Arnold. He touches his earpiece again. "Virginia says proceed as planned." He opens the duffel bag at his feet. "Colt 9mm SMG," he says in reply to Randall's look.

"That's after my time," Randall says.

"It's more accurate than the Uzi."

"Impressive."

A shrill voice in her head cries how can they be so casual when a man might be dying or already dead!

"Who are these guys?" Arnold asks. "Nobody's told us."

"Unknown," Randall answers.

"They're good."

"Very good."

"Why do they want Argonaut?"

"Also unknown."

"How did you get involved?"

"Just lucky, I guess."

"Right."

They laugh.

Molly hates how cryptic men are with each other, how they hide their feelings. Two women would have exchanged a thousand words for catharsis by now.

Randall goes below to tell Rex about the attack. He listens calmly, asks no questions, and rolls back to the bulkhead for more sleep.

"What did he say?" Molly asks when he returns topside.

"Nothing."

"Did he seem upset even?"

"Not to the naked eye."

"Nothing ever bothers him," she protests. "It's like he has ice water in his veins."

The transfer at the marina goes without a hitch and within a half an hour they are taxiing on the runway. It is just possible to relax in this silver tube of luxury. It will only be for a short time, but they are safe. She watches Randall sink into sleep just before she does herself. Dawn is just breaking when they land at Burbank where the advance party waits. Arnold is drawn aside for a whispered conversation.

"Roland didn't make it," he tells them when he returns.

They ride in silence to the studio. If Rex feels anything, it doesn't show; Randall stares out a window and Molly sniffles quietly into a handkerchief. Normally, she would be asleep in bed for another hour before the alarm went off. People with average lives don't know how lucky they are, she thinks. If she had it to do over again, she would run out of that café when Rex came in.

Dickson flew down the night before and is standing a little apart with a knot of smiling studio executives waiting to go to breakfast in the studio commissary. A larger crowd is a few feet behind, lesser figures on the corporate ladder and good looking or comic looking B actors from TV series. They part like the Red Sea when Rex steps from the car like royalty paying a visit to factory workers. In his blocky, cheap suit and a white shirt with tie, the blushing Dickson looks out of place among these sleek Magnificent Pictures executives. His trouser cuffs hang over dull shoes with little domes to allow more toe room. Molly wonders what these Hollywood people thought when he showed up looking like someone who arrived on a Greyhound bus with a sack lunch.

Leah Loraine is at her side, all smiles. "How was the trip down?"

"How did the focus group go?" Molly counters, feeling as haggard as she knows she looks

"Only fabulous," Lorraine says, "they…" She stops with a stricken look as if feeling she has said too much.

"Come on," Molly says, "I knew you wouldn't lose any time showing that screen test around."

The casting director looks around as if afraid of getting in trouble. "People love him on the screen," she whispers.

"What demographics did you test?"

"Truck drivers to post-docs, male and female from sixteen to fifty-four." She hesitates. "Did something happen? You look… "

"Everything's fine," Molly says, breaking off her words. "Who are all the people here?"

"We wanted to give you an idea of the diversity of our platforms. We have content streaming, video game design, the Grand Bazaar Amusement Park and so forth."

White-jacketed waiters were already taking healthy-eating orders for whole-grain toast, plain oatmeal, yogurt and fruit salad. She hears Randall ask at the next table if there are any doughnuts around. "We we could send out for some." Randall says never mind. Molly and Rex are at the power table with Rex, Lazarus and the studio higher-ups, including Leah. Her eyes beg Molly not to mention the focus group screening.

"Where's Dickson?" Rex asks.

"You want that kid here?" Lazarus asks in surprise. He looks around the table. "Hugh, go find him."

Hugh is an older man with a forehead up to the crest of his skull and a thin gray ponytail. He rose to Oscar-winner ranks from his auteur period but now directs movies where aliens blow buildings to rubble. Molly sees sadness in his eyes at this errand-boy treatment. He walks around the room with ponytail bobbing forlornly until he locates Dickson in a clutch of daytime soap opera actors staring with hungry ambition at the power table. "Find another spot, Hugh," Lazarus says when they return. Abashed because everyone is looking at him as they mentally adjust the pecking order, Dickson takes his seat.

"Phil will be your liaison with Molly," Rex says with the beguiling grin he uses when he wants to charm. She has never known it to fail and, sure enough, everyone at the table beams at him.

"Well, all righty, then," Lazarus says expansively, his smile embracing Dickson like a python coiling around a lamb.

"I've thought this through," Rex says. "A billion dollars over ten years, two pictures a year; Phil will work out the details on our side. I'm ready to begin work on *When the Day Comes* this afternoon. I've got some ideas how to make it better."

"Christ," Lazarus cries, "I haven't had a bite of breakfast yet and you hit me with this?" Jaws have dropped all around the table and Dickson is pale and scared. The offer or demand, whatever it was, is on the table and Rex calmly turns his attention to his bowl of yogurt. The impression is unmistakable that it's all the same to him if the answer is yes or no. Molly sees that the arts people at the other tables semse a bomb has been dropped. The faces at the power table are a strong clue.

One of the three burn phones Randall is carrying vibrated a moment before and he had scraped back his chair to take the call outside. The connection with Finnese sounds far away and has echoes. "Alex?"

"Where are you calling from, Timbuktu?" he asks.

"Not so far from there, actually. I just heard."

"I won't ask what you're doing in Africa."

"I appreciate that."

It comes to him in a flashback—low buildings the same pale yellow as the sand they are made from, burning heat under a bleached sky, women hidden in their clothing except for their eyes, and mad fanatics yearning for a glorious death.

"The ink is barely dry on the contract, but I recommend we double the deployment again," Finnese says.

"Okay by me." Overhead is not his department.

"I'll be back in touch."

He walks back inside where he notes people at the power table seem in shock from a jolt no doubt delivered by Rex. Heads are bent toward one another and Mark Aronson is on one knee next to Lazarus.

From words picked up from their whispering, Molly thinks the overwhelmingly negative first reaction undergoes a steady revision when second thoughts evolve around the table. She hears Aronson say "Chinese money…" Conversations trail off and eyes turn to Lazarus.

"Look," he tells Rex with exaggerated politeness, "we can't begin new projects a hundred million bucks in the hole on this one no matter what the potential upside is, and I emphasize potential, because…"

"If you don't project out a one billion two gross based on the opening weekend of *When the Day Comes*," Rex cuts in, "you pay me twenty-five million and we call it quits."

"That's…that's still superstar money."

"Take it or leave it," Molly interjects. "Cohen—"

"Don't say it!" Lazarus pleads, throwing up his hands like someone with a big truck bearing down on the crosswalk. He's in a corner but not even he can make a decision this big. He asks for the rest of the morning to confer with the bankers in New York, London and Dubai.

"Why not put me in touch with the writer while you do that?" Rex says easily. "We can get started."

"Which one?" Aronson asks. "There have been six."

"It doesn't matter."

They stroll with bodyguards to Aronson's office for a conference call to the latest writer. Rex says to her, "I liked how you cut to the chase."

"It was totally spontaneous," Molly says. She had surprised herself, but wasn't that the way people talked in Hollywood? They would have told Lazarus to shit or get off the pot or something even worse."

"Get Dickson fitted out with good clothes," Rex says. "Actors can look like bums but corporate people judge by appearances. Tell him to lose those Buster Brown shoes."

Aronson's office is hung with posters from big movies. There is one from *When You Are Away* about broken romance that Molly took two handkerchiefs to on the advice of girlfriends and wished she'd taken a third; even now makes her throat tight even now it makes her throat tight. Why did they have to…? But most are from bigger action hits like *Punch in the Face, Faster* and its sequel *Faster Than Ever.* Aronson puts the call through to the screenwriter Nick Savvas; the answering machine says leave a message. "Nick, pick up." He calls back time after time in the same droning voice to show he will keep it up. Finally, a clatter is heard on the speaker phone. "What the fucking hell do you want?"

"It's Mark Aronson, Nick. We've got some new notes for the script."

"Oh, you do?" the writer says. "Well, you can—"

"Nick, let's put all that old stuff behind us for a fresh look. We've got a hot new prospect attached to the project."

His silence is sullen. "Yeah? Who is it?"

Aronson looks at Rex and Molly. "Todd Daley Rexford," she says.

"Never heard of him."

"He's going to be big, big, big," Aronson says.

"You said that about Rupert Kingsley and he's six feet under."

"The new guy has ten times his potential and doesn't do heroin. He's here right now."

"Call me Rex."

"Hold on." The phone clatters again and they hear what Molly thinks of as a sinus-y sound. She pictures a line of cocaine being sucked up the nose of a Sicilian type with as much body hair as a monkey, which also described one of her more notable romantic disasters. "Okay, I'm back," Savvos says more businesslike. "What's this all about?"

"Rex has some ideas for *When the Day Comes*," says Aronson.

"We got about a hundred miles of film based on the old ideas, but why not?"

"It's not really funny or enough of a thriller," Rex says. "What's the woman in black got to do with it?"

"Search me; she was in it when it got passed to me. So many scenes are shot with her that she's woven in now. Pull that string and the whole story comes apart. Believe me, I've thought about it for weeks, months! I think she could be a beautiful cyborg who somehow can defy the laws of physics, but the original writer meant her as phantasmagoria. However you slice it, we're stuck with her running or gliding down long corridors—it's been shot both ways—with the hero running after her or holding his fists to his temples because he thinks he's crazy. And that's just one problem. That big Easter Island head with the zither music is another. Shouldn't his lips move when he speaks?"

They go over plot points—the secret to the workings of the universe that are guarded by the giant head; the fantastically wealthy drug lord who seeks it; the ineffectual government leaders who wring their hands when out-maneuvered, which is always; the thwarted chief of Interplanetary Intelligence not allowed to follow his instincts; and many other core ingredients of summer movies.

"Look," Savvos explodes after an hour, "I'm not defending this shit, not one word of it. They brought me in for a rewrite like they did the four or five guys before me. Each one of us made it worse than it was before." The click of a lighter and a big intake of breath are heard over the speaker phone before he continues. "You shoot movies with a finished script, not one that's still being worked on while the cameras are rolling. You learn that in Moviemaking 101." Formerly manic, his voice turns lethargic but doesn't lose its peevish edge. "Where were we—oh, yeah, Rex, do you have any ideas yourself or are you just some Grand Inquisitor the studio brought in and…" It is apparent from the pause that he has lost his train of thought. "And…"

Aronson says briskly, "This has really helped clear the air, Nick. Thanks and we'll get back to you." He looks at them and shrugs.

Rex riffles through the script. "A hundred and thirty-five pages. I think changes on ten or fifteen will reconfigure the story arc to a marketable product. With me as star, you can re-edit what you've got and toss the rest, including the woman in black."

After Aronson leaves, Molly asks where he heard about story arc.

"There's a book in the library I picked up by someone named Robert McKee. It tells you how to write for movies."

"I thought you were learning how to play chess."

"I finished that one."

"I think they bought books by the pound."

The question doesn't interest Rex.

A young production assistant named Barnard, a strapping fellow with a shaved head and a single earring, is assigned to show them around the studio to kill time. "This is where the magic is done," he says, guiding them into a large studio with movie cameras and a large green screen. An actor sits on a stool checking his iPhone between takes. "He's fitted with sensors for performance capture. He literally goes through the motions."

"Then the data is digitalized and massaged to get the effect they want," Molly says. "I've seen it done with commercials—"

"You can do it with facial expressions?" interrupts Rex.

"Sure," the assistant says. "An array of cameras captures them from multiple angles and we use software to create a 3D surface mesh. If face is half the working area of the camera and a camera has megapixel resolution, then sub-millimeter facial motions can be detected by comparing frames. They're working on speeding up the optical flow so motions can be retargeted to other computer generated faces instead of just making a 3D mesh of the actor alone."

A voice on an intercom barks an order and the stool and iPhone are taken away. "Okay, action," the voice says. With five cameras rolling, the actor ducks around with a scared look as if dodging something that could kill him. This is repeated several times. "Cut," the voice says after each take and the stool and IPhone are returned to the actor.

"He'll be doing that all day until they are satisfied," the assistant says.

Back in the office with his feet up, Rex is reflective. "You know how this movie should start?" he asks Molly.

"With you?"

"A full close-up, my face filling the screen. I'm looking for something but nothing registers in my eyes for ninety seconds. Then they narrow because of something I see. Interest turns to alarm and slowly the camera moves to the back and my POV swings into focus. Far off across in the sun-blasted desert we see a column of dust rise on the horizon. My face fills the screen again and I speak for the first time. 'The Trucs.'"

Molly sees it clearly. That perfect face catching and holding the eye of Cineplex audiences all over the world, even from pirated versions projected on bed sheets in the undeveloped world. His long-lashed gaze would mesmerize everyone just as it does in real life. Rex saw that the movie wasn't about the absurd screenplay or special effects; it was his debut as a movie star. That is all anyone leaving the movie theaters around the world would be talking about. Women would forget Brad Pitt and George Clooney, and it would be goodbye to John Wayne and Clint Eastwood as the macho archetypes for men.

"It is ridiculous to go through so many takes," Rex says, "I'll do only one for each scene. Call the Giants and have them send me a catcher. I need to work my arm."

She steps outside to call. "Whoa, so he's going to sign?" Ethan Margolis says excitedly.

"He didn't say that, only that he wants to work his arm. We're in Southern California right now; can you fly somebody down this afternoon?" She hears Margolis talking to someone in the background.

"We got a double-A catcher in San Jose who's about finished with his rehab. We'll shoot him down ASAP."

"Tell him to come to the gate at Magnificent Pictures."

"Magnificent Pictures, right," he chuckles. "Say, the legal staff is really interested in knowing more about our guy. How about his full name for a start? I don't like lawyers, but I gotta admit they have a point."

"Oh, sure," Molly says breezily. "It's Todd Daley Rexford. I'll email you his bio." We'll see how Rock-Steady's identity creation stands up to the bright lights.

"Oh, would you?" Margolis bursts out. "Thanks!" She wonders if he is being sarcastic, but guesses not. He must be getting a ton of pressure from the front office. Five million is a huge chunk of change for someone nobody can find anything about—and they would have been trying really hard.

"How's our guy doing?" Margolis asks. The 'our guy' seems to suggest a comfy relationship has been established between them.

"He's working on the movie end of his career."

"Oh—" It is like a realization has dawned.

Molly thinks Margolis believed until now that the Hollywood talk was a negotiating ploy, smoke and mirrors to fool them into bidding higher. Even asking for a catcher to fly down to a movie studio to take some pitches from him, yes, he could see how they would string it along that far. A man whose career was flying off the handle and shouting into faces was not someone likely to understand a multi-platform wonder like Rex.

"I thought you were kidding about that," he says, humbled.

"Doesn't he look like a movie star?"

"Yeah," he admits, "the guys are still talking about that." He asks uncertainly, "If we make the playoffs, do you think Rex would be available to pitch a few innings in relief?"

"I don't see why not."

"I'll put him on the roster in San Jose," Margolis says, energized again. "He just has to make an appearance and we jump him to our Triple-A club in Sacramento before the call up to the majors."

She is getting fresh air when she sees Aronson approaching with a worried look. She beats him to the punch. "Rex will do only one take for each scene," she says, "is that a problem for you?"

"Frank Sinatra got away with it, so it's not like a precedent. But there's a bigger problem. The New York and London banks are on board, but Dubai is hanging back. It's too risky for Muhammad bin Saqr al-Qasimi."

"That's a mouthful," Molly says.

"He insists on a big marquee name for a July opening on four thousand screens. The people under him are willing to roll the dice after they saw the screen test, but the man is blind—literally blind—and says it's too risky. Unfortunately, his word is, like, law in their clan."

"You can't do it without Arab money?" Rex says mildly when Aronson tells him.

"It's like a stool, we need all three legs."

Rex nods. "Molly told you what I said?"

"Only one take per scene, yes, but we've got a problem getting to that bridge before we cross it."

"What about the Chinese?" Molly blurts.

Aranson looks at her with surprise as if thinking how do you know about the Chinese. "If Dubai isn't in, they won't be. They're very cautious people. And we can't squeeze another nickel out of the Russians."

"Well," she tells Rex, "there's always Cohen."

"Don't say that to Lazarus," Aronson pleads. "It'll give him another stroke. Give us some time for a Plan B."

"How much time?" she asks. "By the way, send somebody to a sports store for baseballs and a right-handed glove. Rex needs to do some throwing."

"Sure, sure," Aronson says desperately. "How about a week, can you give us a week?"

"Let's sleep on it," Rex says coolly. He tells Aronson his idea of how to start the film.

"Just you staring into the camera for that long?" he says.

"Before the credits roll," Molly says. "His face would be the first thing people saw."

Aronson turns eyes to the ceiling to visualize it, and Molly sees excitement building. "Yeah, yeah! People would be so knocked out it would be total surrender. The stupid story wouldn't bother them; they'd just be feasting on Rex after that first minute and a half was imprinted on their brains. It's fucking genius, man." He telephones Lazarus to tell him and gets a cynical look as the conversation goes on. "Great minds think alike, boss," he says before hanging up. "Lazarus says he had the exact same idea an hour ago. I can't tell you how often that shit happens in the industry."

Molly looks to Rex for his reaction; he is unperturbed. "We'll be in Tiburon," he tells Aronson.

The Giants are told of the change in plans and the catcher is reached at the San Jose airport and told to report instead to Bluff Point. The convoy hits the road a half an hour later and they wing north from Burbank. "Mind if I continue on to see my family?" Randall asks. You don't even have to ask, Rex says absently.

CHAPTER 24

THIS IS LIKE WAR, RANDALL THINKS AS HE AWAKENS FROM A LIGHT DOZE, YOU GRAB A FEW MINutes of sleep when you can but you never catch up. Back in his twenties he could drop off with his Kevlar helmet as a pillow. Young bodies adjust to just about anything; no way I could do that today. The jet was over Northern California approaching the Oregon border and he was semi-recumbent on white leather as smooth as a baby's ass. Quite the change from Anwar Province. For all that danger, hardship and general hell he went through, he would still choose that shit hole over this. At least you knew where the threat was coming from.

He checks the news on his smartphone. The grounded ship was still offloading and the government tracing ownership through a maze of shell companies to find out who to sue. Although the crew was Chinese, it seemed that didn't necessarily mean its ownership was. As he was reading this a bulletin crossed the screen. "Jet Fighter Crashes Into Mideast Skyscraper." The warplane had hit the forty-fifth-floor offices of the Bank of Dubai and there were many casualties. Authorities were waiting for some terrorist group to claim responsibility and the country was on high alert.

The sun is setting and the ground already in shadows when the plane lands and rolls to a stop at the general aviation hanger. Abigail and the kids are waiting with big smiles. Even given Satan's power, how could he…

"Daddy!" The thought is driven from him as his kids run up and locking his knees in tight hugs.

"Darling," Abigail says, doing the same with his upper body. She kisses him fiercely.

"Anybody miss me?" he says.

"We did!" the boys chorus.

"No," Abigail says, laughing through tears, "we didn't miss you a bit."

"Yes, we did," Michael and Martin yell.

"Your mom all right?" Randall asks as they walk to the car, the boys clinging like limpets. "Look out guys; you're going to trip me."

"She's not complaining so much," Abigail says.

"They treating you right?"

"Oh, yes. The monks are so kind and thoughtful when they aren't praying or meditating, but I will say they don't waste a word. Mom still has trouble with that; you know how she likes to talk." Her eyes sparkle with the delight of being with him again, and he dreads telling her just how awful the work is that he is doing. He will postpone it as long as possible.

As if reading his thoughts, she says, "How's it going?"

"About the same," he says, "pick and shovel work."

"They're still flying you around on a private jet."

"The Hollywood people want to stay on the good side of Rex."

"That must be so expensive," Abigail says.

"The stewardess told me ten thousand dollars an hour."

"There's a stewardess?"

"Ten thousand bucks is peanuts to a big entertainment company."

"Is she pretty?" Her head is cocked.

"Not as pretty as you."

She gives him a punch on the arm.

"Well, you asked. I'm not going to lie to you."

Abigail throws her head back and laughs. "I've missed you so much."

"Yeah? I'm gonna ask you to prove that a little later."

Brother Mario invites them for a private dinner of soup and thick brown bread that is served by a silent, ascetic man in his thirties in a simple room with white-washed walls. Randall notices the abbot has a worried and preoccupied air.

"Aren't the vegetables in the soup wonderful?" Abigail says. "Everything is organic."

Brother Mario rallies from his abstraction for what seems like a canned speech. "Monks have always chosen remote places that were believed uninhabitable for their monasteries, lands granted to them because they were too hard to cultivate. Over time forests got cleared and marshes drained, roads were built and bridges put over rivers. The monasteries in northern Africa and in western Australia still do the same work today as the monks a thousand years ago. Thank you, Brother Adrian." The monk who had served them nods and leaves the room without having said a word.

"He has a nice face," Abigail says to Randall, "a kind one."

"He was an executive with a company doing mineral extraction in the developing countries," the abbot says. "He was sent on an inspection trip to enlarge his knowledge; by then, he was the chief financial officer, the head bean counter as he put it. The cruel treatment of the workers, mere economic units on a spread sheet for him up to then, surprised and sickened him; he left the company by mutual agreement and, after a period adrift, renounced the world, gave away his possessions, and came to us."

"Does he have a family?" Abigail asks.

"No, he had no worldly ties to bind him, but many monks do and decide to leave them."

"Dumping your family seems pretty extreme," Randall says.

"In a certain light, Christianity is very extreme. One of the early church fathers, Saint Macarius of Egypt, returned to his cell one day to find a robber taking his few sticks of furniture. Having no possessions was seen as a virtue, so he pretended to be a stranger and helped the man pack up and make good his escape. Another monk gave away everything but his copy of the Gospels. Then he sold that and gave away the money, saying in triumph, 'I have sold the very book that told me sell all I had.'"

"No offense," Abigail says, wincing, "but that just seems so—I don't know, too much."

The abbot nods with understanding. "The times were primitive and life filled with peril. A simple scratch or an illness no more than an annoyance today often was fatal; mother and child frequently died in childbirth; savage tribes and criminals made travel dangerous; crops failed and people starved to death; epidemics took one in three lives. People were aware that the Angel of Death grinned at their shoulder."

"They must have been paranoid," Abigail says softly.

"And how much worse before Moses and Jesus Christ brought the law of the

Old Testament and the love of the New Testament to sweep away the household gods and blood-thirsty pagan deities? Still, when we look back at such saintly paragons as Mary of Oignies, the Tenth Century mystic, the modern mind cannot help but wonder if mental illness doesn't perhaps explain her life of perpetual sorrow and longing. She wept floods of tears day and night and became physically frail from devotion to our Crucified Lord. For a long time, she ate only the hardest and blackest bits of bread that even the dogs wouldn't touch; it cut the inside of her mouth and caused bleeding. She often fainted from her fasting and night vigils, according to James of Vitry, an archbishop of the period. The other nuns envied her devotion, but James thought she carried mortification too far cutting off bits of her flesh and burying them in the ground."

"How awful," Abigail says with a shudder.

"Abaddon," Randall says. The name comes to him in a flash.

Both look at him with surprise, "That was an earlier name for the Grim Reaper," Brother Mario says.

"How did you know that?" Abigail asks her husband, soup spoon suspended half way to her mouth.

"I picked it up somewhere. You know how cops are always hearing odd stuff."

After dinner, one of the brothers drives them to the hermitage and waits while Randall tucks the kids in and reads their bedtime story. "They miss their daddy," Esther says in a knife-to-the-heart way.

"I miss them too."

"And you're going again tomorrow," she says, meaning what a cold-hearted bastard. Her husband had been a predictable man with regular habits, which included an hour—not a minute more or a minute less—drinking beer with the boys after work on Fridays. Esther had never understood why Randall was different.

When he returns to the monastery, Brother Mario motions him to a chair in his small office. "Abaddon?" he says carefully. "You don't strike me as the kind of man steeped in Bible lore; where did you hear that name?"

"Camael's got him trapped in California; Abaddon can't get out as long as he's standing guard."

"Trapped!"

"In a big house the world forgot. You can't see it unless you climb a gate and hack your way through thick brush."

The abbot passes a trembling hand across his face. "Do you know anything about Revelations?"

"Not to speak of," Randall admits. "Actually, nothing."

"It's the last book in the Bible, a jumble of Jewish, Roman and Greek symbols and allegories nobody can puzzle out so most theologians ignore it. It's attributed to John the Baptist and is full of angels and devils that go to war before the second coming of Christ and the end of the world. A false messiah called the Anti-Christ rises to deceive mankind. Revelations has seven flaming lamps, seven spirits of God, seven trumpets, seven plagues, a great red dragon with seven heads and seven diadems on each head, a pregnant woman with a crown of twelve stars—oh, it goes on and on. Some interpret those events as having already occurred and pagan Rome was the Anti-Christ, others say they are still in our future and a literal battle between good and evil called Armageddon will take place in the Jerel Valley of Israel. Revelations is really a mess." The abbot was pensive. "Abaddon was a region of Hell in the Old Testament, but in medieval times became personified as the Grim Reaper."

"The Grim Reaper," Randall says, glad for something easier to picture than all those sevens, "there's a name everybody knows."

"The Angel of Death, the skeleton with a scythe," the abbot continues, "the question is what is he doing here?"

They sat in silence for a moment. "What if Rex is the false messiah," Randall asks, "that's worrying Camael... or maybe that was who Rex was meant to be but the process got short-circuited."

"Many believe the all-knowing, all-powerful God who engaged with humans on a personal level disappeared from human history after setting things in motion. Otherwise, how to explain the wars and horrors of history?" He sat silent in thought. "Why would God intervene now unless to level the playing field?"

"Watching Rex or keeping him safe, whatever it is I'm doing, is enough for me," Randall said, shifting restlessly in his chair. "I'll leave the other stuff to you."

"More than sixty million people died in World War Two alone, more than two percent of the world's population. Strife on that scale today would mean far greater death and suffering. I can't begin to imagine the panic if the barest whisper of this got out." Brother Mario crossed himself.

"Besides you and me, only one other person has even a hint. My wife thinks I'm up to my neck in the Templeton Hall case." Funny now how that seems a minor sideshow, something that happened a long time ago.

"The woman, Molly?" the abbot asks tightly.

"She believes Rex is really special—a phenomenon of nature—but that's as far as she takes it. I mentioned that I thought it was something more, but she thought I was being weird."

"I wish there was more I could do to help."

"Looking after my family means a lot to me."

"They're safe here, thanks to our friend." The abbot gives Randall a searching look. "And I hope he's looking out for you, too."

"Yeah, he is." The shame still burns over his narrow escape from the Tenderloin's depravity, and he ignores the abbot's expression that invites detail.

They talk long into the night trying out different ways to explain what is happening, the abbot doing most of the speculating. "And it may be Rex is a blank page, or at least was in the beginning," he says, "but we must remember he was created by Satan; it stands to reason his nature essentially is evil."

"What's reason got to do with this?"

"I take your point, yet here we are trying to rationally discuss something most would dismiss as impossible for any number of reasons."

Randall exhumes a memory from a required college course that had bored him stiff. "What about free will?"

"Interesting question."

"Rex seems to have it, from what I've seen, so maybe he can choose not to be what Lucifer wants."

"As if things weren't complicated enough," the abbot says with a pained look.

Abigail drives him to the airport before dawn and they sit in the car by the general aviation terminal waiting for the jet. They had made love when he returned to the hermitage and afterward fallen into sleep so deep neither heard the alarm clock at first.

"Do you know how much longer this will go on?" she asks in the car.

Randall tiredly shakes his head.

"Being away from home is so hard. We should have packed more toys for the kids." He peels several hundred-dollar bills from his roll. "Buy some new ones."

"Tell me again where all this comes from, Diamond Jim."

"It's expense money, so don't worry about it"

"Oh, it's not just the toys; it's you being away all the time."

"You sound like your mother."

"But it's true."

"These days are long and hard enough without starting off with an argument."

She hears the plea in his voice; she smiles and gives him a kiss. "I know they are, darling. We'll get through this."

Back in California, he is getting coffee in the kitchen at Bluff Point—the security people make it strong and keep it fresh—when Molly walks in. She is in a yellow exercise outfit and has a towel around her neck. Her hair is as untamed as ever.

"Forty-five minutes on the treadmill," she says exuberantly. "How was the flight?" She pats her face with the towel.

"Beats Delta."

"You'll never guess what happened."

"Why even try?" he says with weariness.

"It looked like the new financing for the movie fell through. A blind, old Arab sheik, the head of the bank, put the kibosh on it. Did you hear about the plane that crashed into the building in Dubai?"

"Business as usual for the Middle East."

Molly savors the moment, smiling and fluttering her lashes.

"Is there something else?" Randall says with irritation.

"The old sheik was in the building and was killed. His family lost no time giving the green light. Like everybody else, they think from the screen test the movie will be huge."

He sits down to take this in while she feeds fresh vegetables into a noisy blender; she joins him at the table with a large, frothing green drink he wouldn't touch with a barge pole. "The healthy breakfast," she exclaims and takes a sip. She looks rested and in good spirits for the first time since he met her. Randall thinks being the only attractive female among so many alpha males is having a queen bee effect.

"That plane crashing into the building was an act of God," she says.

"Something like that. What did Rex say?"

"He was noodling away on his keyboard with a music file Mick sent him when I told him. He just said, 'Okay' and went back to it. It's going to be really, really good; it's kind of bluesy rock and roll; I can almost imagine Keith's guitar licks. The sheriff's department is coming about the attack on the convoy."

"They'll bring the FBI with them. Is Finnese here?"

"He arrived with a bunch of new guys while you were still in the air. He's walking the perimeter with them."

"I'm making him our point man on this. I don't want Templeton Hall mentioned if we can help it." They would realize his connection sooner or later, but he would deal with that when it happened. Maybe a passable lie would come to him in a dream.

A man with a gorilla-like build—big chest, stubby legs and long arms—walks in with a big smile and heads for the coffee machine. "That's one of the new inmates of this funny farm," Molly says. "He's Ray Cash, a minor league catcher the Giants sent to work out with Rex. He's never seen an arm like it."

"Like everything else about him."

"It's hard to think clearly when you're testy," Molly says mildly.

"I'm not testy."

"You ought to see your face right now." She takes another drink of healthy breakfast. "I don't know if you've noticed, but Rex doesn't like people to show emotion."

"Thanks for the tip."

Another swallow. "There's no need to be snotty."

He lets that pass. "There are a lot of good-looking guys living with us all of a sudden."

Molly grins. "You think I haven't noticed?"

"Anything else I should know about?"

"Other than the plane crashing into the building?"

"We covered that."

"Dickson said a lawyer already called about the fence."

"That's his problem." If he didn't delegate difficulties to someone else as fast as they showed themselves he would be swallowed by the job.

"Keep me out of it," he tells Finnese when he sees him.

"They're going to want to know who's after Rex."

"Tell them we don't know."

"That's what you said." His tone says he just might have a few doubts about it.

"I wouldn't bring up Templeton Hall, the train, or that ship. And they're going to give that bio you made up for Rex a very close look, so I hope there aren't any holes."

"No worry. We even have a family genealogy that goes back to Scotland and the Eighteenth Century. His people came from a highland clan; we can show letters from cousins from when he was looking up ancestors."

"Rex can learn the bagpipe if you give him ten minutes."

"So that side is all good. I'd feel more comfortable if there was a lawyer sitting in." He paused. "Criminal, not civil."

"I'll tell Dickson."

"I think we ought to lay on drone surveillance night and day."

"Fine by me."

Randall reaches Dickson at Wilkes Bashford where he is being fitted for clothes. "I'll let them know," he says. "I'm pretty sure we don't have a criminal lawyer on staff—I mean, why would we?—but our people will know who to call."

"Make it the best."

"They'll ask what this is about."

"The car that was blown up in Tiburon."

"The news it looked like a terrorist attack."

"They say a lot of things on the news and sometimes they even get it right. This isn't one of them."

"Were they… after Rex?"

"A reasonable assumption."

"But why?"

He sounds like a whiney little kid, Randall thinks. "We don't know."

Someone asks Dickson to lift his other arm. "While I have you on the line," he says uncertainly, "I'm being measured for a suit they say is 'by' someone named Ermenegildo Zegna."

"Never heard of him."

"The thing is Molly wants me to get three or four of them and a lot of stuff to go with them, shirts and ties and shoes. A handkerchief with a monogram is fifty-two dollars. You wouldn't want to blow your nose with it."

"Do you have a question for me?"

"These suits are seventy-five hundred dollars each."

"Take it up with her," Randall says and hangs up. More detail he won't have to bother with. He heads upstairs to talk to Rex.

CHAPTER 25

REX IS AT THE BALCONY IN A THICK BATHROBE WITH WET HAIR FROM THE SHOWER LOOKING OUT at the fog that steals in at night and hides the green hump of Angel Island. He turns to Randall. "You heard the news?"

"Quite a lucky break."

"I don't think so," Rex says, "I think that was our friend."

"Our friend?"

'There is nothing I can't do, not only well but better than anyone else. It's all because of him, isn't it, the old man?" When Randall can't think of anything to say, Rex continues. "I knew he would find a way to get the financing. Only one man stood in the way and now he's dead." Rex closes the balcony doors to the cold air and crosses the room to an easy chair. "Have you talked to anyone about him?"

"Molly blew it off."

"The rational part of my mind doesn't accept what is happening," Rex says. He runs both hands through his hair.

"Her rational part doesn't either. There's kind of an unspoken agreement not to talk about it."

"Have you been thinking about it?" Rex asks.

"Quite a bit, actually."

"I believe I was created for an evil purpose." He rises and walks around the room, shooting glances at Randall as if in hope he has an explanation or a theory—anything at all.

Duck and weave, Randall tells himself. What if I've got it ass backwards and Rex is right? Camael's uncertainty over which side of good and evil Rex was on could be an act. He knows Abigail and the kids are safe at the monastery because he is the only threat to them; he also knew I'd be so grateful for his help that I'd be his patsy. Maybe he wasn't Camael but Abbadon! He could have set me up in the Tenderloin and turn me loose at the last minute so I'd be even more grateful. Even the abbot had been fooled—if Rex is right. But when it came to con artists, wouldn't Rex take the prize? As Lucifer's creation, he would be bred and born to deceit; lying would be as natural to him as breathing.

"Why would he be trying to kill you?" Randall asks.

"Maybe it's dust thrown in our the eyes." He paces more in deep thought... or faking it.

"The only people he'd be fooling at this point are you and me," Randall points out.

"So therefore it wouldn't be worth it? Maybe he's more subtle than you think. A lie with room to grow isn't as risky as one where no groundwork is laid."

Randall has to admit that is subtle. "Why pretend to kill you in that case?"

"To scare me into what he wants when I'm a brand name like Apple?" Rex looms over him like a prosecutor with a witness. "Look, do you have any idea how hard it is to be me? I'm a freak!"

"Most people wouldn't complain," Randall says. "They..."

Rex cuts in furiously. "I came from nowhere, literally nowhere, my mind empty. I was like a child when you picked me up on the road, but look at me now. I'm learning as I go and I'm doing it faster and faster, not just facts but how things relate better than the smartest algorithm. They don't know me, but people love me. Or they love what they think I am. They stare at me like they can't believe their eyes; I don't have to tell you or Molly, you've seen it. They want to be me and because they can't be me, they want to be as close as they can. It's like I fill an inner emptiness they have; they'd worship me if I let them. Why do I look like a god like Narcissus? Perfect features, perfect teeth, perfect hair. My size is perfect, not too big and not too small; I'm a perfect athlete and pick up any skill I want without hardly trying. Music, acting, any of the performing arts. Give me a day and I can dance like Nijinsky or paint like Renoir. Chess, flying an airplane, whatever, it all comes easy. So would math, science or brain surgery. I don't think there is anything I can't do and better than anyone else."

"Like I was starting to say, a lot of people wouldn't mind... "

"And there's more—I have powers that scare me. When I was walking on that road a woman stared at me. Nosy, I thought… and mean. As soon as I thought that, she turned and ran into the house. And I made Cohen trip and fall after Lazarus said he was the worst man in Hollywood. You saw his arrogance."

"I didn't actually see what happened, but he made a lot of noise going down. Women screaming, people running to help… "

Rex cuts in again. "I wanted to humiliate him, make him suffer, to feel what he made others feel. Stories in the media said he was drunk, but he wasn't. It was me, I did it to him."

"The old biddy on that road slammed the door on me. She remembered seeing you and got a bad allergy attack."

"It irritated me that she stuck her nose where it didn't belong, just glaring from her flowerbed as I passed not bothering anyone. So I made her nose run."

"How does it work, do you wave your hand or sometChapter hing?"

Rex shrugs. "It happened that time without thinking about it; next time I willed it. They say people are born with a conscience… are they?"

Randall says he has never thought about it really.

"I don't think I was, otherwise I'd know it, wouldn't I? I decide what's right and wrong without reference to any standard. From what I've seen so far, the cost-benefit ratio definitely favors wrong." He spreads his arms. "So, what's the deal here—does anybody know?"

Randall has seen a lot of blow-ups as a cop, but none with such puzzled intensity. Yet that tiny, stubborn voice in his head still wonders if this is an act.

"That plane crashing into the building?" Randall asks. "Wasn't that you?"

"That was our friend, I'm sure of it. I think I was meant to be the tool of the Son of the Morning Star, but something went haywire. I was meant to be part of some monstrous plan."

"The son of… " Randall says.

"Lucifer!" Rex roars. "The Devil! You can't believe what I'm saying, that's what your face tells me."

Randall again can't think of anything to say. Maybe if he was fresh as a daisy… no, that would make no difference.

"You're speechless," Rex says, more subdued. Silence passes with him pacing back and forth. From far off, a burst of compressed air blasts through the fog horn at the Golden Gate Bridge.

"A monstrous plan?" Randall says finally.

"Vast, huger than minds can grasp, and I'm the key, the only one who can make it happen." He pauses to stare with intensity at Randall. "Do you wonder if I'm only keeping you around as a useful idiot?"

"I'm just an ordinary guy, why go to that trouble?"

"A simple tool is still a tool. Maybe you're needed now but I'll toss you aside later." He paces more and then puts a hand on Randall's shoulder. "But I would never do that."

He wouldn't think twice says the little voice in Randall's head.

Rex turns away abruptly as if embarrassed at showing feeling… or pretending that he is. "I want someone to help with my wardrobe; lay my clothes out for me in the morning and changes during the day."

"You mean a butler?" Randall says.

"A combination valet and butler. He will be my personal shopper, meaning he must have impeccable taste. Tell Dickson."

Randall walks downstairs where Molly is on a telephone. She puts her hand over the mouthpiece and looks at him inquiringly.

"Have Dickson find somebody to be in charge of his clothes," he says.

He checks out the keys to one of the SUVs—the transport pool is next to work underway on a helicopter pad Finnese ordered built—and drives out the gate. He feels like he's adrift on an unknown sea with the wind rising. The scene with Rex is so fresh it is impossible to disbelieve him; but that means the comfortable old party calling himself Camael is a very good liar.

How could he have been so wrong?

If he was.

CHAPTER 26

"MARK ARONSON CALLED," MOLLY SAYS AS REX COMES DOWNSTAIRS IN DECK SHOES, JEANS AND a light gray hand-knitted Italian cashmere-wool sweater from Italy that retails for just under five thousand dollars. "He wonders if you can begin shooting tomorrow."

"Tell him we'll fly down tonight and I'll be in make-up by four-thirty. Everything is set up and the crew ready to go when we walk on the set. No meetings, no delays, no technical chatter, no unnecessary people."

"I'll tell him."

She asks, "Is something wrong with Sergeant Randall? He had a funny look just now." If they had a fight, it doesn't show. Of course it wouldn't with Rex.

"Maybe he misses his family," Rex says carelessly. "It's time we started building a buzz for this movie."

"How is that possible? They've got miles of film, but not an inch of you." She follows him into a room big enough for a sock hop if the parents were waltzing in the grand ballroom. As soon as the words are out she realizes from his look this is more of the foot dragging he doesn't like.

"We're going to redefine 'possible' for this industry." He switches on the wall-size TV screen where a TV personality's head is as big as a hubcap and mutes the sound. "There will be new film in the can by the end of tomorrow; the close-up where I spot the Trucs, remember?" His manner is almost disdainful. "They already have the CGI background that has the British actor in it. Take him out, put me in. Get the picture? It doesn't matter how rough it looks at this point."

"Got it. Fantastic."

"Four-thirty in the morning!" Lazarus cries when she tells him. "The unions penalize us for early call-back and overtime would start before noon. Do you have any idea what that would cost?"

"That's not my problem," Molly says in a sunny voice. She had stifled her own doubts in a talk to the mirror as she brushed her hair. Never question Rex, always agree. "A yes woman, C'est moi," she said aloud.

"And tell me how we begin promoting the guy?" Lazarus continues through gritted teeth. "He's a complete unknown."

"He won't be after people see that opening scene. Rex wants you to send it as a teaser to *GMA*. The other networks will beat down the door for it, and just imagine the YouTube hits."

"You know," Lazarus says calmly after a bit of thought, "that's not a bad idea."

"Rex says your story is he was brought in from outside as a savior for a dog headed straight to video."

"That's not a bad idea, either," Lazarus says, excitement beginning to stir. "I get back from my rehab, see all the problems and realize something crazy is needed to save our asses. Enter Rex, the only guy in the world who can pull this off. We'll phony up a story to feed the media about how I discovered him, some bullshit like Lana Turner being found at the soda fountain. Are you old enough to remember her?"

"I think I saw her on Turner Classics," Molly says vaguely, "or maybe it was Lauren Bacall?"

"That bio you gave us says he's a wildcatter who buys up old leases for frack-ing. Goddard wanted to do his nit-picking on that—wouldn't crude be ingrained in his hands and nails and shouldn't we have a lab check them out?—but I told him to shut his goddamn trap." He thinks for a minute. "I got it! I was out hunt-ing antelope with a guide and came across him and his pickup truck out on the oil patch. I take one look and… no, that's no good. Everybody knows about my health problems thanks to the bastards around here who leak shit, and I'm not a hunter anyway. I'll get my publicity people brainstorming."

Later in the day, a band of investigators arrives to meet with Finnese and the criminal lawyer sent by Rock-Steady. Like everyone, the law men are awed by the splendor of the estate and speak in hushed tones as they are led to the conference room.

"They wanted to talk to Mr. Rexford personally," Finnese tells Molly afterward, "but we said he was a busy man and we could answer any questions. Their first was who would want to do him harm? We said don't know and it went from there. They said the RPG launcher left at the scene is one of a batch we sent to Syria years ago. No idea how it boomeranged back here, but nobody seemed surprised; the Mexican cartels have been using them on the cops across the border. They wondered why the famous criminal lawyer Atticus Noble was there and he gave them fifteen minutes on how Mr. Rexford takes a felonious assault directed at him very seriously and wants to make sure they do their job. They got kind of huffy at that and said they do take it very seriously. Atticus said all well and good, but it was his job to make sure and he'd be in touch on a regular basis."

"He looked like a man who loves to argue," Molly says. Noble was a short, vain man in a bowtie—the chip-on-the-shoulder, ticking-time-bomb, you-lookin'-at-me? type who sucks all the oxygen from a room. He's who she would want for a commercial where an aggressive character stirs things up but finally agrees at the end to buy the product or service amid confetti and high-fives.

"They didn't drive off in what I'd call a good humor," Finnese reports, chuckling. He shifts gears. "The boys treating you all right?"

"Better than I deserve," she says.

"Some of these guys have reputations. Word to the wise."

"I don't have a boyfriend right now, so not a problem. But thanks for the heads-up." Stealing time for romance from a hyper-demanding boss is where the problem would be. When she wearily dropped into a chair with a magazine for a short break, he seemed to sense it and had a job for her. He needed a certain kind of guitar pick only available in Memphis or the piano had gone out of tune. Could she find out what Dickson wanted to talk to him about? He needed the score for Rimsky-Korsakov's orchestration of Mussorgsky's *Night on Bald Mountain* and he needed it, like, right now. The only copy she could find after half a dozen phone calls was possessed by the San Francisco Symphony. She had to plead with them to run off a photocopy and promised a hefty donation to help finance its ambitious next season. When she rushed back to Bluff Point, he said, "Oh, that." He had moved on in the piece he was composing and didn't need it anymore. "That leaf blowing is too loud; tell them to do it when I'm not here."

When she and Rex arrive at the movie set, the grousing by the crew trails off. Some are pale and puffy-eyed as if they had only ended their partying ten minutes ago. A crew member suddenly runs to retch in a waste basket, barking like a seal.

"It wasn't easy rounding everybody up," Aronson says. "Your average creative type is…"

"Are we ready?" Rex cuts in.

He is led to a stool in front of the green screen and the silver-haired director hired to replace Csaba Balušík bends over to whisper to him. Molly sees on a video monitor that Rex nods impatiently. Of course, nobody can tell him anything. Each of the monitors around the set shows him from a slightly different angle.

"Ready everyone?" the new director calls out. "Okay, action!"

Rex gazes directly into the camera, a transfixing presence even on the small screens. Fifteen seconds pass, thirty, and sixty. By ninety seconds everyone has surrendered to his charisma. On the big screen he will be astounding.

"Jesus Christ," Aronson says at her shoulder. "You won't be able to look away not even for the popcorn." Rex's eyes narrow as he registers the first sight of the Truks. Even knowing how cheesy the script is, Molly feels dread.

"Cut," the new director says. "There's no way that gets better."

"Let's go to the next scene," Rex says.

Aronson looks at the Bulgari watch on his wrist. "Fifteen minutes from when he walked out of make-up. Mr. Lazarus is not going to believe this."

"How many scenes is he in?"

"Thirty-eight of the sixty."

"He told me he was going to change the way movies are made," Molly says.

"This isn't change," Aronson replies dramatically, "this is revolution."

The scenes that follow are more complicated, requiring Rex to exactly repeat the movements of the late Rupert Kingsley. This means intense study of what Kingsley had done and precise positioning. After five scenes they knock off work so the convoy can drive Rex to Dodger Stadium to throw from the mound—the Dodgers are on a road trip—and get used to the feel of a major league ballpark. The smack of the ball in Cash's mitt echoes around the stands. The catcher goes to the mound to show Rex how to grip the ball for the two-seam fastball. "Man, this is, like, totally unfair," he tells Molly afterward as Rex towels off. "Nobody's gonna hit them pitches of his 'cept if they get lucky. I'm gonna show him how to hold the ball for the four-seam fastball on the flight back." He shakes his head. "I don't think he needs to mess with a curve ball right now."

They fly back with Happy Hour takeout in a hamper from Cecconi's in West Hollywood. The plan is to commute back and forth is until the filming is completed, and Molly has lined up a half dozen first-rate restaurants for take-out. The hamper holds wild boar sausage and roast peppers, calamari fritti, and lemon and chili aioli. Rex thoughtfully samples each; Molly wonders if food connoisseurship is the next stage. He calls her to the empty seat next to him.

"This plane is too small," he says. "Tell Dickson I'm going to need a bigger one. He can start looking around for the best lease."

"How much bigger?" she asks

"Our pilot recommends a Boeing 767."

"I'll get Dickson right on it." The all-in Molly doesn't ask why he needs one that big.

"After we learn the stadium concert business from Mick and his people," Rex volunteers, "we'll be on the road with a lot of musicians and roadies."

"Absolutely, we will," she says.

Dickson sits at the rear of the plane with coat folded neatly across his knees like a kid afraid of what mom will say if it gets wrinkled. "How's the valet thing going?" she asks.

"We've got a line on one in London. Our people there see him tomorrow for an interview and look at his references." He blushes. "Do you know what qualities he's looking for—I mean beside good taste?"

"Not a clue. Rex wants you to check out leasing a bigger plane for when we're doing musical concerts, a Boeing 767."

"Don't the Rolling Stones people handle that?"

"This might be for afterward."

"Afterward?"

"Mick's no spring chicken; maybe Rex is thinking ahead. You're going to have more balls in the air than a juggler before you know it."

Looking dismayed, Dickson turns his thoughts inward and she goes back to her seat. Her own cell phone vibrates in the new Louis Vuitton handbag. She has been ignoring it for the burn phones, but looks at it now out of curiosity.

Hi, I'm Sarah Marsh of Nyorker. Frnd of frnd of frnd got yr# forme. Hear new mega star to burst on world. Lv to do story frm grnd floor. Call?? Her phone number ends the text.

She would normally ignore it, but these days there is no telling what might catch Rex's interest. "What do you think?" he asks when she crouches in the aisle to tell him. "They're heavyweights in the print world."

"Take a meeting and feel her out."

Take a meeting, she thinks, he's already has the industry jargon. With the crazy hours they have, how can she fit this woman in? *Providence on Melrose 1pm day after tomorrow,* she texts back on a burn phone. She tosses it in the collection box. They all go there for destruction after one use.

To Molly's trained eye, petite Sarah Marsh, young, cute and sparkly in her ironic pixie hairdo with lavender streaks and dimpled chin, looks like she has an Ivy League background and a generous trust fund. She wears a chiffon blouse with a satin self-tie neck and button front and long bishop sleeves, probably hiding tattoos, over a long pastel skirt. The accessories are just right, as are the Prada tartan bow pumps, but Molly thinks the effect is a little too Manhattan for Southern California. She sizes her up as having shed her early mean girl for the common touch journalists develop to snooker innocents. She blurts out bubbly sentences full of exclamation marks, but Molly glimpses a predatory intelligence in the fizziness.

"Nasturtium leaves filled with scallop tartare, this is fucking wild!" Sarah says. "How do people fucking think these dishes up!?"

"Good question," Molly says demurely, feeling like a dowager aunt in sensible shoes next to Sarah's F-bomb exuberance.

"It's awesome to be in Southern California!" Sarah had cried when she introduced herself. "It's already cold in the east."

"I don't like it here," Molly responded, barely withholding a sniff someone like Sarah might associate with slow bowels and Metamucil.

"Oh, I don't either," Sarah said instantly. "The sun is nice, but L.A. is too laid back, don't you think? And shallow!"

"Mm."

They order wine with their meal. Milly has the monkfish with Belgian white asparagus, wild ramps and saffron potatoes. Sarah orders Kamikubo wagyu beef, braised baby carrots and grilled chanterelles. The portions would fit in the palms of their hands and seemed even smaller on heavy wide platters white as bone and decorated in a bold-colored sauce squeezed from a tube.

"Strong presentation," Sarah tells the smocked waiter named Gil, who has his long, dark hair up in a top knot.

When the time is right, Sarah puts her fork down and leans forward in a big-eyed, trust-me way that Molly thinks would only fool a nitwit. "I've heard so many things about Rex."

"Like what?" Molly says. She is pleased to notice that Sarah has plump hands and short fingers. Short as she is, she faces a lifetime of worry about every calorie. As models say, an instant on the lips, forever on the hips.

"Oh, just that he's the handsomest man in the world and he's going to keep Magnificent Pictures from taking a bath in millions of dollars of red ink."

"You hear all sorts of things."

"Is he that handsome?" Sarah presses.

"I suppose some might say so."

"Oh, come on, Molly!"

"Yes."

"And he's going to save *When the Day Comes*?"

"Time will tell." How did this young thing get me into adages, Molly wonders. What's next, proverbs? Actually, one pops into her head at that second: a closed mouth catches no flies. A toothless, ancient woman said that in an Italian movie with subtitles. A dimple on the chin, the devil within—a Gaelic saying, that one. She is aware she's staring at Sarah's.

"People say it's the worst script *ever* and Csaba Balušík went fucking apeshit with it after Lazarus had the stroke. Did you hear that Lazarus tore Cohen a new one at the Polo Lounge? Talk about the battle of titans."

It would sound supercilious to say she had seen the whole thing from start to finish and anyway it would invite a flood of questions. "What's your idea?" Molly asks.

"A long-form article like Lillian Ross did on *The Red Badge of Courage*. It's so famous."

"I... don't think I've heard of that." Now she's made me feel stupid, Molly thinks.

"Really? I would've thought... It's a classic about the making of a movie directed by John Huston. Lillian spent a year as a fly on the wall. The movie wasn't all that much, but her piece was a marvel of non-fiction in fiction form that showed where it went wrong. It was published in five parts and made into a book." Sarah hugs herself excitedly. "That's what I want to do with Rex!"

"I'll pass it on."

"You've have such great hair. What's his real name, by the way?"

"Todd Daley Rexford."

She writes it down in a little notebook with gold pen fished from her purse and cocks her head perkily. "What do you do—for Rex I mean. His manager or agent or whatever?"

"I'm executive vice president of the company." It comes out more haughty than she intended.

Sarah's moue shows she's impressed, but in the ironic way young people have that Molly knows other people hate as much as she does. Older people. She wonders when the usual generational gap became a chasm; the rush of technology must be the explanation. You no sooner master something than it's a museum piece no one else would be seen dead with like an AOL address. If this keeps up, the young will eat the old as a rite of passage with a sauce of mushrooms, rosemary, oregano and red wine.

"If it needs to be cleared with Mr. Rexford," Sarah says, "maybe I could ask him myself." Her pert smile is irksome. "I can be very persuasive."

"That won't be necessary," Molly says, waving to the waiter for the check.

"Oh, this is on *New Yorker*," Sarah squeaks.

"No, I insist," Molly says in this new stately manner she hates. "I must go now." She wants to be away before she starts feeling even more like an old lady with spectacles half way down her nose.

CHAPTER 27

"I HOPE REX DOESN'T AGREE TO THE STORY," MOLLY TELLS RANDALL WHEN SHE SEES HIM, "BUT I guess it's all about building the brand."

They are back at the estate after riding across the bay on a Navy surplus admiral's barge; the darkness is so cold that ice floes wouldn't come as a surprise. To avoid ambush they schedule flight arrivals and departures randomly from San Francisco, Oakland, Santa Rosa and San Carlos; dummy convoys of SUVs leave and arrive at all hours. The watcher on Angel Island has been seen again.

"A journalist underfoot," Randall says from the depths of a pea coat whose collar is up to his watch cap, "just what we need."

"Maybe you could mention that to him," Molly says through a wool muffler. Only her eyes are visible below her fur hat.

"Not my department."

"We're getting so damned specialized now," she protests. "I miss when it was just the three of us."

"You weren't crazy about running over lettuce fields or swimming for your life."

"It's just that we're getting so like a corporation with all these schedules and meetings. Every time I turn around Margie Weston wants to talk about menus or changing the house cleaners. I hardly ever see you except to wave. How's the family, by the way; they've been in Oregon for ages."

"They're having a ball up there," Randall lies. Abigail's mother misses her cat. Keeping her happy, or at least less unhappy, puts pressure on Abigail, and the kids are wearing her down. The meditation thing had gotten old. "I need your help," she had said like it was an ultimatum.

"Are you taking care of yourself?" Molly asks.

"The answer is the same as last time."

"You don't have to bite my head off."

"Sorry."

Molly touches his arm. "You and Rex don't see much of each other; I've been wondering if something happened." Her lowered voice invites confidences.

"There aren't enough hours for the old days when it was just the three of us." Living now at warp speed, they were as long gone as Calvin Coolidge. "I'm just one of the staff; if there was a table of organization, which I have no doubt Dickson will get around to, I'd be half way down."

"But you were such friends."

"That might be overstating it."

"But you were, we both were."

"Really, you and Rex are friends?"

Randall thinks you only got so close and then a force field goes up to stop the process; Rex's mystery and remoteness grew as time passed. Casual remarks were ignored or his face clouded as if to say he doesn't have time for small stuff and why do you?

"No, you're right," she admits. "I could lose this job tomorrow to someone who actually knows what they're doing. It's seat of the pants for me and I'm not alone; I think Dickson is in terror around Rex. The new wardrobe isn't going over well with Rock-Steady; his bosses think it's too show-offy and a conflict of interest because we bought it for him. He…"

"I don't need Dickson or his troubles on my plate, thanks."

"Anyhow, he comes back from lunch with the studio people and throws his weight around. I think he's drinking."

"Wouldn't you if you had to spend time with that crowd?"

"Oh," Molly says tolerantly, "I think they're all insecure."

"Who cares?"

"Margie is worried her cooking isn't sophisticated enough for Rex. He must have said something."

"Reference my earlier comment about Dickson and his problems."

"God, you've gotten hard."

"I'm the same I always was." If he isn't, thinking more or less continuously about the end of the world adds a wee more weight to the load he hauls through his days.

The barge arrives at the San Rafael Marina where the convoy waits half hidden in the fog of condensation from tail pipes; decoy convoys also look ready to go in Oakland and near Pier 39 in San Francisco. He has picked up the phone a half-dozen times to tell the abbot about Rex's self-doubt, but it would take so long to explain that listeners would get a fix and the mole would be reading the transcript before an hour passed.

"That's your second cup and the boys make it so strong," Molly says later at the estate. "If I drink coffee after eight I stay awake so long I'd never catch the flight." As it is, she dozes in car or boat and on the plane even though they leave at four instead of three now because the make-up artist Gretchen flies with them so that Rex is camera-ready. She has developed a mad crush and her eyes follow him everywhere. She has pretty looks and a nice figure and the security guys flirt, but she has no time for them. Her dog-like devotion—it is purely platonic to judge by Rex's indifference—irritates Molly and others have noticed.

"That girl always looks like she's been crying," Margie complained as she stirred a steaming pot of bigoli.

"We've got an op later on and I have to be alert," Randall says now, draining his cup. I won't be going down to la-la land in the morning."

"Op," Molly asks, "what's that?"

"A team is going over to the island when the moon goes down. We think we know where the guy camps that has us under observation." His guard would be down because staying warm is all he'd be thinking about.

A back channel Finnese used got them satellite time for an infra-red scan. There was a chance it would find its way to the mole, but Finnese counted on bureaucratic sluggishness working in his favor. The team was four men chosen by lot because everyone was itching to go on offense. Randall thinks the tension was like being back in Iraq without the dirt and starving dogs.

"What are they going to do if they find him?" Molly asks.

"Ask a few gentle questions."

They come back toward two in the morning with an Arab-looking man gagged and wearing plastic handcuffs; he is shaking and his scared black eyes dart in all directions. "He says he's with Jihad in the Path of God Brigade," says

Andy Gully, an ex-Marine with three deployments in Indian country behind him, "but he could just as easily be with one of them others."

"What's he's doing on Angel Island?" Randall asks.

"He was recruited for his recon skills—he's one of their elite warriors—and was snuck over the Mexican border by the Sinaloa Cartel. The man knows his job; we woulda never found his camp without the infra-red. He showed some pretty good moves before we got him down. Costello's got a fat lip he's putting ice on."

"Who recruited him?"

"Somebody made a really big offer to him and his commanders. He was supposed to be rotated out in a couple of weeks, but more likely it would be a bullet in the head because dead men tell no tales. He claims that's all he knows and I sorta kinda believe him going by my never-wrong instincts." Gully grins. These men have no shortage of self-confidence, but Randall takes a grain or two of salt for swagger.

"What are you going to do with him?" he asks.

"We'll plant evidence and give him to someone in ICE that Finnese recommends highly. He'll be an old man when he gets out of prison and lucky if he still has an asshole to bugger."

"Blessings be upon you," Randall says.

"And *sangha xalda hwa* to you." They bump fists.

Randall gets a few hours of sack time and then drives to the Santa Rosa airport with the ever-present security escort to catch the charter to Oregon. The generosity of Magnificent Pictures seems boundless because of their delight over the dailies of the remastered *When the Day Comes*. He gets another rowdy greeting from a glowing Abigail and the boys.

"You don't look all that harassed to me," he says after they kiss.

"You're just what the doctor ordered."

"Dad! Dad!" the boys shout.

"Where's your mother?" he asks. She's in on every arrival and departure, hatched-faced with disapproval.

"You'll never believe it! She met a man on a walk and it looks like it has possibilities."

"Possibilities?"

"Mom's been alone a long time."

Randall is tempted to say he could think of a few reasons why if he thought real hard. "Have you met him?"

"No, mom has just told me about him. It only happened a few days ago but she can't talk about anything else."

"Where did she meet him?"

"Up in the hills. He was bird watching and stepped out from behind a tree."

"So she was beyond the monastery grounds?" His first thought is does Camael's spell or power extend beyond that?

"Yes, you go through a gate." She peers at him. "What about it?"

"Nothing, I was just wondering."

"Mom says he's a widower and very good looking in a distinguished way like that old TV news guy Walter Cronkite, the one with the moustache? She showed me his picture on the internet. They have heart-to-hearts, mom says. They always meet at that same tree and sit on a blanket he brings. He was in pharmaceutical sales before he retired. Mom says he's a good listener."

"He'd have to be."

She punches him on the arm.

"Don't you think it's strange," he says as they drive to the hermitage. "A guy steps from behind a tree and all of a sudden your mother is in a 'relationship' with him."

"You think mom's an old bag no man would look at twice," Abigail flares.

"You said that, not me."

"I think it's romantic." She has her stubborn look.

"When do we get to meet him?" he says mildly.

"Mom's a little funny about that; I don't think she's ready for introductions yet. Maybe she picked up some vibe he gives off; older women are probably always hitting on him." Randall and the boys pass a happy half-hour at the bathtub filling empty butter tubs with pebbles until they sink. Brother Mario sends a monk named Darrell in a golf cart for him after lunch. As they ride to the monastery, Randall asks if they get birdwatchers in this neck of the woods.

"No," Darrell replies. He doesn't speak again.

The abbot is out front to greet him and they walk to his office where they sit on opposite sides of the plain desk. Randall tells him about the stormy meeting with Rex.

"So he has the freedom to defy Satan?"

"From what he said. He doesn't want to be part of a monstrous plan... his own words."

"But he is the devil's creation."

"If you believe Camael."

"We must believe him."

"You wouldn't be so sure if you listened to Rex."

"Of course he would be persuasive, Satan's cunning is as deep as his evil; he was confident enough in it to tempt Jesus in the wilderness with the glories of the world."

"Camael is pretty convincing too. If Rex gave Satan the slip and he's got free will, that makes Camael the bad guy trying to pull him back, right?"

Brother Mario shakes his head. "No, free will is the gift of God; Satan only wants slaves. He permits lust but not love."

"Camael must have doubts himself; otherwise why keep me on the case. If not, wouldn't he just squash him like a bug?"

"Does Rex seem happy?"

"I'd say more driven than that. He wants to be rich and famous in a hurry."

"That's the goal of so many young people today because they don't trust in the possibility of happiness; they believe they came from nothing and are going nowhere; that is the nihilist culture they have absorbed from the time they were infants parked in front of the television. The modern despair is acted out in promiscuous sexuality and victim mentality. Young people dream of being important without doing anything to deserve it. Old patterns of behavior—morality, belief in family—collapsed and nothing replaces it except the illusions of social media. After Rex has his fame and riches, what then?"

"Wouldn't that be enough?"

"I believe they're means to an end. He said a monstrous plan."

"That he doesn't want to be a part of," Randall reminds him.

"Yes," Brother Mario says distrustfully, "that's what he told you."

"I keep going back and forth on what to believe."

The chair squeaks as the abbot sits back. "Then Satan has succeeded."

"C'mon, I'm too insignificant to waste time on."

"The idea makes you squirm, but what if you are not?"

"Thanks, just what I needed."

"What if you were placed here at this time as the human agent that keeps Lucifer's plan from completion? Great events can hinge on the smallest things." He clears his throat. "Have you ever heard this?" He recites from memory:

For want of a nail the shoe was lost.

For want of a shoe the horse was lost.

For want of a horse the rider was lost.

For want of a rider the message was lost.

For want of a message the battle was lost.

For want of a battle the kingdom was lost.

And all for the want of a horseshoe nail.

"So I'm the nail?" He feels winter in his soul.

"I see it as a possibility."

"So hang in there?"

"Unless I'm wrong, you already decided—free will."

The abbot maunders on, quoting evidently famous thinkers on the subject, but Randall stops paying attention. "Do you get birdwatchers out here?" he interrupts.

Brother Mario, just getting on to an argument by someone named David Hume, thinks a minute. "No, we're pretty far out for them."

"My mother-in-law has been meeting with one beyond the hermitage grounds."

"Oh, well, I'm wrong then."

CHAPTER 28

"MOM HAS DECIDED SHE'S GOING TO LET HIM DRIVE HER BACK TO OREGON," ABIGAIL SAYS WHEN he gets back. "It's like they've known each other for years." Worry fills her eyes. "I want you to talk to her."

"She's never listens to a word I say."

"You're a policeman, warn her about the danger."

"What if he really is a birdwatcher and not just some guy with a thing for old ladies?"

"Don't make this a joke, I'm warning you," Abigail says fiercely. "They're meeting in town tomorrow morning. Mom's in there packing now."

He goes to the door and taps. "It's me."

"Save your breath," Esther calls out. "I'm going and nobody's stopping me."

The twins playing on the floor pick up on the tension and look on with big eyes.

"I'm not sure this is wise," Randall says mildly through the door.

"You can do better than that," Abigail hisses.

"I don't care what you think," Esther shouts.

"Mom!" Abigail cries. "Listen to what he's saying."

"Tell him to mind his own business!"

"Look," he tells Abigail, "we'll check the guy out tomorrow. I'll ask some questions and run his driver's license. If he's got an overdue library book, I'll know it."

She is only slightly mollified. "This is so crazy."

"Everything will be all right," he says soothingly, "watch and see." The subject is avoided through dinner and afterward. He calls the charter company to say he'll be running late. "We still have to charge you by the hour," a voice tells him. Not a problem, Randall replies.

Esther and the birdwatcher—she shyly revealed his name is Matthew Grimaldi but is called Matt by friends like her—are supposed to meet at Dave's Pancake House. The kids are napping and Abigail is in a hot tub with a novel when Esther departs after most of an hour fussing in the mirror. She wears a pale green blouse with the usual sweater and skirt. A quarter of a mile up the trail a grinning man steps out from behind a tree with a red blanket. Randall takes cover as he spreads the blanket with a matador-like flourish. Yes, he does look as if he had just left the CBS anchor chair after telling the country that's how it was. The networks wouldn't allow an anchor with a moustache nowadays unless it was part of the ethnic package. They stretch out and are soon in deep communing. She does most of the talking and the good listener nods steadily.

"You must kill him," Camael says quietly at his side.

Randall jumps. "You did it again."

"He is Lucifer's creature. He will use her against you if you don't stop him."

"He's got to be a real charmer to get to first base with Esther."

"I can't stay long; Abaddon will sense I'm gone."

"Would it work to shoot him?" He shows his Glock.

"Yes," Camael says. "The human part is fragile though the evil spirit it contains is indestructible."

They turn to look at the couple, and Camael is gone when he glances back. Randall considers getting closer to hear what they are saying, but a twig snapped underfoot would give him away. The minutes pass slowly; he gets a cramp in his calf and tries to rub it out. A half hour passes before they get up and the man folds the blanket. He kisses her on the cheek and she heads down the trail toward him with a fond smile. Randall lets her pass and then limps after her admirer.

"Hello," he calls out cheerfully. It seems the role requires showing good humor, so the man waves. Randall inserts ear plugs—there will be no need for conversation—as he closes the distance. When he reaches the spitting image of the trusted old anchorman, Randall pulls the Glock from its holster and shoots it in the face. The thing drops to the ground and Randall pulls out the ear plugs. A moment of startled silence passes and then the ordinary forest sounds come back. Esther will think the shot fired was by a hunter, a breed she despises.

He drags the surprisingly light body, more husk than meat and bone, off the trail and covers it with leaves. The scavengers will gnaw it to the bone and carry what's left off to dens for the kits and cubs. He had killed in combat, but only at long range; he thought it would bother him more. On the way back to the hermitage, Randall wonders if he is in the grip of some madness and has just murdered an innocent man. The joke is on me in that case, he thinks. And the guy back there, of course.

The twins make a sticky mess with the syrup at the pancake house. Esther's face gets stonier as the time passes until they leave at 9:30. Abigail is both relieved and wracked with pity.

"What a bastard," Abigail says when she walks with him out onto the airport's apron.

"Maybe it's for the best," Randall says piously.

"It's easy for you to play the philosopher, but I'm going to have to listen to her. I'm tired of this; I want to be in my own home."

"I know, I know."

"That poor woman," Molly says back at the estate, "getting her hopes up like that. Why don't you move your family in here? I'm sure that place up there is nice, but isn't it kind of limited in a way? I mean, all those silent religious men. It's not like we don't have plenty of room, and it would be nice to have another woman to talk to."

"I'm afraid it's two," Randall says. "The mother-in-law is part of the package."

"I'm sure we'd get along fine; I'll mention it to Rex."

It's no problem for him and the Gulfstream is sent to collect them. "Oh, this is grand," Abigail says. It's still not home, but it beats the austerity of the hermitage. "I'm dying to meet Rex." Even Esther raises a wan smile.

"You might get a quick look now and then," Randall says. "He's generally holed up in his studio when he's not on the road." A digital recording studio with all the bells and whistles was built in two days; Mick and his sidemen exchange music files with Rex over the internet as they create an album.

Having the family safe at Camp Rex, as it is jokingly called, eases the strain all around. Esther asks if she can bring her cat down but changes her mind when she sees the guard dogs that are now part of the scene. "Heeby-Jeeby doesn't like dogs and those look mean," she tells Abigail.

The routine goes on as before except for the variations on the fly dictated by security. They rise in the wee hours for the flight down south and return after dark. "This will gross a billion two or I'll kiss your ass," Lazarus had told a distributor. This was passed on by Regina Welborne-Smyth. Sometimes they depart by fast convoy, sometimes by small boat or the new helicopter that has noise suppression so that neighbors don't file another lawsuit. But Finnese is not satisfied.

"I've been checking out personal submersibles," he says on the scrambler from Virginia. "U.S. Submarines has a doozy in San Diego called a Phoenix 1000. It will take you down to two thousand feet, if you want to go that deep, and does sixteen knots on the surface. It has room for twenty people and gives us another option. I mention it because you told me not to worry about cost."

"Dickson is your man on that. Just out of curiosity, how big is this thing?"

"More than two hundred feet. It can stand off in that channel and we rendez-vous by rubber boat. We drop below the waves and pop up anywhere we want."

That afternoon Molly watches Rex in the snug green suit patiently making minute head adjustments for the cameras when her smartphone vibrates in her purse. She sees it is Dickson and steps outside for the call.

"This latest thing is ridiculous," he says. "Finnese now wants a submarine. They are eighty million dollars new."

Molly tries not to laugh at his exasperation "Is there a used model?"

"I'm glad you think it's funny. We can lease it for, get ready for this, only a million dollars a month."

"Why so hot under the collar?" The reports about Dickson's arrogance are so common the security people have changed his code name from Fawn to Dickhead.

"We're running out of money, that's why. I'm going to have to ask Magnificent Pictures for a line of credit."

"They're going to make eight hundred million from this movie, so that shouldn't be a problem."

"Where did you hear that?" Dickson cries in amazement. "I'm told on very good authority they only hope to break even."

"Lazarus and your 'very good authority' are playing you. They see one point two billion in box office revenue. That's *Gone With the Wind* in adjusted dollars." Welborne-Smyth is a fantastic source of information. She is in love with

Rex, of course, all the women are—including herself, Molly has to admit. The difference is the others live in hope of somehow lightning striking while she knows there isn't a chance. Rex is saving himself for something far bigger.

"Don't give them the slightest hint I told you," Molly says.

"No, of course not," Dickson says. A chastened silence follows. "You're sure of this?"

"A gross of a billion point two."

"Okay, that means we re-open contract negotiations," Dickson blusters. "The movie is three-quarters finished, right? They had less than nothing before Rex, so I say we walk into Lazarus' office and demand half the net."

"Or what?"

"Or we stop work."

"Rex would have to sign off on that."

"Of course." Dickson clears his throat. "You're his liaison with us, would you mind asking? Give me a day and I can make the case with a Power-Point presentation, but to be frank I'm still a little…" He seems to search for the right word

"Nervous?" Molly prompts.

"No, not so much nervous as… well, yes, nervous."

"Rex and I did sign a contract."

"What are they going to do, sue? They would be walking away from four hundred million dollars according to their own projections, which, by the way, they haven't mentioned to us."

Molly stands outside the recording studio until the red light goes off. "Got a minute?" she asks Rex, still at the keyboard.

"I'm taking a break," he tells session musicians listening in from all over the world. "I'll mix it and see what we got."

Their jumbled replies come through speakers in different languages and accents. "It's gonna be great, man." "Thanks, Rex, you're the greatest." "Fantastic." "Awesome." "Haftig." "Super." "Maravilloso." "Sehr gut." "Brilliant."

"I didn't hear Mick's voice," Molly says as Rex stands and stretches as two technicians fuss with the electronic gear.

"He put me in charge after the first track," he says. "The Stones dried up a long time ago." His laugh is scornful. "It's pitiful; greedy old men traveling the world singing songs from when they were young."

"I thought you two liked each other."

"Like?" Rex says as if it is a word he finds as curious as Darwin might a new specimen. "We are making use of each other. I need his fame and he needs new music."

"I'd like to hear what it sounds like sometime."

"When it's all together. I see I have an interview tomorrow with the *New Yorker* writer after the morning's work is finished."

"There's something more important. Regina Welborne-Smyth tipped us that Lazarus is telling distributors the movie is going to gross a billion two hundred million. Dickson says our cut should be four hundred million. If they say no, we think you walk off the set."

"Fine," Rex says carelessly, sitting back down at the keyboard again and noodling something catchy. "This will be one of the cuts."

"This is a big decision," Molly says. "Don't you want to, like, think it over a little?"

"You and Dickson handle it."

Regina is her usual cool professional self when she and Dickson arrive at Magnificent Picture's Art-Deco headquarters. "Mr. Lazarus cleared room on his calendar."

Lazarus in shirtsleeves with French cuffs and loosened tie greets them effusively, meeting them at the door and guiding them to chairs. The screen and projector Dickson carry make him uneasy. "What's with this?" he says, trying for a jokey tone.

"I'd like to make a PowerPoint presentation," says Dickson. He is dapper in a new suit with a handkerchief square but looks young enough with his polka-dot bowtie to be giving the keynote at a Model U.N. conference.

"I hate that shit," Lazarus says, now suspicious. "Just tell me what's on your mind."

"We want to renegotiate the contract," Molly says.

"You want more money?" Lazarus says, his voice rising. "We got a signed contract and Rex is getting top dollar. No actor makes that kind of money anymore."

"What is the biggest profit your company ever made on a movie?" Dickson asks as he sets up the PowerPoint screen.

"That's proprietary information."

"Magnificent Pictures is publicly held and I looked it up. You made three hundred million and change on *Double Trouble Two*, probably more given Hollywood accounting."

"Why'd you ask if you already knew?" Lazarus says, bristling. His dark eyes are beady.

"We want four hundred million or Rex walks when this meeting is over," Molly says evenly. She took an Ativan for nerves an hour before, but she still wipes moist palms on her black silk trousers below his line of vision.

Lazarus looks like he had a jolt of electricity. He pulls a bottle of pills from a drawer and shakes out a small one that he puts under his tongue. "Nitro," he explains. He spins his chair to look out the window. They hear him taking deep, calming breaths.

Molly reminds herself this is Hollywood, land of drama.

Dickson looks for a place to plug in the projector cord. The Mumbai graphic design unit did a fantastic rush job on the pie charts and bar graphs based on data dug up by the research department.

"Okay, okay," Lazarus says to the window after a couple of minutes. He spins back around to face them. "Tell you what I'm gonna do. I'm gonna tear up that legally binding contract and give Rex double what we said—fifty million dollars. I'll have to answer to my board and they might kick me out, but I'm going to take the chance."

"You're predicting a global take of a billion two hundred million thanks to Rex," Dickson says. Before, you were looking at a loss of two hundred million."

"Turn that goddamned projector off." He turns fiercely on Molly. "What have you guys been smoking, crack? Where'd you get a crazy number like that?"

"Your gross before taxes will be in the neighborhood of eight hundred million," Dickson says. "So one way of looking at it is that puts you way ahead of where you were before Rex entered the picture."

"We're expecting a profit, I won't deny that—I couldn't double the pay out to Rex if we weren't, and we were thinking of enhancement anyhow. But you guys are in cookoo land if you think… what was that number? A billion two?"

Molly and Dickson silently nod.

Lazarus explodes. "You pulled that number out of your butts! No movie in modern times hauls in that kind of money."

"*Star Wars*," Dickson says. "*E.T.*" Lazarus goggles at this baby-faced whipper-snapper he had dismissed as no more than a gofer. "More recently," Dickson continues, "*Transformers: Age of Extinction* did one point one billion at the box office. *Jurassic World* did it faster."

"Don't think we're naïve, Mr. Lazarus," Molly says. "Why would you think that?"

"I don't think that, I think you're CRAZY." The last shouted word brings a quaking Regina to the door. "Is everything all right?" she asks.

As soon as he sees her blanched face, Lazarus makes an instant connection. "Get out of here, you're fired." He picks up the phone. "Goddard, send somebody from security to my office right now. I want Regina off the lot in five minutes." She throws Molly a look of panic as she closes the door.

"That treacherous bitch," Lazarus fumes. "I'm blowing smoke up somebody's ass and she thinks it's on the level." He singles out Molly again. "Do you know how much lying you have to do in this business? Do you?"

"Every other word?" she says calmly.

"Yes, sometimes!" he cries, as if happy he got the point across. He yanks at his tie to loosen it further. "If the Russians knew how much I strung them along, they'd come after me, and I'm just not talking lawsuit. They don't bother with that at this level. They put something radioactive in your iced tea or stick you with a needle on an umbrella as you walk down the sidewalk. What I'm saying is these Russian billionaires are all Putin's pals."

"That's nothing to do with us," Molly says.

"We walk off the lot after the morning's work if we don't agree by the end of this meeting," Dickson pipes in a high voice that Molly thinks wouldn't scare a flea.

"I can't believe Rex goes along with this," Lazarus says. "I want to talk to him mano a mano."

"No," Molly says. "He has an interview, then a workout with his catcher and then album work when we fly back. We have full authority for him."

"You're not flying anywhere on the studio jet," Lazarus says vindictively. "Not anymore."

"We'll charter our own," Dickson says. "We've already got it covered."

"What's this about an album?" Lazarus says, abruptly changing tack.

"The Rolling Stones," Molly says. "We told you."

"We figured that was smoke and mirrors, anyhow there's no money in music anymore. The Stones make it on the heritage thing, but that goes away when they're on walkers or have to be pushed on stage in hospital beds."

"We see Rex fronting his own group," Molly says.

"We're talking to Amazon and Google and a couple of others about distribution," Dickson adds.

Molly hopes Lazarus doesn't see her surprised reaction. Why wasn't she told about that?

Much as he'd like to, Lazarus can't bring himself to ridicule the idea of Rex and rock and roll. His mind even kicks in names—Rex and the Kings. Rex and the Kingsmen. Rex and the King's Men. But he will keep these to himself for now. Another idea strikes him: if the music is great, and there's no reason to think it won't be based on the guy's track record, why not toss out the crap score and use the album with the studio taking a cut?

"A hundred million," he says.

"You got off cold but you're still not warm yet," Molly says. She is amazed at her nerve. Is it the Ativan?

After a long silence, Lazarus says, "My last offer, points with a cap of two hundred million." When they still just stare at him, he bursts out, "Do you know how much Tom Cruise earned from all the *Mission Impossible* movies? Some three hundred million!" He can sit still no longer and begins to walk around the room pounding a fist into a palm. "And you're asking for four? C'mon, get real for God's sake. Rex is Rex but the script is shit. The critics..."

"Nobody will care what they say," Molly interrupts. "It will be bullet-proof."

"Make it three-fifty and we've got a deal," Dickson says.

Molly looks at him sharply. Sensing a split between them, Lazarus pounces. "Deal!"

Afterward, she says, "I think we could have got the whole four hundred million."

Dickson shakes his head. "Our strategic committee spit-balled it and came up with four hundred as the opener. Our game theory guy said based on the data and the post-stroke psychological profile we had done that Lazarus might go as high as three point five but don't push him more." He holds his hand out and Molly sees it is shaking. "Man, that was intense."

"Try an Ativan next time," she says. "What's this about Google and Amazon?"

"What about it?"

"I'm Rex's manager, I should be told everything."

"It's just blue-sky thinking for internal use. We're proactive; isn't that want you want from a management company?"

"Tell me everything or you're gone." The words had just popped out. She doesn't really think she has the authority to fire Rock-Solid… no, she's sure of it.

But Dickson doesn't know that. "No problem," he says hastily, "I'll see you're copied on everything." A few steps later, he cautiously asks, "Did I know about the media interview?"

"It just came up," she lies.

"Not to brag or anything, but we've got a great public relations division," he says. "You want me to pull them in on this?"

"I'll handle this one."

Rex only says "fine" when she tells him about Lazarus. Money doesn't interest him, that's clear, or the adoration of the masses. Or love… he remains as distant a moon of Jupiter. What is behind that focused ambition, what goal apart from not being killed by his mysterious pursuers?

CHAPTER 29

SARAH MARSH LOOKS POLEAXED WHEN REX WALKS IN. "OH, MY GOD," SHE SAYS, INSTANTLY GOING from ironic journalist to fan girl. "I heard he was handsome," she whispers to Molly, "but this is madness."

"We get that all the time," Molly replies.

Rex crosses the room with his lithe stride to kiss her hand. "Hello, beautiful," he says, clasping it to his chest and looking deeply into her startled blue eyes.

"Oh..." Sarah says, turning scarlet.

Here is something new, Molly thinks. Sarah is pretty in her zaftig way, but beautiful? She wonders what Rex is up to; it's not as if he needs to go out of his way to be spellbinding. Sarah looks almost paralyzed in the sandals and a belted chambray shirt dress she wears as if atoning for overdressing the other day.

Rex walks her in a mock knightly way to a chair where she looks down in confusion at her lap and the notebook with her prepared questions. "Turn on the tape recorder," Sarah says half aloud as if being stern with herself. She turns her dazzled gaze to Rex. "Tell me about yourself."

"You got my bio?" he says in a Midland, Texas, accent. Why that all of a sudden, Molly wonders.

"Yes," Sarah says.

"It's all in there."

"But... in your own words?"

"Hell, I ain't gonna go through my whole life," Rex says laughingly. "Ask what you want to know." That was Molly's idea to avoid mistakes from ad libbing.

"Yes, right," Sarah says. "Sorry." She is angry at herself for getting off wrong footed. "You came from nowhere and now you're the star of a big movie insiders say was in huge trouble. That story alone could be a movie itself, from the 'Thirties."

"I wouldn't know 'bout that."

"You're not a film aficionado?"

"I don't know what that there word means, but, nope, I haven't seen many picture shows."

This is so unbelievable to someone who has spent so much time in theaters, screening rooms and talking and writing about film that Sarah's mind seems to go into vapor lock. "Ah...ah...ah."

Looking her up on-line, Molly had learned her niche at *New Yorker* is obscure and difficult cinema. She unknots the meaning of reissued European classics by minimalist auteurs like Cristi Puiu, master of the Romanian new wave movement who, she wrote, is now regrettably nearly forgotten. Her reward for this grim toil, usually appearing in meagre paragraphs in the magazine's smallest type, is to be occasionally set free for swings at the Hollywood piñata. Her scorn, also appearing in her personal blog, is treasured by cineastes. "If you don't have acne, skip Backpack IV: Bigfoot Returns..."

Sarah's spinning mental wheels gain traction. "I was going to ask you for your favorites."

"Like I said, I ain't had time to see that many pictures." He throws a leg over the arm of his chair. As she stares at the large bulge at his crotch, he adds, "There weren't a whole lot of money when I was a kid, and we keep purdy busy out on the oil patch."

The Q and A doesn't go well. Sarah, flustered and havering, blushes each time Rex answers a question by referring her to the bio. "Damn," he says with a chuckle, "I'm wonderin' why they bothered printin' it up if nobody reads the dang thing."

"Do you..." Sarah begins a question forty-five minutes into the hour. "No, sorry, that's also covered by the bio." Her forehead has a sheen that makes Molly think of melting butter.

"Well," Rex says, looking at his watch, "I 'spect we'd better be windin' her up quick. We got a plane to catch, darlin'."

"Could I go with you?" Sarah blurts. "I was hoping for more than just a quick sit-down you'd give a newspaper. Didn't Molly tell you?" She shoots her an evil look; the mean girl is back and ready to break up some furniture.

"No," Molly says firmly. "We'd have to run that by PR." Listen to me, she thinks; I'm acting like a big corporation has my back. Actually, I do—it's hard for a small-timer like me to get used to it.

"I know Pauline!" Sarah says excitedly, as if a life raft was thrown to her. "She's a buddy from when she was in New York."

"Who might Pauline be?" Molly asks, feeling the stuffy matron rising.

"Pauline Abramovich! She's Magnificent's head publicist. She'll vouch for me—totally!" She is appealing directly to Rex as if knowing she is in danger of losing the biggest story of her career.

"Sorry, I don't know her," Molly says. But she remembers being introduced to a raptor-like woman she quickly put in the category of those who take a mile if given an inch. Like the other studio executives, she had been frozen out on Rex's order. "We have our own public relations people."

"She'll tell you how important *New Yorker* is culturally."

That gets Rex's interest.

"Do you even know?" she demands, seeing his reaction and directing the question to Molly.

"Yes," she answers, "I told Rex you were big in print, but it doesn't mean anything to the demographic this movie is for."

Sarah sees an opening. "This is not the only film Rex is going to make, not with his acting chops."

"How do you know?" Rex says, his interest sharpened. "We're working on a closed set."

"Out-takes are smuggled and word gets around; you'd be surprised how fast. You can get anything from the Estonian hackers."

"Hell's bells," Rex says in that Midland accent, "we'll think 'er over and get back to you."

"Did she tell you I want to hang out as much as possible?" Sarah says as if Molly is no longer there. "Go where you go, sit in on meetings, have lunch, go to dinner, drink wine together?"

"Nope," Rex drawls with a look at Molly, "I don't recollect that comin' up none, and I shore think I would."

"Nothing published for months, maybe even a year. We think long term at *New Yorker*. You *must* see this is win-win." Her pleading eyes swam with tears pf sincerity.

Afterward on the flight back north, Molly asks, "Why did you talk like that?"

"Jes havin' the sheila on a bit," Rex says in twangy Australian.

Molly stares at him. "What's with the accents all of a sudden?"

"I listen to internet radio late at night," he says in his normal voice. "You pick up all sorts of interesting things."

So just another skill effortlessly acquired. "I don't think it's good idea having her around. She might hear something you don't want her to."

"Ach, I cannae but think the wee lass will be no trouble awrite." The "r" has the authentic Scots trill.

Of course he's right, Molly thinks. It only took the one look and a hand kissing for Sarah to fall like an anvil through a ton of feathers.

"Tell Dickson to have Rock-Steady kick it around," he says, again in his normal voice. "I see upside potential."

Dickson the next day says the corporation's branding experts and public relations staffers agree about Sarah; they will fold her profile into their roll-out strategy for preparing the campaign battle space.

"What does that even mean?" Molly asks.

"*New Yorker* is a big deal with the elites, but a year is too much time. They want us to begin with teasers in the internet and gossip columns and build up to supermarket magazine covers and the network morning shows. When the Big Mo is roaring down the tracks like a runaway freight train, we pick from the late-night comics; Sarah's piece will be icing on the cake." Their advice is that Rex go for a critical success in his second movie; a *New Yorker* profile will lay the foundation for that.

"But it's got to be good with no snark," Dickson emphasizes.

"I don't think we need to worry about that." What she has to worry about is Sarah, who is younger, hungrier and with a better feel for what's cool. Spending as much face time hanging with Rex, it won't be long before she begins to scheming to thin out rivals for his ear. Molly knows the first target will be her.

CHAPTER 30

"SORRY," SAYS CHUCK BREWSTER, MANAGER OF THE SAN JOSE GIANTS, "BUT PLAYERS HAVE TO be here for the whole game. In the dugout or in the clubhouse, no exceptions." Molly has explained on the phone that Rex has to be lead-off batter and is only available to pitch the first three outs of the game with the High Desert Mavericks. "Who does the guy think he is?" Brewster adds. "Supposing he got the side out? What kind of manager would yank a pitcher if he didn't hurt his arm or something? This might be Nowhereville, but I'd still be on ESPN4 explaining."

"So the San Francisco front office hasn't talked to you?" she asks.

"I hardly ever talk to those guys; they're too high up the food chain to bother with us ants. They might be just up the freeway, but it's a different world. All the boss gave me was the email saying your client as of now is on the roster as a pitcher. I had to put Chico Echemendía on injured reserve to make room, and I was already light on infielders. I'll have to move an outfielder to first base if one of them gets hurt and..."

"Listen to me," she interrupts, realizing that this guy might be in the minors but he was major league in pissing and moaning, "I'm going to have Ethan Margolis call you."

"You know Ethan?" he says in a different tone "Hang on; maybe I can work something out for your man. Did you say his name is Rexford?"

"We'll get there in time for him to warm up and we'll leave right after the inning is over. Our security people will be in touch with yours."

"You got your own security?" Chuck is massively impressed.

"See you tomorrow fifteen minutes before the game," Molly says.

"He don't want to meet the team, shake some hands?" Chuck can't believe it. "What about batting practice?"

They leave Hollywood in time for the first game of the double-header at San Jose Municipal Stadium. Rex changes into the team uniform on the flight and Randall listens as Cash briefs him on the Mavericks. "They've got a couple of kids who might make it to Triple-A, but the rest are nobodies going nowhere or guys who maybe had a cup of coffee in the bigs once."

"What does that mean?" Rex asks, interested as usual in adding to his store of slang.

"They played a few games for a major league team before they got sent down, couldn't hit a curve ball or whatever. What I'm saying is this is gonna be no sweat. You won't even have to throw hard for these tomato cans." At Rex's look, he explains. "Bums."

The stadium's straight-back bench seats set close to the field are half full with a couple of thousand spectators for the noon start. Rex strolls from the dug-out to warm up in the outfield bullpen; Molly, Randall and Cash are shown to seats in the press box. The chatter of the fans trails off as the ball pops in the catcher's mitt.

"Man, that guy has some kind of heater," says a sportswriter.

"It's dumb to throw that hard to loosen up," another comments, as he idly scans the stands with binoculars. "Especially when he's the lead-off hitter. Hey, there's Ethan Margolis. What's he doing down here?"

"He's dumb not to wear a hat," the first says, removing a hot dog from its wrapper. "That bald spot is gonna get burned in this sun."

"That's why that guy is throwing so hard, to impress Margolis."

The umpire cries Play Ball.

It takes Rex nine pitches to retire the side, each blazing fastball raising the crowd noise another notch. The Mavericks look shell shocked when he trots off the mound to standing applause. Rex chooses a bat from the rack, takes a few practice swings, and then steps into the batter's box.

"Hey, pretty boy faggot," bawls a stentorian voice from the stands, "who does your nails?" There is laughter from the crowd.

"That's Foghorn Barletta, kind of a legend around the league," one of the sportswriters tells Randall. "He travels on his own dime to razz the other team. He's funny, but he can be real crude. The third baseman went into the seats after him in Fresno." Randall locates the heckler, a fat man wearing a Hawaiian shirt and sweatpants, his Mavericks ball cap turned sideways. He stands and wiggles his rear and does a mincing walk. "You're a zero, Rexford," he yells. "Put that bat down and pick up your dolly."

A Giants fan must have said something because Foghorn yells with out-stretched arms, "Look at the guy, I bet he spends half his time in the beauty shop." The words are no sooner out of his mouth than he falls to his knees clutching his chest. Time is called by the umpire as the standby ER crew rushes to where he lies between rows. As the kibitzer is rolled out on a gurney, he lifts an arm in response to the applause,

Rex steps into the batting box. The first two balls are out of the strike zone, but the pitcher doesn't want to start his game with a walk so the third is over the middle.

Crack.

The ball rockets off the bat in a high arc and soars over the center-field fence three hundred and ninety-five feet away. "That's still in the air," Cash tells Randall as Rex turns for second base. "I bet it's five hundred feet easy." The awed crowd cheers madly. "Tip your hat when you round third," Cash mutters. As if he hears him, Rex does and the roar increases.

He joins Molly and Randall with the security entourage and they hurry through a tunnel with his spikes clattering on concrete to the parking lot where the convoy awaits. Cash gives him a friendly squeeze on the shoulder but drops his hand at the look Rex gives him.

"How was it?" Randall asks as the convoy speeds from the stadium for the flight back to the studio.

"What I expected," Rex says blandly.

"Weren't you nervous, even a little?" Molly asks. But he's already got ear buds in listening to a file sent by a musician in Tasmania recommended by Keith Richards. His head bobs to the beat, not so much appreciating the music as analyzing it.

"Mystery Phenom" says the headline on the San Jose Mercury-News website when the story is filed about the club's 8 to 5 loss to the Mavericks. The deck says, "Fans Three on Nine Pitches, Crushes Homer." A separate story tells how the heart attack victim got flowers in the hospital from Rex. "The guy's all right," he told the newspaper. "I'm sorry what I said." The floodgates open when some smart reporter at the Hollywood Reporter makes the connection between the new baseball sensation and the unknown actor said to be saving Magnificent Productions from Chapter 11 bankruptcy.

"That was a good touch to send flowers to that big mouth," Dickson tells Molly the next day. "Our PR guys say they've never seen anything like it, and one worked for Lady Gaga at her peak. He says everybody wants an interview. ESPN calls, like, every fifteen minutes and so does that *New Yorker* woman."

A heavy, gusting rain is falling that night when they return to Bluff Point. The lights of the lead vehicle pick out Sarah Marsh at the security gate, a pathetic figure in a raincoat clutched to her throat. She pulls the hood back so they can identify her.

"She's been there two hours," Randall says, checking his watch.

"Our guys told her to move it, but it's public property where she's standing," a bodyguard says. "She uses some pretty salty language."

"Invite her in," Rex says easily. The last car in the convoy stops and opens a door for her.

Instead of showing gratitude for being out of the rain, Sarah is furious. "Why didn't anyone fucking tell me he's a baseball player?" she says when Molly brings her a towel. "I could have begun the piece with that scene."

The lifetime of privilege and having others tip-toeing around her moods is showing, Molly thinks. Nothing was too good for her, from Mozart in the womb to a gap year traveling the world. Old money parents no doubt were subsidizing a career that pays peanuts but was full of variety and vivid experience. "Now you can start with 'It was a dark and stormy night,'" she says pleasantly.

"Very fucking funny. What happened to the idea of me hanging out?"

"Rex hasn't mentioned it."

"Isn't it your job to remind him of little details like a profile in the best goddamn magazine in the country?"

"He doesn't need to be reminded of anything." Molly smiles to throw more gasoline on the fire. "He's got it all up here." She taps her temple.

Sarah looks around, toweling her hair. "I couldn't see that well outside, but this place is fucking huge. It just needs a concierge to be an upscale hotel in Copenhagen." Molly suspects the line will be in her story. "When can I see him?"

"Not tonight, he's working on his music." It is such pleasure to say no to this pampered, selfish creature.

"He's a musician, too?"

"He's working with Mick Jagger on a new album."

Sarah's astonishment is so complete she steps back as if struck. "You are *shitting* me!"

Molly wonders if her parents know she doesn't seem able to utter a sentence without foul language. Then she thinks ruefully, I'm so out of it I might as well wear rouge and put up my hair in a bun.

"Why didn't you tell me!?" Sarah stamps a foot, eyes flashing. She walks away and comes back. "My office told me he pitched in San Jose today. And hit a huge home run! They couldn't believe I didn't know. And now you tell me he's writing music with old fucking Mick Jagger?"

"Why do you think that's my job?" Molly says nicely. "We have a public relations department."

"All they do is answer the phone and say they'll get back to me. I thought we had an understanding."

"Would you like a lift somewhere?"

Sarah is instantly transformed from imperious princess to cringing beggar girl. "Molly, please. Let me fly with you guys to Hollywood tomorrow. I need color and, like, granular detail, not the canned shit anybody can get. *New Yorker* expects us to dig way below the surface in our profiles, so I need to be inside, but—this is just between you and me, okay?—I'll let you read the story before I turn it in and you and Rex can suggest any changes you want."

Rex has already green-lighted (it's impossible to avoid movie jargon these days) her going along, but Molly pretends to think. "We leave early and we're pretty full up here, but I can probably find you a place to sleep."

"Oh, thank you, thank you, Molly. You're my friend for life! Any of these sofas will do. I just need a blanket and a pillow."

"Sorry, against our rules," Molly says, creating one on the spot. "There's a place in the kitchen, though." She leads Sarah carrying a blanket and pillow. She points to a spot below a steel utility table opposite a range. "There."

Sarah tries to hide it, but outrage flashes like neon on the Ginza strip. In a strangled voice with a promise of revenge, she says, "Thank you."

CHAPTER 31

"WHY DO WE HAVE TO KEEP THE DRAPES CLOSED UNTIL WE TURN IN?" ABIGAIL ASKS, "IT'S SUCH A BEAUTI-ful view out there." They have come up from dinner, the children are in bed and Esther is in her room where Matlock and Colombo and her other old favorites are back on a flat screen four times bigger than at home.

"To conserve heat and thereby help the environment," Randall says. He takes off a shoe and sock and rubs his foot.

"Don't be a smart ass."

"Doesn't it beat a dumb ass?"

Abigail sighs, in no mood for it. "You're ducking the question."

He gives the other foot the same treatment. "Boy, my dogs are barking." There is never down time on this job except when you go to bed. At least in Iraq you could look forward to R and R in Germany. He would have been off duty hours ago if he was still a cop.

"I still don't understand why the Mafia wants to kill him," Abigail says.

"There's a six-month waiting list to ask that question. What did you think of dinner?" It was ceviche with chopped plantain, avocado, corn and sweet pota-toes. "I don't like that kind of stuff."

"I wonder why Margie doesn't stick to simpler dishes. These are meat-and-potato guys like you; they don't care about fancy."

Randall chews an antacid. "Molly told me Rex wants more sophistication."

"What about the drapes?"

"Finesse's orders; he's worried about a sniper."

Abigail puts hands on hips and gives him a direct look. "I asked one of the guys about the Mafia and he kind of smiled and said it was good as any other theory he'd heard."

"Great answer."

"I don't think even the president has this many bodyguards."

"Some say it was the Mafia that got Kennedy, and he had more than this level of protection. One man with a scope and rifle is all it takes."

"But Rex is just this—what?—ball player and would-be entertainer. Why would anyone want to kill him?"

"Something in his past he can't remember? Maybe you'd rather be back at the monastery with the kids."

"No, of course not. It's peaceful and all that, but you're not there and anyhow it's not the real world, not that this is. This is like living on a really nice military base."

"It's like a five-star hotel where we eat out every night and the boys are in hog heaven. What's to complain about?"

Abigail fiddles with her hair before the mirror. "Oh, I don't know anybody who lives like this. The whole situation is so strange."

"You have a point."

"Molly agrees with me."

"Did she tell you how she met Rex?" he says alertly.

"No, she says she's not supposed to talk about it like it's some big mystery. Mom has never heard of anything like this either."

"Rex is not a would-be entertainer; he'll be an overnight sensation. The world will beat a path to his door."

"They won't get past the gate with all the guards and cameras and other stuff." She changes into her night gown. A great figure still, he thinks; there'll be some hanky-pank tonight. They slip under the covers on the four-poster bed with a red and yellow canopy as high as the crown molding. "Have you noticed each bedroom is decorated in styles from different eras?"

"They spent a ton of money, that's for sure."

"Men don't notice that kind of detail unless they're gay. The mantelpiece in this room is a piece of art. The canopy and drapes are silk."

"I think my years of three hots and a cot dulled my appreciation for the finer things of life."

"When will this movie be finished?" she asks.

"It's seven-eighths done. They know down to the inch because everything is digital. It goes without saying Rex does the green screen better than anyone in history. When there's a wrap, we start to play ball. That will be a whole bunch trickier because we'll be working with big crowds in stadiums instead a few people on a closed studio lot. Let me ask a question."

"Go ahead."

"How does it feel to be in bed with the second handsomest man in the house?"

"You're more my type," Abigail says, turning to him.

After they make love, Randall pulls the drapes open and they lay on their backs in the moonlight and salt air that stream in. Abigail says, "Molly says the makeup artist and that young *New Yorker* woman hate each other."

"Let me guess, they're both head-over-heels with Rex."

"Sarah has the advantage because she gets to talk to him instead of just doing his makeup and being quiet so Rex can think about whatever he thinks about."

"Big thoughts, I guarantee it."

"Sarah hates Molly, too. Do you like Rex?" Abigail asks suddenly. When he doesn't answer, she says, "I don't either."

"I didn't say I didn't."

"Not in so many words."

"There's a there there, but I don't know what it is," Randall says.

"I know what you're saying," Abigail agrees, sitting up in bed. "He always seems so detached."

"You only met him the once."

"That was enough and it's also what Molly says; like you, she's spent a lot of time with him. I'd love to know his history."

"So would he."

"Did you know she had two ex-boyfriends murdered?"

"She told me."

"At the same time. Isn't that strange?"

"Very."

"Do you think she did it?" Abigail says guardedly.

"No."

"Don't ever say I mentioned that."

"Of course not."

"It can't be a coincidence."

"Ask the San Francisco cops, I'm sure they're on top of it."

She fluffs up her pillow and settles back. "She didn't really want to talk about it; it's all bottled up inside. Mom told her she ought to talk to a therapist."

"You're mother is a great one for talking."

"Oh, come on," Abigail chides, "I think she should too, what a trauma that must have been." After a small silence, she asks, "Would you want the boys to be policemen when they grow up?"

"They'll have robots and algorithms doing everything by then. They'll know everything about you from tattoos to DNA and wherever you are within a foot. Nobody will dare do anything, but if they do they'll turn themselves in because escape is impossible."

"What if that doesn't happen?"

Randall thinks about it for a moment, his eyes faraway. "No, I wouldn't want them to be cops; you see too many bad things. It can rub off, change you."

"Did it change you, seeing them?"

"I have to sleep now," he says. He never gets enough to push the needle past half full.

But when he turns out the light, he stares at the ceiling long after her breathing is regular. He has to have a showdown with Camael next time he materializes out of thin air. What if he's playing a double game? Templeton Hall and the convoy ambush were flourishes a magician might do to draw attention away with one hand so you didn't see what the other was doing. But the abbot could be wrong. And what guarantee is there that *he* isn't part of the conspiracy?

He would like to have the benefit of Abigail's clear-headed thinking on this, but he can't do that to her. He doesn't want her to have a red-hot knife twisting in her stomach like he does.

"You seem tense," she whispers, not sleeping after all.

"It's nothing," he says, "just thinking about tomorrow." Not deciding which fork in the road to take is a decision itself, and maybe this torment is part of the satanic plan, a little frosting on the cake for Lucifer's amusement. Tomorrow he will climb over that gate and claw through the underbrush to where Camael has the Angel of Death cornered.

Allegedly.

He is jolted awake when the wake-up call comes. He slips on his robe and goes out into the hallway to tap on Molly's door. She opens it a crack, hair wild and face puffy from sleep.

"Yeah?"

"Tell the boss I won't be going today."

"Lucky dog." She closes the door.

They will ride west over water to Sausalito at the same time the decoy convoy flares out the gate going north at good speed for Napa and the county airfield. The one with Rex will continue on to the Santa Rosa airport in rented vans parked at the Spinnaker restaurant.

He has breakfast with Abigail and the kids and afterward plays with them on the greensward. He is trying to get a kite in the air when Finnese comes through the gate in an up-armored M1097 Humvee and climbs down from the passenger side.

"You don't take any chances," Randall says, impressed.

"I hope you don't," Finnese replies. "We got it from a private party and painted black over the desert tan so we weren't so conspicuous."

"I'm afraid it didn't work."

"It is a real eye-catcher," Finnese admits, "not a lot you can do to disguise them. It came with a CD that has twelve thousand pages of service instructions."

"How long did it take the Arabs to turn the ones we left into junk?"

"ISIS ruined those that still worked. They don't have a lot of mechanical know-how there."

"They know to wipe their asses with their left hand because they eat with the other one."

They share a bitter laugh.

"The FBI is coming for another interview," Finnese says. "I think they like it better here than the Federal Building. I thought you'd be in Hollywood."

"I'll make myself scarce."

"Your name hasn't been mentioned so far."

"They're not all that great despite the PR, but they're better than this," Randall says. "They'll make the connection sooner or later."

"No one will be more surprised than me," Finnese says, "because you never said a single word to me about Templeton Hall." A silver Bentley rolls through the gate with Atticus Noble at the wheel. "Boy, does the FBI have a hate on for him," Finnese says with a chuckle. "He parses every question they ask."

"Hello, stranger," Penny says at police headquarters when he calls on his way to west Marin. "How's Oregon treating you?"

"No complaints."

"Some guys in suits and ties want to talk to you."

"I didn't hear that."

"I didn't say anything, that's why you didn't hear that. I called you stranger in case your name is a key word you know who would home in on."

"Welcome to the police state where even the police are bugged."

"Really." She laughs. "Maybe they can solve the mystery of who's drinking the coffee and not putting money in the cigar box. What's up with you; it's been a while."

"Oh," Randall says smoothly, "just chillin'. Anything new to report?"

"We're still frozen out by the feds; otherwise, it's the same old same old. A church burned down out toward where you live, but that's about it."

An ice pick jabs his gut. "Which one?"

"Let's see," Penny says, a keyboard clacking on her end. "Yeah, here it is. Bethany Primitive Baptist Church and the preacher is missing. It was news on a.m. radio for about five minutes but didn't make the papers."

"When did it happen?"

"About the time you left."

"Keep your ears up for me on that."

"You got it."

Randall drives to the blackened skeleton of the church where men are clearing away charred debris as heavy-set women with a farm look gaze tragically at the disinterring. He introduces himself and they tell him they are members of the congregation. "No sign of the pastor?" he asks after a time watching the work.

"We're think he's here somewhere," one woman tells him in a breaking voice, dabbing at her eyes. "The arson people never dug that deep. He might be in the basement, but that's under ten feet of this stuff."

Randall thinks the mole hidden somewhere in the miles of government corridors devoted to spying led the killers here. The pastor didn't know anything that could help, but maybe he saw them for what they were or gave them some lip; he was a man of strong opinions he didn't bother to edit. He leaves the congregation to their grief and disinterment.

He parks near the gate and forces his way through the undergrowth. There is something he can't put a finger on at first and then it hits him. The creepy stillness that hung over the place is gone; songbirds sing and crows trade mordant comments. Insects drone lazily and one struggles feebly in a big spider's web hung in a bush. He unholsters his gun as he reaches the rise with the view of the mansion below. Instead of the beautiful Southern manse before, he sees a wrecked shell with a caved-in roof. Randall sits on the ground with arms locked around knees. Neglect this complete would take decades. Every window is missing and weather has worn away the paint, leaving the wood gray like a ghost town a century after the ore ran out. And yet down there was showy luxury he had seen with his own eyes. I can be fooled by a clever illusion, Randall thinks, but how could Camael? The explanation comes to him at once: it was Camael who had deceived him through some feat of conjuring, making me see beauty instead of sagging ruin. He gets to his feet and descends the slope to the weedy grounds, scrapes open a slumped door and steps inside. The splintery floor is loose underfoot and faded wallpaper hangs in strips from walls with holes kicked in by vandals. Hypodermic needles lay about in the dirt and refuse and calcified stools lay in a corner; the homeless must have squatted here until the roof gave way.

He returns to the car and telephones the abbot in Oregon. "He has gone away," the voice on the other end tells him.

"Where?"

"He didn't say; he left in the middle of the night."

Randall has never felt so alone. He thinks of that insect struggling in the spider web.

CHAPTER 32

MOLLY FEELS LIKE A DOLLAR PRINCESS PURSUED IN PAST TIMES BY DOWN-AT-THE-HEEL ENGLISH aristocrats hoping to marry an American fortune except her fortune isn't inherited money but access to Rex. It seemed half the world wanted him after predictions of instant stardom came from insiders seeing raw footage of *When the Day Comes.* "The Movie is a Dog, But Rex is King," said the Variety headline. Flowers and candy were to be expected, but some of the gifts offered were so over the top they shocked her.

"The keys to a new Jeep Cherokee?" Randall said. "I would have been tempted."

"I'm holding out for a Rolls," she joked. These were bribes for face time squeezed from Rex's impossibly tight schedule. And it wasn't as if she couldn't buy whatever she wanted with her cut of his contracts, the latest with Rolex. She was certain the accounting firm she hired thought she was involved in illegal activities from the startling sums of money she banked. A photographer took five minutes, all Rex would allow, shooting him smiling into the camera with the Rolex raised to face level. Two million for that and they threw in the sixty-thousand dollar wristwatch for good will.

Two weeks after the rough cut was previewed for industry big shots, Rex had his start with the Giants farm club in Sacramento; he struck out six batters with eighteen pitches averaging 109 miles an hour before leaving the game according to plan. "Unhittable," said the *Sacramento Bee* headline. A website pointed out that the pitches ticked the edges of the strike zone, further flummoxing batters. "Was a better two innings ever pitched?" it asked. The sporting press was thus added to the mix of people begging for just a few minutes of his time. It suddenly seemed his face was on cable night and day, and he had five million Facebook followers and two million on Twitter. Rock-Steady management added three people to post social media updates supposedly written by Rex.

Sarah was collecting a mass of what she called "atmospheric stuff" on her travels with the entourage but kept insisting she needed more one-on-one time with Rex; five minutes snatched here and there weren't cutting it. "I still don't know him," she said with an accusing look at Molly. His bio had gone to *New Yorker* researchers, who confirmed everything, but Sarah dismissed it as the same assembly of factoids everyone else in the media was working from: the dad a drinker and gambler who drifted away, the single mom who brought him up waiting on tables in depopulated towns before her tragic car accident, the need to take roughneck jobs in the oil patch straight out of high school, the start up of his own fracking company on borrowed money—all this was known and already stale and the movie wasn't even released yet.

"Where's the life in all this canned stuff?" she demanded, "it's all two dimensional. I need old friends, cousins or somebody who knew him when he was just a kid. What about the supermarket where he was a bagger after school?"

"It burned down," Molly said. "We didn't think a lot of that petty detail was necessary; he only worked there fourteen months."

"What about his co-workers?"

"Scattered to the wind, but feel free to look for them if you can find their names." Molly seriously doubted she would go to that trouble. "Rex has always been the loner type, so I don't think they'd be able to tell you much even if you find them."

"Yes," Sarah had said, "the loner people said was so quiet, what a cliché. They say that about every crazy maniac who kills people in a mall; it doesn't really mean anything." She took out her gold pen, wrote something in her neat handwriting and then drew a line through it. *Sports Illustrated* had already hit the loner angle hard, interviewing every sports psychologist they could find. "Parasites," she said half to herself. She glanced up from her notebook. "Did I say that?" she said sweetly. "I meant staff."

"I know you did," Molly said just as sweetly.

She had thought more than once of telling Sarah no more traveling privileges, but each time she came close Rex casually asked how the story was coming along. It was as if he picked up on the hostile vibes between them.

"She wants more one-on-one time with you," she says now as they drive to AT&T Park for his Major League debut. "She wants more than the bio says, including talking to people from your boyhood."

He is as relaxed as ever, looking out the backseat window at the heavy game traffic. The local media have been reporting scalpers getting playoff prices for tickets. "We don't want her doing that, do we?"

"Sergeant Randall said this morning he's afraid your cover story might spring a leak if there's too much pressure on it."

"So tell her I'll give her more time."

"That's the story of her life," Molly says, tossing her hair. "She always gets what she wants." She is sorry she said it when he doesn't reply.

A mad crush of photographers is at the player's parking lot entrance and the convoy, horns blaring, inches through it amid pleas and shouts to roll down the tinted windows. Noses are flattened on the glass by the pressure of the throng behind; mucous from a red-haired photographer unable to lift his arms in the crush leaves a slow smear like a snail's track across the windows from front to back. "What is the common term for that?" Rex asks. "Snot," Molly replies. Only fragments of shouts from the yammering horde can be made out. "Rex…" "C'mon guy… "Just one…"

Molly and Dickson take the elevator to the owner's luxury box that has theater seats and big-screen TVs. Strangely, he wears You Can't Bust 'Em jeans with turned-up cuffs, a plaid wool shirt and stiff, new lumberjack boots. Molly wonders if the look was his mother's idea. Randall and three bodyguards continue on to the dressing room where Rex is to meet his teammates; the Giants had feebly objected to the security detail, but Molly instructed Dickson tell them that was the way it was. He had lately worked up a tough-guy look for business conflicts, but she thought it only came off as sulky.

"Rex came, he saw, he conquered," Randall remarks, joining her as the Giants warm up on the field, "Everybody is his buddy now, some of the players even asked for his autograph."

"Did he sign them?" she asks.

"Yes," Randall says dryly, "he was very gracious."

"Dickson said only eight thousand or so people in San Jose and Sacramento have actually seen him in person and maybe thirty studio people on top of that, and yet here he is a world celebrity. There's a TV crew here from India."

"Do they play baseball?" he asks.

"Cricket is their game, but they're great movie fans. Lazarus says the Indian distributors are in a bidding war for the movie."

Lazarus and Dickson detach themselves from a knot of Giants executives and come to where they stand near the buffet table with chefs in crisp white smocks and toques. The studio chief is in a dark business suit and no tie but wears a foxy grin. "Woo hoo! Are you ready for some baseball?" They dutifully respond to his high five and then to Dickson's. "I'm a Dodger fan," Lazarus says, "but today I'm pulling for the Giants. Woo hoo."

Molly and Randall drift to the big window that looks down on the jewel of a ballpark. She sees the area she used to sit in with her old boyfriends and a swell of sadness sweeps over her.

"Are you okay?" Randall asks, putting a hand on her shoulder.

"I'm fine," she answers, brushing away a tear. "I was just thinking of something."

Randall is pretty sure what it is. It is his professional opinion those cases will be solved the same time as the Templeton Hall massacre is—meaning never.

"I could walk to my old apartment from here in half an hour." There are some personal things she would like from there, but there has never been a minute since she first saw Rex in the old ladies' café with chintz curtains and fake flowers. Her landlord has the rent in advance for the next six months; in that time she surely will be able to wrench herself free from this never-ending circus for lunch with the friends that Randall warned her against calling for their sakes, even from a burn phone.

The teams take the field for the introduction of notables and the singing of the National Anthem. Molly sees Sarah stand and look at the owner's box from a seat on the first-base side of the field. Ray Cash appears at their side with a plate of crisp chicken drummettes he eats from as he talks. "I told him if his arm feels loose to throw extra hard to scare the pants off them."

"Wow," an awed voice says near them, "the radar gun clocked that one at 112 miles an hour." The play-by-play announcer and color commentator on TV are equally impressed. "This guy is unbelievable," the color guy says.

Cash winks at Molly.

The Dodger's lead-off batter never gets the bat off his shoulder and goes down after five pitches, two of which the TV graphic showed were in the strike zone but got called balls. Anger is stirred in the owner's box and profanity yelled at the screen. The next batter lays down a bunt on the fourth pitch and reaches first on a throwing error. Another strikeout and a towering pop fly end the inning and the crowd cheers as Rex saunters to the dugout.

The Giants score three runs in the inning and a man is on base when Rex picks a bat from the rack. "They say he hits as well as he pitches," the play-by-play man says. "That is doubtful," the color guy replies, "the guy pitched a perfect inning not counting those bad calls." Rex rips the second pitch into the waters of China Basin and a great roar goes up from the crowd. A camera catches Lazarus throwing his arms in the air with joy.

Rex strikes out in his second at bat and leaves the game in the fourth inning when he walks two batters. "He was still throwing as hard but just missing the strike zone," the color announcer says. "So Rex is just human after all."

They leave the ballpark and get a police escort to San Francisco International where the jet waits for the flight to Burbank. Rex is back before the cameras before the game ends. The post-game press conference turns rancorous when he is not there for questions.

"He's got another job," the Giants PR man says weakly into the storm of shouted questions and cries of incredulity.

As they wait in the darkness at the Santa Rosa airport that night for the chopper ride to Bluff Point, Randall says, "I'm going to guess you deliberately walked those two."

Rex gives him a measuring look. "And the strikeout. A few human flaws make you more loveable, right?"

"Is lovable what you want?"

"Doesn't everyone? Is Sarah here?"

"She's in the decoy convoy out front."

"Tell her she can ride with me in the helicopter."

After the film wraps with the traditional party that Rex skips for a Skype session with Mick, Magnificent Pictures books the Dolby Theatre, home of the Oscar ceremonies, for the premiere of *When the Day Comes*. It is a gala with red carpet, searchlights, movie stars alighting from limousines, fans screaming from bleachers, jostling photographers—the whole nine yards, as Lazarus puts it—the biggest opening since *Gone With the Wind*.

A police helicopter circles overhead with the media choppers darting like dragon flies. Marty Cohen, the only Hollywood luminary not invited, had left for Europe, pleading urgent business. "He's not fooling anybody in this town," Lazarus gloated in the reception before the screening, Rex in his Henry Poole tuxedo with peaked lapels had moved through the Hollywood royalty, smiling and nodding as if acknowledging the courtesies of lesser sovereigns. Extravagant compliments were showered on him by industry brown-nosers who advance and recede like a waves on a shore. Taking the red carpet honors at his side, sometimes slipping her arm through his, Sarah was in a Versace sheath the same lavender color as the streak in her hair.

"Sarah looks ridiculous in that dress," Molly tells Randall, who wears a rented tux. Sarah's share of Rex's day has been growing and her own getting smaller, which Molly was sure was the scheming bitch's plan.

"She looks all right to me," Randall says.

"It makes her look like a sausage."

He doesn't need female rivalry right now. The security force is augmented by the studio's and their chatter is in his earpiece. Bomb-sniffing dogs searched the building earlier and the crowd in the bleachers went through metal detectors. Unlike the baseball stadiums where risk analysis had identified threats to guard against, there are random elements to this event that worry him. Beyond the small, protected perimeter, Los Angeles sprawls like a vast amoeba that throbs with ominous possibility.

One of the networks bought the exclusive right to live coverage and Rex stops for a few words with a man and woman who ask the pre-approved questions and thrust microphones in his face for his rehearsed replies.

"Isn't it an amazing night?" the woman asks.

"It's great," enthuses Rex, "really amazing." He tells her that as a beginner he learned a lot about acting from his study of the late great Rupert Kingsley. What a loss to acting, he says. "I hope one day I'll be as good. The guy was amaaazing." The stretched-out vowel is Hollywood's homage to the superiority of British thespians.

"This is by Versace," Sarah tells the excitable man who has asked about her backless and strapless evening gown. Molly is pleased at her plump shoulders. They'll be as solid as Smithfield hams when she's my age, she thinks.

Randall looks up as the helicopter gets louder. "What's that asshole doing?" Finnese asks in his ear. Different voices shout into the earpiece as Rex and Sarah are about to enter the theater entrance. "It's comin' down!" shrills the loudest.

The black-and-white Bell 206 chopper with LAPD on the side skims deafeningly over the bleachers at a tilt, dazzling upturned eyes with its flashing strobe lights. It hits the red carpet with a clang like a hammer on an anvil, crushing the TV interviewers and crew that froze at the sight of death rushing at them. Then it blows up.

Analysis of dozens of smartphone and other videos afterward show the flying blur that is the amputated head of the male interviewer that seems to pursue Rex and Sarah as if to ask just one more question. The separation from his body was so swift that his smile remains. People said afterward it was a miracle a hundred more weren't killed and injured by the crash and the bomb on the helicopter.

CHAPTER 33

"HORRIBLE AS IT WAS," LAZARUS IS SAYING TWO WEEKS LATER, "AND 'HORRIBLE' WAS THE EXACT word most people in our industry use—I personally never experienced anything worse or even close—it was a shot in the arm for the box office. We added a thousand screens for the domestic roll out." His eyes cut to Rex. "But that was the last thing on my mind at the time; in fact, the distribution people had to talk me into it and believe me I was no easy sell."

What a liar, Molly thinks.

They are in the game room at Bluff Point. Beside Lazarus and Aaronson and Goddard the lawyer, Randall, Dickson, Finnese and Sarah are gathered. She is now a constant presence, scribbling notes with her gold pencil and being free with her opinions.

"The blast would have knocked me down if it wasn't for Rex," Sarah says with an adoring look at her lover. Nobody has said much on the subject, but one of their late-night conversation lasted until Sarah came downstairs in a silk kimono for his breakfast tray. Slaving over a hot stove, Margie Hartley had blown a tendril of hair out of her rosy face and cocked an eyebrow at Molly.

"Do they know any more about him?" Randall asks Finnese.

"Same as before. Solid cop and good family man kayos his wife in a big blowup before his shift, shoots the co-pilot and takes the chopper down. His timing was off by ten seconds."

"He just flipped out, that's the best they can do?" Randall asks.

"Unless they're holding out something, and I can't see why they would with all the pressure on them to produce."

"No luck yet on the bomb?"

"They admit the log wasn't kept up the way they should."

"Somebody put it in the helicopter before Thorgeson got in," Randall explains. There are sharp intakes of breath. "He wasn't carrying anything but a clipboard."

"You mean it's some kind of conspiracy?" Lazarus says. Understanding dawns. "So that's what's with all this big-time security thing you got going. Who's behind it?"

Rex nods at Randall to explain.

"That's the problem, we don't know."

"We should have been told about this," Goddard says. "When word leaks this wasn't just a cop who snapped but an assassination attempt, a thousand lawyers will sue the studio for negligence the following day."

"Shut up, Goddard," Lazarus snaps.

"Why wasn't I told about a conspiracy?" Sarah says with a glare at Molly.

Molly has been wan and pensive since the premiere, but Sarah's indignation focuses her mind. "Didn't you ever think it's funny how we come and go?" she says. "All these armed men and that prison fence around the place? You're a journalist, aren't you supposed to be curious?" Sarah's look at Rex asks if he is going to let Molly talk to her like that.

"Good question," Rex says as if admiring a long putt on the Golf Channel, his latest interest.

Sarah is astonished. "You… you…" she stutters. "You're a fucking celebrity, the biggest!" Her glance sweeps the room for confirmation. "Everybody knows the world is full of crazy people."

"That's the defense, Goddard," Lazarus says exultantly. "He's not only a celebrity, he's on course to become the biggest ever in the history of the world. The right lawyer can make case law with this, and I'm speaking as one myself. We had a bunch of security that night; you might even say excessive security. The right lawyer could argue requiring more would be unreasonable restraint on something… he'd figure out just what. Did anyone sue the Boston Marathon over those two Muslims? You're not the right lawyer, Goddard, but you could find who is."

"Do you know how much money we'd be on the hook for if we lost?" Goddard asks.

"That's defeatist talk, Goddard. Leave the money to people smarter than you."

As they talk and the despondent Sarah blows her nose softly into a handkerchief with hurt looks at Rex, Randall's mind goes back to the scene that night. He hit the ground and took Molly down with him, thanks to some instinct still alive from Iraq, and they weren't hit by the metal that slashed through the air as if a ship-of-the-line in the days of sail had cut loose with grapeshot. The concussion wave from the explosion sucked the air from their lungs.

"Meet me at the lead car," he yelled when lifted his head. She was dazed and uncomprehending as he helped her up. "The lead car," he shouted over the ringing in his ears. "Tell them we'll meet them on the other side. Go now!"

He watched her stumble off as wailing rose all around, another reminder of Iraq and the mosque blown up a short block from where they patrolled. His own legs were wobbly as he made for the entrance. The air seeming to thrum from the explosions. The lobby doors had been blown open and people cut down by the razor-sharp slivers of glass lay in their own gore. Those still upright but about to fall were in shock, blood welling from the wounds that darkened their fancy clothes. The people inside the theater were on their feet shouting and screaming as plaster dust drifted from the ceiling like a light snow. He spotted Rex on the stage hurrying Sarah for the wing and and caught up outside with his gun out. They stood over Sarah trembling on the ground until the up-armored M1097 Humvee rolled up with Molly ashen-faced in the back. They made for the airport, passing sirening police cars and ambulances in the other lanes headed for the theater.

Lazarus opens the bulging leather satchel Aronson carries and pulls out movie scripts, one after another. "The Giants are going on a long road trip, so I thought you might have a chance to look at these when you're traveling or in hotels. They're the ten best our readers came up with from the submission pile. We got full financing for whichever one you pick, no questions asked by any of our backers. Just between us, we're cutting back on partnerships for self financing."

"I'm not interested in another cheesy CGI epic where I swing a sword," Rex says lazily.

"Thanks for your input, that makes it easier," Lazarus says, removing three scripts from the pile and returning them to the satchel. "That leaves a psychological thriller; an action-thriller like the Bourne movies; a crazy-genius thing like *A Beautiful Mind* that would let you show your acting genius and win us an Oscar, guaranteed; a man-against-nature survival opus; and so on—your choice."

Rex takes a nut from a dish, casually tosses it up in the air and catches it in his teeth. "I'll take a look," he says, chewing. He ambles out the door.

When it closes behind him, Dickson stands, shoots French cuffs and tells Lazarus, "We'll get back to you on that." He has become even more self-important since Rock-Steady made him a vice president with a big bump in salary and deal points. "Molly," he says in the deeper voice he now uses, "could I see you and Sergeant Randall?"

"No," she says firmly. She sees Lazarus and Aronson exchange secret smiles as she leaves; little things show they find the new Dickson as obnoxious as everyone else. Randall, who has taken to wordlessly waving him aside like a gnat, does not bother to reply.

Esther lays in wait for him upstairs with an angry look. "She might not show it to you, but my daughter is a bundle of nerves," she says accusingly. "She worries all the time."

"We all do," he says.

"We want our normal lives back. When does this end?"

"You know, Esther, I ask myself that from time to time."

"Abby says you can be so sarcastic."

"Well, that's my answer."

"It's not a good one."

"Best I can do."

He walks away so as not to give in to a mad urge to squeeze that scrawny neck until her eyes bulge. Everybody is on edge. Things were serious enough before, but now the security guys are grim; one told him always waiting for something bad to happen reminded him of Falluja.

"Tell your mother to stop bugging me," he tells Abigail.

"What did she say?"

"You're a bundle of nerves."

She hugs him. "We all are." Michael and Martin look up from the floor where they are playing with their toys. "Except them," she says. "They like to wave from the balcony at the photographers." An item about neighborhood ire over Camp Rex had appeared in a gossip column, and that brought paparazzi shooting with long lenses from land, sea and air.

Molly is liking one of the scripts, a romantic comedy that takes her mind off the horror at the premiere, when a tap comes at her door; it is Sarah, weepy and red-eyed. "Molly, can we be friends again?"

"Like before?"

"I blame myself for scewing things up between us. I'm really, really sorry I've been so fucking snotty. That's not me."

Molly thinks it is exactly her, but invites her in to sit down anyway. "You're upset." She waits for the sudden storm of sobbing to pass.

"Yes," Sarah says, tears spilling down her cheeks. "It's Rex, he's so different now."

"You mean after sleeping with him?"

"That's never been a thing for me before. I've always been fuck-and-run, no big deal."

"You're going to tell me Rex is a ten in bed," Molly says. She hopes her envy and jealousy don't show on her face.

"He's a twenty!" She sobs again, harder, as if another defense had given way and deeper sadness engulfs her. "But that's not it. He was so warm and tender when it was just us, but you saw him in the meeting. He was so cold and distant then and... af-af-afterward."

"What happened?" Molly says, all business.

"I followed him to the music studio—I had to almost trot he was going so fast—but the door was closed right in my face! I'm supposed to see you from now on."

"See me about what?"

"A fucking appointment."

"You mean..."

"No, no—for anything." She is crying more, her handkerchief sodden. "I don't mean anything more to him than..." Sarah searches for some comparison. "...than that dust bunny under the chair."

Molly bends to look, glad for the chance to hide her gloating, and goes to the in-house phone to catch Dickson before he leaves. "Fire the cleaning service and get another one," she tells him.

There is unfriendly silence. "O-kaaay," he says at last. The way he draws out the word gives the message he is worlds above that now, but will indulge her this one last time. "I'd like to talk to you..."

"Send me a memo." If they are now a bureaucracy, so be it. She hangs up and turns back to Sarah. "Is this going to be in your profile?"

"No, of course not," Sarah says indignantly. "I love him... I can't tell you how much."

"Was there anything else?"

"Are we still... friends?" Sarah sniffles.

"Honestly, I don't think we were like you and Gretchen before you got Rex to fire her."

"We didn't need a makeup artist anymore."

"We could have found a job for her."

Sarah drops her eyes. "Can I go on the new submarine tonight?" she asks in a little voice.

"I'm afraid not, seating is limited. If you're going to Chicago, we'll see you there."

It is like Sarah was expecting the refusal. She lifts her chin and walks out the door. It isn't quite slammed, but she does close it harder than necessary.

Long after darkness falls, the traveling party is rowed against the tide to the new submarine almost invisible in the black water. Finnese is along for the ride to the rendezvous with the Monterey fishing boat that will ferry them to Fisherman's Wharf. The Golden Gate Bridge in the fog is illuminated like a vast movie set for a gothic movie. "Is this cool or what?" Finnese says delightedly as the sub gains speed and slips underwater. "We could pop up anywhere." This is the first time Randall has seen him show anything but a cool professionalism.

"It's a good thing nobody's claustrophobic," Randall says.

"I am a little," Molly admits. "Actually, a lot." She closes her eyes and concentrates on the deep breathing she learned in yoga. That has helped keep the movie premiere from invading her every thought; but she still worries that she's a prime candidate for PTSD.

"One of the FBI guys is wondering if there might be a connection between these attacks and what went down at Templeton Hall," Finnese tells Randall in a low voice.

"Like I said, that was a matter of time."

"Not necessarily, the guy was doing some what-if thinking over a cup of coffee. He pointed out what both have in common is out-of-the-blue and callous disregard for human life. It was off-the-cuff like guys do when they're shooting the breeze; I don't think he's passed it on to a supervisor."

"Wait until they find out what they have in common is me. He's going to remember that conversation."

"Yeah, well... I won't."

The next sixteen days on the road are a blur of travel and hotel rooms. Rex is 3-0 with two saves at the end of it, but has perfected the look of not quite being the best pitcher who ever put on spikes. He fills the bases with walks when it seems he has lost control of his fastball. He paces around the mound, taking off his hat and mopping his face with his sleeve. Then it seems he reaches deep for the three-and-two heater on the corner that strikes out the batter just as the manager is about to yank him for a reliever. He even gives up a grand slam in Yankee Stadium with the Giants ahead by eleven; he is pulled and leaves the game kicking at the grass.

"I just didn't have it today," he says in the brief appearance at the post-game press conference. Sarah sits with the other journalists, pale and her eyes begging him to look at her. The frustrated sportswriters yell questions as he ducks out with a grin and a friendly wave. His modesty endears him to baseball fans as far away as Japan. Bags of fan mail collect at Rock-Steady where interns send replies from a menu of choices, including messages to the sick and dying. Each bears a photo of Rex and an authentic-looking autopen signature. Giants merchandise with his name and number fly off the shelves.

The Giants make it to the playoffs but lose to the Washington Nationals; Rex's two shutouts are the only wins the Giants get. After the home run in his first at bat, he is walked each time he comes to the plate. Randall sees his consoling presence in the clubhouse after the final game, mingling freely for a change, showing his regular guy side and cheering up downcast teammates.

"We'll get 'em next year, guys," he repeats over and over, pounding shoulders and punching arms. He even gets the catcher Buddy Grant in a headlock for a playful noogie. Faces light up and everyone agrees that Rex pitching a full season means they'll go all the way to the World Series next season.

There are a number of events scheduled to celebrate the team's near-miss at the World Series that must be fitted in with the Hollywood galas that are a part of the awards seasons. Invitations come from the Academy Awards, People's Choice, Golden Globes, Critics' Choice, Screen Actors Guild, Grammy and a string of lesser events. Abigail nags Randall to buy a tuxedo instead of renting each time. "I keep hoping Rex will tell me my presence is not necessary," he tells her. He has always been lukewarm about parties but now detests them.

"I don't know how to be a celebrity," Rex tells Molly one day. He is at the wheel of a seventy-one-foot ketch returning from a day's sail outside the Golden Gate Bridge. A famous photographer rides with them, three cameras around his neck for close-ups and wide-angled shots of Rex with the city and the tawny hills of Marin as backdrops for a spread in GQ. He wears sunglasses and is in designer jeans and a white turtleneck sweater under a blue windbreaker; his hair is artfully ruffled by the wind. Molly has no doubt the pictures will turn out beautifully, the god-like skipper lit by the setting sun off the blue water, the white sails, the hovering gulls.

"Just be yourself," she says.

"No, I've seen on TV there are exact ways to enter a room when people are applauding. You point at someone in the crowd like you're surprised and delighted and keep walking. Other times you put your palms together and give a little bow like you are honoring the people honoring you. There are a lot of little tricks I need to learn. I don't think my waving is right."

Molly learns there are people who coach celebrity demeanor, and a spry former Londoner comes highly recommended. "Modesty is the key," explains Ian Oliver. He is a talkative sort, older than he looks, with a tipped-up nose and the lower-class accent now more fashionable in Britain than the posh one. His father was a member of Herman's Hermits and Ian had studied entertainer mannerisms in childhood until obscurity reclaimed dad and the rest of the group.

"You can't let people think you're too far above them," he tells Molly, "which is a real danger in Rex's case as anyone with eyes can see. You want to seem above them, yes, but not so much that they can't imagine being in your shoes and waving themselves if a few things in life had gone another way. You know, different parents, different body shape, smarter, better looking."

"You mean if they were different people," Molly says.

"Well, yes, you might put it that way. But everyone can imagine, can't they? That's where celebrity magic comes in." He teaches Rex the stagecraft of the famous: the clasped hands with a fluid bow from the waist, the arms spread wide and head lifted when the applause is rapturous, the shy glance at the floor when goes on too long, the wry look when it becomes sycophantic, also the soft-shoe step entering a talk-show set with the house band playing. Rex learns every permutation of celebrity protocol,

"He's the best student I ever had," Ian says when the lessons are over.

"Somehow I was hoping he'd be the second best," Molly says wistfully.

"My second best—I won't mention his or her name because of the confidentiality agreement—doesn't even come close, luv."

Rex's appearance on *Talkin' 'Bout*, the afternoon show featuring five catty women who bicker about current events, shows the mastery he has gained. As the band plays music from his blockbuster hit, he does the heel-and-toe to the sofa where he whirls each of the ladies in a dance step and then plumps down in the middle of the sofa with a broad aren't-we-having-fun grin. The ecstatic studio audience won't be silenced until he stands and lifts his arms up and down in the cool-it signal that Ian taught him.

"It's great to be here," he tells the women, taking his seat again. "I love you," he calls to the audience, bringing on more cheers that he must stand and silence it as before. When they are finally calmed down again, he looks at his wristwatch with fake panic.

"Is it that late? Gotta go!"

He pretends to leave the set as the ladies—two whites, one black, a Chinese and a Native American—break up with shrieks of laughter and Nooooo comes from the crowd. Rex is coaxed back to the sofa, throws an arm over the back and says, "Now, where were we?"

Molly and Randall watch from the control room. "He looks like he's been in show business all his life," she says.

The women lean toward him, as soft as butter melting in the glow of his glamorous presence. He gives the speeded-up version of his background, soon to appear in an autobiography by a wordsmith hired by Rock-Steady and titled *From the Oilfields to Now*. It has a first printing of five hundred thousand, but nobody thinks that will be enough.

"And you learned about oil drilling by hands-on work?" the maternal co-host asks, cocking her head and lifting a finger to adjust her eyeglasses.

"Somebody told me I had, like, a doctorate in shale oil. I wish I had! Instead, I learned from every mistake I made, which were plenty." Murmurs of approval rise from the audience at this confession of human failing.

"But look at you now," exclaims Peggy Wong. "A big movie in your first role and a star pitcher."

"I've been lucky," Rex says humbly.

"I'd say it's more than that, baby," croons Destiny Jackson, making goo-goo eyes at him.

Ahhh, the crowd agrees, there being no doubt what she is referring to. The women pepper him with fan magazine questions.

"Has your heart ever been broken?" asks Debbi Hawk Flies Schmidt.

Rex looks into the camera with sadness. "Hasn't everyone?" Molly absurdly has the impression he is talking directly to her, a feeling repeated in millions of households where the show is streamed live. Molly is sure somewhere Sarah has begun crying,

Norma Deen, the maternal co-host, moves quickly to fill the silence that falls. "Where did you get all your brains and ambition?"

"I don't know about the brains," Rex scoffs, "but I got the ambition from my mom. She wanted me to go as far as I could." A long burst of applause follows.

"That terrible tragedy at the premiere," Norma says tenderly, "how did you feel?"

"At the time?" Rex says, "Scared out of my wits. Afterward, awful, just awful." For a few seconds it seems he is too overcome to continue. "The man must have been insane. They tell me any crowd of people would have served his purpose."

Randall shakes his head in admiration. Like everything else Rex does, he is a superlative liar.

CHAPTER 34

REX AND HIS ENTOURAGE ARE BACK IN WASHINGTON IN ROOMS AT THE HAY-ADAMS HOTEL. "I FOR-get, why are we in D.C.?" Randall asks Molly in the Off the Record Grill. A framed caricature of a long-dead chief justice smiles down on their table as if about to render a favorable decision.

"He doesn't say, but we obey."

"You sound like O.J. Simpson's lawyer."

"This being Washington, my guess is somebody in politics wants to talk to him." Molly has a ninety-dollar glass of Gaja Barbaresco merlot before her. This is how the one-percenters live, she thinks.

Dickson flew in with his new assistant, Linda Atwood, an early-thirtyish woman with short dark hair in a tailored gray suit and silk blouse who looks corporate to her fingertips. She has eyes as cold as an alpine lake and speaks in a clipped way as if words were money and she was putting away for retirement. She strikes Molly as a health fanatic and probable germophobe who shuns makeup except for a pale shade of pink lipstick; a thin gold necklace is her only jewelry.

"Hi," she says to Molly in voice as icy as her looks when Dickson introduces her as a new deputy assistant vice president at Rock-Steady. "We got her from Goldman Sachs," he says proudly. "Princeton and Wharton before that."

First impressions always work best in casting, and if an agency was looking for someone to play a ruthless Medusa type clicking in high heels across corporate floors I'd send her, Molly thinks. "Nice to meet you," she says as they shake hands. "This is Sergeant Randall, our head of security."

Apparently, Dickson has not been clear about where Randall fits in the scheme of things, and the title says insignificant underling. "Yes," she says, jerking a nod but not offering her hand.

Randall nods back, amused. If there is a table of organization, as he suspects, Dickson has obviously put his box somewhere in the limbo of middle management. A clothes horse now, Dickson has taken to look-at-me bow ties and power suspenders and wears his hair slicked back. Randall believes Dickson doesn't see the threat in this pale-eyed woman. She will have his job within a year and would be already sizing up prey higher in the organization.

"Linda spent a lot of time with the Goldman Sachs team in the Capitol," Dickson says. "She'll be going with us to the meeting this afternoon."

"No, she won't," Randall says. "I want Finnese's people to vet her first, number one. And, number two, Rex likes 'em short with a minimum of people. I'm not even sure he wants you there."

Dickson's face flushes and Ms. Atwood instantly recalibrates her understanding of the power relationships. Molly detects a movement that slightly reduces the space between her and Randall.

"I've gone to all the meetings," Dickson objects hotly. "This one is really big." He looks around as if afraid of eavesdroppers and drops his voice to a whisper. "They want him to run for president. I sent him an email."

"Did you copy it to me?" Molly asks.

"I'm pretty sure I did." It is obvious he is lying.

"Well, for some reason I didn't get it. Send me the email." Dickson gives a surly nod.

"I'll talk to Rex and get back to you," Randall says.

"I want to be there," Dickson insists. "I want to make the case for Linda and me."

"Sorry," Randall says.

They leave Dickson seething under Linda's cool gaze and ride the elevator to Rex's penthouse suite where the view across the street is the White House. He shows them an email saying Mick broke his left femur and the tour timed for the release of the album is off.

"I guess he's lucky it wasn't his hip, a man his age," Rex says. "How did it happen?"

"He was walking on the sand at Larry Ellison's island in Hawaii and his leg just gave out under him. Amazing, a man that fit. Maybe we'll release the album without the tour, or I could do it on my own." A magazine poll a couple of days ago showed he was as well known as Donald Trump, now said to be writing his memoirs with the help of writers who are fired one after the other.

"Dickson has a new assistant," Molly says now. "He wants to bring her to this political meeting."

"Is she necessary?"

"I wouldn't say so."

"How about Dickson, should we have him sit in?"

"Let's see how serious this is first," Molly says. Dickson will think twice before he tries another end run, she thinks.

"Fine." Rex turns back to the *Washington Post*.

"It would be interesting to find out what time Mick broke his leg," Randall says afterward.

"The time?" Molly asks. "What difference does it make?"

"His people don't know me from Adam, could you find out?"

She calls his room later. "He broke his leg at 3:05 in the afternoon. Satisfied?"

"What time did Dickson send Rex that email about the people who want Rex to run for president? Our time, not Hawaiian."

She checks her smartphone. "He's already sent me the copy. Let's see—wow—a minute before."

"I'll leave you to think about that. See you at the meeting."

Four middle-aged men whose commanding bearing says they are accustomed to submission arrive punctually at Rex's suite. The CVs they sent in advance identified them as men with influence in and out of government, but even without those credentials their manner would deliver a strong power-broker message. Three of the four are billionaires; they are short, tall, even taller and tallest—sort of like the music scale, Molly thinks. Randall pats them down for weapons before introductions are made. "It's because of the premiere," he apologizes.

They nod and murmur understandingly. Don't blame him at all, would have somebody do it themselves, horrible tragedy, where are all these maniacs coming from? They all sit, Rex throwing a leg over the arm of the chair as usual. He wears his baseball jersey, pre-faded jeans, and moccasins without socks. If he wanted to give a relaxed impression in the face of a powerhouse lineup like this, he has succeeded.

He waves off their compliments about baseball. "I understand you want to talk about something else."

The others turn their eyes to Josiah Walden, a ruddy outdoor type with curly gray hair and smile lines who looks like he'd be at equally at ease taking a horse over a hedge or at the wheel of a sailboat in heavy weather.

"You know how screwed up things are in this country," he says.

"I read the papers," Rex replies in his easy-going way. "Watch the news."

"Baxter there is a Republican like me, Ronald and Morgan are Democrats. There aren't a lot of things we agree on except the nation is in trouble and needs a strong leader the people can get behind. We're not going to get that person the way the two parties are set up; both are in the hands of their extremes. We need somebody voters know and trust, someone with a big name to lead a third party."

"And that would be me?" Rex says.

"If you're interested."

After a long pause. "I might be."

The men quietly let out breaths they have been holding. Randall and Molly exchange looks. The roller coaster is climbing for another Loop-de-Loop.

"You don't need to know much about the inner workings of the system," Walden says. "We have enough know-how in this room to show you the ropes and if there is something we don't know, we know the people who do. This third party, call it the Good Citizens Party until we come up with another name, would have as good a shot at winning the Electoral College as either the Republican or Democrat nominees, people are that fed up with the endless crap in Washington."

With a glance toward him, Walden hands off to Ronald Robosh. He is a narrow-faced, ascetic-looking man in rimless glasses who Molly sizes up as dry and humorless. She would cast him as the buzz-kill school principal who gets introduced to a candy brand and is so won over after a taste that he joins the kids dancing around the room.

"We have done polling that shows the right person would have an excellent chance," he says, "but it can't be someone who has spent his life in our poisonous politics; those people acquire enemies like a ship does barnacles. They are spent forces by the time they're ready to run for the White House; a new face with a carefully crafted message will be a breath of fresh air."

"What is the message?" Rex asks.

"We need a fresh start," says Baxter Vargas, known in Silicon Valley circles for a mind somewhere between a sponge and steel trap; he soaks up data and makes fast decisions. "We need a charismatic figure that can blow out the cobwebs and get this country on the move again." He is slender and the tallest, a rail-thin fitness buff by the look of him. He yanks at his tie as if by nature he's an open-collar guy. "In the interest of transparency, we'll say straight out we had your background examined for skeletons."

"I got a ticket for speeding once," Rex admits with a shy smile that Molly and Randall know is purest actor's artifice.

"We found that. Doing ninety-five on the interstate; other than that, clean as a whistle."

"I was always too busy to get in trouble," Rex says, the smile leaving his face for introspection. "Dad was long gone and mom was sick a lot. I had to grow up in a hurry." It's straight out of the bogus bio. Randall wondered at the time if Finnese and his people weren't laying it on too thick and did manage to talk them out of the Eagle Scout embellishment.

The fourth man speaks, Morgan Kessler, a short, heavy-jawed man with thick eyebrows and a paunch that says the only gym he sees is from a car window. "I told these guys you sounded too good to be true and to dig deeper." Randall had Googled all of them as soon as their CVs arrived. Kessler gives away his money as fast as he makes it, the reason he is the non-billionaire. "Lazarus was there before us, did he tell you? He's a smart guy; nobody pulls the wool over his eyes. His people couldn't find anything either."

They bat around why a new face is needed, a rejuvenating someone to shake the country out of the doldrums. The military has been weakened, the borders are a farce, the national debt is a time bomb, the economy is like it had another heart attack, failed states, Muslim terrorism—the list is long and familiar... and tedious. People have been talking about these things forever, Molly thinks, and it's a big turnoff except for politicians and people like Sarah who make livings writing or talking about them. How Sarah would love to be a fly on the wall at this historic moment; she still calls every day, leaving messages. Her story is late thanks to a horrendous writer's block and there's pressure from the magazine. Could Rex please, please help her? She needs just a half an hour more alone with him.

After forty-five minutes the sales pitch is over and the men settle back in chairs for the verdict. "You guys can do a lot better than me," he says after a moment, "I'm just a jock and actor."

It's the perfect thing to say, Randall thinks.

"You're a celebrity," Walden emphasizes. "That's everything these days."

"Politics is show business for ugly people, so they say,'" Kessler remarks. "That gives you a huge head start over anybody in sight."

"You're better known than Arnold Schwarzenegger at his peak, and he would have gone on to be president if he wasn't born in Austria," Vargas says.

Robosh takes off the rimless glasses and massages the indentation on the bridge of his nose. "This is almost a no-brainer. You can be the most powerful man in the world. We'd have a government-in-waiting with policies and plans; all you have to do is make the right noises in the campaign and take the oath of office."

"A trained monkey could do the job," Kessler agrees. "Look at the string of mediocrities we've had; they wouldn't last a day in any well run company."

Rex stands at last and rotates his muscular neck to loosen it. "Thanks, guys, you sure gave me something to think about."

Walden is beaming like he dropped a stag at three hundred yards with a 100-grain bullet. "So you'll seriously consider it?"

"No, I said I'd think about it," Rex says, "seriously consider is a horse of a different color." His increasing command of slang now extends back in time now. "Give us a few days, okay?"

They grasp the offered straw and file out the room in good humor. Garza pauses at the door to hold up crossed fingers and Rex makes a funny pushing motion that says, C'mon, get outta here already. But he is all business when the door closes.

"It's ridiculous," Molly says with a toss of her thick red hair.

"Why?" he says imperturbably.

"Right out of the blue? The election is fourteen months away! The Democrats and Republicans have been working on it for years. They're totally organized and everything."

"Sergeant?" he asks.

"If you want the job, those guys are right. The parties are pushing the same old tired faces, a governor and a senator. A lot of people are turned off and won't bother voting, but you could get us off the sofa."

"But what do you know about the country?" Molly cries. "Your memory only goes back to that... that horrible thing that happened."

"I don't need to know much according to those gentlemen," Rex says. "They handle everything."

Randall knows he has already made up his mind; he probably did it as soon as he read Dickson's email. Mick's broken leg eliminated a problem like the plane that hit the building. Rex won't be at the Giants training camp in the spring, he will be on the campaign trail making speeches and kissing babies. The Secret Service will handle security then, so adios to keeping an eye on him like Camael wants. Nobody ever got around to what we should do if Rex turned out to be under Satan's control.

As Randall now knows he is.

And whatever those men are thinking, he won't be a mere figurehead president doing what they tell him.

CHAPTER 35

"SO IT LOOKS LIKE WE'RE GOING TO SEE HISTORY MADE," MOLLY SAYS OUTSIDE IN THE CORRIDOR.

"You don't like the idea."

"Even though you were encouraging him, it doesn't look like you feel like handsprings yourself."

"I wasn't encouraging him, just telling it like it is. Tell me what you're thinking." He thinks it's time he had more company in his circle of hell.

"Six months ago I was checking out old ladies for a commercial and look what's happened since. My life is something between Cinderella and a Coen brothers movie."

"You don't know the half of it."

Molly is wary. "What do you mean?"

"Let's take a walk around the block."

It's a gray day under heavy clouds spitting rain that could turn to sleet if the temperature keeps dropping. Three different groups across the street demonstrate with chants that cancel each other out. Matching his pace with her tomboy stride, Molly waits for him to speak.

"Want to know why I was interested in when Mick broke his leg?" Randall asks.

"Why?"

"Rex broke it."

"No, really. Why did you want to know?"

"Remember when you and he left that hotel in San Francisco and those thugs were coming at you?"

Molly shudders. "Of course."

"Then they started fighting?"

"Yeah?"

"Rex did that."

Molly stops and looks at him.

"I tried to talk about it at the time, but you didn't want to hear it because you're a rational person. I used to be myself, so I understood. The plane that crashed into the building in Dubai? Rex did that."

Molly has the poleaxed look of a cage fighter who took a kick to the jaw. "I don't understand what you're saying."

"He made Cohen fall down at the Polo Lounge."

"How could he do that?" She stares into his face. "It was an accident, I saw it happen."

"Rex did it to humiliate Cohen because he's an asshole."

"Rex was at the table with me and Lazarus and the others. It isn't possible. "

"How possible is what you said before? Six months ago Rex walks into a café and look at him now. He's going to run for president and win."

"It's not the same thing," Molly says. "I've got to sit down," They find a bench beneath a bare cherry tree. Small birds with feathers puffed up hop and peck at invisible things on the sidewalk.

"Rex has special powers," Randall says.

"You mean like in DC Comics?" She feels what she knows is a hysteria rising in her.

"If that helps you to get what I'm saying, yes."

There's a keen wind and he hunches on the bench and jams his hands in pants pockets; they should have put on heavy coats before coming out. He looks drawn in the winter light; she notices more gray in his hair and the lines in his face are deeper. It's all this killing pressure, she thinks, it never lets up. "No, I want to know what you mean."

"I tried to tell you this before."

"Tell me what?" she demands. Molly is so intense she doesn't notice the cold.

"The old guy, the one I said was an angel?"

"Oh, that. You were pulling my leg."

"Telepathy explained how I knew my kids were in danger, that's what you said."

"I haven't thought about it since."

"He warned me Rex was created by Satan."

"Oh, my God, Alex," she cries out, "that's just crazy."

"Life would be a lot simpler if it was. Camael is his name."

"Whose name?" Molly asks. Both are aware she is inching away from him on the bench.

"The angel." Randall is staring straight ahead. "But I've been thinking maybe I'm wrong and he's one of Satan's, too. His job might be to mislead me."

After a moment, she asks, "Do voices tell you that?"

"You can knock that shit off," Randall says curtly. "I'm not nuts."

"But don't they always think that… the mentally ill? That they're not?"

"I tell you what's crazy, sitting out here in this cold. Let's go back inside."

Molly wonders if she should. What if the voices started up and he got violent? Traffic is heavy but she would run out into the street and hope the cars stop. But he doesn't look that kind of crazy; it's more like sad desperation.

She walks warily alongside, aware of the cold now and hugging herself. They go into the lobby warmth and down to Off the Record, where they order hot toddies. The chatter around them is all about politics. Both lost in thought, they do not speak until the waitress returns with the drinks.

"Did you have religion growing up?" Randall asks.

"I was a Catholic—I still am, I suppose, but I don't go to mass. The patriarchy thing and all those priests molesting boys."

"Pope Francis talks a lot about the Devil. He says he's not a symbol but is alive and well."

"I read something about that." The pope in his big hat addressing crowds was not something that interested her, but she was glad they picked someone who wasn't another Italian, or dry like that German. The snarky article said the idea of Lucifer was so medieval and embarrassing it made modernizing elements in the Vatican uncomfortable, and they ignored it like the Pontiff farting in public.

"What we originally came up with—Camael and me—was Rex got loose at the last minute and Satan is trying to get him back under control. Or kill him if that isn't possible and start all over. That what Rex thinks, too… or did."

"You talked to him about this?" Molly says with amazement.

"At the time he was afraid he was going to be the key player in some monstrous plan and wasn't going along with it. Now, I'm getting this feeling he's changed his mind."

"What's the evil plan?" Molly asks. Her stomach is twisted in a knot.

"All the big religions and probably a lot of the small ones say time will come to an end, the only questions being when and how we'll know it's coming. It will be bad versus good for the last time, God's forces against Lucifer's. The Devil loses, but there's hell to pay before it's over."

"I'm going to look this up," Molly says, taking her smartphone from her purse. "What do I search for?"

"End Times," Randall says.

"Look at all this stuff," she marvels, looking up from the Google website.

"There were half a billion hits when I looked it up," Randall says. "It's got to be millions more by now."

"It's the same as Judgment Day, which I have heard of. Oh, look, somebody named Harold Camping who owned radio stations predicted it would begin May 21, 2011. A lot of people sold everything to get ready; he got a ton of money from them. Five months of fire, brimstone and plagues were supposed to come with millions dying each day. Then on October 21, 2011, the final destruction of the world was supposed to happen. When it didn't, he said oops, I made a mistake and need to study the Bible more. Then he went silent and died at ninety-two."

"I was a beat cop at the time," Randall says. "I don't remember the lieutenant mentioning this at roll call, so I'm guessing what you mean by 'a lot of people' were a few snake handlers in backwoods." He inhales the honey and spices in the hot toddy before sipping.

"I'm just reading what it says," Molly says intently, still scrolling. "It all has to do with chaos in the Middle East. Israel is destroyed in a war and Jesus returns." She clicks some more. "This other website says after Israel is destroyed, the Twelfth Imam, the Muslim messiah, shows up to force the world to submit to Islam." She puts away her smartphone and gives him a level look. "You don't believe this stuff."

"I talked to a preacher who told me there are signs that point to End Times, the Middle East being where it all kicks off. I'd have him tell you himself, but his church burned down and he was in it. The only other person I mentioned this to was the abbot of the monastery in Oregon, and he's gone missing. So is my friend, Camael the angel, for that matter."

Her eyes widen. "Oh, my God."

"So if you throw in the people who are after Rex, Camael and all the rest of it—the plane, Jagger's leg—yeah, it sure looks like something weird is going on, and, yes, Satan is in on it in my humble opinion." Randall takes another sip; the Jack Daniel warms his insides. "They say this is good for colds, but I can think of one or two other things." Liquor was called Dutch courage once, he reflects, but you can't say stuff like that anymore.

"Why would Rex even want to be president?" Molly asks plaintively. "He's got everything already."

"You're joking, right? It's the most important job in the world. You can start a war big enough to make the world unlivable except for a few things on the bottom of the ocean. That happened when the big meteor hit Earth; it was lights out for almost everything." Was that the first round between good and evil, he wonders. Is this the finale?

Molly puts hands to ears. "Please don't talk like that."

"Welcome to my life."

"You haven't told Abby this?" She would have said something.

"Good Lord, no. She'd tell her mother and who knows what would happen when Esther got that mouth working." He wouldn't wish this on Abby anyway; in the right mood one of the twins skinning a knee could send her up the wall.

"Shouldn't the government be told? We're right here!"

"Go ahead, you have my permission."

Molly thinks about this. "They'd think I was on crack."

"They sure wouldn't let you near Rex when he runs for president. You'd be in a locked ward to keep you from making trouble." Or maybe, he thinks darkly, they'd go for a more permanent solution.

"I don't think he will, do you?" she says, hope in her voice. "He's flattered, of course, but it's just talk… don't you think?"

Randall slowly shakes his head. "The movie, the baseball, and the rock tour were to make him famous enough to run for president. You heard what those guys said about celebrity—media and brands are all that count today. Make a name in sports or entertainment and transfer the buzz to politics and the next thing is you're hearing Hail to the Chief."

"It's like you're saying someone like... oh, let's say Lady Gaga could win just because she's famous.."

"They could be elected to the House or Senate on their names alone, but they've got too much baggage for the White House. Rex doesn't, we gave him a bio Abe Lincoln would be proud of. He'd be a blank slate for people to pin hopes on; picture what he'd look like in the spotlights in a huge stadium when he accepts the nomination. The crowd on its feet roaring their love, Rex raising his arms as if blessing them."

Molly thinks about it. "The country would go wild for him."

CHAPTER 36

"I'D LIKE TO DO SOMETHING DIFFERENT," ABBY SAYS RESTLESSLY. "THIS IS A NICE PLACE AND ALL that, beautiful and so on and the kids love it, but as mom says we never go anywhere." They have paused the nature movie on the birds of Micronesia that is putting Randall to sleep.

"Your mother…" he flares. Automatic lockdown engages his jaw, stopping the words before they spring like tigers from a cage.

"I know you're mad when you breathe through your nose like that," she says. "You got out all the time going to those baseball games and Hollywood, but I haven't left Bluff Point since we got here."

"Believe me, that was work not pleasure."

"I long just to look in a shop window; I know that's hard for a man to imagine. Or go to a restaurant in San Anselmo or San Rafael—just the two of us—they're close and we wouldn't need all that bodyguard hassle. Or Tiburon is just down the road."

"I'm not very good company right now."

"I know, sweetheart. Mom says you're wound tighter than a spring, and have you noticed how much gray is in your hair?"

"Could we agree on something?" Randall asks.

"You're breathing through your nose again. What?"

"No more telling me what your mom says."

"She loves you!" Abby cries.

"Deal?"

Abby sighs but he knows that does not mean agreement, merely that the discussion is postponed to another time.

"Finnese wants bodyguards to go where we go," he says, "and I agree. We can't let our defenses down even a little." Ground sensors had detected an attempt to tunnel under the fence through a shaft dug from under a home on a nearby hillside. The property was being watched, but no one had been seen since the discovery. Finnese's experts had mined the tunnel with small explosive devices that would go off without anybody hearing. If anyone survived, they'd be buried in the tunnel collapse.

"Anyhow, I think Margie puts out damned good chow," Randall says, "even Rex says it's okay, and you know what a food snob he is now."

Master chefs and sommeliers from celebrated restaurants fly in to prepare feasts and uncork rare wines on weekends for hustlers and fawners from Hollywood and Washington eager to board the Rex Express, the name that came up tops in focus-group testing. Margie had stepped up her game as a result.

"I'm not saying it isn't," Abby says. "It's just that I'd like a change of scene; this is like being in prison, a nice one but still a prison, and mom notices the guys aren't as happy-go-lucky as they used to be. She says they're actually like prison guards sometimes."

"Maybe she gets on their nerves."

"Oh, pish," Abby says. "Why did you put so much butter on the popcorn?"

"It's more unhealthy that way. Believe it or not, it's possible for your mother to rub people the wrong way."

"I think they're just stressed like everyone except The Great Rex." That was what Abby had taken to calling him; she had resisted the power of his gravitational pull from the start. "Beneath that charm he turns off and on he's cold as ice." she said once. Abigail unpauses the bird documentary.

The narrator is discussing the common pochard. "Females give hoarse growls. Males have whistles cut off by a final nasal note aaoo-oo-haa." Randall feels his eyelids growing heavy again.

"They've got money to burn," Finnese says the next day on the encrypted line from Virginia. "We just traced the new owner of that house with a tunnel through a dozen cutouts to a dummy corporation in the Cayman Islands. Our people think they used a cartel professional for the digging."

"Didn't the neighbors wonder about all the dirt?"

"The story was the new owners were digging out a basement for a game room. Money being no object, as you told me, I'm putting guys on the Angel Island ferry to monitor the passengers. We don't want someone going over there with a mortar tube and hoping for a lucky hit."

"Run it by Dickson."

"He's got an assistant that I liaison with now, Linda. Is she a real person or a robot?"

"I haven't made up my mind."

Later that day, Randall gets a call from the acting abbot at the monastery. "We've heard from Brother Mario," he says excitedly. "We were so worried."

"Is he back?"

"No, not yet, but he gave a number for you to call." There was a pause. "He didn't sound right, Mr. Randall. He sounded rushed and... and I would say scared."

"Did he say where he'd been?"

"He didn't have time to talk; he just said to call this number." Randall dialed from a burn phone but the call went straight to a voice mail. "Hi, this is Kenny. Leave a message." At eight that night, the phone vibrated in his pocket.

"Hello?"

"Is this Alex Randall?"

"It sure is."

"This is Kenny Marshall. I was out of cell phone range when you called back. A guy I met on the Lost Coast Trail wants you to meet him there."

The Lost Coast.

Randall had hiked it as a teenager, no dumber than other kids his age. It was five hours north on Highway 101 and then you traveled more than an hour west to the coast on a harrowing road as ancient oaks gave way to redwoods and deep shadows. The state had thought of pushing Highway One through decades before, but it was more rugged even than Big Sur so it remained lonely and foggy coast visited only by hardy backpackers and surfer dudes. You had to time your hike between cliff and narrow beach because parts of the trail were under breaking waves at high tide. Sometimes a sneaker wave rolled in like a big hill of water.

"His name is Brother Mario," said the caller, "a real nice guy, older guy, really religious; I think he's on a pilgrimage or something. A retreat? He said for you to meet him at the first shack after the Mattole trailhead." They didn't even deserve "shack," Randall recalled; they were the gray skeletons of small vacation cabins left to fall apart when the lovers of solitude who built them died.

Kenny hesitated. "I think you ought to get to him as fast as you can, Mr. Randall, he was really hungry. I gave him my trail mix and all my energy bars, but that cold wind and the rain this time of year really take it out of you."

"Did he say what he was doing there?"

"Well, praying is what I'd say. He was on his knees and crossing himself when I came on him."

"Why didn't he come out with you?"

"He just shook his head when I asked him."

"And what took you there?"

"I go down there once a month to measure the radiation levels from Fukushima. This time of year it's rare to see anybody but a ranger. Take a can of pepper spray."

"Aren't the bears hibernating?"

"They're supposed to be, but I saw fresh tracks; it's a big one by the look of them."

Randall goes to the room used as Bluff Point's unofficial armory; it is presided over by Brad, a burly ex-Marine. His inventory ranges from a slingshot powerful enough to throw a quarter-inch steel ball that would down a drone to RPGs in case word came about a truck on the way that was going to ram through the gate and blow up at the front door. Some of the stuff Brad had was illegal in civilian hands, but hopefully they would never have to answer questions about it.

"Think a Glock would stop a bear?"

"About as much as a bee sting," Brad says. With his pale eyebrows and shaven head he looks like Mr. Clean. He won a Silver Star in Afghanistan.

"What would?"

"A twelve-gauge shotgun with military-grade buckshot is what I'd want."

"How about bear spray?"

"If it's not too windy."

"I'm thinking handguns in that case."

"A Smith and Wesson 500. It has a helluva kick, though; a little guy will sprain his wrist. You get off another round sometimes because the recoil makes you squeeze the trigger again. It's five pounds unloaded, meaning you're not gonna get it out of the holster as quick as your Glock. I just happen to have one if you're interested." He hands Randall a clipboard. "I need your John Henry."

Randall takes off before dawn from San Carlos in a chartered twin-engine Cessna for the tiny Shelter Cove airport near the start of the trail. The pilot, Jim Tonci, a balding former airline pilot lucky enough to retire in his mid-fifties, notices his hand is shaking as he pours coffee from a thermos. "You afraid of flying?"

"You'd be surprised the things that scare me."

"Private planes are safer than driving, but people don't know that. I called the hotel and got somebody out of bed to see if it's raining or fogged in," says Tonci. "He wasn't too happy about it."

"It sounds like barnstorming days."

"The weather bureau only gives you a general idea, and forget the webcam they got there; it isn't working half the time. If fog rolls in while we're on the way we'll have to divert inland."

But the fog bank is still offshore when Shelter Cove comes in sight like a nail at the end of a green finger. The airfield appears to be built in the middle of a golf course. Sheer cliffs to the north and south are under ceaseless attack from the ocean; white surf leaps above the rocks, and farther out dark reefs are punished by the ocean. "We're early enough so no golfers are out," Tonci says.

A van from the inn drives out to meet him and Randall steps into a cold wind that puts a bite in the damp salt air; he doesn't feel its sharpness thanks to thermal pants and shirt and a fleece-lined jacket. He has a baseball-style balaclava in the backpack with camping gear and the heavy Smith & Wesson revolver.

"Gettin' an early start," says the sleepy kid driving the van. He doesn't fully wake up until they reach the trailhead. "Watch out for a bear that's not hibernating like he's supposed to. Somebody reported him a couple days ago." Hikers are supposed to get a permit and carry a bear-proof container in the backpack for food storage, but Randall plans to put on a goofy look and plead ignorance if a ranger stops him.

The low tide is going out and a six-foot high tide isn't due until two o'clock, plenty of time to reach the ruined cabin. The teasing trail that disappears and returns ranges from black sand to pebbly beach and farther on to round stones like shiny bald heads gathered in conference. The slippery rocks, black and worn smooth by decades of tidal washing, are harder going than when he was a teenager and everything was a lark. His joints feel like they had a cement compound injected and his muscles are like rubber bands stretched to the snapping point. What if a hamstring pops as he hops over these damned rocks? How would he… he pushes the thought from his mind. There is a long stretch of deep sand that sucks at his boots and then a field of more wet rocks to scramble over. Shit, he thinks, already winded—I knew I was getting older, but this?

The wind brings the gray fogbank closer to shore and a few minutes later it is hard to tell whether it is that heavy or if it's lightly raining. He takes a breather with hands on hips, studying what the withdrawing water lays bare in the intertidal zone: strands of brown kelp festooned with bulbs, dark gray mussels and pale sea stars clinging to rocks, green algae, empty shells as white as bone, spiky purple anemone. People devote lifetimes studying these things, he thinks.

When he rounds a point of land, he sees a segment of the cliff has collapsed and rubble extends out into the water; seismic activity is another reason highway engineers decided against pushing Highway One through here. Examining the scree closer up, he sees it is too unstable to cross. That means returning to a narrow creek bed a quarter mile back and following it to the top of the cliff; it is a stiff climb, tiring and time consuming. He rests a few moments, almost panting, before continuing inland along a game trail that parallels the cliff; he has to crawl on all fours under fallen trees at points. Beyond the rock fall, he descends through heavier fog to the trail, following a second little creek whose eroded sides say winter storms make a mighty cataract.

He is aware time has passed, but he's surprised how much when he looks at his watch. He has fallen far behind schedule, but can't force the pace any more or he will take a fall for sure. The incoming tide begins to worry him when the water washes over his boots. There are places above the tide line where he could pitch his tent and wait until it turns again, but also stretches where the trail bumps up against sheer cliff and there is a danger of being trapped by rising water. Then there is the matter of the abbot; from Kenny's description, he is a candidate for hypothermia. Also the bear prowling around that should be sleeping until spring. He slogs on and more time passes.

The land juts out to another point and when he can see ahead he feels a stab of panic. The land drops off more steeply and the white caps are the only color in this gray world where he can't tell where the water ends and the sky begins. He struggles through the water, now up to his knees, bracing against surges rollicking in as if they are happy the long journey across the Pacific is over at last. A small comber sweeps in chest-high and he feels the backpack rise on his shoulders as if about to float free. It is a quarter mile to where the trail, having had its joke, resumes on solid ground. But his reserves are close to empty and his legs as heavy and stiff as bollards. He saw this many times in failed candidates for the SEALS; they wanted to climb the rope after the long forced march with a heavy pack but just could not no matter how angrily minds lashed bodies. The trail inches slowly closer But the ocean is now at his waist; he shrugs off the backpack and it bobs away. A few steps on he is knocked under water and uses his hands to keep off the boulders as the wave carries him forward. He surfaces coughing and spitting and tugs the sodden balaclava from his face to see. His peripheral vision is gone for the single-minded focus he has on the trail, now close enough for hope… he can reach it only his legs can keep moving. He is bowled over again and claws forward for the narrowing band of wet sand. 'God help me,' he cries. A breaking wave makes him look behind in time to stretch out and body surf; it carries him to firm sand where he rolls like a plank washing ashore. The backpack has already beat him there; when a little strength returns, he drags it to solid ground and collapses. He pulls out the flask of brandy and he mixes a healthy pour in a cup with Red Bull, his shaking hands spilling half. He gulps it down and pours another. Feeling slowly returns to his legs.

After he rests, he gets up, shoulders the backpack and pushes on for the cabin; it comes into sight after forty-five minutes. At first, Randall thinks it is being buffeted by the strong wind, and then he gets a glimpse of something black through an empty window. He drops the backpack at his feet and takes out the heavy revolver. The walls shiver inside from heavy impacts and he wonders if the slanting roof is about to come down. He circles to where the rear wall fell in long ago and sees a bear tearing something to bloody pieces.

Randall has no doubt it is Brother Mario.

As if sensing his presence, the bear turns and drops the abbot after a final shake. It slowly advances on him, snarling with head lowered; strings of slobber hang from its jaws and teeth make a clicking sound. Then it busts into full gallop at him. They are faster than a race horse over a short distance—the thought streaks through his mind.

Wrist braced with his other hand, Randall fires. BLAM. The blast makes a Glock sound like a toy popgun. The animal gives out a surprised grunt and stops as if it hits an invisible wall; the heavy bullet struck a non-vital area, but with stunning effect. BLAM. The next one is a heart shot and the bear slowly topples over on its side, legs jerking and jaws snapping. Randall puts a third bullet in its brain as he passes.

The abbot is torn open like a rag doll; bloody clothes and the skin beneath are ripped away to reveal white bone under exposed ligaments and coils of gray viscera. What power that animal had; a grizzly couldn't have done more damage. As Randall looks around the blood-spattered scene, he spots something pinned below a board. It is paper covered in minute handwriting, the kind a prisoner would use if he had a lot to tell and wasn't sure he had enough room. He stuffs it in an inside pocket of his jacket and zips it up.

He is sitting looking out to sea when a gangling ranger with a long white neck emerges from the fog in a watch cap and a jacket with a fur collar and a Bureau of Land Management patch. "Afternoon, sir," he says. He is apple-cheeked and young and clearly proud of the authority his uniform gives him.

Randall nods.

"I heard gunfire a while back, three shots. You wouldn't know anything about it, would you, sir?"

"That was me."

"The possession and discharge of firearms are illegal on the Lost Coast Trail at this time of year, sir. This is federal land."

"I shot a bear over there by the cabin."

The young man looks at him sternly. "I take it you don't have a license to shoot a bear."

"No, I don't."

"If you did, you would know the season ends in December. It is clearly stated on the license."

Randall is silent.

"How did you expect to pack it out, sir?"

When Randall doesn't answer, the ranger gives a sigh that says: Sorry, fella, but the law is the law. Randall is still gazing out to sea when he hears the ranger cry, "Oh, my God!" That is followed by vomiting and then the dry heaves. "Christ!"

After a few minutes, scuffling boots approach and the ranger sits down heavily, head between knees. Then he lifts it to also look out to sea. "What happened?" he asks in a shaky voice. He appears to have aged ten years when Randall turns. The apple cheeks now have red patches like rouge on his blanched face

"The bear got him and I got the bear."

"It looks like it's over seven hundred pounds." He offers his hand. "I'm Arnold."

"I'm Alex. That's Brother Mario Roberti over there."

Arnold nods vacantly.

He's in shock, Randall thinks, his well-ordered world of enforcing small-bore rules blown to bits. He will recover from the immediate trauma but he won't go back to how he was before, not after what he has seen. In combat you learn to distance yourself like a photographer behind his lens. He shows him his police badge.

A long silence. "Was the... the deceased a friend of yours?"

"I knew him."

"You look like you've been in the water."

"The rock slide forced me out."

"I was coming out to see if we need to close the trail."

"So it's new, the slide?"

"Yeah, it was just reported to us. These tides can be dangerous if your timing is off."

"If it wasn't for that, I might have got here before the bear." What was the difference, ten minutes, five?

Arnold swallows hard. "I should have touched the body to see if it was warm, but I..."

"It was warm, but he was dead."

Arnold puts a hand on his shoulder. "Sorry for your loss."

"You better call this in."

"They'll send a Coast Guard chopper from Arcata-Eureka." He looks up at the rags of fog blowing past. "They can land in this. There was a woman with a broken back once."

"Remind them to bring a body bag... make it a couple."

CHAPTER 37

TONCI HAS FLOWN THE CESSNA OVER FROM SHELTER COVE AND STANDS GRINNING IN WELCOME at the airport when Randall walks from the helicopter. His smile fades when he sees Randall's face.

"Is something wrong?" he asks. Then he sees the body bags being unloaded. "What happened?"

"A bear killed a man."

"God Almighty." The pilot is silent until they are in the air. "Did you see it?" he asks at last.

"I don't want to talk about it." They fly the rest of the way without speaking; they land at San Carlos and he is driven to Bluff Point.

Abby and the kids and her mother thankfully are at the movies in San Rafael with their security detail. Ordinarily, Randall would laugh at the thought of those burly warriors with shaved heads and tattoos watching a motion picture for little kids, but a gloom has settled on him as dark as smoke from a stack of burning tires. He goes upstairs to shower and change and then to one of three studies on the floor; he settles in an easy chair and smooths out the pages Brother Mario wrote. The writing is so small he goes to Esther's room for her reading glasses.

Alex, I am in an old cabin (what's left of it) writing these words. They will remind me when we meet of what has happened, which I hope is soon because the cold wind makes this ruin shake and I am very weak. To begin with, I flew to Rome to talk to a friend in the Vatican archives who knows as much as one human possibly can about the contents of its fifty-one MILES of shelves. His job is indexing but his passionate inter-est is the paradox of evil in a universe created by a loving God—or so we must assume otherwise our lives are without meaning. As he explained to me, the early church fathers, the closest to the Disciples, explained the dichotomy thus: angels, like humans, had free will and could choose evil over good. He reminded me that St. Gregory said in Dialogues, "In this visible world nothing can be achieved except through invisible forces." Origen likewise held that such things as famines, plagues and natural disasters were the work of fallen angels. Tertullian said disease and calamities were caused by demons bent on the ruin of mankind. Clement of Alexandria said creation doesn't always reflect the Creator because it is corrupted by demonic forces led by Satan. And so on and so forth. He kept bringing me volume after dusty volume—in Latin! (mine is rusty to say the least) that made this point over and over: Satan is using his free will to create pain and misery. These are forgotten books by and about forgotten theologians. There would be even more on the shelves except most from the first twelve hundred years of the faith were lost because of upheavals in church and society. It wasn't until Pope Innocent III… well, I'll leave that to later if it interests you. As time passed, study of the source and nature of evil gave way to how it might be mitigated by charitable acts. This was a good thing and untold numbers of people have benefited from it over the centuries, but a result was to draw attention away from Satan to the agents who do his will: vile criminals and wicked rulers. Rather than its wellspring, Satan became merely a symbol of evil like the scepter in the hand of a king that represents authority but is without power itself—in short, he became a metaphor. He told me Satan's greatest achievement in modern times has been to foster disbelief in his existence, even becoming a comic figure in festivals and parades. When you're laughing, you're not thinking. This, of course, is not an original thought, but so avid was he in pursuing the point that I felt it would be discourteous to say so. Even though as a monk I am accustomed to self-denial, I think about food almost constantly, another reason to occupy my mind in writing these thoughts. It has been two days since I had anything to eat except for a little trail mix from a Good Samaritan. I drink from a small creek, so far without ill effects. Fasting for spiritual reasons is different from this; hunger is more easily managed in quiet contemplation than when one is a hunted fugitive. Eventually, I begged my friend to show me no more ancient tomes or crackling scrolls, beautiful as they were with their calligraphy and illuminated initials and biblical scenes. How medieval monks in scriptoriums labored year after year on these works! Now they might be opened perhaps only once in a generation; they have become quaint objects for aesthetic admiration rather than sources of God-inspired wisdom. We were stopped as we left for dinner by a haughty French priest, my friend's superior, who demanded to know why I had been allowed to enter the secret archives. Permission is granted only to credentialed scholars whose research must be approved in advance, and access to archival resources is limited to what is stated on the application. What they request from the shelves is brought to where they sit at a table. I was informed of this as my friend was reprimanded for his grave breach of regulations. It appeared the haughty Frenchman had been observing our conversation from concealment, and when we were getting ready to leave he sprang. We could not have been treated more rudely if we were shoplifters. We were ordered to leave. "Hors de ma vue!" the Frenchman cried. We left Vatican City and walked to Via Famagosta for supper. My friend's fallen spirits rose under the influence of the penne all'arrabiata and a glass of wine from northern Italy. The priest, he told me, was one of many in the Vatican who are scornful of the pope's ideas on Satan. They have fostered the belief that the church remains tied to medieval superstitions and is incapable of a modernizing spirit. That opinion is not expressed publicly, only among themselves. My friend said many but not all holding this view are homosexuals who have advanced in ecclesiastical rank with age and are now even in the College of Cardinals. One day, he said, there will be a gay pope although this will not be revealed until the Africans have become reconciled to homosexuality. My friend believes the infestation of the church by pederasts shows Satan's power. This is not a popular view in the Vatican, as you might guess, so he must be careful even though he believes it is shared by Pope Francis himself. The Curia has long experience in handling difficult popes and will bide its time until this one is replaced by one not so concerned with satanic influences. I told him of my hope of meeting the pontiff and telling him of our strange experiences with Camael. He said it was doubtful His Holiness would have time for it, so busy is his schedule. I told him if anyone could interpret the visitations and understand whether we should see Camael as friend or enemy, it is the Holy Father. He promised to try to get word to him.

"I think you should know the granny-glasses look is not for you." Molly stands in the doorway with a smile.

Randall peels them from his face. "They're Esther's; I need them for this handwriting."

"Whose is it?" she asks, coming closer. "Gosh, they look like ant tracks."

"You know that abbot who took in my family at the monastery in Oregon?"

Molly sinks into a chair with an apprehensive look. "You're going to tell me something awful, I just know it."

"He was killed by a bear this morning."

"Oh, my God!" A hand goes to her mouth.

"I'm reading Brother Mario's last words." He passes her the page he had finished.

"Are you going to tell me what happened?"

"He sent me a message to meet him on the Lost Coast."

"Nobody goes up there."

"By the time I reached him, the bear already had him. Then it came at me and I shot it dead."

"Does this have anything to do with Rex?" Molly asks in a flat voice.

"Everything does, doesn't it? But I haven't come to the explanation yet." He resumes reading; she stares at him bleakly before picking up Brother Mario's first page.

I got a telephone call late at night at the small hotel where I was staying. It was my friend from the Vatican speaking in a voice barely above a whisper. Hello, Brother Mario, he started to say, listen carefully... but there was noise as if a struggle had begun and the phone was hung up. I called back, but the line was busy. As I sat on the side on the bed wondering what to think, a gentle tap came at the door. Brother Mario, a voice said, let me in. Recognizing it as Camael's, I opened the door and he told me to leave at once. My bag was already packed for departure in the morning, so I threw on my clothes and followed him out of the hotel.

He led me into a shadowed doorway just as a car turned onto the alley with lights off. Four men entered the hotel in silence. There was a flash of blue light in the window, but no gunshot; the night deskman fell, mortally wounded, according to the story I read later in Il Tempo, Camael hurried me to a passageway and through a door on a rusty hinge which he bolted behind us. It was some kind of lodging for religious pilgrims that dates back centuries; I followed him up dimly-lit stone steps to a room scarcely big enough for a narrow bed and chest of drawers; the toilet was down the hall. The room had light from a streetlamp through an opening in the wall like an archer's slit. Rome is full of people welcoming to Lucifer, he whispered, the Holy City is sick with their wickedness. I was to take the late train to Brindisi and the ferry to Corfu, sparing no expense to return to the safety of the monastery. He pressed a thick roll of currency into my hands. There was bread and cheese in the room and bottled water; I was to stay two days, seeing no one, until the search in Rome eased up. As if to emphasize his point, we heard running footsteps and voices in the alley. Never assume they have given up, he warned. I will help when I can, but there will be times I cannot leave my adversary. He connects Rex to the End Times, but certain things must happen first. What things, I asked, but my answer was a shake of the head as if even he can only guess. And then he was gone.

I will tell you those two days were very hard for me. There was nothing to do but lie on the bed and think. Would a plague go forth from one of the dozens of bio-warfare laboratories where men patiently refine their deadliness? Or perhaps it would be an infestation of self-replicating nanobots. Would a nuclear warhead explode in the atmosphere for an electromagnetic surge that would hurl us back to a new Dark Age where the living would envy the dead? My mind ceaselessly looped through apocalyptic possibilities. Earthquakes, great storms, crop-devouring diseases, bone-dry droughts, ocean poisonings, volcanic eruptions. Now and then I heard voices in the narrow hallway, a polyglot of languages. I made out English, French and Spanish, of course, but also Germanic and Scandinavian and Asian and African. They were poor and pious, occupying the warren of small rooms behind mine. No doubt the church owned the building and refused princely sums for it over the centuries. I was glad when the time came to slip out of my prison for the night train to Brindisi.

"Fifty-one miles of shelves," Molly says looking up from the page, as impressed as the abbot had been.

"The Library of Congress has eight hundred and thirty-eight miles of shelves," Randall replies.

"How do you know that?"

"It's one of those facts that sticks like gum to your shoe. I must have a million of them, all useless."

"He reads Latin, that's really something."

"Read, not reads. It's all past tense for Brother Mario now."

Molly flinches.

I slipped out the creaking door to the deserted alley at nine and walked to a plaza still crowded with Romans and tourists strolling and sitting at outdoor cafes. I caught a bus to Tiburtina Station in the northeast of the city where the last train to leave connects the following morning with one to Brindisi. I took the overnight ferry from there to Paxi, which is a short commercial flight from Corfu. There were incidents I should mention. At the train station in Rome a man on the same bus fell to the ground a short distance behind me and called out in agony that his ankle was broken. I normally would have gone to his assistance, but I had already begun to suspect he was following me. On the ferry ride, a deck hand who also took an unusual interest in me was ordered into a whaleboat let down into the water to assist a leaking boat with migrants from Africa. He argued long and loudly before the officer evidently gave an ultimatum. The ferry continued on its way, not waiting for the coast guard to arrive. There was no mistaking the malevolent look the man shot at me as he went over the side. A woman I felt was observing me in an open market in Paxi where I bought fresh fruit for the ferry ride was accosted by a stumbling-drunk man who gave her slobbering kisses. She pulled him to the floor by his hair and gave him several rapid kicks to the ribs; meanwhile I blended into the crowd. At Gatwick a man peering at me over a newspaper was seized by two policemen who accused him of being a shoplifter. Indignant, he tried to pull away from them to follow me and was hit with a taser dart that made him jerk like a puppet on strings. At LaGuardia, someone in a Spider Man costume tried to cadge money from the man shadowing me, occupying him so much with his wheedling that he didn't see when I followed a custodian into a secured area. I waited there until I thought it was safe; it was clear by then that Camael was protecting me, but I remembered his warning that I couldn't always count on that. I changed my flight from Portland to Sacramento, not bothering to turn in the old ticket, thinking chances were greater they would watch flights to Oregon. I rented a car and drove north on Interstate 5 in the belief that between us Camael and I had outwitted the pursuers. But an eighteen-wheeler tried to run me off the road south of Redding, jack-knifing and overturning in the process, and I turned east off the interstate to continue north on Highway 101. I had my eyes on the rearview mirror as much as the road ahead so I was aware of the headlights that followed me off the highway at Garberville when I turned off suddenly to a rural road that became the twisting route to the Lost Coast. It is a terrible road, frightening in stretches, and I believe whoever followed miscalculated and plunged over the side because suddenly his lights were gone. I was frightened and continued on, arriving at dawn to where the road ends and hikers leave their cars to walk to the Lost Coast. I am in despair that I didn't reach the Holy Father having come so (relatively) close and more so when I think how Satan's agents have burrowed into the Vatican's innermost chambers and no doubt plot against him. The amused off the record remarks by "high ranking Vatican sources" over His Holiness's warnings of Satan's modern presence are at the very least suggestive of his influence. I met a young scientist when I reached here whose job is to measure radioactivity in the ocean. He took pity and promised he would let you know of my whereabouts. I think I will be safe when I reach the monastery because Camael made it a sanctuary for your family.

Randall passes the final page to Molly, saying, "Then comes the bear that is supposed to be hibernating."

When she comes to the end, she is ashen. "Did Satan... take over the bear somehow?"

"I don't know," he says. "Maybe it was Rex. Any wild guess will be as good as any other."

"What are we going to do?"

"I don't know that either."

"I think we should tell Rex," she says after a moment. She dabs at her eyes with a handkerchief. "Don't you think he should know what's going on?"

"All he has to do is look at your face and he'll know."

"I'm very careful about that," she says. "Faces were my business, remember?" Then she adds sadly, "A hundred years ago."

"Satan doesn't trust Rex since he went off the reservation and we know our guy is leery about being a tool in a conspiracy. It might be he wants to do things his way on his own timetable. He's got a colossal ego and maybe now he sees himself as Lucifer's equal."

"You're saying they're both evil, so trust is impossible."

"We have two suspects and either one could have killed Brother Mario. Both had reasons, Lucifer because he doesn't want word about End Times getting out before all the boxes are checked, and Rex because voters just might hold it against him if word gets out he's the devil's creation."

"Where does that leave us?"

"Where we've been all the time, square in the middle."

CHAPTER 38

"IT BOILS DOWN TO THIS," REX SAYS TO THE POLITICAL CONSULTANTS AND POLLSTERS SITTING alertly around the table, "would a rock tour hurt or help my chance of being president?"

Dickson was looking like someone from the Roaring 'Twenties in a wide-brimmed Borsalino hat and an ankle-length raccoon coat over an ice cream suit; Molly wouldn't be surprised if he pulled out a silver hip flask. It wasn't so long ago he was a blushing young man in funny shoes and clothes his mom picked out for him; she has never seen someone transform himself so quickly. Having shed hat and coat, he sprawls carelessly with an arm flung over the back of the chair.

There had been the customary stunned awe when Rex entered the room, and now it seems no one is willing to be the first to share an opinion. Finally, a heavy, florid-faced man, balding, with a deep Southern accent speaks up. He has a pointed chin like a bird perch in a goiter-like bib of flesh that pours down to the knot of his tie. "I don't see how one concert would hurt, but a whole tour?" The flesh above the tie throbs in syncopation with his words. Molly is reminded of a frog on a lily pad. "Not so sure 'bout that," he says. Heads around the table nod in assent.

Molly is not impressed by this assembly of politicos. The florid-faced man with bright blue eyes looks like there might be a problem with drink or high blood pressure, probably drink, though; another wears a suit and run-down shoes that could use some of the shine the elbows of his coat have; a third has close-bitten nails and a busy facial tic. The Republicans and Democrats had skimmed the cream and these consultants are what's left, the best that could be drummed up so late in the political season by the Good Citizens Party; the name has yet to find an admirer. They look like veterans of delivering bad news with quick sideways looks. Googling them told her they ran minor campaigns that generally finished out of the money unless they were lucky enough to be pitted against one another, in which case there was the hope a coin toss brings.

"Everyone else is locked up," Josiah Walden had apologized. "We should have got to this sooner."

Russell Kornhouser, the Southerner, doesn't like to be squirming in the spotlight with Rex's question still in the air. "What do you think, Charlie, good or bad idea?"

Molly thinks Charlie Parsons would be a natural as the salesman trying to put something over on a young couple, but his hound-dog face shows familiarity with rejection and accepting it as natural. Belatedly noticing the state of his shoes, he tucks them under his chair. "Ah, that's the question, isn't it?" When there is no response, he wings it. "It would kind of depend on the kind of music in some sense, wouldn't it? Heavy metal, for example; there's a lot of people don't like it. Older people, I mean; feedback into hearing aids and so on. Unfortunately, they're more likely to vote than the young folks, and…" His voice trails off as if it has occurred to him that heavy metal might be Rex's ruling passion.

"My music will be a huge hit with everyone," Rex says comfortably. "There will be millions of downloads the first day."

Parsons is clearly a man accustomed to working around the grandiosity of political aspirants, most deluded to one degree or another. "Yes, but then we have the concerts themselves."

"Charlie has a point," Kornhouser says.

"What is it?" Molly prompts.

"Charlie's sayin' troublemakers from the Democrats or Republicans or maybe both. When it gets out you gonna make a run at it, they won't confine themselves to oppo research. They'll be disruptive and there'll be incidents, the kind the media plays up. They might have somebody rush the stage, some phony group with a cause somebody rents for the occasion. Fightin' with your security people, that sort of thing. A stink bomb or a box of mice let loose in the crowd. Boom! On defense right out of the gate."

"You would know about that, wouldn't you, Korny?" Charlie says bitterly.

"Let bygones be bygones," Kornhouser says quickly. "The point is Rex announces his candidacy at the first concert and there's no chance to put a fox in the henhouse at the next one 'cause there won't be a next one."

"Let's be honest," says Raymond Drexel, an up-tight sort who has slicked-back hair and muscles knotted like marbles on his jaw line. "All the talent is already on board with Maxwell or Hanson. They can't even lend us staff under the table for fear of getting caught. All the pollsters are tied up with the exception of maybe a few doctoral candidates at backwoods universities. Same with the mailing houses and media buyers, and anyway the ad time from prime time to early hours was booked months ago. The best creative ad agencies are locked in. Every big name you'd want for endorsement is taken. The governors and senators are in one camp or the other. Both parties have yard signs and grass-roots volunteers ready to go door-to-door."

Molly doesn't see him as someone who carries you to victory. He would insist on control, a total my-way-or-the-highway guy who would lose sight of the big picture because he obsessed over every little detail. His contempt for the others was clear from the moment he walked through the door, showing anger to be lumped in with these losers. Drexel's eyes are scornful as he takes in the room. "I appreciate the honorarium and the first class ticket, so I'm going tell it like it is, Rex. You've been in a movie for teenagers and you had a good season in baseball—okay a great one—and you seem to think you've got a hit album on the way, which is not the big thing it used to be, but no way are you going to pull this off even running against worn-out hacks like Barney Maxwell and Dolly Hanson. People might not like them very much, but as Jews used to say 'Better the czar you know than a new one.' That's your typical voter, very cautious. So my advice is save your money and enjoy being the world's biggest celebrity."

A great hiccup bursts from him like a shout. HICK. Then another and another and another. HICK. HICK. HICK-UUUUP.

When they show no sign of abating, Molly hurries for water. The hiccups echo through the building and people come out in the hallway to look. When she gets back, everyone is on their feet and Drexel is worse than before. HICK. HICK. HICK-UUUUP. They are like sobs wrenched from deep within. The others are transfixed as if witnessing a rare form of performance art.

"What is...?" HICK. HICK. HICK-UUUP. "...is happening to me?"

"Drink this," she says. Drexel takes a long swallow but it comes up almost right away, a fountain riding another HICK-UUUP." Kornhouser dances clear, showing quick feet for such a heavy man.

"You hear of people getting these and they don't go away," Charlie says unhelpfully. "They go on year after year, night and day."

Randall comes in and sizes up the situation with a glance. "Where's Rex?" he asks.

"He left the room," Kornhouser says urgently, his wide throat wobbling like small birds inside are trying to get out. "Y'all better call an ambulance."

Rex is standing in his room at the balcony window looking out at the lights of the Bay Bridge. "I'm thinking of taking up painting," he says.

"You've proved whatever the point was," Randall says. "That poor bastard is going to die from a heart attack, which would make two dead today."

"He tried to discourage me." Rex seems privately amused.

"I don't know why you bother asking people for their opinion."

Rex turns from the window. "What do you mean, two?"

"The abbot from the monastery was killed this morning. By a bear."

Rex tilts his head. "A hundred and eight people die in the world every minute of every day and night; tell me why I should care about him."

"He just got back from the Vatican where he was asking about Satan."

The indifference evaporates. "You think it's Camael?"

"Camael helped him get away from bad guys in Italy, so why wait until he returns and why then kill him and use a bear to do it?"

"How do you know about Italy?"

"He left me a letter where he was killed. I got there just a few minutes late." Randall explains the delay by the rock slide and how he nearly didn't make it in the rising tide.

"To come so close," Rex muses. He takes a turn around the room and returns to Randall with a look that says he has the answer. "Camael is playing you, and the bear has some symbolic meaning."

"You think it was him?"

"Who else?"

"I'm thinking of the plane that went into that building in Dubai."

"Oh, that," Rex says as if it is some niggling detail. "The blind old man was standing in the way. He was financing terrorism in the Middle East, by the way. A very major actor."

"Who told you that?"

"It wasn't a little bird."

"Finnese?" He would have contacts who knew.

Rex looks at him without answering. If it was Finnese, Randall realizes, he would ask that he not be named.

"So I did everyone a favor and got the last part of the movie financing," Rex says. "It was win-win."

"Except for the pilot of the airplane."

"He was Shia and the banker was Sunni, mortal enemies since the Seventh Century. Both believed they would collect a reward in Paradise for helping cleanse the world of each other. What did the abbot find out in Rome?"

"There's opposition in the inner circles to the pope making a big thing about Satan. Brother Mario hoped to use influence for a private audience about your situation, but they got to his contact and then came after him."

Rex rounds on him. "My situation?"

"The monstrous plot," Randall says nimbly.

"You talked to this abbot about that?" Rex says. His manner turns freezing. "That was between us."

"You have to be pro-active to stay ahead of problems and that means reaching out. Security and intel go together." Like *love and marriage…* the song pops into his head which right now he needs to be clear as a bell.

Rex's expression is uncertain, something Randall hasn't seen since the early days. He isn't sure if I was doing the best job I could or lying. The song continues with its see-saw rhythm… *dum de dum like a horse and care-idge*. It's like an escape valve on a boiler, the mind letting off pressure when it builds too high. Everything, he thinks, will be decided right now. Rex doesn't need a bear; there is any number of ways to kill me. *Ask the local gentry and they will say it's el-la-men-tree.*

"Did you tell Molly about this?" Rex asks softly.

"She'd think I was crazy."

After a few more seconds, he relaxes. "Yes, that's true. No matter how long you looked, you could never find anyone who'd believe this."

The song goes away in Randall's head.

Dickson says "Finally" down the hallway when Drexel's hiccupping stops as suddenly as it started.

"I've never had this happen before," Drexel says pitifully in the chair where he had collapsed, all his contempt and arrogance gone.

"Five minutes," Dickson says coldly, looking at his watch to note how much valuable time had been taken. "You ought to see a doctor about that."

"Waal, now, looka here," Kornhouser protests, "the man…"

Dickson cuts him off. "Getting back to business, all those problems he mentioned don't matter at all." He has one hand in a trouser pocket, as casual as an old-time crooner. "You know why? They're old-school ways of thinking— obsolete, dead as a doornail. Rex is not an ordinary candidate; in under a year he's become one of the best known people on the planet, so ordinary rules don't apply to him. He doesn't begin small and get big, he begins huge and gets colossal. When I go back to my office, there'll be another ten or fifteen endorsement offers. Nike and Adidas are in a bidding war that will guarantee him a billion dollars over his sports career. Do one of your polls," he says with scorn, as if that is a tool little people use to impress other little people, "and you'll see his name recognition is already thirty points ahead of either of the candidates, and that's before the album release our hiccupping colleague seems to think won't matter. I've got news for you, friend, I've heard some cuts off that album and it's going to go down in history as the greatest ever. Trust me on that."

The men seem cowed by his grandiosity, but Molly isn't—far from it. She has noticed lately that Dickson has a dissipated look that makes her think he has has taken up shocking vices. What a figure he must cut around his office, she thinks, brutal and boasting. He'll push things too far and Linda Atwood, that viper in the long grass, will sink her fangs into him when he least expects it. Dickson will be out the door before he knows what hit him.

"So you don't need us?" Charlie asks. He acts like he knew it would turn out like this.

"That's not Mr. Dickson's decision to make," Molly says firmly.

Heads whirl toward her, including Dickson's. It rankles more than ever that she stands between him and Rex with veto power over what he wants, like being spared the iris scanning at the front gate. He thinks he is too important and well known now to be subjected to such petty rules. Molly insisted because Randall told her to—he seemed to like sticking it to Dickson—but let him believe it was her decision so he didn't get the idea he could push her around. But the message evidently hasn't got through yet.

"Can I have a word with you?" Dickson says in a way that sounds like a warning she is about to get a dressing down in private.

"No," she says blithely, "but I'll let you know when I can spare you some time. Better yet, give me a memo."

She tells the others to liaison with the Rock-Steady team for ideas that blend their thinking with the celebrity-is-everything concept. "Do you want them to go through Linda Atwood or handle it yourself?" she asks the seething Dickson.

"I'll handle it myself," he says in a strangled voice.

"I'll leave you boys to it, then," Molly says as she breezes out the door.

Later, she sees Randall standing at a window looking down on the raked gravel circle in front of the mansion with the dormant hydrangeas that form a square in the center. They'll be lovely in the summer, she thinks. The politicos are getting into a van that will take them to their hotel in the city. "When did Dickson trade his Porsche for the Lamborghini?" he asks.

"He's quite the showboat these days," Molly says, watching him shed the fur coat and Borsalino before getting into his glossy, low-slung sports car. "One of the security guys said that car costs four hundred and fifty thousand dollars."

"Not bad for a young pup," Randall says. "Is his Rudy Vallee look coming back?" The clothes and the car make him think about what Camael said about Lucifer's love of show.

"He doesn't look so young anymore, have you noticed?"

"I try not to look at him."

"He still had his baby fat from before, but now it's like he's aged a decade and a half. And there's something creepy about him."

"Does he still live with his mother?"

Molly says she doesn't know or care.

"I took a chance and told Rex about the abbot."

She turns big eyes to him. "What was his reaction?"

"He thinks Camael was acting through the bear."

"No, I mean his reaction to you?"

"He wanted to know if I'd told you, and I said hadn't. I watched him as he thought it over and it was scary. Then he decided no one in his right mind would believe me about any of this."

"What happens now?" She thinks how much she yearns to return to a normal life and how it seems more and more impossible.

"We keep putting one foot in front of the other."

It's the best he can come up with.

CHAPTER 39

"SHE NO LIVE HERE," THE YOUNG MAN SAYS IN A HEAVY CHINESE ACCENT AND CLOSES THE DOOR.
Hong Kong money has been investing heavily in San Francisco real estate for
decades and lately has been joined by the mainland rich fleeing environmen-
tal pollution.

Randall goes next door and knocks. An old and dignified Italian woman in
a flowered dress and gray hair in a bun with silver combs shuffles to the door, a
little yellow dog yapping at her feet. He shows his badge through the sceen and
asks if she knows where Mrs. Dickson has gone.

"Quiet, Mitzi!" The toy dog stops its yapping.

"He put her in a rest home," says Mrs. Allegretti, who is a widow like
Dickson's mother. "One day she was there talking to me over the fence sharp
as a pin and the next she was gone. Mitzi!" The toy dog stops its yapping. "We
were neighbors seventeen years and no goodbye or nothing. The mailman told
me her mail is forwarded to Pineview-by-the-Sea in Daly City."

"Was it something sudden, a stroke?" he asks. "A fall down the stairs?"

Her black eyes snap. "He walked her out to the street, two months ago it
is, and put her in a car, and that's the last I saw of her. His hand was holding
her arm like he was forcing her. If one of my kids... " The threat trails off. "Is
she all right?"

"I'm just checking on some unpaid parking tickets."

"Those are his," Mrs. Allegretti says. "She didn't drive; she took the bus when
she needed to go somewhere." She looks around and drops her voice. "He was
a nice boy before, but now he acts like his shit don't stink."

Randall stops at a flower shop for a bouquet and drives through the fog to the
rest home, low buildings with a 'Fifties look in a dull suburban neighborhood.

Inside, the strong disinfectant doesn't quite cover the smell of urine. Old people with vacant looks sit in wheelchairs.

"I brought these for Mrs. Dickson," he tells the woman at the reception desk. The wicker basket has lilies, red roses, gold and burgundy chrysanthemums, solidaster, brown copper beech and salal.

"Aren't they lovely," says the woman, a pleasant and plump woman in the rest home's blue uniform. "I'll see she gets them."

"I was hoping to see her just for a minute," Randall says. "I'm just in town for the day and I wasn't around when she... you know." He gives her a pleading look.

"She's not supposed to have visitors," she says doubtfully.

"Thirty seconds, then. She's always been my favorite aunt."

"Roseanne to the front desk," the receptionist says over the paging system. "No more than thirty seconds," she says. "I don't want to get in trouble."

As Roseanne, younger but also plump, leads him down a hall with walls painted in primary colors like a pre-school, he says, "Is everything all right with Mrs. Dickson?" He stops and pulls out a roll of currency with a rubber band around it. "A thousand bucks to see she's treated right."

Roseanne's eyes get big. "Oh, yes, sir, everything is fine with her." Not for the first time he thinks how pleasant you can make it for everyone when you have an unlimited supply of somebody else's money.

"Spread it around if you want or keep it yourself, our secret. You know, just so things are hunky-dory."

She glances around and drops her voice as she pockets the cash. "You know, to be truthful I don't really think she belongs here. They keep her on a dose of anti-depressants that would drop a mule. Us techs talk about it among ourselves, but doctor's orders." She gives a what-are-you-gonna-do shrug.

They look in on Mrs. Dickson who sits in an easy chair staring at a TV comedy from long ago. She is gaunt and wan in a housecoat; she wears a ribbon in her pale blond hair the same blue color as the rest home outfits. "How are ya, darlin'?" Roseanne says cheerfully. She whispers to Randall, "She isn't eating." Raising her voice, she says, "Here's a nice man who brought you some beautiful flowers." Mrs. Dickson slowly moves her gaze from the television to Randall and the flowers and then back to the screen. "Holy macaroni," cries a long-dead comedian in a checkered sports coat.

He telephones Inflexible Security from his car and asks Finnese to scope out Dr. Eldon Reykauser, the medical director of the rest home, and gets a call back before he reaches the Golden Gate Bridge. "He lost his license to practice medicine in Kentucky and works as a consultant to chains of rest homes," Finnese reports. "He was involved in several personal injury suits, is what we found out; a few patients suffered intracranial bleeding from anti-depressants. You want details?"

That's good enough, Randall says; he doesn't need another rabbit hole to go down. Back at Bluff Point he catches Molly on her way to the conference room for a meeting with a concert promoter. "Just so you know, Dickson put his mom in a nursing home," he says.

"What's wrong with her?" she asks, making sure her skirt is straight.

"A neighbor says nothing, but a quack has her under what the mental health people call chemical restraint."

"That explains the new wardrobe, but why do that to his own mother?"

"Maybe mom was cramping his style. Working for Rex made him rich in a hurry, but he couldn't spread his wings with her still in the picture."

"Rex's made me well off, but I hope it didn't make me a monster." She does a quick personal inventory. She was pretty sure she wasn't one; her nerves were ragged and she could be sharp with people, but a monster of selfishness like Dickson—no.

"He's young, maybe Hollywood went to his head," Randall says. But there is another explanation, he thinks, recalling the force that pulled him to the Tenderloin. Only Camael saved him from the walk on the wild side that one day brings with it the full horror of what you have become. When that happens, men run onto the freeway without clothes or tear gas grenades smoke them out of a barricaded room.

"Or maybe it's the same thing that got into that bear." Molly is only joking, but the look Randall gets scares her. She has an urgent itch on an arm. If I'm getting hives now, she thinks, I'll ask for a medical leave. Rex probably wouldn't allow it though; he'd fly in the world's leading authority to treat me at Bluff Point. Despite all the people he has met since the cafe, Sergeant Randall and I are still the only ones he trusts. We were there for him when he was weak and defenseless, now everyone he meets wants something from him.

But we'll be thrown on the junk pile when he no longer needs us to watch his back, she thinks.

"I've got a meeting," she tells Randall.

"Abby wants to go house hunting, so I'll see you at dinner."

"It's a celebrity chef tonight. I saw the menu, roast lamb with green almonds and cauliflower cream, baby turnips and carrots embedded in what he calls 'edible soil.'"

"You mean dirt?" Randall asks. "I'm not eating dirt; I did enough of that in Iraq."

"No, according to the menu notes it's made with malt, hazelnut, and other flours, and butter."

"Wouldn't you like to have a plain cheeseburger sometime? The guys are getting mutinous."

"Desert is a gooseberry sorbet with elderberry foam over a toasted corn cake."

"The kids will probably eat that," Randall says, "if they put ice cream on it."

The concert impresario is an extremely black man, Jaivon, who looks like he graduated from the skinny guy counting the house to heavy-gut prosperity from booking stadium acts featuring blue smoke and light shows and the audience lifting candles in little cups overhead at the end.

"Z'up," he says, enfolding her in the hug that at some point became a duty even between strangers meeting the first time; in the old movies that she loves a simple handshake was all that was required. He is so black it seems his skin absorbs light. His partner is a twentyish white dude named Foster, who is in an ironic Beatles T-shirt that shows thousands of dollars worth of intricate tattoos fitted as tightly as puzzle pieces on his arms. Molly guesses they are symbols of a dense personal narrative he will discuss at the drop of a hat. "And I got this one in Thailand when I…" A whole evening could spent on personal milestones if he took off his shirt. She wonders if the tattoos are compensation for his uninteresting face, the average-man type you forgot as soon as you look away.

"You real careful who you let into this place," Jaivon says.

"It's as bad as the airports," Foster complains.

"Thought they was gonna put on the glove and make me bend over," Javion adds. "Haven't had that done to me that since Rikers, and I was gonna say no way, we do our talkin' on the damn phone."

The door opens and Dickson insinuates himself into the room with a slowness that she is sure is meant to be menacing. "Don't get up," he says, although no one showed any sign of it. It is the Great Gatsby look today. A linen shirt, light gray vest, an oatmeal-colored textured blazer, and dark gray trousers. The unbuttoned vest allows a peak at royal blue suspenders. He carries a man purse made of hide from some rare animal. All Molly can think of is his poor mother; what did she do to deserve this? After the men have hugged one another, Dickson sits down and raises a knife-edged trouser crease with forefinger and thumb, a prissiness that draws attention to custom-made alligator-skin shoes with tips like stilettos.

"Those are some kinda threads, my man," Jaivon says admiringly. He is in a dark three-piece suit with chalk stripes and flared lapels, a big diamond pinkie ring his only show business touch. The memo Molly got said you had to go back to Don King and Bill Graham to find his match as a show promoter.

Dickson ignores the compliment. "Let me ask which is the best way to attract public attention, a series of speeches or rock concerts?"

Jaivon and Foster trade surprised looks. "You serious, man?" Jaivon says.

"The reason I ask is there is a disagreement within our organization."

"There's no comparison," Foster says as if he can't believe what he heard. "Speeches? C'mon, dude."

"So you're saying concerts would be better," Dickson says with a look at Molly.

"A hundred times better," Jaivon says.

"A thousand times," Foster says.

"Okay, I go with that," Jaivon says.

"A thousand times better," Dickson says triumphantly, throwing her another look.

"But the music gotta be dynamite, a course," Jaivon cautions.

"Goes without saying," Foster says. "It has to be strong as that song on the sound track."

"I was hummin' that mofo for a week," Javion says. "Couldn't get it outta my haid no way. Why we even talkin' about speeches? Rex got more like that sound track song? Let's be hearin' them before we go on any mo'. We lookin' at a three-hour show with the intermission." Molly senses a shrewd business intelligence behind the chuckling Uncle Remus front.

Dickson gives each man a smartphone with ear buds. "These are just a few cuts from the album." They plug in and begin bobbing their heads, Javion with eyes closed. "I'd like to listen," Molly says.

"You haven't heard them yet?" Dickson says with a look of pleased surprise. Foster is on his feet doing dance steps to the music in his head. He whirls and dips his knees. Javion, still nodding, hasn't opened his eyes.

"No, I haven't."

"Sorry, but I only brought two. I thought you people would've heard the tracks by now." He rubs it in. "People at corporate are blown away; I played them at a meeting. Most were on their feet like him."

"Fine, I'll hear the whole thing after this." She digs her fingernails into the tormenting itch on her arm.

Javion removes the ear buds after the last track and is quiet for a moment. "Ten concerts will bring in half a billion dollars easy. We'll get two hundred bucks for nose-bleed seats and—woo—concessions? Ten bucks for a ten-ounce Bud and twenty-five for a shot of call liquor. Stop that dancin', fool, I'm talkin' bidness here."

Foster takes out the ear buds. "Wow," he says, "I've never heard anything this good."

"Sound like every instrument in there," Javion says. "What's that one the man play with the monkey?"

"The hurdy-gurdy; yeah, I heard it too. Slack-string guitar, every brass horn, a pipe organ, harmonica, a string section, drums, sitar—shit, I could go on and on."

"And can the man do hard-knock rap? I guess he can! Remind me some of Lil Wayne. What can I say 'cept the man got soul."

"A whole lot of influences all mashed up," Foster says, his face alight. "Sergeant Pepper, Willie, Dylan, Frank and Dino. Kean, Bono; even the Weavers for God's sake."

"I heard like a Ray Charles and the Raelettes riff against a Duke Ellington lick," Javion says. "It take a shitload of musicians to pull this off unless it done with computers and synthesizers. That keep the overhead down, a course, we do it that way. You want me to start workin' on dates? We got ballgames we gotta work around in a lot of cities."

"Yes," Dickson says. "Get right on it."

"No," Molly tells Javion firmly. "I have to run it past Rex."

His shrewd gaze switches between them. "Who da boss here?"

"I am," Molly says.

Dickson silently looks at the sharp points of his expensive shoes.

"You gonna explain what this speech shit is?"

"Not right now."

"Okay, you get back to us, then?" Javion says.

"Yes," she replies.

"They gonna search us on the way out too?" he says, chuckling.

"We love you, man," Foster says.

There are farewell embraces as they leave and Foster adds the increasingly common peck on the cheek. Are we all becoming French, Molly wonders. Submitting with ill grace to the hug, Dickson roughly pulls away when Foster attempts this additional courtesy.

After they have gone, Rex leafs through the thick binder Javion left for a proposed concert tour. There are tabs for stage design, professional crew, logistics and transportation, accommodations, insurance, trucking and equipment leasing for staging, risers, props, lighting, electric distribution, backline, PA, special effects, video projection and so forth.

"It's like moving an army around," Molly says.

"I've been wondering why more than one concert is necessary," he says.

"The promoter says a series would bring in a half a billion dollars."

"It's not about the money, it's about being president. They say politics is show business for ugly people, but why should that be?"

"I think it's supposed to be a joke, like saying somebody has a radio face."

Rex doesn't seem to hear. "Why shouldn't politics be for anyone whatever they look like?"

"To be honest," Molly says, "I don't think an ugly person can be elected today. Abe Lincoln sure couldn't with his long, sad face."

"Why should my looks be held against me?"

"Are you kidding? Who does that?"

"Has someone like me ever been president?" His eyes seem to be on some faraway thing.

"I don't think there has ever been anyone like you."

"I wasn't given all I have for nothing." He turns to her with a look so intense she feels she will shrivel like an ant with the sun through a magnifying glass. "Do you ever wonder why?"

"No," she says faintly.

"I think I know."

"Yes?" She cannot breathe.

"I was chosen by God."

"You... were chosen?"

"To help the people of the world."

CHAPTER 40

"PLEASE HELP ME." HER PLEA IS SO TRAGIC THAT MOLLY THINKS IT WOULD TAKE A HEART OF stone to hang up. "I feel like my life is over and I want to kill myself." Sarah Marsh is crying into the phone. "Will you see me?"

"I'll tell them at the gate," Molly says after a hesitation. How can she say no to someone so broken?

"No, I can't come there. I don't want to see Rex, it would be too hard."

Molly agrees to meet her before the evening rush in the bar of a restaurant on Fourth Street that is fairly smart for the suburbs. She locates Sarah sitting alone at a table and her bodyguards fall behind to give them privacy. Molly hardly recognizes the forlorn figure hunched over a drink, alone in the room except for a codger at the bar. The youthful cuteness and sparkle are gone with the lavender streaks in her unwashed hair. She has dark circles under her eyes and wears jeans and a wrinkled top with as much fashion flair as a body bag.

"Hi," Sarah says wanly. "Thank you for coming. Yes, I know I look awful, so we don't need to talk about it."

"No, not awful," Molly says, feeling a surge of sympathy for this poor creature who was once so cocksure, so certain she was climbing to where the air was so thin only a fortunate few breathed it. "Just, I would say... tired."

"Well, I'm not sleeping, so, yeah."

"Is there something I can I do?" Molly asks.

"*New Yorker* doesn't like my piece and I don't think they'll renew my contract, so I am so totally fucked. I was the youngest person they ever hired and they got excited by the Rex story I stumbled on; but I blew it and it looks like I'll be the youngest to ever be let go."

"Why don't they like your article?"

"They say it reads like something in a fan magazine. I toned it down as we went back and forth, but my editor still didn't like it. Everyone beat us to the punch about how awesome Rex is, all those suck-up feature stories based on hearsay crap; she says all I gave them is more detail about his awesomeness."

"But you were with him when that bomb went off."

Sarah shrugs indifferently. "Yeah, well, it seems like I gave away too much stuff in interviews. Looking back, I shouldn't have talked to the media. What happened seems stale now and nobody was charged and the investigation is stalled. She wanted to know without coming right out and saying so if I slept with Rex; little things she said, like, you know, hints? It was like a total fucking invasion of my privacy."

"Well, you did sleep with him," Molly points out.

"I know, I know, but I was professional enough so it didn't compromise my work."

Evidently not, Molly thinks. "What was it like, sleeping with Rex?" It was twenty on a scale of ten before, but she wonders if Sarah revised her opinion after she was jilted.

Sarah raises downcast eyes. "The absolute best," she says, her mood lifting. "He knows every position in the Kama Sutra from a book he found in his library. I'll never have sex that good again. He's just…" She searches for words. "Well, the best." Sinking back into listlessness, she catches a waitress's eye for another drink. "You want something?" Molly orders water from an iceberg sold in a fancy bottle for fifteen dollars.

"Could you get the round?" Sarah says. "I don't have money right now. I sold my car for living expenses and my parents are pissed." She adds in a voice near tears, "They cut me off."

Molly knows of many a modelling career shortened by drugs and recognizes the symptoms, the hopelessness, the slovenliness, and now the acrid body odour that reaches her.

As if she knows what she is thinking, Sarah says in a flat voice, "I'm doing heroin." She pulls a sleeve back to show needle tracks.

"Oh, Sarah."

"When I'm high, it makes me feel like when I was with Rex and you guys." She thinks for a moment. "I'm sorry I was such a bitch."

Molly believes her contrition is genuine. "You're young, that's all. Young people make mistakes; I made my share." Nothing this bad, she thinks.

"I don't feel young anymore, I feel like an old junkie. I don't even brush my teeth."

The old man behind his basket of pretzels and beer stein takes an interest in them in the mirror's reflection behind the bar. Next, he'll turn on his stool and openly stare, she thinks. Why is it so hard to mind your own business after a certain age? Women are worse; they live to pass on gossip. It's not even necessary to cast for a curtain-twitching archtype for commercial work as it's understood all old ladies do it.

"You need to go home and go into rehab," Molly says firmly. "We'll pay the airfare."

"I'd still be a failure without a job." Her voice is lifeless.

"What if there was something new for your story?"

"Like what?"

"Something big."

Interest flickers. "It would have to be huge."

"This will be."

"You don't mean his album launch?"

"No, but that's part of it."

"There'll be a tour?" Sarah straightens in her chair, listlessness falling away as her focus sharpens.

"Even bigger."

"Omigod, what is it?"

"Does it sound enough to get your article in the magazine?"

"If it's as big as you say, Sarah exclaims, "they'd put it on the fucking cover!" The kickass journalist is back. "Tell me, tell me, tell me."

"You have to go into rehab first," Molly says coolly. "Then you get the story, which I guarantee you is earth shaking."

She hesitates, the addiction very strong. "I'll do it," she cries suddenly. "When?"

Molly calls the woman at Rock-Steady who makes their travel arrangements and tells her to book a seat on the next flight to Boston. "One of our guys will drive you to the airport and see that you get on the flight."

Sarah is stunned things are happening this fast and then overcome by emotion. She bursts into tears. "Why are you being so nice to me?"

Molly is at a loss for an answer. "I guess something just got into me," she says with a laugh.

"Can it be tomorrow?" Sarah says.

Molly knows what she would do with the twenty-four hours. "Tonight or never, honey," she says firmly.

"Yeah, you're right," Sarah says. Molly motions over the lead bodyguard. "Take her to the airport for a flight to Boston. Someone will meet her there. No stops between here and the airport no matter what she says. Wait until the airplane is in the air."

They start to leave together, and then Sarah comes back. "You have every right to say no, but could I ask one last favor?"

"What is it?"

"I'm going to go through rehab and come out clean on the other side," she says bravely. "And when I do I'll be able to rework my profile so *New Yorker* publishes it and my career will get back on track. But if you give another writer the kind of access I had, it'll be spiked for good. That's what I have that no other writer does, all those hours of being with him. Is that asking too much?"

She looks so bedraggled and forlorn, so at the end of her string that Molly can't say no. "Deal," she says.

"Thank you," she says simply before leaving, her shoulders heaving from her sobs.

Molly meets Randall when he comes back from house-hunting with Abby; they sit in the game room where the trophy heads stare glassy-eyed from the wall. She tells him about Sarah.

"Maybe she can turn her life around," he says. "I thought you two were enemies."

"She asked why I was being so nice, and I couldn't think of a reason."

"How did she get on smack?"

"It took Rex's place in her life like rebound romance."

"Maybe it's part of the plan," Randall says.

"What plan?"

"You don't think there's a plan here?"

"I know you do."

"I have no doubt about it. The only question is whose?" A thought occurs to him. "Anybody else in the bar?"

"No."

"You sure?"

"There was a nosy old man. I hope when I'm that age…"

"That probably was Camael," Randall cuts in.

"Your angel?" Molly says with a half laugh. "No, this was just some ordinary old guy."

"That's what he looks like, ordinary."

"Angels stand out in a crowd, don't they? Wings or a halo, cherubs flying around them."

"Maybe they looked like the old paintings at one time, but that's too over the top today. People would think it was being ironic."

Molly wishes she'd paid more attention to the old coot. "That just wasn't my image of an angel."

"Did you see him leave?"

"I wasn't paying attention."

"But he wasn't there when you left?"

Molly thinks, twirling a thick lock of red hair in her finger. "No, I don't so."

"That's how he operates, there one second and gone the next."

They pursue private thoughts for a moment. "Rex said something funny to me today."

"I haven't seen a sense of humor," Randall replies, "so it must be the other kind of funny."

"He said God chose him to run for president."

Here we go, Randall thinks. "Did he say more or was that it?"

"He asked did that bother me and I said no. I was afraid to ask him questions."

"I get the willies, too."

"Look at my arm." She showed him the rash. "I know that's from nerves."

"My mother-in-law told Abby she's never seen a man age as fast as me. She thinks I've got cancer and I'm hiding it."

"Do you think he'd let me take a medical leave?"

"No."

"I don't, either." They fell silent again. "He wants to take up painting next; he told me to find an artist to show him how."

"He'll be as good in two days as those old Dutch masters."

Randall wonders how to interpret things. Was Sarah led into drugs by Satan on the chance she might re-enter the picture or was there some even deeper level of complexity at work here?

The next day, Molly is on the phone to a dean at the San Francisco Art Institute. "I'm looking for someone to teach Rex how to paint."

"Good Lord, *the* Rex?"

This reaction is common and every door flies open for him. "He wants the best to come to our place on a daily basis for an hour or so." She still gets a thrill from saying money is no object.

"The best teacher or the best artist?" the dean says after thinking.

"Just the best for the job." A cosmetologist is working on her nails and a stylist on her hair; security doesn't want her going outside the compound for such mundane things and sometimes she feels as trapped as Rapunzel in the tower. A bunch of the guys are chanting as they double-time around the property. Their lives seem to consist of exercising, staring at the hills and water with binoculars, eating and sleeping. She thinks she would go crazy from the boredom.

"Someone like the old Dutch masters," she tells the dean.

A dry laugh. "Well, they're not making many of those these days." He mentions several names that mean nothing to her.

"Cutting to the chase," she says, "whose paintings make the most money?"

"That would be Vargas." He says the name with distaste. "For what it's worth, I think the man is a whore and a charlatan." After Hollywood, she thinks, that's no problem.

The Vargas Gallery is just off Union Square where a line of tourists is at the door. A junior executive from Rock-Steady has made arrangements for Molly to be admitted without waiting; he stands outside when she and two bodyguards in their wrap-around sunglasses are let off at the curb.

"He's the Thomas Kinkaid of the day," a gallery attendant says proudly as she leads them to a back office. "Kinkaid had his work in one of every twenty homes in America and we're on track to better that record."

Vargas is a diminutive man in a grandiose get-up that proclaims a scorn for the ordinary conventions. He has Buffalo Bill's golden locks and Van Dyke beard and moustache and wears a shirt with puffy sleeves tucked into silk pantaloons. A Wellington boot rests on a cluttered desk and his arms-crossed posture shows insouciance.

"Hello," Molly says.

Vargas does not answer at first as if studying her for hidden condescension; the early years of artist poverty supporting himself cleaning restrooms in government facilities have left their mark. What filthy pigs people are!

"Who are these men?" he asks finally.

"They are my associates," Molly says nicely. She is well-acquainted with the touchiness of the artistic temperament from television commercials. She rather liked his work from what she had seen on the internet even though but his mother-and-child paintings in pastoral settings are punching bags for art critics. They are offended by the sentimentality shown of farm animals bathed in sunset's hues as lamplight glows from cottage windows. His paintings are denounced as pastiches of Kinkaid and Norman Rockwell; she gathers they are two of the more despised figures in the art world. "You can almost smell the manure," one critic wrote of the glisten Vargas put on a cow pie. Molly thought that should be seen as a compliment though obviously it wasn't. She explains that Rex wants someone to teach him to paint.

Vargas is stunned, insulted. "Do you think I teach beginners?"

"Rex is talented and learns fast," she says.

"I have heard of the man, who has not?—nor am I surprised that he has heard of me. But when Vargas picks up a brush he earns three thousand dollars an hour until the painting is finished." He puts his Wellingtons to the floor and rises to his small height as if the number is so daunting it will end the conversation.

"We'll pay you six thousand dollars an hour," Molly says calmly.

Flabbergasted, he puts a hand to the desk for support. Three thousand dollars was not the strict truth, or even close. "I... I accept."

"Can you come with us now?"

"You mean this very moment?"

"You're penciled in for three o'clock," Molly says. "You don't have to bring anything; we have set up a studio with everything including the bowl of fruit he wants to paint first."

Regaining his Grande Artiste manner, Vargas dons a satin robe as colorful as Joseph's coat and strides through the gallery in an Australian bush hat; he carries a New Guinea head-knocker staff festooned with talismanic charms and tinkling bells. He nods and smiles at customers buying prints of his work and pauses for a single autograph, waving off other seekers.

"How did you know Vargas would accept?" he asks in the car.

"Nobody says no to Rex," Molly says matter-of-factly.

"If I do not find the situation—what is the word?—congenial, Vargas will not hesitate to refuse." He takes a pinch of snuff from a small silver box.

"I didn't know people still did that," Molly remarks. She thought it went out with powdered wigs.

"People don't like cigarette smoke, but I will have my tobacco." He looks prepared to argue the point, flourishing a large silk handkerchief from his cuff and sneezing into it. He stares at her with intensity. "You are not as happy as you want others to think. The artist knows when the subject tries to hide the truth."

"I'm exactly as happy as I want people to think." She dislikes amateur psychology.

"There is tension in your face and how you hold your head. Vargas knows massage techniques emphasizing acupuncture meridians." The smile that shows long canines reminds her of Bela Lugosi in the Dracula film.

"I'm fine, but thanks." She is certain he is too weird looking for steady work in TV advertising.

"The offer is there."

He is visibly impressed by Bluff Point and does not object to the pat down or the sniffer dog's inspection for explosives. "Ah, yes, that terrible thing," he says when Molly explains. "Vargas does not follow the news, but our young people—how I love the young people!—told him what happened."

Entering the new studio, Vargas throws up an arm as if struck by a blinding light when Rex turns to him. "But it can't be," he cries, "such perfection is not possible." Rex receives the tribute with his usual indifference, as does Molly, both being used to it in their different ways. Vargas bows, sweeping off his bush hat in a theatrical way. "Only an artist can appreciate such manly beauty."

"You're going to teach me to paint," Rex says abruptly. A small canvas is on an easel in the good light from the balcony.

"It will be my pleasure, but you will not approach what Nature has already created in your own person."

Rex says, "I've been doing some work to get ready." He goes to a closet and returns with pen-and-ink sketches.

"Why, these are superb," the artist gasps as he looks through them. "They are the work of a mature talent."

"They're not bad," Rex concedes. "Now I need to learn about color. Let's start with a still life."

Vargas notes the large canvas leaning against a wall. "That is meant for a full-length portrait? You are very ambitious."

"Let's get to it," Rex says with a glance that tells Molly to go.

An hour later the lesson is over and Vargas finds his way downstairs, crushed. "I have spent my life as an artist and I don't have a tenth of his ability. You should have seen the work he began on a bowl of apples and pears. They radiated the very essence of those fruits, the tartness of the apple and the sweetness of the pear seem to come through, and yet there was a tiny flaw in the perspective I mentioned. None but an expert eye would have noticed and that eye would have instantly forgiven the error, but he saw it at once and threw the canvas in the fireplace and up it went in flames. If it hadn't happened so fast, I would have begged to let me sell it in my gallery under my own name if that was the only way to preserve such a… well, in its finished form I would have called it a minor masterpiece. But of course he would've refused, wouldn't he?"

Molly sees that his grandiosity, developed as armor for the art world's malice, has fallen away. He is meek as he puts on the bush hat and gives her a timid wave at the door. "Rex told me to return tomorrow at the same time."

"Who's the Disney character?" Randall asks after he leaves.

"He's the famous painter Vargas," Molly says.

"Not famous enough for me to hear of him."

"Do you want to know what he said about Rex?"

"As a wild guess, he's a genius."

"He's says he is ten times the painter he is, and this is a man with an ego as big as he is little—or it was before today."

"Where did he come from?"

"I called an art college, why?" She sees he is annoyed.

"I want to know who's coming and going, that's my job. Tell me next time, okay?"

"Don't get your nose out of joint."

"Has Rex made his decision about one concert or a bunch?"

"Rock-Steady is putting together options."

He gaze is steady. "You're not going to let Dickson squeeze you out."

"Rex will make up his own mind," she flares, "but why wouldn't I want to let myself be squeezed out if I want to? I'm in the middle of everything down to approving menus for—what is it now, forty-two men with big appetites?—and seeing that the house cleaners do their job."

"Tell Rock-Steady to send an assistant."

"That would just be someone else for me to manage."

"It's called delegating; people do it all the time."

Molly storms out of the room with a fiery look thrown over her shoulder. "You just don't get it, do you?"

Of course I get it, he thinks. We're breaking down mentally and physically, everyone except the ringmaster of the circus. The security force has a steady rotation in and out because of the strain of constant watchfulness.

"You used to drink a glass of wine with dinner," Abby had said as they got ready for bed the other night. "Then it went to two and tonight you had three. Mother noticed, too."

"I wonder how she finds time for her own business."

"I hate it when you're like this. She worries about you and all the stress; you have to be around when those boys are growing up."

"Heap some guilt on these shoulders, I'm staggering but I can take it."

Abby ignores his reply. "Which house did you like better, San Anselmo or Greenbrae?"

"San Anselmo," Randall said, turning out the light, "those Greenbrae hills will be murder when I'm old and decrepit in six months."

"You know, you can just walk away from this job. People do that all the time."

"Actually, I can't, I signed a contract with a penalty clause," he lied.

Abigail had sat up in bed. "Without telling me?"

"It didn't seem important at the time, just some formality; that'll teach me to read something before I sign it. I'd have to give back most of what I've been paid."

"I can't believe you did that!"

"The Templeton Hall shit storm was going on at the time, remember? I was distracted by a million things." He guided the conversation to redecorating if they chose one of the houses. One was built on Craftsman lines and the other was ranch-house style, both way out of reach if he was still a flatfoot. The real estate agent had four more lined up to look at.

He telephones Penny at headquarters. "You are one hard dude to catch up with," she says. He feels almost nostalgic hearing the background noise, the droning voices over the police radio, phones ringing, people bitching. "Do you ever check for messages?"

"I can never remember the code on the answering machine."

"If you're too cheap for voice mail, you ought to write it down and put it in your wallet."

"If I want abuse I'll talk to my mother-in-law. I was calling to see what's new with Templeton Hall."

"The FBI is already acting almost like it's a cold case file. They're re-interviewing everybody and want to talk to you. I told them you're in a remote fishing camp in the woods. How're Abby and the kids?" Randall tells her they are all in the pink, never better. "Tell everyone Penny said hello," she says. "Gotta run, there's an accident with injuries."

Randall makes an appointment to meet with Atticus Noble, the flamboyant criminal lawyer, and drives into San Francisco where he has Georgian-style offices in a small building almost in the shadow of the Transamerica Pyramid. His chamber is all mahogany and brass with a fireplace and fender. The bow-tied lawyer is coatless, his starched two-toned shirt has French cuffs that Randall has a feeling are never rolled up no matter how warm it is.

"I thought the head of security was Finnese," Noble says, starting out in a tone he would use on an uncooperative witness.

"He's the subcontractor."

Noble has unblinking, hawk-like eyes that Randall thinks don't miss much. "Why hasn't your name come up before, Mr. Randall?"

"I keep a low profile."

"And why is that?"

"Personal choice."

Noble assesses the answer with a skeptical tilt of his head. "How can I help you?"

"The FBI wants to talk to me."

"A number of attempts have been made on your employer's life; I'm surprised they haven't got around to you before now."

"They want to talk to me about something else, the Templeton Hall massacre."

Noble's manner sharpens. "What is the connection, Mr. Randall?"

"I was one of the investigating officers."

"You are a policeman?"

"I retired when I took the job with Rex." Under Noble's rapid questions, the story quickly unfolds. "So you were initially suspended for complicity in those terrible crimes but then quickly reinstated?"

"That's it in a nutshell."

The lawyer gazes at him. "I'm more interested in the meat of the nut than the shell. The man with amnesia you took to Templeton Hall vanished without a trace?"

"He's long gone." That's true, if only in a Clinton it-depends-on-what-your-definition-of-'is'-is sense, Randall thinks. The Rex of today is not the man he found walking down that country road.

"Why did you retire from the police force?"

"I didn't like the way they treated me."

"How did you get your present job?" Noble sits on a corner of his desk so he's looking down on Randall.

"Through a friend, Molly Simon."

"I know Miss Simon, a very competent woman. She is Rex's assistant, I believe."

"More than that."

"Most of my dealings have been with Mr. Dickson."

"She hired him and can fire him, just so you know."

"Really?" Noble looks amused. "He gives a different impression." Randall says he has no doubt of it. "You were interviewed about this once, why do you object to another?" the lawyer asks.

"I don't want to give them something that would drag Rex's name through the mud. If you think he's big name now, wait a bit."

"He's on just about every magazine cover and talked about on TV incessantly; I've never seen anything like it. How can the man get bigger? And what interest would the government have in damaging his reputation?"

"They can find a reason to do whatever they want, you know that."

A slow smile spreads. "You sound like someone who believes in conspiracies, Mr. Randall."

"Don't you? Look at the tobacco industry. Look at Watergate and 9/11. Obamacare and Hillary's emails. And that's just the stuff people know about." Those are minnows, Randall thinks, compared to this whale that could break the surface without warning.

Noble takes a gold coin from a drawer and begins passing it between the fingers of his hand like a magician—an aid to thinking, Randall guesses. "There is no reason for them to know you work for Rex."

"They're going to ask for the names of everybody."

"Of course," Noble concedes, "just a matter of time. When I was a federal prosecutor I would have demanded it in the first twenty-four hours, but this U.S. Attorney is rather thick-headed and has a clown posse for a staff. It's the old story; second-raters hire third-raters. Still, this is a pretty big mistake even for him."

"It would be bad if my name came up." He wonders if some power—Satan, Camael, Rex himself—caused the government's blunder.

"That's easy, get off the payroll." He gives him a sheet of paper and a pen. "Write 'I resign' and sign your name. We'll leave it undated for now. There's no reason anyone needs to know you and Ms. Simon entered into a private employment agreement."

"That sounds shady," Randall says.

"The law has shade as well as light otherwise there would be no need for lawyers. I'll resist their request for records as a matter of course; they're used to my cussedness and will assume it's more of the same." The smile lengthens his nose into beakiness. "I love to yank their chain; if I don't make a prosecutor turn purple with rage I haven't done my job."

Randall writes out the resignation and pushes it back to Noble, who folds it in half and puts it in an envelope. "If I was advising your people on this, which I'm not, I would recommend that your salary be paid henceforth by an off-shore bank with two or three dummy corporations in between. Mr. Finnese will know what to do."

CHAPTER 41

JAIVON IS PHILOSOPHICAL ABOUT STAGING ONLY ONE CONCERT. "WE JACK UP THE PAY-PER-VIEW and concessions so we get back some of the scrilla we walkin' 'way from." He clinches a seven-inch Montecristo cigar between his teeth, unlit at Molly's request, rolling it from one side of his mouth to another.

"That's fucked up, man," Foster protests, "leaving all that cash on the table." His blue T-shirt front and back says Save the World, Save the People, Save the Animals.

Molly wonders what's left to save. She decides it must be more of the modern irony that goes right over her head.

"You're talking fundraising, we're thinking political impact," says Kornhouser. "The political media won't cover ten concerts, the message would be diluted."

"What fundraisin' got to do with it?" Jaivon asks. "You folks talkin' about speeches last time and politics now. What happened to show business? There somethin' Foster and me ain't gettin'?"

Molly explains that Rex will make an announcement of a political nature. "I'll leave it at that."

Concentrating on balancing a pencil on the knuckles of one hand like it's the most important thing in the world right now, Dickson has not taken part in the discussion and wears his sulky look.

"Politics is fucked, man," Foster says. "You don't go to a concert to hear somebody make a speech and shit like that."

"Music and politics have gone together forever," declares the aroused Kornhouser. "It goes back way before Roosevelt and Happy Days Are Here Again."

"Huh?!" Foster says.

Molly doubts he has heard of either the man or the song. Rex hasn't said what policy ideas will be in his announcement, but the state of the public schools is there for the taking. Kids seem dumber than ever.

Kornhouser and Foster quarrel over what is more important, politics or popular culture. Rex takes it in with an expression of amused scorn; she thinks of it as his what-fools-these-mortals-be look that he has more often these days. "What's the best venue for this?" he interrupts

"Dallas," Jaivon and Foster say in unison. "You got Cowboy stadium," Jaivon continues, "and a huge parkin' lot for Jumbotron screens."

"You price the parking lot tickets at a third of the stadium seating," Foster says.

"Half," Jaivon says, taking the cigar from his mouth. "We got some ground to make up."

"Better," Foster agrees, nodding.

"New York," says Kornhouser. "It's the media capital of the world, perfect for what we want. Half the country hates Texas."

"Ain't no parking lot in New York or New Jersey can touch Dallas," Javion says. "Then there's the mo-fo taxes; if the lady wasn't here, I'd say sumpin' stronger..."

"I think the middle of America would be best," Rex says. "St. Louis?"

"Flyover land," Foster snorts. "They can't afford what we're going to price tickets. The coasts are where it's at."

"Hang on, kid," Parker says, ducking a look at Rex, "we don't want to price out John Q. Citizen and his missus." His shoes have a bright shine today.

"We could raffle off a few thousand tickets so's the poor folk can come," Jaivon suggests. "Throw in some free chicken and ribs."

"Not free," Foster says, leaning forward on his elbows.

"But reasonable," Kornhouser insists, the great expanse of flesh below his chin pulses in syncopation with the words. The pencil falls from Dickson's knuckles as he watches with horrified fascination; Molly has noticed he can't keep his eyes from it when Kornhouser speaks.

"We raffle the barbecue off like the tickets," Jaivon says, the cigar back in his mouth.

"Dallas," Rex decides, rising from the table. "I'll leave you to work out the details." He leaves to go upstairs for his painting lesson with Vargas.

Vargas stays longer than usual and Molly catches him on the way out the door to the waiting SUV. "Everything go all right?" she asks in a chipper way that she is far from feeling. Men can let their moods show, she thinks, but women are always expected to look upbeat—another of life's unfairness. Vargas glances around before he replies. "No one can have such talent; it's not humanly possible to develop such gifts so quickly. I'm learning new things about creating light on canvas from him."

"He's good at everything," Molly says.

"No, no." Vargas gives another look around like a man who is frightened. "It is literally impossible."

"And yet he's doing it, so it is literally possible. He doesn't let anyone but you see the painting, so I probably shouldn't even have an opinion." The lock has been changed and Rex has the only key; a guard sits outside scrolling the internet on his tablet so he doesn't go mad from boredom.

"It is a full-length portrait," Vargas says, "and I compare his work to such masters as Cericault and the Holbeins."

"What's the reason for all the secrecy?" she asks.

"It might be that he wants to wait until it is perfect in every detail before he reveals this astonishing genius to the world. A movie star who is also a baseball star…" Vargas falls silent.

"It's a first," Molly says.

"But to add to those an ability equal to the greatest artists in the history of the world…" He trails off again. "He is painting bottom up from a mirror; the lower half has already been completed. The fold of the cuff, the thread of the fabric, and the gleam from the shoes are exquisite. Most artists begin a self-portrait with the head, which he has not even roughed in yet. But the hands, they make me shudder with horror and disgust. You've noticed his own hands, beautifully shaped with long fingers."

Molly nods. "Everything about him is perfect."

"The hands he has sketched are thick and gross, the fingers like thick sausages with stiff black hairs on the back; they are grotesque ape hands holding his coat lapels in a way… it's hard to describe… that say there is no tenderness in them, no human feeling, only brute strength for crushing."

Molly thinks it is weird way to put things, but artists see things differently.

"Critics are fools; my own work shows that. Words cannot do justice to what the eye sees, but as you see I've fallen into the same trap. The hands Rex sketched are those of a monstrous being… and yet it is a self-portrait."

"Maybe you're reading too much into them," Molly ventures.

"No," he says, more subdued. "They terrify me." He arranges the bush hat carefully on the flowing Buffalo Bill locks.

"How long before it's finished?" She finds herself wondering if completion will unleash whatever havoc Randall's angel friend predicts. Stop it, she tells herself. These are the crazy thoughts mentally ill people have.

"The hardest work is yet to come when he begins on the face; that is when he must capture his own soul. I think it has made Rex tense, this most certain of men. His technical skill will carry him further than any living artist, but not to the very summit of artistry. That will require a willingness to fully understand himself and the inner struggle everyone wages between what is good in him and what must be hidden from the world. If he has given a hint with the hands, even so noble a countenance as his must reflect the hidden side for his art to be true and great. If not, the portrait will be merely wonderful, a triumph of technique but no more. People will praise it while wondering what concealed message the hands convey, but it will not be counted as among the great masterpieces of the ages. And when great art is the goal, as his is, you see the dilemma. He can eclipse the greatest artists who ever held a brush, but only if he is honest. This is what Vargas believes."

"Why does it matter?" Molly asks. "Why care if he falls a little short when he's got so much else going on for him."

"Do you not know him?" Vargas asks incredulously. "You see him every day, how can you not see him for what he is? I swear to you it is not human this zeal to acquire every secret that art has. It is like some kind of supernatural being who has taken human form for a purpose that has it divided within. The conflict is right there in those hands, those monstrous, ugly hands swollen near to bursting with evil intent." He takes off the hat and runs a hand through his mane. "I told him he has learned all I can teach him and this is my last lesson." He trudges to the SUV without a look back.

Molly finds Randall on the roof where he watches the slingshot specialist take a bead on a drone flying overhead. Seeing she is about to speak, Randall motions for silence. "He's missed twice already," he whispers, "and he's pissed."

The ball bearing is launched, hits its target and the drone twirls to a splash-down in the bay.

"Probably media," the grinning slingshot man says.

"Vargas isn't coming back," Molly says when she draws Randall aside. "Do you want to know why?"

"No, but from your face you're going to tell me anyhow."

"He doesn't think Rex is human, he's some sort of spirit that has taken human form."

Randall's look says is that all? "Tell me now how that moves the ball down the field."

"He thinks there's a war going on in Rex."

"What brilliant insight."

"But it's, like, confirmation," she says. "It shows in the hands he's painting in the self-portrait." Seeing his puzzlement, Molly bursts out, "Oh, you had to hear him." But she can't stop the skeptical tape running in her head from loop-ing back: if she could only know for sure. Two people could be fooling them-selves, digging the delusional rut deeper, but a third?

"I don't need confirmation," Randall says. He jams his hands in his pock-ets and walks away.

I need to talk to someone, Molly thinks. She has lost touch with friends, the ones she used to let her hair down with. Even her rushed, just-checking-in texts have stopped. Tuning them out has made them think they've been dropped; no longer part of what they assume is her new glamorous, exciting life. If only they knew how she envied them! Even Eli Pico, who hoped that Molly could help her jazz up her going-nowhere career, has stopped trying to reach her. Business as usual she must be thinking. Every day thousands of names drop off hundreds of lists in Hollywood. Good luck, adios. No, not even that, just a line through the name or the delete button pressed. And even if her old friends were still available, how could she talk to them about this? They would sit across the table, impressed at first by the great clothes and the new hairstyle touched up so the gray is gone. But as she went on the jitters would begin. Molly has gone so far around the bend, they'd think, she's never coming back. They were prac-tical, down-to-earth women like her... or what she used to be. Word would get around, and some would be glad for her comeuppance.

Hal Spiegel, a hyper man with enormous white teeth, is the head of public relations for Rock-Steady. The thickish lips that bare those teeth in frequent smiles remind her of awnings that roll up and down in shop windows. The effect is too Bugs Bunnyish for work in commercials. He telephones as she ponders not having a friend she can talk to.

"*Der Spiegel* is the latest to request a one-on-one with Rex."

"What's that?" Molly asks.

"A very important news organization in Germany."

"How many are on the list now?"

"Let's see, a hundred and eighty-seven. We get four or five new ones a day; *Ceylon Today* in Sri Lanka is another. The editor is coming here on a holiday, it says here. Very flexible as to time and place."

"Add both to the list."

"The thing is the German request came from their Washington bureau chief, who it seems is well connected. That means word is beginning to get around the political world; how much longer do we have to wait on the *New Yorker*?"

"I'll talk to Rex." She hasn't told him about Sarah being in rehab.

"Why are we waiting? Is there some kind of, er… relationship I should know about?"

"You didn't ask that question."

"A question?" She pictures his lips lifting, revealing the enormous teeth. "Did you hear a question? This must be a bad connection."

On impulse, she asks, "Does your company have access to a shrink? One of our people needs to see somebody on a rush basis."

"No wonder with all the pressure you guys are under! Yes, I think we can fix you up, a woman we use on a consulting basis. She's on Bush Street in the Financial District. How soon?"

"Today."

"Hold on while I call her." He is back within thirty seconds. "Five o'clock okay? She will see your person at the end of her business day. Is there a name?"

"He'll just show up," Molly says. "He's a little sensitive about this stuff."

"One of the macho guys? Fine, I'll pass the word."

Psychiatrist Evelyn Logan has the sort of inner calm Molly has always envied.

She is middle-aged with dark hair that has highlights and wears a skirt and blouse with an expensive designer scarf in earth-toney orange and white that brings things together. She has glasses in chic frames that match her shoes; it is a well-planned and executed look that says she is thoughtful, dependable and discreet. Molly would book her for a commercial as a financial adviser or health plan executive. She accepts her invitation for a cup of chamomile tea.

Dr. Logan explains she isn't a clinical psychiatrist but more on the academic side of the street; she works with Rock-Steady on the integration of corporate cultures after mergers and acquisitions. But if it was a case of any port in a storm right now, she would be glad to listen and point her to someone better suited to her needs.

Comfy chairs in a tweedy fabric face her desk that has a circle of family photos—her two girls are in college back east, one a freshman and the other a sophomore. "Tell me a little about yourself and then we can get into what brings you here. Mr. Spiegel said there was some urgency—he also said you would be a he." She has a nice laugh.

"I had a career in television advertising until last year," Molly says. "I found faces for roles in commercials—new faces, different ones than the same old odds and ends from the casting agencies. I traveled all over the country, usually by myself."

"Oh, how interesting."

"I don't have a husband, as you can see from my finger, and my two old boyfriends are dead." She surprises herself by bursting into tears; she had thought all that was under control. "They were murdered."

Dr. Logan's poise is shaken and her dark eyes fill with sympathy. "I'm so sorry," she says, pushing a box of tissues toward her.

"But that's not why I'm here," Molly says, blotting her eyes with the tissue.

"Oh."

"I got another job last year… by accident. That's what I want to talk to you about."

Dr. Logan takes a deep breath, adjusting from the murders. "What is the new job?"

"I work for a famous celebrity."

"I don't need to know his or her name if you don't want to tell me, but I understand that kind of work can be stressful given all the demands a difficult personality can make."

"He's Rex."

"That *is* famous," the psychiatrist exclaims. "My girls are just crazy about him. They were so upset by that awful thing at the premiere that we did a conference call, the three of us. It was hard to get them settled down; and all the girls they live with were like that." She looks more closely at Molly. "Were you there?"

"Yes, but that's not why I'm here, either."

"There's more?" Evelyn makes another adjustment. "Just those together would seem to…"

"I work with someone," Molly interrupts, "who is a very good person, but he has a strong feeling, well, it's more than that, something terrible is going to happen. The thing is I'm starting to believe it too."

"Something terrible did happen," the psychiatrist points out, "the helicopter crash that killed all those people."

"I still jump when I hear a loud sound," Molly says. A bolt of adrenalin shoots through her system, making her heart leap, and it takes a long time for her nerves to quiet down. Randall told her years might pass might she gets over it. "It's given me hives."

"It hasn't been all that long," Dr. Gordon says warmly, "and I understand the police haven't…"

"No, I'm talking about something far worse."

Evelyn is perplexed. "Far worse?"

"Do you know about End Times?" Molly asks.

It takes a few seconds for that memory to be unshelved from her mind's library of misfiled and irrelevant data. "Oh," she says, "do you mean the Biblical thing, what's it called? Revolutions? No, Revelations. I didn't think people still talked about that outside of…" A tactful silence as she looks away and then back. "Is this individual a member of a cult?"

Wouldn't some expert say that they do qualify as a cult, Molly wonders. Rex and the two of them—three if you counted Vargas, which you couldn't really— the mysteries about Rex, the sergeant's experiences with an angel (mental air quotes here), the intimation only they share that some calamity that will overwhelm humankind if something isn't done. It's classic cult behavior.

"No," Molly says.

"So it's an individual's obsession we're dealing with and you're afraid you'll also fall under its power?"

"No," Molly says, shaking her head. "That's not it."

"We know the end of time *isn't* coming, so it has to be one or the other," Dr. Logan insists gently.

"I don't know that, that's the problem. And it's not the end of time, it's End Times."

Dr. Logan frowns. "Perhaps I don't exactly understand what that means."

"As *I* understand it, it's the final battle between good and evil when things are put right forever. Virtue is rewarded and wickedness punished."

Dr. Logan says dryly, "And what happens then?"

"I'm not clear on that," Molly confesses.

"Well," Dr. Logan says briskly, all business, "let's look it up." She turns to the computer at a right angle to her desk and taps rapidly. "Okay," she says, "massive cataclysms, earth changes, economic woes, evil threats, wars, a complete unraveling of society. Nation will rise against nation and kingdom against kingdom. Famines and pestilences, terrors and great signs from heaven. It does sound awfully grim," she says with a wry glance at Molly. "Really bad for women who are pregnant or nursing infants."

Molly walks to the window with the cup of tea still too hot to drink and looks down on the street scene many stories below; people just now are headed home or still grinding away despite corporate lip service about balanced lives. Nobody leaves for home on time, she thinks. The computer keys are clacking rapidly behind her. "Christianity traditionally depicts the End Times as full of tribulation—great word you don't hear very often—and, let's see, the second coming of Christ, who will face the Antichrist and usher in the Kingdom of God. The oceans roaring, people fainting from fear. Some uncertainty as to when, however. Jesus said, 'The precise time, however, will come like a thief in the night.' Also said, 'But concerning that day and hour no one knows, not even the angels of heaven, nor the Son, but the Father only.'

"Jews say God returns the Jewish people to the Land of Israel—well, that's already done, isn't it? He resurrects the dead and creates a new heaven and earth and so forth. 'They shall beat their swords into plowshares and their spears into pruning hooks; nation will not lift sword against nation and they will no longer study war.' There's no hunger or war, no jealousy or rivalry, all delicacies are as available as dust, which I guess means they're really common. The only job people will have is to know God. 'For the earth shall be filled with the knowledge of God, as the waters cover the sea.'"

Molly sees orderly lines form below at the stops for the Peninsula and Marin buses. People board with tablets and smartphones ready to be pulled out, hoping to get more work done before reaching home to catch up with the kids and have dinner. Then they buckle down to more work before bed. Down time is disappearing, Molly thinks; if you are unable or unwilling to put in the time after work and weekends, there is someone who will. The computer keys rattle on merrily, as Dr. Logan continues.

"In Islam, the Day of Judgment follows the appearance of the Mahdi on a white stallion. He is the Muslim messiah and defeats another false messiah with the help of Jesus, who the Jews think was a false messiah. This is interesting: there is another white horse in Hinduism, ridden this time by Kalka, the final incarnation of Vishnu. White horses are definitely a thing. Let's see, who is Visnu?" The keys clack furiously. "Okay, he's pale blue and has four arms. He is all present, not limited by space, time or substance. Moving on, Buddha predicted that his teachings would be forgotten after five thousand years, then comes more of that turmoil. Then a bodhisattva, one of the four sublime states a human can achieve in life—very compassionate it says here—appears and rediscovers the teaching of dharma. Okay, what is that?" The keys rattle. "No single definition it turns out."

There is a manic quality to her typing that nibbles at the edge of Molly's mind. "In Hinduism, dharma means behavior considered to be in accord with rta—I probably mispronounced that—which is the order that makes life and universe possible, including the right way of living. Buddhists call dharma cosmic law and order, which sounds pretty much like the same thing. For Sikhs, it means the path of righteousness."

"Woo hoo, the Zoroastrians believe in a final clean up of the universe when good destroys evil and everything is in perfect unity with God as it was at the time of creation." The woo hoo makes Molly turn back to Dr. Gordon. She nearly drops the cup.

While she gazed at the street below, the psychiatrist has changed. Her face is empurpled, her hair sticks straight up like a fright wig, and her eyes bulge with supernatural fury. Her body, burst from her clothing. is grotesquely swollen and oozes a shine like an insect metamorphous in time-lapse photography. "You stupid, fucking bitch, don't you get it?" she yells. "They're all dreamers! Evil will always be." A smell like an open sewer, ripe and revolting, fills the room.

A knowing smile of crooked, black teeth appears below a nose like a rotten potato; the psychiatrist slides back the chair and rises. The move breaks the spell and Molly dashes the tea in her face and bolts from the office. "Hee!" the thing laughs, and Molly knows she is following, moving rapidly for something so grossly misshapen.

"Hold that elevator!" Molly cries at the woman peering from it as if expecting her. Small and plain as a sparrow, she looks without expression at the thing that thumps behind Molly; its footless limbs squirt corruption against the walls.

"Oh, God, hold it!"

Molly is running so fast she hits the mirrored back of the elevator and falls on the rebound. In the reflection, Dr. Logan's fingers—beclawed, black and textured like asphalt—squeeze between the doors that stop closing as a buzzer begins. The little woman steps forward and strikes them with her bare hand and they turn gray and fall like ash tipped from a cigar. Dr. Gordon shrieks with pain.

"First floor?" the woman asks Molly and the elevator begins its descent; it's an express and they drop quickly. Molly rises and steadies herself with the help of the hand rail.

"How did you do that?"

"She was a demon and they can't stand to be touched," the woman explains with a smile. An angelic smile, Molly thinks instantly. "They are happy to rend and tear flesh, but they cannot be touched by another. The pain burns like acid."

"It was a nightmare," Molly cries, holding her head with both hands and feeling she might faint. "I can't believe that happened." The woman puts a steadying hand to her elbow and Molly feels immersed in sudden warmth. "Who are you?" Molly asks.

"Oh, just a Friend."

Something about her serene presence. Molly feels her nerves fall back into place like when a film is reversed and puzzle pieces spilled from a box fly back up inside in perfect order. "What happened to her?"

"She was possessed."

"Will she... will she be all right?"

"It's not given to Friends to know that. We're Friends, not Deciders."

Molly blurts, "Are you a guardian angel?"

"Only in a small way. When you stray into the next lane on a narrow curve and another car is coming, we warn so you can avoid it. Or when you get a 'funny feeling'—that's what a lot of people call it—and change your mind about something and it's the right thing to do, that's us. It happens millions of times a day; many think of it luck or instinct, meaning without our help, but none of us mind just so long as the job gets done." She dusted her hands with a humorous look. "Sometimes, like now, we intervene directly because otherwise... well, you saw. Other times, we just watch because the Deciders made up their mind something must turn out the way it does."

"This wasn't a little thing in life to me," Molly protests. "It was huge; I've never been so scared in my life."

"Oh, I know, dear," she says soothingly, "of course it wasn't a little thing to you. But I was always there the other times, even though you didn't know. When you were in the sea and the time the helicopter went down. When you fell from the apple tree just nine years old I was there watching out. A Decider did not want your neck broken, so it was only your arm. The tree branch only had to be moved a tiny bit to make that happen."

"You mean I didn't have to worry?"

"I wouldn't say that," the Friend says with a laugh. "You never know."

The elevator reaches the lobby. "Well, you take care," the little woman says as if their encounter was no weightier than a light give-and-take between checker and customer in a grocery store. She breezes out the doors that divide silently and disappears into the knot of people waiting to get on.

CHAPTER 42

THE BODYGUARD IS WAITING FOR MOLLY AT THE CURB. A PART OF HER MIND DIMLY REGISTERS HIS joviality; he probably knocked back one or two while waiting even though the rule is no drinking on duty. Normally, she would ride in the passenger seat if there was only the driver, but she sits in back to try to slow the speed of her spinning thoughts. Her rational mind rejects as impossible the tsunami of impressions that overwhelm her. That couldn't have happened, no how, no way. She stares zombie-like at the beautiful pastel homes in the Marina district on the way to the bridge.

As they cross the Golden Gate Bridge, she telephones Randall. "I'll be there in a half hour, meet me in the room with the water buffalo." Then she has a ludicrous attack of good manners. "If you're not too busy."

"No, we just had dinner and Abby's giving the kids a bath."

Molly feels a deep craving for stablity, to know when something happened each hour of the day instead of the tumble of dread and uncertainty that pulls the cold knot tight in her stomach. Meals, playing with children, kissing them and putting them to bed after storytime… it would be paradise. It had always been a question of finding the right man among the numberless bad ones she met who thought the sun rose and set on them, but somehow she didn't try hard enough or set her sights too high. She had noticed that friends who married and had children changed. Their smart, funny conversation got shaved down to talk about kids and household matters—the dryer went out, the dog got loose—that they thought must interest everyone. Molly had rather scorned the soccer moms but saw now the appeal of their ordered lives.

"Something awful happened I want to talk to you about," she tells Randall.

The sigh on the other end is weary. "Okay," he says, "don't say anymore; I'll watch for you from the window."

He stands at the one with cushions and a view of the tawny hills you could look at forever. Down below is the circle where the SUV pulls up a short time later and Molly steps out. He heads to the room where the water buffalo's pricked ears indicated an awareness of the lethal threat hidden on the savanna; a brass plaque beneath has the details of when and where it was killed. Lesser horned beasts on the walls show the same alert sense of self-preservation yet they too had missed what was coming. The thought makes his spirits drop like ike a stone in a deep well. Sometimes the best is not good enough and the price is paid. What had he already missed or wouldn't see when it happened? A twitch of the ear by these animals might have caught enough hint of the concealed hunter to bolt and escape the bullet.

Randall can't shake his everlasting resentment at being the point of the spear. Why me? The feeling was worse at times like now when bad news was on the wing. He sometimes daydreamed of packing up the family and striking off for the wilds, Alaska maybe; they had more money now than he ever dreamed of thanks to Rex's generosity. Or maybe that's the wrong word given that Rex didn't seem to care about money. Randall thinks about a place so remote from civilization that only wild creatures are around; there they would wait out whatever happened when the End Times kicked in. There were strong arguments in favor but a mind-boggling number of details to worry about including basics like food and shelter. No doctors, no medicine, predators unafraid of humans because they had never seen them. Whatever dehydrated stuff they humped in would run out eventually, leaving a diet of game and whatever unpoisonous green things came up from the ground in the short growing season; those would have to be learned like in primitive times by trial and error. Flies and mosquitoes would be a continual torment. Their teeth would rot and fall out; they would begin to smell but not notice or care after a while. They would dread winters that came early and stayed late. They would have to make candles from animal fat when the ones they brought with them ran out like the batteries had long before; they would give only a dim, sputtering light so it would be early to bed in the long nights with worry and fear for company. Wolves would howl; some nights they would whine and try to dig into their bunker in a hillside. The grizzlies were bigger and stronger than the bear that killed the abbot. The boys would grow up laconic and hard-bitten, barely civilized… if they survived at all. So, a tropical island? No, it would be a magnet for people fleeing the chaos, people more than willing to resort to violence to get what they wanted. Even if he could teach Abby to shoot, there would only be the two of them to defend their stronghold —Esther would refuse to come and would be useless if she did..

Molly rushes into the room like her hair is on fire. "You're not going to believe this…" Then she sees his face and stops. "Yes, you are," she admits, "nothing surprises you."

Randall drops into a chair. "Go ahead, I'm all ears."

When she finishes, Randall tiredly asks, "What happened to the doctor?"

"I wasn't interested to tell the truth."

"So you're finally all on board." A statement, not a question.

"It was the most horrible thing that's happened yet." She grips her head with both hands as if that is the only way to keep it from exploding.

"That bar is a pretty high one."

Molly shudders. "But this was so… personal. So in my face. Omigod, the smell." She puts a lock of hair under her nose and her throat tightens; she would have to shampoo twice to get it out. "Her eyes looked like they were going to pop out of her head." Randall waits with folded arms for her to continue. "Do you think I should tell Rex about this… and the little woman and the Watchers and Deciders?"

"It would have to be the right moment, that's for sure."

"How will I know when that is?"

He shrugs. "Look for a chance." They sit in silence for a moment. "Your driver came through that gate pretty fast."

"What's that got to do with anything?"

"Just a thought," Randall says. "Anyhow, we're finished talking about the psychiatrist, aren't we? It happened and it's over."

Molly looks ready to spring at him. "How can you always be so calm!"

"If climbing the wall helped, I'd do it."

She walks to the window and looks out. "I think the driver might have been drinking."

"It seems discipline is getting a little loosey-goosey."

"Is that a big deal?" Molly asks. It seems like a small thing to her; he wasn't actually drunk, just a little relaxed. They do so much waiting around.

"No, but it's something different. Something different is always a big deal in a situation where you're trying to keep out someone who wants in." Esther had complained about loud voices downstairs the other night, but he blew it off. I'm getting a little slack myself, he thinks.

When he gets back to their suite, Abby cries, "There was just a bombshell on TV. One of the networks, the one with the young and good looking anchorman, said it learned exclusively that Rex is considering running for president."

"It had to get out sooner or later," Randall says.

"You might have told me."

"You didn't need to know," he says with a shrug. "Need to know is a thing in a situation like we're in."

"Isn't it wonderful?" Esther bursts out.

The two of them give her stony looks. "You know I don't like the man, Mother," Abigail says reproachfully.

Esther has a defiant look. "Oh, yes, I know, and you're entitled to your opinion and all that, but I think you're wrong about him. Those other two candidates… I don't know, they're so ordinary and predictable, especially the woman, what's-her-face. You know what they're going to say the minute they open their mouths. The people I talk to back home feel the same way; it's time for a change."

Straight from the beak of the canary in the mine, Randall thinks.

"There's just something about him," Abby protests.

"You keep saying that," Esther says peevishly, "but you never say what."

"Do you think he'd be a good president?" Abby asks Randall.

"It's not a good time for a greenhorn. There's a lot of crazy stuff going on around the world that…"

"Oh, posh," Esther interrupts, glaring at him. "It's never a good time for some people." Abby is surprised at her mother; she never gets this worked up unless it's about kids or animal welfare…

"I know, I know," Esther says at Abby's look, "you think I don't think about anything but domestic stuff and the boys, but I do sometimes think about bigger things like what's going on in the world."

That throws Abby off balance. "I know, Mom, you've got a good mind, every-body knows that."

Esther cuts a look at Randall. "Maybe not everyone."

"I have to make a call," he says.

"Woah," Finnese says when he comes on the scrambler phone downstairs, "you've been keeping a big secret. One of the guys just called." He pauses. "Assuming it's true?"

"It's true. I want you to rotate a new crew in here ASAP."

"That'll take a couple of days. What's the problem?"

"I want a whole new crew, that's the problem."

"Okay, okay, keep your shirt on," Finnese says. "I'll get on it right now and you should see the first tomorrow morning." He pauses to see if there is a response. When Randall is silent, he says, "As soon as Rex files the legal papers saying he's a candidate, we're out of the picture and the Secret Service is in charge."

"Fine, it won't be my worry then."

It seems someone is on every phone in the huge house as Randall walks through the rooms. As soon as a phone is hung up, it rings again. News travels faster than ever, Randall thinks, especially when it's bad. A bodyguard approaches to say Rex wants him and Molly. He collects her and they take the elevator to his corner suite where the propped-open balcony doors quiver in a gusty wind through the Golden Gate. They are surprised to find Dickson, hands jammed in a heavy camel-hair overcoat buttoned to the top with the collar turned up. He can't hide his glee.

"Why is it so cold in here?" Molly exclaims.

"It's healthier," Rex says. He lounges in an easy chair in chinos and a casual shirt with long sleeves. The light from the lamp makes his profile glow like a Russian icon.

She goes to the door and asks the guard outside to bring her warmest coat from her room. "The fur," she says, "and there's a hat that goes with it on the shelf above."

"Are you all right?" Rex asks Randall. "Need a sweater?" He never shows interest in the comfort of others, so the sergeant guesses he is being tested.

"I'm fine," he says. "Want me to open a couple of windows?"

"We put that leak out to the network." Rex means he and Dickson did,

Randall realizes. They have been working a back channel he and Molly weren't told about.

"I would have appreciated a heads-up," Molly says, hugging herself for warmth. Her teeth start to chatter.

"Because we're moving into a new phase, we're going to change the ways we do things," Rex says. "Rock-Steady did studies of other presidential campaigns and we need to ramp up."

"I thought the idea was all you needed was for people to see you," Randall says.

"Yes, as far as it goes," Dickson says. "That's why you and Molly could do so much before we came into the picture. Rex being Rex let you defy what I would call the branding laws of gravity. But what is ahead are orders of magnitude harder. It's more complicated and the world expects more than this bob-tail outfit you put together on the fly. The optics would be damaging to establishments that like organizational order and predictability." His manner is pompous and patronizing. He pauses at a beep to check his smartphone for an incoming text. There is a knock at the door and Molly is given her fur coat and hat and gratefully snuggles into them.

"Here's an example of what I mean," Dickson says, looking at the text. "Sergeant Randall ordered a complete overnight switch of our security force." He looks at Rex. "Were you informed of this?" Rex gives a shake of his head. "Why was this done without consulting anyone else?" Dickson demands.

"Call it a hunch," Randall says.

"A hunch?" Dickson is working up a huffy indignation. "A hunch? Do you have any idea how much money this costs? Travel, payroll, overtime, penalty clauses—it will be enormous. What happened to give you this hunch?"

"Just a feeling," Randall replies calmly. "That's what a hunch is. You get them in combat. If you're smart, you pay attention."

Dickson spreads his arms to Rex as if to say, Can you believe this guy? "A hunch! Do I have your permission to cancel this?" He is poised to thumb a text.

"Mm," Rex says. "I'm going with the sergeant on this one."

Dickson is stunned, looking like he might cry. How he had plotted and schemed to put them on the sidelines and then loses the ball on the first play from scrimmage. Molly thinks he pitched his plan to senior executives, telling them of the guaranteed riches in Rock-Steady's connections to the next president. Lobbying, legal work, management contracts—profits would shoot over the moon, putting shareholders into a state of bliss. A fine academic background, a meteoric rise at a big management company with every resource and networking connection, already a seasoned veteran of Hollywood intrigue and backstabbing, all had worked to put Dickson on the inside curve of the fast track. Why wouldn't he think he could outfox a cop and a woman who did casting?

"They've been with me from the start," Rex tells Dickson with glacial detachment. "Molly hired you and it was a good call. Okay, see you later." He jerks a thumb and Dickson slinks from the room.

Randall wonders if superstition played a role in Rex's decision. We were there when he needed us and he wants us see him through to the end. No, he thinks, that can't be true. Rex is not sentimental so he figures we must have some future use for him.

"But I am going to follow the recommendations in his memo," Rex continues, tapping a folder. "We're going to move operations South-of-Market where the tech companies and talent are. This will be a campaign more technologically savvy than any dreamed of before. Every time somebody opens a refrigerator door or turns on a car engine a message at the subliminal level will say vote for me."

"Wouldn't that, like, be against the law?" Molly wonders. "Privacy and so forth?"

"People make laws and change them all the time, people with money and power. If your lawyers are smart enough, they find loopholes or work-arounds." Rex taps the folder again. "It's all in here."

"So when I go to the refrigerator at midnight to make a ham sandwich, I'll hear 'Vote Rex'?" Randall asks.

"You won't be aware of it," Rex replies, "Like the other things in a house connected to the internet, it will be just a fleeting impression thrust into your subconscious."

"I don't think you need tricks to win," Molly says loyally.

"I don't either," Rex says with a smile. "But I'll go along with the experts." They sit in silence in the cold wind, Randall resisting an impulse to rub life back into his numb hands. "Tell Rex about your exciting adventure today, Molly."

Rex fastens his laser gaze on her as she relates what happened. "That was Camael's doing," he says when she is finished. "It was a warning to Molly and to you, sergeant."

"What is the warning?" she asks.

"That he means to interfere with my plans and no one will stand in his way." Rex thinks about it more. "You two are tied into what's happening in some deep way." He stands and reaches a hand out for theirs like before teammates before a game. "Promise you'll stay by my side."

The pressure of his hand has an almost electric tingle that makes this seem a transcendent moment. Randall sees from her welling eyes that Molly is overcome. He would be too if he didn't have that cold bead of doubt that won't go away.

Abbey is yawning in front of the TV when he gets back. "You know that funny little man who was teaching Rex how to paint?" she says, alert at once.

"I always thought he looked like one of those garden gnomes," Esther says, rising to go to her room.

"The news said he died of an overdose," Abby says. "He left a note that said if someone found him before he was gone, he didn't want resuscitation."

Esther pauses in the doorway for solemn reflection. "Some people just don't want to live."

CHAPTER 43

WITH ROCK-STEADY IN CHARGE OF EVERYTHING FROM CONCERT AND POLITICAL PLANNING TO MOV-
ing operations South-of-Market, there is little for Randall and Molly to do.

"At least my rash is gone," she says as they sit in the weak sunshine watching the bundled-up kids play on the smooth lawn with their toy dump trucks; their function seemed not to transport alphabet blocks from one pile to another but to smack into one another with as much noise as possible. Abby and her mother have gone to the hairdressers and to shop for clothes for the big concert. Esther said she hopes the music won't be too loud.

"I could get used to being paid to do nothing," Randall says.

"No, you couldn't," Molly responds.

He stretches out his legs. "Yeah, you're right."

"I'm kind of at loose ends myself," she admits. It has gone from working sixteen hours a day with sudden massive jolts of adrenalin to a cruise-ship life. She is quiet for a moment watching the fog ghosting in on a stiff breeze. "Wasn't that a magical moment when Rex took our hands? I just felt such a flash of warm go through my whole body."

"I felt something," Randall admits.

"I don't see how Vargas could be right about Rex just from the hands." She shakes her head. "The critics are as vicious about his work as when the poor man was alive."

"I heard that you sometimes find jealousy in the art world, but I never believed it."

"You're such a joker. That must be a problem with people without a sense of humor."

"I dodge them when I can. The problem is there are so many of them."

An argument breaks out between the boys and Randall tells them to knock it off. "I've been wondering if Vargas really committed suicide," Molly says, looking at the fog patches hurrying overhead.

"The autopsy didn't find anything fishy." Penny got a copy and read it to him over the telephone. "Straight up suicide."

"So you wondered yourself?" Molly says.

"Of course."

"But you never mentioned it," she says accusingly.

"It must have slipped my mind."

"How does Abbey put up with you!"

"I used to think it was my looks, but now I think it's my charm."

Molly ignores this. "Vargas was so deflated when he left. I think that what was so hard for him was learned by Rex in such a short time."

"Or maybe he he had a sense something bad was coming at us and he didn't want to be around for it. It would be interesting to take a peek at the painting," Randall says.

"There's always a guard at the door."

"I don't know any of these new guys, not even to nod at."

"Did you get good seats on the charter to Dallas?" Molly asks, pulling her coat tighter. She doesn't at all miss the freezing boat rides after the flights up from Burbank. When she wonders what the future holds for her, she hopes it includes a warm climate.

"Dickson put us in the back with the music press," Randall says. "We're not supposed to talk to them, though. It'll be a hardship for Esther."

He takes the twins in for their nap and stretches out himself on a sofa. He doesn't know how long he slept but wakens to the kids talking to someone. He hurries to where they sit opposite one another on the floor. They look up at him in surprise.

"Were you talking to someone?" Randall asks. His heart beats faster.

The boys look at one another. "No," says Michael.

"Yes," says Martin, the more honest of the two.

"He said not to tell," Michael warns his brother.

"Where did he go?" Randall asks. The boys gaze around. "Where did he go?" they chorus. "He was in that chair," Michael says.

"What did he look like?"

"Like a funny wittle clown with sticky-uppy hair," Martin says, "and really big these." He points to his lips. "Red!"

"He was funny!" Michael agrees. "He could roll over and jump up. And walk in the air!"

"He said he would teach us out there." Martin points to the balcony.

"Mom and dad said never go there when we're not here, remember?" Randall says, his throat tight. "That's why the doors are locked." It's a long drop to the seawall.

"He says he can open them," Martin says brightly. "He says it's easy."

"Is that how the wittle clown got in?" Randall asks. He goes to the doors and finds they are locked.

The boys look at each other. "We don't know," Michael pipes up. "He was there when I woked up." "Me, too," Martin agrees.

We are in an armed camp, Randall thinks, I'm in the next room and still someone gets to the boys. He shakes with rage. "You look mad," Martin says worriedly. This usually means someone is going to the corner to think about a wrong choice.

"No, I'm fine," the sergeant says huskily, pulling them in for a tight squeeze. He rough houses with them until they go back to crashing their trucks into each other. Molly and now this. He calls the nanny service and cancels them for the Dallas trip. He tells Abby in a casual way when she and her mother get home.

"When did you decide that?" Abby says, laying down an armful of garment bags on the table.

"It's not as if they need me in Dallas; Finnese is personally in charge." He'd had a quick exchange with him on the phone about going behind his back; Finnese started giving him the old it's-just-business-not-personal bullshit when Randall hung up.

"I wouldn't miss it for the world," Esther had vowed. "I have never seen history in the making and I want to be able to tell the twins I was there."

"You go too, darlin'," Randall says to Abby. "I cancelled the nanny so I'll watch it on pay-for-view with them. Be sure to wave at the camera."

"Are you sure?" Abby says doubtfully.

"Go with my blessings."

"Why all of a sudden?"

"I've had it with travel for a while." He is much better at a convincing lie than when all this started.

"It does sound fun," Abby says. "I bought the prettiest new outfit, so did mom. Shall we give you a fashion show?" She is elegant in the long sleeveless dress with a low V-neck bodice that has sparkling crystals on an illusion background. The sleek floor length skirt has a high side slit and a sweep train and open back V-neck. Randall calls up a wolf whistle. Esther looks like a garish tropical bird with layered flounces that give the effect of ruffled feathers; it needs only a banana headdress like Carmen Miranda wore in 'Forties.

"I decided to go for it," Esther says.

"You certainly did," Randall agrees. Abby's look warns him not to say more.

When they are putting the twins to bed, Martin asks, "Where did Bub go?" They had been vague about it—he ran off and will come back one day—and quickly changed the subject. Randall thought Bub had dropped off their radar long ago.

"Well, we don't real know, sweetheart," Abby says. "We just have to keep a good look out." When she leaves the room, Randall bends low over Martin and says in a jolly, just-between-us-guys way, "What made you think about Bub?"

"The wittle clown knows where Bub is. He'll take us to see him!"

"If you see him again, will you promise to run and tell me? I'd like to meet him."

"Sure, Daddy."

"You're more tense than ever," Abby says later, coming up from behind and kneading his tight shoulders. "I thought it was supposed to get more relaxed now that you'd don't have to run security."

"It takes a while to loosen up, darlin'," he says. "But I'm getting there."

"I'm not going to Dallas," Abby says. "I told mom."

"You look gorgeous in that new outfit; it's a shame to waste it."

"Oh, it won't be wasted," she says brightly. "We'll go somewhere nice when we're on our own again and I'll wear it then. I know! When we move into our new house we'll have a party. You can wear a tux and mom..." Abby flashes a grin. "She'll be back in Oregon then."

Five convoys leave Bluff Point before dawn to confuse the enemy; a helicopter plays a blinding light on the ground at the gate as they pull out. Randall watches the submarine submerge in the darkness with Rex and a small party that boarded from a rubber boat. Traveling on the music press charter, Esther is in a high state of excitement. She telephones from the aircraft to say the goody bag each person got includes an iPhone with the new album downloaded, a half-dozen little airline bottles of liquor, Belgian chocolates, perfume, gift certificates, and lots of other things. "They say each bag is worth twenty-five hundred dollars." She calls in regular updates from the flight, having been surprised to learn there is no charge for it. In the first hour everyone listened to Rex's album A Call to Us All. "People were really quiet with their eyes closed. When it was over, they began saying it was the greatest album ever and drinking those little bottles." She lowers her voice although the din in the background makes it unlikely she would be overheard. "A lot of them are drunk already and it isn't even noon. The flight attendants are trying to get them to eat lunch."

The live television coverage has stories through the day about how many satellite TV trucks are at AT&T Stadium in Dallas. It is clearly a light news day, no massacres or disasters to speak of, and the networks have difficulty filling the time with fluff, "Fifty-six of them from thirty-seven countries," Molly tells Randall from Dallas where she landed in the smaller jet with Rex's party. "Usually there has to be something terrible to bring that many. Dickson is being a real shit, by the way. He didn't like it when Rex switched me to his plane."

"We're at the press center now," Esther reports in another of her updates. "I get to wear one of those laminated plastic thingies that let you in places." A boastful note enters her voice. "I have one of the highest levels of access they tell me."

"Good for you, Mom," Abby says. "It must be really exciting."

"It's a jazz," Esther says in a youthful way, going on to confide: "I don't think the political reporters like the music ones; I believe they see themselves as higher up the pole."

"Oh, well, everyone likes to have someone to look down on," Abby says.

"They say Rex is better known than the pope," Esther says. "People just take a step back like they can't believe it when I tell them I know him personally, and before I know there's a circle around me listening to the conversation."

"Mom," Abby says carefully, "you don't actually know him; you were just introduced that one time with the twins."

"I live in the same house with him," Esther blazes.

"It sounds like she's on a big ego trip," Randall says afterward.

"Oh, so what," Abby says, "let her have her moment in the sun."

"Fine by me," Randall says, raising his hands in defense

One of the networks proclaims the concert a MEGA-EVENT and the others quickly fall in line: THE MAIN EVENT, THE BIG EVENT with other variations on the theme. One talking head compares it to the Super Bowl, the World Series and Oscar Night rolled into one. The sports channels explore the baseball angle of the THE REX STORY featuring Giants teammates and analyses by Hall of Fame players; some say scornfully that a part of a single season is way too soon to say Rex is a lock for Cooperstown. The entertainment columnists and bloggers can't deny his movie was a huge popular hit, crap for the masses. But there is agreement, as one critic says, that Rex spun gold from dross. The perky E! anchor woman needs the expression explained to her. She makes a comic face for the camera. "Where's that saying from? Like, a hundred years ago?" A graver tone is taken by the political punditry under pressure to speculate on what Rex will say and irked that they will learn the big news at the same moment as couch potatoes and retired folks who watch re-runs starring actors dead and buried decades ago. All the time and effort devoted to cultivating sources on and off the record, receiving and passing on political gossip, spinning for one party and exposing spin for the other; the privileged insider-status authority carved out with such pain and effort, years establishing their voices and these bona fides and for what? They denounce the "circus atmosphere." Bald heads and scalps peeking from under swooping comb-overs shine with perspiration from the stress of forcing empty chatter. There are guesses that Rex will endorse one of the candidates for the Oval Office. "It smarts, it really hurts," crows a media analyst unfriendly toward his former colleagues. "The so-called experts don't know what they don't know."

Molly wanders with two bodyguards trailing inconspicuously through the vast encampment outside AT&T Stadium; the air is blue with barbecue smoke from a thousand grills and heavy with the mouth-watering smell of beef, pork and chicken cooking outside luxury RVs and elaborate tents with genera-tors ready for the evening chill. Lines stretch from the food trucks circled like a wagon train; it looks like every cuisine under the sun is available. She overhears debates over whether the experience will be better inside with its shockingly expensive food and drink—Javion and Foster drove hard bargains—or watching the big screens in the parking lot from the comfort of padded folding chairs with drink holders and no worries about the traffic afterward.

Her phone rings in her purse and Molly answers as she saunters through the excited crowd. "Hi, Molly, it's me, Sarah." She sounds like the old Sarah, not the drained and defeated young woman the last time they talked.

"Where are you?"

"I'm still at the rehab place, but I'm doing so much better. The awful craving for smack that all I thought about is gone. There are great people here and the nicest staff. They want to watch me a while longer before they let me go."

"I was worried about you."

"Could I ask you something; it's okay to say no! *New Yorker* is running my piece in the next issue. It still has stuff nobody else knows about Rex, a lot of stuff actually, personal stuff, including about me and him when we were a couple, or at least *I* thought so"—she laughs at herself, which Molly thinks is healthy—"and they're not so worried it reads like a fanzine because he's all anybody is talking about. They're so pumped they're adding a hundred thousand to the press run."

Molly gently probes. "So all is forgiven?"

"Yes! They're giving me a job where I decide what to cover and they'll send me wherever I want to go. Do you want to know what you can say no to if I ask you for it, and really, really feel free to say no? The issue closes in a couple of days. All I'm hoping for is you'll tell me if something earthshaking happens at the last minute so I can squeeze it in before the presses roll."

"Well," Molly says, "there is his announcement tonight."

"I don't mean that. Everybody at rehab will be watching along with the rest of the world. I can't think of anything that could possibly be bigger than that. This is just a make- sure-all-the-bases-are-covered thing my editor wants."

"I promise," Molly says.

"You are the best!"

CHAPTER 44

THE GREAT STADIUM GOES DARK FOR TEN SECONDS AND THEN A SINGLE SPOTLIGHT IS ON A TINY figure up high in a skin-tight tunic and leggings the sapphire color of a tropical lagoon. Then the mighty chords from the film blast out, a detonation of sound now better known to the mass culture than even Stairway to Heaven. Jumbotron screens flash on giving a close up of Rex raising his arms with the slow deliberation of an Olympic diver. The Cirque du Soleil specialist who choreographed the stunt closes his eyes as Rex dives into the dark emptiness. Followed by a new spotlight that gives a nimbus of divinity, Rex rides an invisible wire around the stadium like an avatar searching for a place pure enough to land. The ancient toccata recorded at great expense by Dolby Labs at the Sydney Opera House's world famous organ plays thunderously until suddenly silenced.

A stage rises on the playing field in front of a symphony orchestra that bursts into the doom-ridden dirge in *When the Day Comes* as the vast army of hideous Truks advanced on Rex and his brave but outnumbered warriors. When he lands as lightly as a butterfly, the orchestra gives way to Rex's all-star band augmented by Mick and Keith rocking out Locked On, the anthem that thrilled movie audiences in the battle sequences that Rex mimics with ninja leaps and rolls.

"This is fantastic," Abby says in the Bluff Point screening room where they watch with off-duty bodyguards. "Awesome, man," one says. "Better than awesome, dude," another replies softly. "Nkhukutemwa," says a Bantu maiden in a live shot inset on the screen from a forest glade in east Africa; the show is projected on a sheet hung between a tree and the camera crew's truck. The caption translates her words: "I love you."

"That was my idea," Dickson shouts in the sky box.

They had partaken of a pre-show feast, courses of lobster and stuffed Long Island duck and other delicacies prepared by famed chefs introduced by a trumpet fanfare each time a dish was presented. The wines were chosen by a suave celebrity sommelier with oiled hair and dramatic dark eyes that he flashed when uncorking a bottle—a definite cad, Molly thought. The gluttony is so redolent of late Roman decadence that she feels disgust. I'm becoming a common scold about everything, she thinks.

But that is forgotten as she watches Rex's consummate performance, one instant hit from the movie after another sung in his marvelous voice except when lip-synching during his spectacular twirling stunts and balletic leaps as high and graceful as Nureyev at his peak. The rapid inset of videos on the screen show famous faces with dumbstruck looks.

"Those reaction shots," Dickson cries, "my idea again."

Not even his crassness breaks the spell that Rex weaves for ninety hypnotic minutes until disappearing into a swirling melee of dancers. Hidden by the moving bodies, the wire is secured by a technician in costume and he ascends in a spotlight that fades and at last disappears with the thunderous hymn-like finish that celebrated the final defeat of the vile Truks. A stunned silence like at the opening stretches for what seems an eternity before the crowds in the stadium, the parking lot, and all around the world climb to their feet for rapturous applause that continues at the stadium for ten minutes with shouts of "Encore!" The inset videos return in full screen now to show the faces from before now exultant or wet with tears of happiness. "There has never been a greater triumph on stage or screen," a crusty Baltimore critic taps on his laptop, shoulders shaking with sobs. "A blessing it was to be there." Reading those words on a screen back in the office, an editor too busy to watch the performance says, "Warm somebody up in rewrite, Boswell has been hitting the bottle again."

Rex at last appears on the stage in a single spotlight wearing an impeccable tuxedo and mopping his brow with a towel he flings into the audience; it causes a mad scramble that the cameras turn away from after a brief look. "Thanks, everyone," he says. "I'm running for president of the United States!"

The cheers are deafening and he tries to quiet them, pointing to his wristwatch time after time. When finally he bows and maintains it, they die away and he finally straightens. "Anything you can do to help," he says simply. And the spotlight winks out.

"Well, we're screwed," says Russell Kornhouser as the screening room lights come on at Bluff Point. "If we had a thousand campaign headquarters around the country, there'd be a thousand people pounding at every one of those door asking to volunteer." His gaze is on Randall. "Know how many we have?" He uses a thumb and forefinger to make a circle. "Zero."

"Dickson says it doesn't matter because this is a new kind of campaign."

"The man don't know shit from Shinola; I saw that from the start. You gotta have boots on the ground, my friend."

Charlie Parsons is thoughtful. "Between us, we have contacts in every one of the states. I bet if we pulled in people tonight, we can peel off plenty from both parties and have them working for us in two days. This isn't going to go away overnight, you know."

"We better get started," Kornhouser says tiredly. They leave minutes later for their hotel in San Francisco.

Randall is sleeping lightly with the twins between him and Abby when he feels his arm touched. Awake instantly, he sees Camael in the faint light with a finger to his lips. He beckons him to follow. "They'll be safe."

He leads the policeman to the studio where the bodyguard slumps in his chair sleeping soundly. The locked door springs open to Camael's touch. "It is more complicated than I thought," he says inside.

"I don't know how much more complication I can take."

"You and Molly have been heroic, but there is more to do."

Randall thinks he looks nearly exhausted.

"The struggle has been difficult," Camael says as if reading his thoughts. "The Angel of Death is harder to confine as Lucifer hurries us toward the end." Seeing Randall's look, he explains. "I mean the End Times, when all is chaos and confusion and he imposes his evil on the world."

Randall's stomach feels like it is diving to the center of Earth. "And the complication?"

"Rex sees himself as Lucifer's equal or perhaps even greater. He thought he was creating a perfect evil, did Satan, but he is not capable of perfection. That is his flaw, the one that will put him in the lake of fire forevermore. Instead of a willing tool to complete his end game, he created a usurper." He goes to the easel and pulls away the cover of Rex's self portrait. "Satan's revenge is to have Rex paint his replacement."

"But he's painting himself," Randall points out.

"Look more closely," Camael says.

Randall sees what he means. It looks like Rex in some sort of elaborate black uniform with a yellow sash, medals, decorations, epaulettes and brass buttons, a repellent evocation of some murderous emperor from the past. Rex's fluid lightness and grace are gone, replaced by an impression of thickness and density, meaty and solid, not capable of engagement with others but only of overpowering resistance by brute strength and demonic cunning. The eyes are dark reservoirs of fury and malice, the lips parted in a disdainful smile. The hands have fingers as wide as snakes and look strong enough to snap elephant bones.

"Is this how Rex sees himself?" Randall says with disbelief.

"He sees what Satan wants him to see. You can imagine what glee Lucifer takes in deceiving his deceiver. He will have no trouble managing the creature on the canvas; there is no misleading hint of goodness there, no superficial charm to beguile others; Satan learned from his mistake. This thing Rex is painting could not be elected to high office, but he could bend nations to his will by brute force."

"Rex doesn't see this?"

Camael shakes his head. "Such is his pride he thinks it is his work alone, yet his every brush stroke is guided by Lucifer's hand."

"There's not much left to do, what happens when it's finished?"

"Oh, he will be killed by the thing he is creating and ages of pain will follow for his disobedience. He will be a blackened cinder with only the smallest pulse when the last measure of his suffering ends except for its memory, which for him will be eternal. Satan is very good at punishment; it is where he approaches perfection. At some point Rex recognized the risk he was taking, but it was worth it to him. His infernal pride drove him to rebel, which was the very undoing of Satan himself. Does not God work in wondrous ways?" He replaces the cover on the painting and they walk outside past the sleeping guard to the room with the mounted heads.

"What happens now?" Randall asks.

"The future is hidden even to angels on high," Camael says. He seems to harken to a voice only he hears. "I must leave you now, Abbadon stirs again."

"But…" The question dies on his lips for Camael vanishes like a pebble dropped in deep water, leaving Randall to wonder at first if it was a dream. But he knows it wasn't, it was just another phase of the ongoing nightmare. He walks out into the hallway where the guard, now alert in his chair, stares at him.

"Staying awake?" Randall asks.

He guard holds his stare a long beat and says, "Not a problem for me, sir. How's about yourself?" His curtness makes it plain that Randall is just another civilian to him.

The chartered jet lands the following morning at Sacramento and Rex and his party travel as tourists on a Napa Wine Tour bus back to Bluff Point where the gate slides open with military precision seconds before they arrive. News choppers hover overhead watching for his triumphant return, but the tour disguise works and nobody is sure if he is back or not. A courier from Rock-Steady arrives with a thick binder of printouts of the overnight reaction by the foreign media.

"Bom," is the big headline in De Telegraaf of Amsterdam. "That means 'bombshell' in Dutch," Dickson says after looking up the Google translation on his smartphone. "Obuz," according to Actualitatea Romaneasca in Romania. "That means the same thing," he says. "Let's see what the Brits say. 'Fantastic,' the Guardian. 'Great Act, Huge Announcement,' the Express. 'Fantastique,' the biggest French paper." Dickson pages quickly, 'The Next American President?' asks the Australian. 'Следующий лидер,' in the Moscow Telegraph. Hmm, let's see. That means 'The Next Leader.' This stuff is crazy good."

Molly watches his avid eyes as they consume the headlines. He will claim credit everywhere except when with Rex; he is always as humble as a cart horse with him even though he is like a snorting stallion lashing out with sharp hooves everywhere else. "Bookers from every hot network show are begging me in tears to put Rex on," he says. "Jobs are at stake."

"It's all because of you," Molly says sweetly.

"I know you don't mean it, but thanks anyway. Maybe you'll think this is important: our Washington office says the other candidates already reached out. They want to knock out Rex with a one-on-one debate and get on with beating up on each other."

"Rex will kill them."

Dickson's smile is Machiavellian. "See, they they're stuck in the old ways of thinking. They see Rex as a lightweight, just an actor okay at reading lines and making the right faces to go with them. They think an hour with the heat from their candidates and he'll be smoke and ash."

"So they both have death wishes? What about Rex being up thirty points in the polls?"

"That's just name recognition. They think when he's shown up as a nothing burger on national TV those numbers will melt way. But that's not our problem, lady," Another courier arrives with tapes and news printouts of the domestic coverage and he withdraws to gloat over them privately.

The debates are arranged swiftly with a bidding war for rights that is won by PBS thanks to a huge donation by a combine of wealthy patrons from both parties as interested as the candidates themselves in putting Rex's candidacy into an early grave. The first up is Gracie Ashcroft Weber, a short and thick-legged woman with blond hair who has devoted her life to continuing the dynasty that put her paternal grandfather in the White House. Although resorting to what the media calls Graciegab when backed into a corner, she knows enough to pass as informed on most issues, and likeable enough if questioners don't press too hard. Rex orders that only Molly and Randall are to be with him in the green-room before the debate in Cincinnati.

"You don't look a bit nervous," she observes.

"Why should I be?" He is humming *The Advance of the Lancers* from the movie.

"It's a big deal," Randall says.

"It's been a big deal from the start."

"We didn't know that at the time."

Rex frowns. "It sounds funny, but I just didn't know I knew it."

"That country road seems like a century ago in a different world."

Rex indicates with a motion that the subject is closed. He has little patience for disagreement these days.

Randall didn't tell Molly about Camael's visit because he thought her fear for Rex would leap from her face when next they met. She doesn't want him president, but she doesn't want him dead either; she would want to find a way to save him. Then Rex would ask why I didn't tell him about Camael myself. In time of war that falls under the heading of trading with the enemy. He gave me one pass, but there wouldn't be another.

Rex picks up the different vibe in him. "You all right?" he asks Randall. Molly and he had both noticed how quick and sure his instincts were becoming, the way he sorted strangers into useful, useless and doesn't matter.

"Great," Randall says. "Opening night nerves, I guess."

"I've got them, too," Molly says, in her case meaning it.

Molly's interjection deflects Rex from the feeling he picked up on from Randall. Smiling tightly, he says "Trust me on this, it'll be a piece of cake."

With half the country and a global audience expected to watch, it made the movie premiere seem like an opening at the Roxy in Smalltown, America. Sarah's *New Yorker* profile was so huge they ran off two hundred thousand more copies, twice the original estimate, and she is now a bona fide media star, appearing frequently on afternoon television and a 60 Minutes segment where she talks about issues; there is talk of a Sunday interview show of her own.

Dickson and Kornhouser were in the talks with PBS and the two presidential campaigns over how audience seats were to be split up for the debate. Old school on the subject, Kornhouser wanted half for Rex's followers, but Dickson pulled the rug out from under him. "We don't care whose butts you put in the chairs," he said as he worked on a hangnail with small gold scissors. Kornhouser's head turned to him so fast that throat and jowls rippled like Jell-O in a bowl. "Huh?"

Ignoring his bewilderment, Dickson told the meeting, "It doesn't matter, Republicans and Democrats, right or left, everybody likes Rex; so, really, it doesn't matter to us. I keep telling my friend here this is a different kind of election, but it hasn't sunk in yet." Nobody arguing over it was fine with PBS and the political party people, so first come, first seated was decided on and the meeting ended early. Dickson and Kornhouser left separately without speaking.

CHAPTER 45

KORNHOUSER WAS AT THE DOOR WITH A GENTLE TAP. "FIVE MINUTES, REX. GRACIE ASHCROFT Weber's people say she's not coming out until you're behind your podium." With a wink at them, Rex strolls out with the panache of a boulevardier on his way to the afternoon assignation. The screaming from the audience begins as soon as he comes from the wings with a head-ducking arm wave that is a perfect expression of humble modesty.

"Raaa-*eeex*!" they begin to chant.

"Her people are on their feet too," Molly says, studying the big TV screen, "you can't tell the difference. Omigod, that woman just threw panties at him. Didn't they screen these people?" They watch as security hustles her off the set. Kornhouser comes through the door. "People are bananas out there." Assistant directors try to calm the crowd so Gracie can come out. Finally, one speaks into Rex's ear and he goes into his palms-down, cool-it routine until the raucous welcome tapers off into an expectant buzz.

Gracie enters from the other wing to more restrained cheers, looking poised, even youthful for a woman in her middle fifties; she wears a designer scarf and a dark suit to de-emphasize the weight that even diet and exercise won't take off. She waves and points to people in the crowd as if surprised and delighted they came all this way to see little ol' her. Then she walks straight to Rex and plants a kiss square on his lips that goes on and on until he flaps his arms comically.

"Mwah," Gracie says, breaking it off and brightly turning back to the crowd. "Is there any one of you who hasn't wanted to do that?"

"That was a big wet one," Molly says.

"A big mistake I'd call it," Kornhouser says. "Hell, they just met this minute."

The shots of the crowd show a mixed reaction. Some men are laughing and women here and there jump and scream, but others of both sexes seem sympathetic to the mild dismay Rex puts on with actorly skill as he looks into the blinding lights. Gracie's next surprise is grabbing his lapels and peering up into his face. "Is my lipstick all right?" she says coquettishly. When he nods with a stagy helplessness, she turns with a wave to the crowd and strides to her podium.

"Well," says the moderator humorously, mastering his surprise, "I've never seen a start to a debate quite as... as friendly as that."

"You never have to worry about Rex handling a situation," Randall says with a significant glance at Molly. Her expression says she remembers Cohen's fall in the Polo Lounge, the jet into the Dubai building, the thugs fighting in the street.

As Gracie begins her opening statement, a slight confusion clouds her face as if she is asking herself, Did something happen just now?

"She's already regrettin' it," Kornhouser observes, scrolling on his smartphone, "as well she should. Look how the social media is lighting up."

Gracie hits all the usual notes in her well-polished talk—the need to reach out, to show greater compassion for the misfortunate, America cannot be an island unto itself, we can do better as a nation, and so forth. Puzzled sound technicians watch needles register animal sounds interwoven with her words that are almost below human hearing. They twiddle the dials and hear a coyote's yip, a chicken clucking, and a donkey's hee-haw. "Why is she doing that?" one asks another. "It's not outside interference; you can see she's doing it."

What gets everyone's full attention is when Gracie turns to conditions in the Middle East with the now clearly audible sound of a pig's squeal; the camera on Rex registers his shocked reaction. "The reconciliation of stakeholders in the region"—it is grunting sounds now like a razorback rooting for acorns, and the concerned moderator breaks in. "We seem to be having some technical trouble; Mrs. Weber, would you like to take a short break?"

Irked at the interruption, Gracie says, "Of course not" and makes a sound like a barn owl. Woooo. She puts a hand over her mouth, shooting a panicked look offstage where her advisers are frozen in shock. One hurries to take her elbow and lead her to the wings.

"Anybody got any ideas?" the moderator is heard asking the control room.

He stuffs his tiny earpiece in tighter for the reply and looks at Rex. "Okay, we suggest you go ahead with your statement and take questions afterward for the rest of the hour."

Rex looks tempted but shakes his head. "No, that wouldn't be fair to Gracie Ashcroft Weber and the fine people who support her. Let's wait until she's... recovered. Then we can do it the right way." His kindness and generosity—the obsolete word "chivalry," banished these many years, is dusted off by commentators—moves the crowd to cheers as he gives a wave and departs.

Gracie's meltdown and retreat into seclusion were all people talked about in the run up to the second debate with Buster Keegan, the Republican. Her camp issued a statement that blamed pain medication for a bad back, but said she is recovering and eager to get back on the campaign trail.

"That old chestnut," scoffs Kornhouser. "It's like when famous people used to go to the hospital for 'nervous exhaustion'"—he makes air quotes—"when everybody knew they'd been on a bender. She's finished anyhow; Rex and Buster are splitting the numbers Gracie dropped in the polls."

If Gracie blew it, it is evident from Keegan's grinning cock-of-the-walk stride as he bursts from the wings, powerful chest stuck out and arms swinging, that he is not someone to squander an opportunity. A former governor and senator, he is broad-shouldered, glowing with health, abrim with animal spirits; his expensively cut salt-and-pepper hair is in the Bill Clinton league. In other circumstances, he would be the handsomest man in the room.

He doesn't wait coyly for Rex to come out first, but dives into the crowd for hugs, fist bumps and high fives. "I love you!" he cries in his Happy Campaigner voice, a wondrous instrument tailored to the venue with a range from flugelhorn to warm cello. When Rex does emerge, Keegan bounds back to the stage to grip his hand and upper arm and pull him in tight in a show of macho domination. Rex gets a big laugh when he gives the camera a waggish look, shaking his hand as if to say that really hurt.

"I'm givin' that point to Rex," Kornhouser says in the greenroom.

"He didn't used to have comic chops," Molly muses.

"He's better every day in every way," Randall says in a defeated voice.

Buster Keegan uses every second of his time in opening remarks to list his myriad accomplishments in political office, ending by gleefully turning to Rex to say, "All my experience is in the real world, but I have to admit I've never been in a movie for teenagers."

It is a brilliant thrust and Rex smiles gamely into the storm of groans and cheers until they subside. "Well, governor, I've got friends in Hollywood who can help you out after the election." This also brings groans and cheers, and Buster good-naturedly snaps off a hand salute that says "well done."

"I'm gonna call that a draw," Kornhouser says. "Of course, Buster knew what he was gonna say and it was probably focus group tested, whereas Rex came up with his answer off the top of his head. That kind of shit impresses the political pontificators."

There were no more fireworks after that, the two men talking wonkish policy points developed by the governor's experienced staff and Rock-Steady. "Boy, was that a snoozefest except for the start," says Kornhouser, "but we established our guy is deeper than the establishment thought."

"You took it easy on him," Randall tells Rex when they are alone for a moment. "I thought he'd have a coughing fit or blow a snot bubble. You know, something subtle."

Rex doesn't smile. "I want to keep the race close so people don't lose interest, but maybe you'll see something unusual in the last debate."

A blur of travel and campaign events in flyover land follow in the weeks afterward. They seldom see him except when he leaves his private compartment on a plane, train or bus—he is composing an opera—for a quick speech to awestruck hayseeds astonished someone so famous has found a path to their insignificant burg.

"Why is this necessary, these piddling states?" Molly asks Randall crankily. They are traveling on a chartered luxury bus through the endless Dakota badlands followed by a string of identical vehicles where bored and resentful journalists stare through tinted windows at swales and hills of prairie grassland, goddamning the sheer size of this fucking country.

"Kornhouser says it has something to do with the Electoral College," Randall replies. "The way he scopes it out, Rex needs every one of the votes he can get and this has three."

"They must count the deer and the antelope as people," Molly complains, sandled feet tucked under her and hanging on to the arm of her seat as the bus jolts and lurches. "It's been a half hour since I saw even a pickup truck. All these ruts!" The buses raise a tail of dust a quarter mile long.

"They've got us going down back roads for security, that's why the ride is so rough; it's pretty smart of them, actually."

Sometimes fences must be taken down to let the buses clank over cattle guards and then put up again. Their bus begins and ends in a different spot in the convoy and changes places in the lineup in case of snipers in the stands of Ponderosa pine that rise from the moraine; a helicopter gunship circles overhead for that kind of surprise. After the rodeo or picnic or whatever other event ends the day, they stop beyond the town for the chopper whose rotors flatten the grass. The three of them transfer and fly miles deeper into the countryside where they spend the nights under brilliant stars at isolated ranches with rural folks dazzled by their glamor; the buses continue on to the next town, no more than a dot on the vast plain. Sparks generally fly between the news people who jam into the one or two honky-tonks where they complain about slow service and the rot gut liquor poured into expensive brand-name bottles. Shoving and punching generally break out with the locals when everybody is loaded. Black eyes and chipped teeth are nursed with the bad-booze hangovers on the buses the following morning. Network anchors chopper in wearing jeans and western shirts with snap buttons for interviews with the folksy Rex ("I'm lovin' seein' this great country of ours up close and personal") and with rustics in dusty boots and sweat-stained cowboy hats. They tip them back and utter laconic country wisdom. "If you're not makin' dust you're eatin' it." "Always drink upstream from the herd." The media eats this up. After the Big Foots fly out they leave seething producers to drag themselves back on the buses for the long ride to the next town big enough for its own school and hardware store, which are Kornhouser's inflexible principle on where to stop.

"I never heard of the Electoral College before Trump," Molly says. "I think I had it confused with the College of Cardinals."

"I maybe heard of it in social studies when I was in high school," Randall replies.

CHAPTER 46

THE CHOPPER SETS THEM DOWN AT SUNSET NEAR A LOVELY OLD HOUSE ON A BUTTE WITH A LONG view of a valley that could have been the setting for a Vargas painting titled Peace at Sundown. Holsteins browse in a meadow, horses watch with erect ears from a paddock, and soft light glows in every window as if a set designer was in charge. The only jarring note is the jumble of government trucks bristling with quivers of aerials.

A man and woman stand in welcome on the wooden porch; a barbecue pit glimmers with red coals, and a lamp-lighted table inside with a blue-and-white oilcloth is spread for dinner. Introductions are made with the Stephens, brother and sister; Rex shakes hands quickly and goes off to the Secret Service communication van for his nightly video conference with advisers.

The sister is dark-haired, pert and freckled with lines around her eyes from squinting into long distances; the hand she gives them is hard from outdoor work. "Welcome to First Light Ranch," she says to Molly. "I'm Gert and that there is Robert, but call him Rob and he'll answer."

Rob steps forward with a smile. "We haven't had this much excitement since the pig ate my second cousin."

"Rob has a strange sense of humor," his sister says. "It helps to keep that in mind."

Molly feels a small earthquake of desire as he takes her hand in his. She likes men who make her laugh. He is blue-eyed and so handsome in a Gary Cooperish way that he could have stepped from the cover of a Harlequin Romance, though his mop of gray hair looks like his sister cuts it with dull scissors. Something makes her sense contained sorrow as he fixes drinks and small talk is made.

"Thanks for giving a roof over our heads tonight," Randall says, accepting a glass dark with a hefty pour of Maker's Mark.

"We would have offered without being asked," Rob says, "but as it happened the Secret Service spotted us from the satellite as pretty far from everything, which I guess they like. They approached us and we said why, sure, no problem. I don't follow politics much, but Rex doesn't seem like the usual run of the mill."

"Far from it," Randall says, chewing an ice cube.

"Think he's going to win?" Rob asks Molly.

"We think so."

"But you don't want to go out on a limb?" he banters, touching his glass of wine to hers.

"A week is a long time in politics, let alone two months before an election." There is more light cocktail talk until Rob says to her, "You any good at barbecuing? I think it's time to get those steaks on."

"Below average," she says with honesty. Her boyfriends always insisted on having custody of that rite as if it was sacred to males. Randall excuses himself to call Abby and they are alone in the gloaming, the stars just starting to come out.

"I thought I'd be cooking steaks for the whole bunch, that's why the barbecue pit is so big" Robb says, "but the Secret Service is afraid of poisoning and they tote their chow with them." He forks inch-thick slabs from a platter and they flame up on the coals.

Molly smiles. "They have a lot of rules and regulations, those folks."

"The smell will drive them nuts, but more for us, right? Gert makes a dynamite potato salad, and the agents gave us fresh tomatoes from somewhere." He grins at her. "Flown in at small cost to the taxpayer, I'm sure." The flames from the fat die down and they watch the steaks sizzle.

"It sure is quiet out here," Molly says, feeling more relaxed than she can remember. Life seemed complicated before Rex, but looking back it really wasn't. It was heart-breakingly simple and ordinary.

"This is a city right now compared to normal," Rob says. "Listen to those generators; every one of those trucks has one sucking up gas. You should hear what it's really like out here when… " He stops as if something came out he didn't mean.

"I'd like that," she says, surprised by her boldness. "Sometime."

"Just give a shout."

To cover her forwardness, she says, "You know, I'm not really in politics, I work in advertising. You could make a living doing commercials with your looks."

Rob stares at her with astonishment and then bursts out into laughter. "Sure, lady."

"I'm serious, that was my job, scouting for faces. You'd be a natural for shaving cream and after-shave lotion. Call me Molly, by the way."

"If I had to make a living from this mug, Molly, it'd be a damn short one. A har har har. I think I'd better stick to ranching, but thanks." He had laughed so hard he wipes tears away. "Wait'll Gert hears that."

"What'll Gert hears what?" she asks, coming out the screen door.

"You'll tell her," he says.

"I was saying," Molly says somewhat defensively, "that he could do TV work shaving or slapping on after-shave. Outdoor clothes, too."

"He's good looking enough," Gert agrees, "but I thought that was for sissy boys-—those male models you see in magazines looking so pouty. Get a reputation for that out here and you might as well hit the road. They rank about equal with sheep molesters."

When the steaks are charred outside but pink inside, they take them to the table where Randall joins them. "Where'd you get the candles?" Rob quietly asks his sister.

"I had a couple stashed away," Gert says. "Rob's wife Ginny died last year. They always had candles with dinner."

"Not always," he says softly.

"Every time I was here," she explains to Molly. "I moved from Portland so he wouldn't get so lonely he'd put a gun to his head."

"I'm sorry about your wife," Molly says.

"Yeah, that's rough," Randall adds. He never knows what to say in these situations.

"How long were you..." Molly starts.

"Fifteen years," Rob says. "We couldn't have kids." Randall changes his mind about showing pictures of the twins.

"My three boys are grown up," Gert says, "and they don't want anything to do with ranch life, so it looks like after four generations of our family on this land we're the last."

"At least they'll be well off," Rob says, clearly making an effort not to be a wet blanket. "We get wealthy guys in here three or four times a year asking to name our price, but I plan to hang around into my nineties shaking my cane at strangers if I'm not too blind to see 'em."

They are finishing their meal—the potato salad very strong on dill and pickle is as good as advertised—when Rex comes in. When he turns on the charm, as he does now, Molly thinks rooms must fill with negative ions that bring more oxygen to the brain; everything seems sharper and brighter as if a lens is twitched for better focus.

"Let me throw a steak on for you," Rob says, scraping back his chair. Rex holds up his hands. "No, thanks. I had a bite with the boys in the van. Filled to the top, though maybe there's a little room if that's blueberry pie I see."

"It certainly is," Gert says.

"It's an honor to have you here, sir," Rob says with formality.

"I'm Rex to my friends, which I hope you two are." He gives them a quick smile and charming little bow and the Stephens are captivated. It always happens so quickly it is like magic by a shaman who has mastered his act so completely he barely needs to go through the motions.

"Rob and I drove three hours to town to see your movie," she says. "We thought it was great."

"Three hours one way," her brother emphasizes. "There's no streaming out here and we didn't want to wait a year for Netflix, not the way people talked about it."

"Glad you liked it," Rex says, seeming touched. Pure genius, Molly thinks. Has anybody in history ever faked sincere humility better than he does?

"Just following the news," Gert says, "the world's not in such great shape today. The Middle East…"

Rex finishes the sentence. "Is a powder keg and the fuse is lit, sad but true."

"It was bad enough when all they had were bombs, guns and knives," Rob says worriedly. "But now everybody's got nuclear weapons. What can one man do, even a president?"

"That remains to be seen," Rex says. "It depends on the man, of course. Or woman. Ma'am—Gert—this is the best blueberry pie I ever tasted."

"Oh, please," she says, flustered but pleased. "The berries were frozen because the deer got all mine."

"As your president," Rex says grandly, "I'll see that doesn't happen next year." Everyone laughs.

The men adjourn to the family room while she and Molly clear the table. "Thank God for dishwashers," Gert says. "My grandmother used to boil water on a wood stove and made her own soap." She laughs. "The dishes didn't always get as clean as they might."

Molly asks the question she has been thinking about through dinner as she cast covert glances at Rob. "So, is he ever going to marry again or is he one of those types that carry a torch to the grave?"

"He never meets any women way out here, so your guess is as good as mine." Gert gives her a frank look. "Why, are you interested?"

Her cheeks feel hot. "Am I blushing?"

"Yes, as a matter of fact."

"Well, I guess that's your answer."

"I wish he would find someone," Gert says wistfully. "I'd like to get back to Portland. I've got a kind of steady guy, but I'm getting the message the heart doesn't always grow fonder with, you know, too much absence."

"Are you still afraid Rob is…"

"No, he's much better now. He was just so haggard before; he lost so much weight he was a scarecrow.

"It doesn't look like it now."

"I didn't have to resort to spoon feeding, but it was close." She sighs. "I bet you lead an exciting life."

"All this here looks pretty good to me right now. Exciting lives are not all they're cracked up to be."

Gert's smile is warm. "I'd wave a magic wand if I had one."

Drowsy from bourbon and the wine with dinner, Randall half-listens to Rex and Rob talk about cattle breeds. "My dad was a Black Angus man, but I've been doing some cross-breeding with Herefords; they're hardier and more efficient at converting pasture to prime beef."

Rex takes this in with a nod. "What about the Piedmontese? They have less marbling and higher protein content." Randall wonders as usual where he learns this stuff. Is there a Google microchip implant to go with all the other advantages he's got? Satan must be keeping up with all the latest stuff.

"Yes," Rob says, leaning forward with interest, "but a narrower birth canal, which means more damaged calves or dead ones. I don't need that with only three ranch hands."

"On the other hand…"

"Gentlemen," Randall interrupts, "I know you won't mind if I leave you to this interesting discussion. Another long day tomorrow." He goes upstairs to his room; when he comes out of the bathroom Camael is in an armchair.

"One of these days I hope not get the shit scared out of me by you," Randall says.

"Things are not going well." Camael always looks concerned, but now things are evidently worse. "The Angel of Death is loose in the world. Already, there is a variant of Ebola more deadly than before. It will make the first outbreak look mild."

Randall sinks down onto the bed with head between hands before looking up, "Can't you pray to God to stop it?"

"God doesn't always listen."

"How did Abbadon get loose?"

"Lucifer appeared to me in all of his gorgeous satanic pomp and majesty with a temptation he said I couldn't resist. What he meant was I could not resist listening in order to reject it utterly, as he knew I would. The details of the offer are unimportant, less than for Jesus if you want to know, but still very handsome. He puts on a dazzling show, to give him his due. As I listened, my contempt for him was so clear it provoked a mighty display of anger. You know about the volcano eruption in Indonesia?"

"The press people on the bus were talking about that," Randall says. "A bad one."

"It killed ten thousand people who suffered the greatest terror and pain, all of it keenly felt in the angelic host. In my distress over an event I had provoked with my contempt, the Angel of Death slipped away." He shakes his head sorrowfully. "You think you know all his tricks and then Lucifer shows a new one. That vile look of vindictive triumph as he withdrew into the sulphurous cloud that carried him away… well, I can never forget it."

"They stopped Ebola the first time." Randall says hopefully.

"The virus learned and is changing," Camael replies. "It won't be beaten so easily this time, and the same is happening with other diseases. And that's not even the worst. In lands where murder and suicides demonstrate piety, a few people are a restraining hand on mad rulers. One, a general of the army, had his throat slit today in Pyongyang. They will blame an agent of American imperialism, but it's Abaddon's work. Each of these will be removed until the truly insane or demonically possessed have no check whatever on their actions. It will take only a small incident for the rockets to begin flying. The entire world will be aflame. Rex will flourish in those conditions."

Randall has a feeling Camael is working his way around to something he won't want to hear. Mouth dry, he says, "I've got my Glock in the suitcase; you want me to walk downstairs and shoot Rex in the head?"

Camael shakes his head. "You don't understand, you can't kill him, no human can. I doubt now that even Lucifer has the power. Rex has become his own evil force. Only that creature he transfers his essence to with each stroke of the brush can do that, as Rex will learn at the instant the portrait is finished." Camuel stops as if a thought occurs to him. "Or perhaps they will embrace one another as brothers. That would be more like Lucifer; two would be controlled more easily because he would have one constantly intriguing against the other."

As the angel ponders this new alarming new possibility, Randall speaks. "We haven't been to Bluff Point for weeks, but we're heading back tomorrow. Do I still have time to get my family to safety before all the shit comes down?"

"Safety?" Camael marvels. "Where would you find it?"

"I was giving some thought to Alaska. Find some spot in the wilderness, you know, build a bunker and hole up."

"You and your family would be hunted down wherever you hid and your days and nights would be spent waiting for it." Camael puts a warm hand on his shoulder. "Besides, I need you and Molly."

"For what?" Randall asks, the feeling of dread stronger.

"To Rex you are nothing, but he believes you think you're friends. You could have stopped him when he was new and vulnerable, but you stood by his side and kept him safe."

"That was your idea," Randall reminds him. "If I had to do it all over again…" The angel's hand presses tighter on his shoulder and his blustering stops.

"You'd do the same thing again, my friend."

The grudging admission is forced from him. "Yeah, well, maybe."

"A hundred times over," Camael gently insists. "It's the kind of people you and Molly are."

"She doesn't like to get into it, but I don't believe she really knows how deep this is. She goes with the flow because she doesn't see a way out."

"She's a good woman, that's the important thing. A policeman loses perspective; there are many bad people, but most are good."

"I'd have to take your word on that." The hand on his shoulder is firmer. "Fine," Randall says. "I'll take your word, but remind me why 'good' is better than naïve in the real world." Randall pauses. "Well, real is not quite the word, is it?"

"Yes," Camael replies, his mood more somber than ever, "that is exactly what it is."

"You always want something, what is it this time?"

"The same as before, continue watching. When the time is right, we will strike." Then he is gone as if he had never been there.

At the possibility of action, Randall feels a little encouraged. This passivity has been like keeping a drug house under surveillance. He and a partner would check out a different undercover car and find an inconspicuous place to park. Then they waited for time to drag past. Check your watch after what seemed an eternity and the second hand had only clicked off ten minutes.

They travel fast the next day with cops from the jurisdictions serving as outriders until the county line is passed and they are replaced by the next group. They roll into a raucous welcome at Bluff Point after dark where a new rota of Secret Service agents waits to relieve the traveling contingent. Abby is radiant and the kids hop around like kangaroos. Even Esther smiles. "It's been a long time away this one time," she chides, "but I'm a believer in Rex's cause." A campaign badge on her chest says Rex Is Ahead and So Are We.

"Rex is her cause now?" he asks Abby in bed later, every trace of travel fatigue gone thanks to their lovemaking.

"He's replaced The Young and the Restless as her main conversation," she says impatiently. "It's like idolatry; she just cannot understand why Buster Keegan sticks so close in the polls. Rex is so great and Keegan is nothing. I swear sometime I'm going to blow my stack."

CHAPTER 47

MOLLY OBSERVES DICKSON STARING WITH REVULSION AT KORNHOUSER AS HE STROKES HIS throat, which seems to swell from this attention. Kornhouser had made a sound that indicated speech was imminent.

"Yes," Dickson says brutally, stabbing a look at his watch as the politico continues his unhurried search for words, "you're going to say something?" He is in a dark gray double-breasted Saville Row suit with chalk stripes that would say investment banker except for the black limited-edition LeBron high-top athletic shoes from Nike signed by the basketball legend himself. This detail would not be noticed except he has insolently put feet up on the conference table with ankles crossed. He is with his assistant Linda Atwood, as still and watchful as a cat. Molly has noted she wears either black or beige with her quiet jewelry and accessories. Absent the evidence of any warmth or other signs of personality, Molly thinks her value to a company must be a super-smartness that delivers logical options uncorrupted by emotion.

Kornhouser never speaks to Dickson now; his words at meetings are directed to walls, the ceiling, the table or another person, in this case Molly. "My gut tells me barrin' the unexpected, it's going to come down to who wins the debate. The focus groups said it was dead even last time."

"I don't think you need to worry," Molly says wanly. The sharp look from Dickson reminds her she has to keep up the pretense of backing Rex to the hilt. What an expression, she thinks; it doesn't have to mean total support. An image fills her mind of a knife struck in a back as far as it will go.

"I don't worry about Rex," Kornhouser says, "a 'course he'll do his usual great job."

"Then what's bugging you?" Dickson demands.

"I'm worried Buster Keegan is gonna pull off the performance of a lifetime in the final debate, leadin' to another dead heat," Kornhouser tells Molly. "That would leave things up to our dodgy electorate."

"I wouldn't worry about that either," she says, wondering what Rex will do to sabotage his rival. Make Keegan stumble when he approaches the podium and he has to be helped up with broken teeth and a nose that won't stop bleeding? Eyes rolling and showing the whites as he topples backward in a faint? Perhaps he will take on an effeminate lisp and flop his wrist when the debate turns to the military. Or a heart attack, incapacitating but not fatal to keep the sympathy vote down. Really, the possibilities are limitless. She remembers the fat man who abused the waitress and hopes it won't be something Keegan never lives down, a Poirot-like clinched-buttocks waddle to the wings with everybody knowing he's carrying a pants load.

"Well," Kornhouser says, carefully selecting a nut from a dish and chewing—the motion adds a lapping motion to the goiter-like neck-chin amalgamation that Dickson goggles at—"worryin' is what I get paid for."

Dickson brings shoes from table to floor with a loud stamp as if he is going to lunge across the table at Kornhouser. She wonders if he is on a street drug, one of the new ones the papers say bring out a person's vicious side.

"I can't take any more of this shit," Dickson shouts. Atwood's pale eyes cut to him coldly; she is so obviously reporting to someone behind his back, Molly thinks.

Kornhouser fastidiously chooses another nut from the bowl as if he hadn't noticed, holding it up the light like a connoisseur. "Unfortunately," he tells Molly when he is satisfied it passes muster and pops it into his mouth, "Rex has associations with Hollywood, which is a stench in the nostrils of decent people."

Dickson says, "For crissake, he wouldn't be where he is if it wasn't for Hollywood." He glares at Molly. "I'm recommending that we cut ties with this guy." Kornhouser selects another nut with the same care. Atwood catches Molly's eye and gives a slight shake of her head, telling her dumping Kornhouser isn't going to happen; it also means it's a matter of time before Dickson is marched out of Rock-Steady carrying his private belongings in a box.

"The horns of our dilemma," Kornhouser explains to Molly, "is what brought him this far might just well stop him goin' all the way, leastwise as I read the data. Barrin' the unforseen, of course."

"What do you mean by that?" she asks.

"Bein' caught in bed with a dead girl or a live boy, as a Louisiana governor said back in the day."

"What a sickening sack of shit you are," Dickson yells as Kornhouser begins another discriminating hunt for a nut in the bowl.

Unable to restrain himself any further, he slams out of the room, leaving Linda Atwood behind. "That boy's got a temper," Kornhouser says mildly. "Ah, a filbert."

"We'll get back to you," Linda says calmly, picking up her matching Gucci purse and briefcase and following Dickson.

That night just before midnight, Molly is putting cold cream on her face when there is a light knock at the door. Slipping on her robe and wiping her face with a towel, she finds Randall with an older man in work clothes. She wonders if there is a plumbing problem. "Got a minute?" Randall says. "There's someone I want you to meet."

She is enchanted at once by the stranger's kind eyes and the strange warmth he brings with him like a tropical trade wind off sun-dazzled waters. "This is Camael," Randall says simply.

"The... the angel?" Camael takes her hand when the room starts to spin. He seems to float her to the nearest chair. "I didn't think you were real," she says in a small child's voice.

"Didn't I say?" Randall tells Camael.

"It was easier to believe in us in times past," Camael says in his soft voice. "Believing is much harder today, except in evil—it has a way of always reminding you it exists." He touches her arm, "Jimmy and Al are just fine, and so is everyone else you loved and lost in life."

Molly buries her face in her hands and cries for a long time. "Thank you," she says at last.

"You are lucky that you haven't known bad people until now," Camael replies. "Others are not so fortunate, but they never again will see those bad people who hurt them and damaged their lives. No one will except the demons and fiends who will exact a just punishment. Many of these names resound in history, genocidal murderers and the like, infamous for their cruelty. Stalin who lay on the floor for hours after his stroke threw up his hands in horror when he saw the terrible revenge that advanced on him for the millions he callously and in some cases even merrily slaughtered."

"You said until now," Molly says, brushing away the tears with her hand. "Do you mean Rex?"

"Yes." Once again, gently.

"I've had such mixed feelings about him."

"Yes, of course," Camael, "Satan is the great deceiver." A thoughtful pause. "The double cross becomes the triple cross and more; so absorbed is Lucifer in his own cunning it is our good fortune that his plots and conspiracies cancel out each other and he is lost in the very chaos he creates. His rage is terrible to behold at such moments. He takes out his failures on others. Instead of the earthquake occurring on a remote archipelago, it strikes a densely settled area. A well-watered plain goes to desert from one year to the next, that sort of thing."

"But why doesn't God do something about it?" She feels tears on her cheeks.

"I don't know," Camael confesses with a simple honesty that touches her in a deep place. "Perhaps it began as a principle when He created the world. If there was good, there must also be evil… at least until the end when all Creation is judged. Perhaps he will see it was a mistake to create evil, but perhaps without the freedom to choose one over the other there is no meat on the bones of goodness. Wouldn't life be meaningless with only one choice?"

His admission of not knowing the profoundest mystery is so humble she doesn't want to be like a prosecutor badgering a witness. I'm such a coward, she thinks. Why are there pain and suffering—it's what everyone wants to know. Why do people die for no good reason, leaving hearts broken that are never mended? Religions came along to try to answer the questions, but their explanations don't hold water for everyone.

"The point is," Randall says impatiently, "Camael thinks matters are coming to the boiling point fast. If Rex wins the debate, he goes to the White House and has all that power to do what Lucifer wants."

"Unless Rex has another goal he must accomplish first," Camael ventures, "which is overthrowing Satan and reigning in his place."

"Would that be better or worse for us?" Molly asks, half in hope.

"We don't know," the angel replies. "We do know that the portrait he is completing would be infinitely worse than Rex himself."

"You don't want to see it," Randall tells her. "It's a lifetime of nightmares."

"Then let's go up there and cut it to pieces," Molly cries, "drag it out on the balcony and set fire to the fucker."

"Camael says it's our ace in the hole," Randall explains. "They don't know we know. That gives us our only chance to spring a surprise when they're not expecting."

"But first," Camael says, "we must stop Rex from winning the debate."

"How is that even possible?" Molly objects. "He can crook his little finger and Buster Keegan suddenly becomes the village idiot. Look what he did to poor Gracie; her political career is dead. People give her that hee-haw donkey sound wherever she goes; the poor thing never leaves her house."

Camael returns to the point. "Whatever we decide, the blow must be struck before the debate." They talk for an hour until a plan begins to emerge. Then one second Camael is there and when Molly turns her head he is gone.

"I'm sorry I didn't trust what you said about him," she says tragically.

Randall stands to go. "I probably would have thought you were crazy if you did."

"Do think this plan will work?" she asks, twisting a handkerchief wet with tears in her hands.

"Probably not, but it's the best we've got."

CHAPTER 48

SARAH MARSH OF *NEW YORKER* IS NOT THE SMUG, IRONIC YOUNG WOMAN THEY FIRST MET AND still less the skinny, strung-out addict. The makeover by the celebrated television team on the syndicated Look Your Best—Now! plays up her best features and de-emphasizes those Sarah wasn't crazy about. Underlying the cosmetic changes seems a glowing wholesomeness.

"The skinny-lipped look is gone," she says. "They said it made me look judgmental, so I get Botox injections every two months." She gives a pooched-out pout to emphasize how pillowy her lips are now. "All the A-list media go to Dr. Feldman for their work."

"I thought you were pretty before, but you look good now."

"Only good?" Sarah says, her face falling.

"No, great," Molly says. "You look fabulous, way better even than before."

Sarah is mollified. "Well, thank you. I'm sorry you had to fly all the way to New York City, but my schedule is fucking hell; I've had to hire my own personal assistant." They ordered wine and appetizers at Jean-Georges Restaurant, a slow-cooked egg topped with caviar for Molly and Santa Barbara sea urchin lightly breaded with black bread crumbs for Sarah. "Between us," she says, lowering her voice. "One of the independents has me in mind for a late-night talk show going up against the comedians. It will be, you know, serious but not fucking boring. I am so pumped." She sips water. "How's Rex?" There is longing in her voice. "People can't believe he was my boyfriend."

"The biggest story in the world is about to get bigger," Molly says.

Sarah is disbelieving. "How is that *even* possible? He's going to mop the floor with Buster next week, and then it's clear sailing to the White House."

"This is bigger than that," Molly replies in an even voice. "Do you want the story?"

"Are you shitting me? Hell, yeah! Anything with Rex's name is pure platinum."

"Because we can take it to someone else." She knows the hint of an iron hand in the velvet glove never hurts in dealing with the media.

"Oh, please, please give it to me. Gimme, gimme, gimme! What is it?" Her eyes sparkle.

"There are guidelines."

"I agree to them all, so you don't even have to tell me what they are."

"It's not exclusive; you have to agree to share the story."

"If it's as big as you say, everybody will pick it up afterward. The networks, the wires… "

"No, I mean live. Everybody gets it at the same time."

Sarah is mystified. "How would that work?"

"Your crew does the video and the afternoon of the debate the package is delivered to everyone who agrees to our conditions in advance. An hour later the embargo lifts and everybody puts it on the air and it's streamed live." She doubts any of the media will hesitate; the herd instinct is too strong.

Sarah thinks this over. "If everybody gets it at the same time, what's in it for us?"

"You're the host and ask the questions. If you think you're well known now, wait until you're on all these platforms at the same time all over the world."

She actually shivers at the prospect, but then Molly sees doubt creep in. "You know," Sarah says, "I don't really have the authority to say yes. I work for A Deeper Look Productions and a guy named Basil Chambers. He has to say okay."

"Get him on the phone."

"You mean, like, right now?"

"You don't want this to slip away, Sarah."

Sarah hesitates a beat and then, looking determined, fishes out her smartphone and dials. "I need to talk to Basil," she says commandingly. She listens to the reply. "I don't care who he's with, get him on the phone; tell him this is not big, it's Yuuuge." Thirty seconds pass. "Simon, it's Sarah. I'm sitting across the table from Molly Simon; I don't need to tell you who she is, right? Good.

She's offering us the biggest story ever about Rex. No, I don't know what it is; no details yet because there are conditions before she tells. Yes, absolutely trustworthy. We're at Jean-Georges, which is twenty minutes from you." She hangs up. "He's coming right over."

Sharp-faced and intense as if he used his narrow head to go down hidey-holes where the soon-to-be-disgraced hoped to escape exposure, Chambers has the rushed, rumpled look of a man who wears the same clothes two or three days in a row because he can't get home for a shower and change. Sarah had warned not to judge from appearances, saying he is one of those louche journalists who climbed the greasy pole of the London tabloids before crossing the Atlantic for better money. "He's really news smart," Sarah said, "in a way you don't see over here. He says American journalists are smug and lazy and wouldn't last a minute on Fleet Street."

He introduces himself to Molly in an accent that mixes Cockney with another region she can't identify, the north perhaps. "Gawd, what's that muck?" he says, recoiling from the appetizer placed with a flourish before him by the epicene waiter.

"Sea trout sashimi with trout eggs," Sarah says. "I thought you might be hungry." He does have a hungry look, Molly thinks at once, but it isn't for food.

"Take it away and bring me a pint of Guinness," he orders the waiter, who is in a white coat so starched it crackles.

"But… yes, sir." He picks up the plate and departs in a busy-buns walk that expresses indignation at the low-life people one must deal with even at a high temple of cuisine.

"So, what's this about?" Basil Chambers asks Molly without preliminaries.

"The inside story on Rex."

"I wasn't aware there was one, and I bet I've read a hundred thousand words about him without going out of my way; everyone has had a go at him. Oil man turned Hollywood god, baseball great, and savior of the nation, all of it hashed over and over."

"There's more," Molly says, "much more." Beneath the pose of cynical knowingness and indifference, she senses a keen attention under tight control. "He's not what he seems."

"Who is in public life?" This is put almost scornfully.

"The difference is he is running for the White House. Don't you think people ought to know everything?"

"Okay, theoretically. But you should know in my personal experience the public is as stupid as an acre of dirt. But tell me what you've got."

Molly takes the page from her purse with the few paragraphs of conditions. Working with Hollywood types and their lawyers has been educational.

Reading them swiftly, Chambers nods as he mentally checks off each one. He looks up. "Each copy of the video that goes out has Courtesy of A Deeper Look Productions at the bottom of the picture—clearly legible, mind—at the beginning, the end and every sixty seconds. Some of these bastards will try to edit it out or hide it with pixels. And Sarah does all the narration, not some voice-over they squeeze in with cutaways to their people. In short, all credit to A Deeper Look Productions… and Sarah, of course."

"Fine," Molly says, "we'll put it in the contract."

The Guinness arrives and, holding up a finger to detain the waiter, Chambers drinks half the pint straight away. "I'll have another, mate." He gives Molly a penetrating look. "And the story is?"

"Do you remember Templeton Hall?"

"Please," Chambers says scornfully. "I'm in the business for crissakes, remember?"

"He was there."

"Oh my God!" Sarah cries out, drawing looks from other tables. She blanches and her hand goes to her mouth as if to stop herself from saying more. Chambers drains the rest of his pint, more slowly to give him time to think.

"Can you prove it?" he says, putting the glass down.

"Yes," Molly says, looking him straight in the eyes. "We have a video when a policeman stopped him for questioning. Afterward, he drove him to Templeton Hall and left him there. Rex remained there until just before the killings began."

"So he wasn't actually there at the time?"

"He left just before; I met him the following morning. He couldn't remember anything about what went on before the officer stopped to see if he needed help. The video shows him being interviewed in the back seat of the police car. His mind is a complete blank."

"Why didn't you tell me this?" Sarah wails.

Ignoring her, Chambers asks, "Is Templeton Hall connected to the other attempts on his life?" Chambers asks.

"Yes, and there are even more nobody knows at this point. We can give you all the details."

"This policeman will agree to our on-camera interview?"

"Yes."

"Got a name?"

"All in good time. Incidentally, if you leak this before everything is ready, I'll deny everything." It's time for a bluff. "I should tell you the other party is very interested."

"But you said..." Sarah begins.

"Don't be stupid, of course they have someone to play off against us," Chambers snaps. He chews his lip as he stares at Molly as if trying to read her mind.

"You don't want him to be president, obviously."

"Obviously."

"May I ask why?"

"Yes, why?" the anguished Sarah echoes.

"There is too much nobody knows about him."

"What about his official biography?"

"It's totally fabricated by experts in the field, but once you find a loose string it will pull right apart."

"Why is he running for president?"

It's time to play the ace in the hole with the twist that Camael and Randall agreed was sheer brilliance. "He says God wants him to be president." Their stunned looks of disbelief are just what she hoped for. No one would believe Lucifer, a comic figure brought out for Halloween and carnivals, was behind everything evil. Wars, mass atrocities, suicide bombings, beheadings and the like always were done in the name of God. The demonic possession phenomena were explained as some sort of mistake in brain chemistry.

"I never heard that from him," Sarah says, "he..." A withering glance from Chambers stops her. "Why does he think God tells him to be president?"

"It has something to do with End Times."

"Eh?"

"It's in the Bible."

"I never read the Good Book myself; never was exposed to religious stuff. My parents, either. England isn't called the land of empty churches for nothing." He shakes his head. "It's different here, of course. I'll Google it myself, but give me the short version."

"Something happens in the Middle East to set off the final battle between good and evil. Civilization collapses and millions die."

"Jesus, it's that bad?" He broods for a minute. "Things are looking crazier than ever over there. The Israelis say some splinter group of Muslims has got its hands on a nuclear weapon. My pals back home tell me the Times is doing a big Sunday piece on it." He yanks at his tie to loosen it and signals to the waiter.

Sarah checks her watch and looks back at him, all but saying aloud, You've only been here twenty minutes and you're having another?

"The newsagent placards have already been printed," Chambers says. 'The Race to Doom's Day.' Brilliant, that. They'll sell millions. It's a great time to be in the news racket."

"This is bigger, wouldn't you say?" Molly asks.

"Apples and oranges." He mulls it. "But, yeah, on balance I'd go with you. Shoo-in as president revealed as mystery man with bogus past who thinks he has divine guidance to do… what?" He rubs his head. "Put his foot on the brake or the accelerator in the Middle East? Stop or start these end times?" He looks at Sarah. "Sweetheart, this is going to make you the biggest name in news. Ever. Try to stay humble."

Molly sees Sarah adjust perspective almost instantly. Instead of loyalty to her former lover—who heartlessly dumped her now that she remembers—a vision of global fame is expanding in her mind. She will be as big as Oprah. "I'll admit on camera that I was taken in by Rex; I'll hold up the *New Yorker* issue as my mea culpa."

"Yes," Chambers says, a born coach to young media talent, "that establishes credibility with the audience. What woman hasn't been taken in by some bastard at some point?"

Sarah casts a glance at Molly. "Maybe not some."

"Don't kid yourself. I fell for it, too."

Chambers beckons to the hovering waiter. "Can I get some bangers and mash with peas?"

After a supercilious pause the waiter replies in a poisonous voice, "That is not on the menu, sir,"

"Send the manager to me." Understanding this flourish of force majeure, the waiter turns in silence to put in the barbarous order.

"Can you have your people ready by midnight to go to the Coast?" Molly asks. "That's when I'm flying out."

"No problem," Chambers says, getting out his smartphone.

Later as they are driven to the airport, he says, "That waiter was a bit on the snotty side, but I'd go back. For Frenchman, they do a good job on bangers and mash. I'll ask them to cook the peas just a little longer."

It is still dark when they land in Santa Rosa; Sarah and Chambers and his crew of four is dropped off at the Tiburon Lodge just as rain starts to fall. Randall meets Molly when she arrives at Bluff Point. They whisper with hands covering their mouths in case someone is watching on a monitor screen with some state-of-the-art spy software.

"Everything go all right?" he asks.

"They interview us at the lodge at ten o'clock. Here are the questions. The program airs the afternoon of the debate. Did the family get off okay?"

"They're at the monastery already, except for Esther. She won't budge until the debate is over; she's got this idea in her head that she's on the outer edge of the inner circle."

"Did you tell her where Abby and the kids went?"

"I said they're in San Francisco a couple of days for *Nutcracker* and early Christmas shopping."

The fewer who know, the better; you can't leak what you don't know and the rapt look Esther had these days was worrying. "History's being made," she sings out at odd times as if she had a contrapuntal voice in a baroque fugue that starts up in her head. Abby had said she still talks wistfully about the man in the woods. "She knows they would have had a good life together. He liked cats, too. Did I tell you that?"

"Once or twice."

"Was it hard to talk Abbey into it?" Molly asks now.

"This place is like a prison to her; she doesn't think the Secret Service crowd is as friendly." They were uptight lawyers, accountants and former cops unlike the friendly ex-military guys in the old security detail. "When are you leaving?"

"Before Sarah's interview is on, that's for sure."

"Don't cut it too fine."

"And you?"

"We better keep details to ourselves." He pauses, looking straight into her eyes. "Just to be on the safe side."

She hugs herself against the chill that creeps up her spine. "It's finally coming to the end, isn't it? You and me."

"Looks like it."

CHAPTER 49

DICKSON ANNOUNCES HIS ARRIVAL IN THE FORECOURT AT BLUFF POINT BY SKIDDING TO A STOP AND gunning the snarling engine of his Lamborghini. Molly thinks of it as like a trumpet flourish to draw attention to his importance. Today he wears a tight-fitting white jump suit with zippers everywhere and a World War I leather flying helmet and goggles which he peels off as he walks to the entrance with his leather man purse.

"Who are you today, the Red Baron?" she asks when he comes into the room.

Ignoring that, he says, "You flew a video crew out here and they're staying at the Tiburon Inn. I'd like to know why."

Molly is shaken but keeps it from showing. "What business is it of yours?" she says. She goes on the attack. "Does Rex know you're spying on me?"

"I have been given a very large grant of administrative authority. You were sent a memo to that effect."

"I never read the stuff you send me."

"If you did, you'd know," he says. He would have a paper trail with all the requisite counter-signatures, routing slips and boxes checked.

"Does he know you're spying on me?" she repeats more loudly.

"He knows I'm examining every expenditure on this account to make sure they conform with the goals and missions of the Rex Express. There has been a lot of loose spending, as I'm sure you know. It's in the memo you were sent, a copy of which I brought to refresh your memory." He takes it from his man purse and hands it to her. She deliberately tears it in two and the pieces float to the floor. Dickson is surprised; he was not expecting eye-flashing defiance. Game theory predicted submission.

"You haven't answered my question," Molly persists aggressively. "I used my personal credit card for the hotel. Are you watching what I spend my own money on? Do you know you what trouble you could get into for hacking my privacy. I don't think Rex would like it, in fact I know he wouldn't." She senses a sudden deflation in Dickson as if he wonders if he has misjudged the situation. "Let's go up and see him right now."

"I... I don't see any need to bother him. He's in the middle of his debate preparation."

Molly is not at all sure what side of the question Rex would come down on. She had definitely gone off the reservation in hiring a video crew without telling anyone, and he would want to know why. She decides to push it harder and starts out of the room. "C'mon, let's get this cleared up."

"Hold on," Dickson says, "I can explain this better. Finnese's people are still on contract as security consultants..."

"I thought the Secret Service was in charge," Molly interrupts.

"... and through some abundance of caution or due diligence, whatever you want to call it, Inflexible Security is watching everyone's credit card transactions."

"Except yours, I bet," Molly says. That struck home. "There's probably some pretty interesting stuff you wouldn't want to get out." Dickson flushes and then turns pale.

"How much are you paying Inflexible Security for this consulting?" Molly demands. "I bet it's plenty."

"That's proprietary information," Dickson says weakly, now in full retreat.

"I'll ask you in front of Rex, or maybe you think he doesn't need to know that either."

"Look, I was just curious about the video people."

"I'm making a documentary about the last days of the campaign," Molly says brightly. "I don't have to clear that with you."

"We have people doing that."

"Mine is going to be a documentary about making the documentary. We'll be shooting your people shooting Rex. Cinema verite, ever heard of it?"

Dickson clearly wants to end this showdown. "Let's just forget we had this conversation, okay? I'm sorry and all that."

"Tell Finnese I don't want any more surveillance of me, and I think I speak for Sergeant Randall as well." She turns on her heel and strides from the room. When she reaches her room, she has to lie down until her heart slows down. The Lamborghini starts up outside with an angry howl and roars away. Dickson had realized he overplayed a strong hand when she said let's go see Rex. He forgot or downplayed the bond of friendship Rex maintained would always be there because she and Randall were with him from the beginning. Dickson's confidence collapsed like tissue in rain with the sudden awareness he couldn't be sure that carried more weight than the unauthorized spending. But it had been a close thing, she thinks. Dickson's fatal flaw, one of them anyway, was he was lousy with people; pissing everyone off is risky if your goal is the top of the ladder. Dumping his mother at a rest home under heavy sedation showed his emotional IQ was around zero; it was no wonder Linda Atwood was scheming at his downfall so easily. She might not understand emotion herself, but she had analyzed their effects and drawn the right conclusions. It's lucky Linda isn't serving from the other side of the net, Molly thinks. She wouldn't make Dickson's dumb mistakes.

She finds Randall outside watching the heavy rain from the shelter of the portico; it is drumming down so loudly she doesn't think a listening microphone could pick up their words. "A good storm," he says. "We need the rain." Head down so her lips aren't read, she tells him about Dickson.

"I've been operating on a cash-and-carry basis for a while now," he says. "There's no need to make it easy for them."

"I just wasn't thinking."

"It sounds like Dickson is back in his cage until the next time. Did you get the call asking if you're flying down to L.A. with Rex and the rest?"

"I said I'd meet them there and fly back on the plane; I gave Esther my seat for the flight down. She's in seventh heaven at being what she calls an 'eyewitness to history.' I think she got it from TV."

"Camael wants me here when Rex gets back." His voice had came to him in a dream. "He thinks that's when he will put the last touch on the portrait. I'm staying rather than take a chance on getting stuck on a dummy convoy that gets back too late."

"Rex will be mad we're not there; he thinks of us as good luck charms."

"He's reached the point where he is so sure of himself luck doesn't matter.

He's a runaway train blowing down the tracks through all the red lights. He thinks nothing can stop him now."

"He must know Camael is waiting for his chance."

"I think he's dropped him threat-wise to a buzzing fly, irritating but not serious." Randall gazes in silence at the falling rain. "It would be nice if it rained for a week so we got a good snowpack in the Sierra."

CHAPTER 50

SARAH IS DUMBFOUNDED WHEN RANDALL WALKS INTO THE HOTEL ROOM WHERE SHE AND MOLLY are forcing conversation to pass the time. "Wait a minute, you are the cop who found him?"

Chambers gives her a sharp look. "What's going on?"

"He's the head of security for Rex! He and Molly were with him from the start."

"Good," Chambers says, relaxing into a grin and extending a hand. "That gives us more weight and shall I say authority."

"Was the head of security," Randall corrects. "The Secret Service runs the show now." He hands over the Cannon video camera. "Don't pay any attention to the cat in the tree."

"You have my word." He gives the video for a technician to make copies, and a makeup artists fusses over Randall in a chair. "Don't make me orange," he jokes. His Q and A lasts twenty minutes with only a couple of retakes when he stumbles over a word.

"Yes," one of Chambers' assistants confirms as she studies her laptop. "There are quite a few stories on YouTube about that train stopped the middle of nowhere, and a huge amount about the ship that went aground."

"If you can't download them directly, get on to New York and L.A. and have them email the video files," Chambers replies.

"There was a woman who drowned."

"Get what they have on her, too. You've got the story on that, right, Molly?"

"She was the skipper. The ship went aground because it was trying to run us down. Rex pulled me out of the water without a stitch on either one of us. Alex picked us up the following morning."

"Here's the story about the airplane that crashed into the building in Dubai," the assistant says excitedly. "And, okay, a whole shitload of them about the premiere and the police helicopter. Some shots of Rex pitching and half a dozen trailers from the movie."

"Deal with their libraries, not some newsie who might ask what we want them for. If anybody does have questions, we're doing a Top Stories of the Year recap for New Year's Eve."

"Don't do that from here," Randall says. "There are a bunch of internet cafes in Marin. Use a different one for each request."

"Because?" Chambers says, raising an eyebrow.

"Big Brother is watching; that might confuse him for a while."

"Got it." He looks at Randall with new respect. "How do we tie Rex to that Arab killed in the crash?"

"He was blocking his family from putting money into the movie, so Rex told me he had him killed."

"He told you that?"

"Yes, he said the man was secretly involved in terrorist financing, so you might say two birds with one stone."

"I'll add that to the questions to ask him."

Randall and Molly had decided not to throw Vargas and the psychiatrist in the hopper; that would push things too far into Crazy Town. Leave them to the enterprising journalists who come along later with the fact-checking Pinocchio-nose gimmick. What they find out will keep the story alive.

"How would he know about terrorist financing?" Chambers asks.

"Ask Inflexible Security, they've got a lot of ex-spooks on the payroll. They'll stonewall, but it plants the seed. Or maybe a chance to question Rex himself will come up in the debate."

"We need some aerials of Bluff Point to show how it looks like an armed camp."

"Our guys got pretty good at shooting drones down with a slingshot, but local TV must have chopper shots." As soon as the federal government took over protection duties, the lawsuit to tear down the security fence was put on the back burner so it still stood.

"How about that house where the tunnel was being dug?" Chambers asked. "I can't believe how fantastic that is."

"I saw some video at the time, but I doubt they'd let you have it. And I wouldn't try to go inside; no telling if it's still booby trapped."

"We'll just shoot exteriors and get the graphics people to show what the tunnel must have looked like. Anything I'm missing?"

Time for the second part of the plan. "Rex's strange mental powers."

"Ha ha. No, I'm serious."

"He made Gracie Ashcroft Weber do those animal sounds in their debate."

There is a silence as Chambers takes this in. "How, by hypnosis? Voodoo? We'll need to pull that video, too," he tells one of the technicians. "The shrinks put her through every test in the book and said it was a possible case of clinical lycanthropy, but they couldn't be sure. They said it was rare and probably never happen again, but once was enough for you Yanks."

Randall lifts his shoulders. "He didn't explain how it's done, but look for something bad to throw Buster off his game."

"If people know that from the video going in, Rex won't dare. You're up next, Molly." Chambers checks his watch. "C'mon mates, we've got a lot of work to do and not much time."

She gets through her interview smoothly and they are about to take away the small mic pinned to her front when Chambers says, "One more question for Sarah to ask." She looks at his scribbled note and then at Molly.

"What do you think explains Rex?"

Without hesitation, Molly says, "I don't think he can be explained."

"Cut. Alex," Chambers orders, "back in the chair. Sarah, same question."

"I agree," he answers when she asks again. "The guy comes from nowhere and look at him now."

"You make him sound so strange," Sarah objects.

"Didn't you?" The looks that rapidly cross her face to final agreement say it all.

"There's our close," Chambers says jubilantly.

"That wasn't as bad as I thought," Randall says afterward.

"The questions were right on the money. I can't think of anything we missed."

"Except for coming right out with the devil's spawn angle," he says.

CHAPTER 51

"YOU MEET ALL KINDS IN THE FLYING BUSINESS," JIM TONCI SAYS AS THEY FLY OVER THE DRY AND seamed Tehachapi Mountains. He glances down at the arid prospect. "I suppose all of California will look like this in the future, Mrs. Hope."

"Oh," says Molly, "you can call me Denise." That is the name on the phony driver's Delaware driver's license and passport that Inflexible Security made for her when they were first hired. Randall's farseeing idea, it was a perfect counterfeit, proof of the quality of their work, but no doubt it and the other two bogus IDs and passports in other names were on a secret list in a server somewhere ready for a watch list. But nothing now was without risk.

"Yeah," Tonci continues, "all kinds of people. I flew a guy up to the Lost Coast a while back. A bear killed another hiker and you should've seen his face—the guy who flew with me, not the dead one. He could hardly talk from the shock. There was an article in one of the little papers, on their website, and that was it."

When Molly doesn't reply, he moves on, undiscouraged. "I'm going to stay in Las Vegas just long enough to gas up. They say what happens there stays there, and in my case it was my money. It cost me my first marriage, but I'm in Gamblers Anonymous now. A great organization if you ever need help."

"That's not one of my problems," Molly says.

Tonci waits to see if she wants to open up about what hers are, which many do under his casual questioning in the droning intimacy of the Cessna cabin. Cheating husbands and wives, domestic violence, addiction, rehab and recovery, kids that went bad. What problems people have! He thought about writing a book about them and already had the title, *Things My Passengers Said to Me*. His wife was pushing for *Revelations on High*, which he admits to himself has more punch. Mrs. Hope is a nice-looking woman who takes good care of herself; he surmises she is probably older than she looks. "What takes you to Vegas," he asks lightly, "business or pleasure?"

If Molly was scouting for the Middle Ages cardinal type whose twinkly manner masks cunning she would rate him high. Or maybe as the fly fisherman with smiles creasing a face seamed from decades outdoors who tells how an extra-strength chewable antacid works like magic.

"A little bit of both," she replies after a studied silence by way of warning.

Tonci doesn't take the hint. "What business are you in?" he says pleasantly.

"It's none of yours," she says just as pleasantly.

"No offense, ma'am," Tonci says, reddening. The rest of the flight passes in a silence as deep as with the man who shot the bear. He has to admit sometimes there is a dry well; he'll put a sentence or two in the book when he writes it to warn other authors.

After landing, she wheels her small suitcase to the taxi stand for the ride to the Bellagio, which she chose as the most vulgar and garish of the hotel-casinos in a city with many pretenders to the crown. She checks in and the FedEx package she sent herself waits at the desk. It contains 20.201 pounds of Benjamins, or a million dollars. Before leaving, she rented safe deposit boxes at Bay Area banks for nine identical boxes containing coupon bonds, bearer notes and warrants—negotiable securities in short—and more currency. Cash and carry, Randall had said. Another hundred thousand dollars in various denominations are in the suitcase with wheels. She puts the valuables in the room safe and takes a long hot bubble bath, feeling the tension drain away; she even falls asleep in the tub. Dinner in her room and then she watches *Sleepless in Seattle* for the millionth time. Tomorrow is the first *Sarah Special!* It is to be followed an hour later by the debate, enough time to for the country to absorb the shock of the video. Except for the odd contrarian here and there, the media has already agreed that Rex will win the debate and election in a walk.

She has a sleeping pill with a glass of wine and sleeps soundly through the night, rising early for a run before the sun is too harsh for a redhead's skin. She has a light breakfast at one of Belagio's cafes and later the lunch buffet. She had forgotten what it was like to be around people so busy with their own affairs, talking, eating, drinking, whatever, that they pay her no attention. In Bluff Point's common rooms or on their incessant travels there were always eyes reading her, wondering what she was thinking, looking for direction, hoping for encouragement, fearing disapproval—something. She had forgotten how comfortable it is being just another face in the crowd.

In one of those moments of group-mind synchronicity that occur in the media, old anchors and commentators are brought back from retirement for the debate and the before-and-after chat; perhaps it is to add gravitas to successors who mostly got their starts in comedy, the modern path to the anchor chair. Molly is shocked by the changes. There is no hiding that frail Wolf Blitzer hardly has any of that white hair left, and his neck rising from a too-large collar looks as thin and vulnerable as a flower stalk. George Stephanopoulos has put on enough blubber to play Big Daddy in Cat on a Hot Tin Roof, and Bill O'Reilly seems unaware he is leaving words out of sentences. "He going be good," he says of Buster. "Mark words." Why did Anderson Cooper dye his hair coal black, she wonders, and plastic surgery has frozen his features into a tight mask of inscrutability. Megyn Kelly looks ready for a role in a revival of The Golden Girls, and ESPN talking heads returned to the sets back have jowls and dewlaps under golf tans. It's hard for them to bring off the old jokey raucousness with the quavers time has put in their voices.

At two o'clock news crawls at the bottom of the screens begin promoting the Sarah Special! airing before the debate. "Sensational revelations," says NBC. "Documentary claims Rex not who he says," according to ABC. "Disturbing questions about Rex," CBS proclaims. Gaunt and stooped, Tom Brokow has the air of an ancient sage who has shuffled from the temple with disturbing portents from the innards of the goat sacrificed on the steps. "I've seen the documentary," he says hoarsely, "and in my opinion this could be bigger than Watergate." Molly notices people are checking smartphones and crowds in the vast gambling halls thin as people head for the big flat screens in their rooms upstairs.

Sarah looks pretty and poised in the opening shot. "Hi, I'm Sarah Marsh and I wrote this profile of Todd Daley Rexford, who everybody knows as Rex." She holds up the New Yorker cover split between drawings of him delivering a fastball and felling a monstrous Truk with his sword. The magazine opens to show the article with her byline. "I'm going to tell you how I got it and him all wrong. Then I'm going to ask for your forgiveness."

The documentary moves smoothly back and forth in time from Rex's first burst into public awareness to his most recent political speech in Iowa, a masterly job of finger-jabbing rhetoric calling for A New Beginning; he makes the tired old troph sound new and scintillating. "He's good, isn't he?" Sarah's voiceover says. "Better at getting the crowd on its feet than Obama or Trump, according to the professionals. You know why? It's because everybody thinks they know him." Sarah fills the screen in a close up. "Rex and I were a couple for a short time. And you know what, I didn't know you, Rex—not at all."

After the first glance, Molly thinks it's better to listen than look at herself when she's on screen. Who's she been kidding? She has the face of a woman hanging on by her fingernails to the last of youth. Her neck! It seems all cords and vein like her hands. She pushes this to a corner of her mind and admires the professional gloss Chambers gave this documentary with such a fast turn-around. It cuts from a flyover of Bluff Point that shows its combination of luxury and military base to crowds cheering Rex to a drone shot of the container ship that ran aground.

"What does this ship on the rocks have to do with a candidate for the president of the United States?" Sarah asks. "Just this: if we can believe the executive vice president of his company, she was with him on a small sailboat when this vessel went after them." A still shot of Gayle Hunnicut flashes on the screen. "The skipper drowned when the sailboat was driven onto the rocks." Molly looks away again when her face comes back on. "I would have drowned if it wasn't for Rex," she hears herself say.

"So you think he's a hero?" Sarah asks off camera.

"Definitely."

"What happened before?"

"They stopped a train in a lettuce field to look for us and we had to run for it." A newspaper headline and story about the enigmatic event is on the screen. "There was never any explanation, was there?" Sarah asks.

"No," Molly hears herself say. She steals a peak. She had overreacted; she doesn't look all that bad. Intent, serious, focused; nothing wrong with that.

"Who are 'they'?" Sarah asks off camera.

"Rex never said."

Randall looks gruff and honest like Tommy Lee Jones in *No Country for Old Men*. Jones was good looking as a young actor, but later became as homely as his name. Men become attractively rugged with character lines instead of wrinkles—another example of life's unfairness to women. Maybe it's their take-it-or-leave-it attitude, Molly thinks. They don't primp for an hour in front of a mirror before a date at a vanity covered with tiny, hideously expensive pots of cosmetics or smooth on anti-aging creams at night; they don't pluck eyebrows or worry over lipstick shades or a dozen other things a woman does. They give their hair a lick with a comb after a shower and that's it. At least that was the case with Jimmy and Al and the other… pay attention, she reminds herself.

"Something happened even before the train and ship incidents," Sarah says, the camera back to her. Then there is a lurid montage of Templeton Hall, the police and ambulances casting a strobe-light effect on the classic building, and later the procession of bodies wheeled into the gray dawn. Drawn faces discuss the massacre, bits of the governor's press conference are shown where he promises to find and prosecute those responsible.

"You were an officer on that case," Sarah says to Randall.

"Yes, I took Rex to Templeton Hall for evaluation when I found him walking on a country road." The interview in the backseat of the cruiser is shown.

"You were suspended for breaking regulations."

"For a short time, yes."

"Why was that?"

"I should have taken him straight to headquarters."

"Why didn't you?"

"I felt sorry for the guy. If you knew what holding cells in cop shops are like Friday nights, you'd know what I mean."

"Was Rex at Templeton Hall when the killings took place?" A prosecutorial edge is in Sarah's voice now.

"He was gone by then. A matter of minutes or seconds."

"Why hasn't this come out before?"

"We didn't want it to. He wasn't involved in the killings, but we figured he was the reason for them. We had to go in deep cover to keep him alive."

"Making him a movie star doesn't seem like deep cover to me."

"I didn't have anything to do with that."

"It was an accident?"

"I guess you might say that."

"You're not a policeman now, are you?"

"I was chief of security for Rex until the Secret Service took over."

"Still on the payroll?"

"The last I looked."

"Some might see that as a payoff."

"I wouldn't blame them; looks fishy, doesn't it?" His chuckle is good natured. "The truth of the matter is he liked me. I helped him when he didn't know who or where he was because of his amnesia and he was grateful to me and Molly."

"Amnesia," Sarah repeats, drawing the word out to show her skepticism. "That could explain away a multitude of sins, in fact just about anything, couldn't it?"

"You'd have to ask an expert."

Footage shows the house where the attempt was made to tunnel into Bluff Point. "Talk to us about this strange incident."

"Somebody bought that place and tried to dig their way into the grounds," Randall says. "It was detected and stopped." There is a shot of the anonymous building in Virginia with the small sign that says Inflexible Security. "Do you recognize this name?" Sarah asks.

"Yes, I hired them."

"To protect Rex."

"That's correct."

"They're like a private army, aren't they? Bodyguards, chauffeurs, sentries and so forth, all of them former special services people. I saw them when I was at Bluff Point."

"They do good work," Randall responds.

"One of their drivers died when a convoy"—Sarah turns her head to directly address the audience—"was attacked in this country by an RPG traced to a Mexican drug cartel." There is video of the wreckage.

"We kept our comings and goings random so they couldn't lock in on Rex," Randall says. "That one was a case of bad luck."

"I guess that brings us to the big question," Sarah says. She lets a long, dramatic silence fall. "Who wants Todd Daley Rexford dead?"

"We never figured that one out," Randall answers.

"Could it be the drug cartel?"

"That's as good a guess as any."

"Do you have any theories?"

"One or two."

"Do you want to tell us about them?" She lifts an eyebrow—rather theatrically, Molly thinks.

"Not at this point."

"You were in the news another time, weren't you?"

"I shot a bear on the Lost Coast that killed a friend."

"This friend was the abbot of a monastery in Oregon."

"That's right."

"What were the two of you doing meeting at such a remote and isolated place?" A panning shot captures the foggy, windy coast with crashing waves and flying spume as birds utter lonely cries.

"It was his idea and I went along."

"There has to be more to the story than that."

Randall settles back in his chair with a look that says plainer than words that is all Sarah is going to get from him on the subject. "No comment," he says.

It's back to Molly. "Molly Simon, you got Rex into the movies."

"Only indirectly."

"Please explain."

"They were shooting scenes in San Francisco of what later became his big blockbuster. A friend got us on the set, he was noticed by the director and I guess you would say nature took its course."

"How did you first meet Rex?"

"In a tea room where I was scouting for faces for TV commercials. He wondered in and all the conversation stopped. He sat down at my table and it went from there."

"And he was suffering from amnesia."

"It was very obvious."

The closing comes where Sarah apologizes for her *New Yorker* profile and flings the magazine over her shoulder. "I wanted to believe, so I did. The magazine wanted the money so they printed it—a million extra copies, I heard. What can I say except I'm sorry." The credits roll.

The live feed picks up at all the networks where their cameras are focused on the empty stage with the two lecterns. Molly switches back and forth for reactions. It is the second time the on-camera talent has seen the documentary, but a stunned confusion is still clear. It is shared in the faces of the polling groups each network has gathered for their response to the debate.

"Well, I've never seen anything like it," says Chet Nutley, the lordly NBC anchor. "I'm asking myself who is this guy, Rex Rexford?" replies his new co-host the gamin-like Polly Popkins. "This raises serious questions about the Rex candidacy," the CBS anchor Franklin Nunley says gravely. The ESPN old timers seem at a loss for words until Andy Powell, the color man for decades for the St. Louis Cardinals, pipes up. "I'll tell you this, that fastball of his was no phony."

CHAPTER 52

BUSTER KEEGAN ERUPTS FROM THE WINGS, BURLY AND BURSTING WITH AN AGGRESSION THAT brings to mind a Miura bull charging from the tunnel onto the sand of a sun-blasted arena for death in the afternoon.

Molly hears a deeper chord than mere encouragement for the underdog as he pumps a fist. For the first time, they are louder and longer than for Rex when he makes his graceful entrance with a hand raised in casual acknowledgement. She can't tell if he has noticed the difference, but of course he would. Nothing got past him.

He had won the coin toss and his opening statement is a model of tight reasoning and eloquence. "It's time we returned to our days of greatness…" "America used to be respected, but now we're despised by our friends and scorned by our enemies…" "With your help, we can return to the Years of Glory…" The applause at the end is sustained, but lacks the true-believer passion of before except from the claque Kornhouser put in the seats.

"Not much new there, Polly," Chet Nutley says, as grave as a judge about to pronounce sentence.

"No, we've heard it all before," she agrees. "Look! Buster Keegan is tearing up his opening remarks."

"He's certainly tearing something up," Nutley says more cautiously, "but we can't be sure…"

"Instead of my opener, I want to ask Rex a few questions," Buster says into the camera. He turns to Rex. "First of all, did you see the documentary?"

Rex is loose and relaxed, shifting on the balls of his feet like a boxer ready to bob and weave. "No, but I certainly heard about it," he says jokingly. "I…"

"Long story short," Buster butts in, "it makes the case you're not who you say you are."

The crowd is startled into laughter when Rex says with a humorous look, "Like Popeye used to say, I yam who I yam."

"This is as a serious subject," Buster admonishes him, "and I think you owe it to the American people to take it seriously."

"I'll have an answer for you as soon as I see it," Rex says. "From what I've heard, it's the work of disgruntled employees who want revenge for being fired."

"One says he's still on the payroll. I'm referring to Alex Randall, who was in charge of your security until recently. Is that correct?"

"I'll have to check with the management company that handles that detail," Rex says in a bantering tone. Despite everything, part of her winces. Jokiness is the wrong slant to take on this, Molly thinks.

Buster Keegan was a prosecutor at one point in his career and knows how to put together an argument. "Can you tell us if you know Mr. Randall?"

"Of course I do," Rex says, an edge creeping into his voice.

"Do you remember the interview conducted when you were in the back of his police cruiser?"

Rex appeals to the moderator. "This is not a debate; it's an interrogation about something that has nothing to do with the future of our great country." There are some boos and catcalls from the audience. "Answer the question," bellows a foghorn voice.

"Mr. Keegan still has sixty seconds left on his opening statement," the moderator tells Rex. "Under the rules, he can use the time any way he likes, including singing God Bless America if he wants."

"Tell us about your amnesia," Buster says.

"I had it and don't know why. I'm afraid that's the best I can do."

Buster drills deeper. "First question, why are we just hearing about it? Second question, could it happen again?"

"I'm fit as a fiddle, in good form, in fine fettle, hale and hearty; I'm in the pink of health." His continued levity is jarring and the audience stirs restlessly. "Tell you what," Rex offers, "let's both submit to a battery of physical and mental tests by experts and see who does the best."

"That doesn't answer my questions," Buster says with a stern glance into the camera that asks viewers to confirm this.

Molly sees uncertainty in Rex. He had never quite got the hang of humor; it was foreign to his driven nature. Why risk it now—to show he is a well-rounded guy, someone you could have a beer with? The idea is so idiotic it had to come from Dickson after he pored over focus group data looking for even tiny ways to build on his appeal. She can tell Rex knows now he planted a foot wrong, but is unclear how to undo the damage. Some kind of meter-like visual the network she watches shows viewership mounting almost exponentially as people tune in. It began at twenty-two million and already has hit fifty-four million. And that is not counting foreign viewers, Nutley points out in the hushed voice of an Augusta golf analyst as a player is addressing the ball. "This debate is going to set records," Polly Popkins whispers back.

"So the second question, is this going to happen again?" Rex asks. "You're not saying you know the future, are you? I sure don't."

"I may not know the future," Buster booms, "but I do know these are dangerous times and the American people cannot put their trust in an unstable leader who might at any given time…"

"Your time is up for your opening statement," the moderator interjects.

"If I may conclude," Buster says, biting off his words, "… who might at any given time forget who and where he is. The president is the commander-in-chief and his is the finger on the nuclear trigger. We cannot take that risk. It's clear Mr. Rexford has some sinister and powerful enemies responsible for the atrocity at Templeton Hall, but we don't know who they are and why they have made so many attempts on his life. Like many, I happened to be watching that premiere when the helicopter crashed into the crowd. It is a memory I can never forget, unfortunately. I call on my opponent to step aside until we have the results of a thorough investigation, however long that may take. Let no stone be left unturned." There is long applause.

As Rex waits with a tight smile for it to subside, Molly imagines the panic in the spin room where his political and public relations team must gape at the banks of televisions in disbelief. Before the documentary aired, there had been no warning this meteor would streak across the sky and hit the ground so hard it would shake from the impact.

"And give voters one choice on the ballot named Buster Keegan?" Rex drawls. There is laughter and some applause at his adroit reply.

"She has problems of her own, and they might be serious problems," Buster says even more deftly, "but I'm sure Gracie Ashcroft Weber would consider restarting her campaign." The man is on a roll.

A screen split shows Josiah Walden, one of the billionaire founders of the Good Citizens Party, hurrying from a hotel room where cameras were set up for his triumphant post-debate comments. A pack of journalists pours after him; there is no sound but they appear to be yelling questions. His back to the pursuing cameramen, he lumbers down the corridor at a good speed for a man his size and age. "The rats leaving the ship?" Polly whispers gleefully.

Nutley rebukes her in his Augusta voice. "We don't know that."

"This is a calculated distraction by Mr. Keegan from the serious issues I've raised in this campaign," Rex says. "But as long as he is throwing mud, maybe he can explain as a lay minister and Sunday school teacher a single young woman he supports in Minneapolis, apparently without the knowledge of his wife and family." This might be more of Dickson's dirty tricks, Molly thinks, but the fingerprints could just as easily be Kornhouser's.

Buster seems to have known this was coming. "I'm glad to have the opportunity to lay to rest a lie by your people. Miss Margaret Terry is the daughter of an old friend who has fallen on hard times. She has an incurable disease and I'm supporting her in her final days." Oooh comes from everywhere in the audience. "I was asked not to speak of this to anyone, but you forced my hand. I hope you're satisfied and you have the decency to personally apologize to Miss Terry after this is over." There are indignant cries from the crowd that Rex tries to outwait. When they continue, he raises and lowers his palms in the cool-it gesture that has always worked before. It doesn't work this time, and it is Buster who quiets them by pulling his wallet from an inside pocket and taking out a photograph.

"This is Margaret," he says to the cameramen, holding it up. "Can you focus on it?" It shows a wan young woman, clearly ill, with hair like straw and huge suffering eyes. Buster says to Rex, "She loved your movie, and I bet until a minute ago she was your biggest fan." He walks over to the wary Rex. "Would you like to see the picture?"

"Tell her my people will be in touch," Rex replies in steely voice. The callous kiss-off triggers more outrage and boos rain down. "What I mean is," he shouts over them, "is they'll set up a meeting for me and Margaret."

Buster waits until the ruckus dies down. "I'm not sure she'll be interested; but here, I'll make a call." He takes out his smartphone and the country waits breathlessly for what comes next. "Hi, Margaret. Yes, I knew you'd be watching. You just heard Rex say he'd like to meet." He nods at her answer and puts the phone away. "She says thanks, but no thanks." The applause is thunderous.

Rex is never going to be president, Molly thinks. At last it's over.

"Let's get back to business," the moderator pleads and the two candidates revert to the safe ground of their standard speaking points as the running meter registers a rapid fall off in viewers.

A wave of relief floods her: she and Randall have won against impossible odds. It makes her realize how all this has left her like a cracked, dry river bed that thirsts for the flood that hurtles down channels from a storm in the high country. "Thank you, God," she says, tears beginning to stream down her face.

The networks and cable talks shows she switches back and forth to agree the call Buster made to the young woman, who they swiftly learn suffers from a rare blood disease, was a masterstroke. As one talking head says, "it seals the deal for him." Experts marvel over the plunge in Rex's favorability ratings in the snap polls. "It's unprecedented," one says.

"Hollywood is going to notice," perky Polly Popkins says. "A lot of people are gonna be turned off. It's like James Dean."

"I don't get the comparison," Chet Nutley says with a touch of asperity, "wasn't he killed in a car crash?"

"Meaning he never made another movie."

"That's apples and oranges," he tells her. "Hold on, there's breaking news." He presses on his earpiece to hear better. "One of Rex's senior aides choked another in full view of reporters, and it took three people to pull him off. Holy smokes, what'll happen next? Do we have the names of the victim and the alleged assailant?" He shakes his head at viewers. "No names as yet, but you'll know as soon as we do." A few minutes later, another network shows the Rex Express jet already taxiing onto a runway.

"That was fast," Polly exclaims. "Wasn't he supposed to have a press conference? The must want time for the dust to settle."

"Indeed," Nutley says, giving her a poisonous look. The dust-settling line was his, brazenly stolen by her from the teleprompter.

Molly's euphoria gives way to an instinct that she should get moving. She was planning an early departure in the morning, but packs quickly and takes a cab to the Enterprise agency; she is headed for the wide-open spaces of Texas an hour later. Two days from now she will be in Neuquén in Patagonia, a place remote enough to discourage all but the most dogged of pursuers, but it is an energy boom-town big enough for all the modern comforts. Molly has it all thought out. Working through a dummy corporation, she will buy an apple farm and nice farmhouse with a rack over the fireplace for a shotgun. She will keep a pack of dogs, of course—nosy terriers because they don't miss much and Rottweilers for muscle. She remembers Randall's last words to her. "Don't keep in touch."

CHAPTER 53

"HE'S ON HIS WAY," CAMAEL SAYS IN REX'S STUDIO WHERE HE AND RANDALL SIT BEHIND A PALE
Japanese screen with a delicate mountain scene. "He is a true son of Lucifer and
his fury has no bounds. He is so blind with rage he will fall into Lucifer's trap
and finish the portrait to release an even greater evil on the world."

"Except you're going to stop it," Randall points out.

Camael turns his level gaze to him. "No, Alex, you're going to stop it."

"Me!"

"Rex and the demon Satan had him create will have a life-or-death struggle
in this room. When the creature in the painting wins, there will be the tini-
est window to kill him before Rex's powers complete their transition to him."

"All I've got is my Glock."

"It is enough if you time it right—just as the unholy spirit leaves Rex and
enters his creature."

"How will I know?!"

"Watch his eyes, you will know. Remember, not a second too soon or too late."

"Where do I shoot the thing when it comes out of the painting?"

"In the head."

Randall feels all two million sweat glands in the human body start to pump.
"That puts a lot on me," he says in a voice that shakes. "What are you going to
be doing?"

"The Angel of Death will come unseen by Rex to escort him to his eternity
of punishment. It is my job to stop him from interfering with your job."

Randall tries to swallow but his throat is dry. "Can you handle him?" He
wipes away sweat already trickling into his eyes.

"We will see," Camael says evenly.

"You mean there's doubt?"

"Don't you understand yet that doubt is part of the plan?" He holds a finger to his lips. "Now."

They hear running feet in the corridor and the door bursts open. The lights come on and Rex snatches the cover from the portrait and screws open a tube of paint. Camael touches Randall's arm and nods.

Randall peers around the Japanese screen; Rex's back is to him, but then he half turns to mix dabs of paint on a palette. "This will take just a second, the small highlight on the cheek," he says to himself out loud. "And then, together…" He dips a tiny brush in the paint and positions himself carefully.

Randall has the Glock out and silently moves closer. Rex is too intent on his work to notice.

And incredibly he doesn't seem aware of the inky darkness that is instantly met by a bright light, the see-sawing combat between Camuel and Abbado, one stronger and then the other giving a strobe effect. Although ready for it, Randall is as astounded as Rex when he touches brush to canvas and the thing he created erupts into the room like a diver breaking the plane of the water. Its malevolence is horrible, felt as much as seen, and Randall barely stops himself from emptying his gun at it from sheer revulsion. Despite being a superb athlete, Rex has no chance against this thing. Its monstrous hands with those thick fingers are around his neck squeezing off oxygen. Rex tries a hard slap to both of its ears, the martial arts countermove, but it only makes the thing squeeze harder. Rex's face darkens and his eyes begin to lose focus and then move up into his head until only the whites show. The thing takes a deep breath for more strength and Randall sees the forearms under the sleeves bulge to their huge limit.

He draws closer, using a quick brush of a sleeve to mop the sweat from his forehead; the Glock is slippery in his hand. The light show in the room goes on, first dark and then light stronger. Ignore that shit, he tells himself, moving around the struggle like a referee in a cage fight.

He sees Rex going limp as a guttural sound of gratification comes from the demon. Up this close, Randall sees lumpy earlobes like sacs of poison attached to the thick carapace of skull where bristly hair grows in clumps. The smell pouring from the canvas split is like wet leaves that moldered for months and were mixed with some vile chemical.

Almost gagging from the stench, he moves his gun to within inches of the head as the creature throws its head back for a crow of victory. He fires every round in the magazine and the room suddenly blazes with a glorious light. The thing that came from the painting to kill Rex shrivels to ash from some inner combustion. Randall looks to where Rex's body had fallen to the floor but it is gone.

CHAPTER 54

"IT SEEMED LIKE THE WHOLE WORLD WAS IN THE ROOM WITHIN SECONDS," RANDALL SAYS.
"Everybody had their gun out; they were so surprised to find me alone that it was comic. I started laughing and damn near couldn't stop. Boy, were they pissed. Later, they recognized it was from shock."

It is three years later and he and Abbey sit on the veranda with Molly and Rob Stephens, the Montana rancher. It is a graceful old stone home a century old with ivied archways and a red tile roof. They arrived in an elderly Lincoln sent for them that smoothed out the bumps in the miles of dusty roads from the little Patagonian airfield.

"The apple trees go as far as the eye can see," Abbey marvels.

They have all put on a little weight, but still look pretty much as they did at Bluff Point. Rob sports a better haircut. "I cut it but with sharper scissors than his sister," Molly explains with a smile.

Molly and Rob go to the edge of the veranda to wave at a flatbed truck carrying their farm workers and household staff. "Everybody's going to the town for the carnival," Molly says. The women in sparkly costumes and the men in fancy dress wave back merrily. "They don't go as wild as Brazil, but there'll be drinking, dancing, and music all night long."

"From the sound of them, they already started the party," Rob grouses good-naturedly. "We won't get much work out of them tomorrow."

"I often wonder what happened that night," Molly says to Randall. "There were a million news stories and a thousand every anniversary, but you know how they get things wrong."

"A lot of people wonder," Randall says, "the investigation is still open. A missing presidential candidate is not something that goes into the cold case file."

"She didn't tell me any of this until our first anniversary," Rob says.

"I was afraid you'd think I was a lunatic," Molly says.

"What makes you think I don't?" he replies with a straight face. She gives him a kick with her work boot. "He never changes," she says. "He'll be telling you next the pig ate his cousin."

"This weather is wonderful," Abbey exclaims. "I bet you've forgotten what winter is like."

"Pretty much," Molly admits, smiling. "We're here when it's winter in North America and there when it's winter here." It was teeth-chattering cold when the Randalls left San Francisco two days ago, but it is in the mid-seventies in Neuquén.

"We're lucky to have first-rate managers running both operations when we're not around," Rob says, "though I've become a fair apple knocker since we got hitched. We're strictly organic and ship all over the world. We grow the Cripps Pink variety from Western Australia. It's a cross between Lady Williams and the Golden Delicious."

"We're pretty proud of them," Molly says. "We have some of our own beef from Montana ready for the grill and guess what dessert is?" Molly says.

"Apple fritters," Randalls says dryly.

"Close," Molly laughs.

"I'm mad about anything with apples in it," Abbey says.

The afternoon light is beginning to fade and they fall silent for a moment to watch the sun lower behind distant mountains. It is a lovely, peaceful scene that Molly thinks Vargas would find good for a dozen paintings.

"C'mon, Alex, I want to know more about what went down that night," Molly says over drinks when they go inside.

"Not much to tell," Randall tells her.

"It's like pulling teeth to get him to talk about it," Abbey interjects.

"That thing came out of the painting and choked Rex. I shot it and it turned to ash. The Secret Service people rushed in, put me under restraint, and asked what I'd done with Rex. They finally decided he had never been in the room, disappeared from shame or something, and I emptied my gun at Angel Island and didn't recall doing it. It was the only"—he smiles—"rational explanation. They spent months with metal detectors looking for slugs in the trees. That's pretty much the story."

"What about Camuel?" Molly asks. "That's the angel," she says, turning to Rob.

"I never saw him again," Randall replies, "but he must've won the big battle the way things turned out."

"What about the painting?" Molly asks.

"I guess it's in a government storeroom somewhere. It was scorched from back to front at the place where it was ripped so they couldn't tell who was in it. I told them I didn't know, it was done before I got there."

Rob shakes his head ruefully. "If it wasn't Molly telling me, I wouldn't have believed a word of this." He looks apologetic. "And I'm telling ya, darlin', I still sometimes have my doubts."

"I'm with you, Rob," Abbey says. "Alex kept me in the dark all through this. As I said, it's still like pulling teeth to get anything out of him."

"Coming this far, you really wanted to get away from it all," Randall tells Molly.

"See," Abbey says with triumph, "changing the subject as usual."

"I know what you mean," Rob says, grinning. "It's not the end of the world, but there's a place not far from here that advertises that it is."

"Tierra del Fuego," Molly says, "it has the most southerly town in the world. It's actually quite a way from here."

"It ain't all that far the way these people measure distance," Rob insists.

He's used to bossing a ranch and having his word being considered the law, Randall thinks; good luck on that with Molly. Her compressed lips confirm this. "Anyway," she says, "it's like the end of the world, just what I wanted at the time. I was so tried of being around people, even nice people."

"If we didn't have the boys, I might have been interested myself," he says. That's the signal for Abbey to bring out the photographs. "They don't fight as much with Alex around more. In fact, they're pretty nice boys if I do say so."

"You can tell from the pictures," Molly says in an admiring voice.

"They're at the monastery while we're gone; my mother is watching them. They love it there and so does she." She checks her watch. "It's time to call mom and see how things are going."

"The phone's in the room two doors down that hallway," Rob says. "There's no signal this far out."

Abbey comes back a few seconds later. "The line's dead."

A little alarm goes off in Randall's head. No, he thinks, it's nothing.

"That means no internet," Molly tells Rob. "We'll have to drive to town tomorrow and report it." She explains to the visitors this is the time of year they get orders from global distributors.

The talk turns to President Buster Keegan. "I can't see much difference between him and the standard run-of-the-mill politician," Rob says.

"Mediocre is a good word," Randall agrees.

"At least there isn't a really big war in the Middle East and Israel is still safe," Molly says. "I don't think that would've been the case with Rex."

"Really?" Abbey says with a glance at Randall. "He was that bad?"

"Worse," Randall says with a shortness that shows he'd like the conversation to shift to another subject.

Rob scratches his long Gary Cooper jaw in puzzlement. "Why were you helping him, then?"

"We were watching him," Molly says.

"Surveillance," Randall corrects.

"So at some point you realized he was bad news?" Rob asks.

"It took a while, but yes." Seeing the doubt in Rob's eyes, Randall adds impatiently, "You had to be there."

"It took me longer," Molly says. "Alex had to convince me."

Randall rattles the ice in his glass. "I might squeeze back another."

Molly leads him to the drinks table to recharge his glass as Rob and Abbey drift outside to the veranda. "Do you think about him much?" she asks.

"Yeah," Randall admits.

"Do you think he's really dead?"

He pauses before answering. "I thought I saw a shadow go out the balcony when I shot that thing from the painting, but it was just the corner of my eye. I'm not really sure I saw it, but I sometimes think of it."

Her eyes are big. "So do you think… "

"Hey," Rob shouts from the veranda, "you want to see something strange? There's a guy dressed like a knight walking down the road our way. It looks like he's carrying a big ol' sword. Molly, you know what? He looks like Rex in the movie."

Randall calmly takes the shotgun from the rack on the wall. "Get the women in the Lincoln and drive like hell," he tells Rob in an even voice. "I'll go out and say hello to our old friend."

That old song starts up in his head as he steps from the veranda.. *Love and marriage, love and marriage go together like a horse and carriage...*

Jauntily passing the sword from hand to hand as if to show he's relaxed and has all the time in the world, Rex stops and turns as if he suddenly sees something surprising to his right in the apple trees.

ABOUT THE AUTHOR

Jerry Jay Carroll is a former feature writer and columnist for *the San Francisco Chronicle*. Nominated twice for the Pulitzer Prize, he is the author of *Top Dog*, a *New York Times* bestseller that earned an "A" from *Entertainment Weekly* ("A captivating romp"). Recently revised, it is available in print and as an ebook. He also wrote *Inhuman Beings, Dog Eat Dog* and *The Great Liars*. His most recent book is *The Horror Writer*.

www.ingramcontent.com/pod-product-compliance
Lightning Source LLC
Chambersburg PA
CBHW031943260626
47157CB00017B/2090